HUNTING VAMPIRES FOR FUN AND PROFIT

VAMPIRE INNOCENT
BOOK THIRTEEN

MATTHEW S. COX

DIVISION ZERO PRESS

CONTENTS

TILLOA

Coping is such a weird concept.

I mean, how does a person really 'get over' being killed and discovering they didn't really understand the world at all. Everything—well, *almost* everything—people think is made up nonsense is real. Like vampires. Turns out, there's also magic, leprechauns, demons, and other strange creatures. To be fair, death isn't usually an event a person needs to cope with themselves. All the difficult and painful parts usually fall on the shoulders of their friends and family.

It's weird to say, but having my mind opened to the existence of so much stuff I used to think of as made up stories shocked me *more* than dying. Since I still exist, it's fairly easy to kinda brush the whole murdery stabby bit aside and pretend it didn't really happen. It's the first week of July and I've officially been a vampire for more than one year now. Feels like a lot longer, but not in a bad way. The first few months did suck—pun intended. Emotions are gonna 'emotion' no matter what, but hey... I've stopped crying on my stuffed animals due to random sad storms and fits of nostalgia. As long as Dad doesn't remind me they canceled *Firefly,* I'm done with the crying.

So, yeah. About as much as it's possible for anyone to cope, I've coped.

Sarah 2.0 has arrived. Better, stronger, faster... or whatever they say in that cheesy old TV show my father liked as a kid. Growing up in the Eighties, most of the shows he watched pre-tween came from the Seventies. Have I mentioned he's a massive fan of old movies? Specifically 'Eighties cheese' as he calls them. Back in the day, he took them all seriously and adored everything. His favorite had to be *Airwolf.* I think he still secretly daydreams about flying it. Pity his adult brain knows slapping jet engines on a helicopter won't magically bend the laws of physics and allow it to go at Mach 2. No longer being an easily impressed child doesn't stop him from continuing to love those old shows. But now, they're awesome for being silly and funny. I'm sure he gets the same sort of nostalgia kick from them I do from looking at the life-sized picture of my former bedroom window. My new basement bedroom has no windows—kind of the point of moving downstairs. So, Mom printed out a three-and-a-half by five-foot-tall poster for me. It's the view I used to have from my upstairs bedroom out into the yard during summer.

I know... I know. I'm eig—technically nineteen now, so shouldn't feel nostalgia at all.

The 'rents and my friends think it's odd for someone my age to have such an emotional reaction to the end of childhood. Neither Ashley nor Michelle miss being younger. Both of them are full steam ahead, looking forward to joining the real world. Ash wants to be a vet, and she also wants to have kids seriously bad. She does, however, have the willpower to wait on producing spawn until she's established herself job wise. Michelle hasn't said anything about starting a family. She's totally focused on her law degree and becoming an attorney. Except for a stray imp making her life at the office hellacious for a week or two, it seems to be working out for her so far. Sure, she's merely an intern-slash-helper. We all only have one year of college done, so it's not like she's doing any actual law stuff, just working in the environment.

That leaves me, the Super Slacker. Pump me up and watch me... do nothing.

For three years of high school, I worked various summer jobs. Had I remained alive, there'd likely have been two more years of summer job in my past. Alas, having a sun allergy and enforced sleep schedule incompatible with mornings gets in the way of gainful employment. Though, to be fair, my sun allergy is improving. My bloodline's ability to tolerate daylight is a 'power' just like any other vampire ability. It can be developed. Paradoxically, it's one of the most difficult ones to work on since we have an instinctual aversion to the angry ball of fire in the sky. Some obliging assholes decided to play personal vampire trainer and chained me to a tree, *forcing* me to practice not incinerating when the sun came up.

Buttheads.

No, they didn't do it to help me overcome the powerful, instinctive drive to run away from morning. The bastards wanted to destroy me, but failed. And yeah... it *completely* sucked. I haven't experienced that much pain since the grandparents gave my sister Sophia a recorder flute to play when she was six. Did you know the frequency of sound required to shatter glass is not as intense as the frequency required to shatter eardrums? About the only thing I can think of more painful than being tied to a tree as the sun came up would be being tied to a chair and forced to marathon the Dr. Phil show for forty-eight hours.

Anyway, fate gives lemons, make pie.

Or something.

Many things in this world are tradeoffs. For example, if I take advantage of my ability to tolerate the sun, I get really hungry. If I behave myself like a good little normal vampire and avoid all daylight, feeding only needs to happen about once a week, maybe two weeks if I take a big meal and seriously get my lazy on. Since those idiots obligingly kicked me in the butt and helped me flex my powers of sun tolerance, I'm taking advantage.

When I first became a vampire, moderately bright days hurt too much for me to tolerate. My skin would start smoking and... yeah, just generally a bad idea. Now, the brightest it gets around here is 'uncomfortable' but doable for short stints. I can put up with a clear, cloudless summer afternoon in Seattle for about an hour before screaming uncle and retreating to the shade. The more common partially overcast days are tolerable with only a constant needling sense of discomfort—like having Uncle Hank over for holiday dinners. Wait, no... that's *more* uncomfortable.

Regardless of my powers developing, my body still won't wake up any earlier than around 2:30 p.m. Even that's crazy early for a vampire to open their eyes. Everyone else is stuck enslaved to the solar cycle. They can't wake up earlier than about ten-ish minutes prior to sunset. I imagine they stir a bit earlier if it's gloomy. Still don't understand it fully. I mean, they 'sleep' in complete darkness but still don't open their eyes until right before sunset. And yeah, they *can* wake earlier but only if threatened. It's a weird sort of quasi-magical sixth sense type deal. And yes, they *do* see dead people.

Fortunately, I don't make a habit of sneaking into the lairs of sleeping vampires with intent to destroy them. Okay, it's happened, but only because I was ordered to do it. Going back to the whole summer job-slash-slacker thing? Yeah... I'm technically employed but not in the sense of any mortal employment.

Being one of Arthur Wolent's 'people' isn't a forty-hour-a-week gig with accrued time off and benefits. It's a 'hey can you do this for me' type arrangement with a bad habit of coming out of nowhere and biting me in the ass at inopportune moments. Sometimes I wonder if he has people watching me. Nothing for two weeks, then the day I absolutely need to take Sophia to dance class or drive Sierra to her sword training sessions, one of Wolent's people calls me with an assignment.

Gonna regret saying this, but it's been quiet lately.

Attending college lets the summer feel somewhat normal. I dunno if I'm ready for adult life. Like... my 'rents—and every other working adult—no longer think of summer as anything really special the same way I used to. Wouldn't it be cool if jobs had summer break like school? Maybe not. Be kinda weird if everyone just stopped working during the summer, especially medical people and cops. Ack. Civilization would shut down for three months. Oops, so maybe my idea's impractical.

Back to making lemon pie. I've been taking advantage of my increased ability to cope with sunlight by spending time out of the house during the day. Usually, I hang out with Ashley, Michelle, and/or Hunter when they aren't at work, asleep, or busy. Michelle's taking one class over the summer —girl's always been an overachiever. Both Ashley and Hunter are focusing on work. Bleh. They're adulting so hard, making me feel like a slacker.

Tonight, Hunter surprised me with tickets to a concert in Seattle. He figured I'd like it since my Dad is super into Eighties stuff. We're at an 'Iron Maidens' concert... an all-female cover band. I think Hunter and I are the youngest people in the venue. Yeah, sure, I've heard some Iron Maiden before thanks to my father, but I'm not so into it that hearing a woman sing those songs sounds weird. As far as I'm concerned, they're really good. At least being a vampire, my eardrums will regenerate if the loud music blows them out. Even concentrating on turning down the metaphorical volume knob on my ears doesn't help much. I get why Amy, Dante, and Luke always hang out at the far back end of any concert they go to. Hearing sensitive enough to pick up the creak of human muscles moving doesn't really get along too well with concert speakers.

While the ladies are in the midst of a rousing version of *Run to the Hills,* I slip away from Hunter—he knows—and feed on the nearest, most convenient person. It's quite dark to mortals in the concert hall and we're in the standing section, so surreptitious feeding is possible. Still, it's kinda crowded and I don't really want to fight my way too far through the crowd to find someone. Generally, I try not to bite women if I can help it. Unlike some vampires, I do my best not to take the act of feeding in a sexual way. Honestly, though... lips to neck is pretty intimate. Maybe I *should* cling to the discomfort. If I detach emotionally from the act too much and start thinking of people as walking cupcakes, it might lead to me becoming inhuman.

Right, so biting this fiftyish woman dressed like she's a teenager playing hooky from high school to go to a metal concert is ten tons of awkward. Something about her dye-green hair, crop top, and overall presence makes her blood taste like cotton candy and Vicodin. Just kidding. I have no idea what Vicodin tastes like. Sounded funny to say. The cotton candy is real, though. Bleh. Still, the crowd around us is too into the music to notice. Good thing, too. This woman's old enough to be my mother. Ugh. Another layer of awkward.

Hunter pretends not to notice. He knows a girl's got certain needs. Dating a vampire obligates him to put up with some unusual behaviors, like drinking blood. I'm really surprised he doesn't get jealous at all when I bite other guys. According to Amy, one of the local Lost Ones, biting a romantic partner during sex is supposed to be insanely sensual. I haven't gone there with Hunter yet. I don't think we will. Just like biting my family feels completely *wrong* in every sense of the word wrong, biting him does, too.

The middle-aged punk goes straight back to reveling in the music once my mental derp slap wears off her brain. I slip back under Hunter's arm. He smiles at me. At the tip of his brain, he wonders what the woman tasted like. You know, totally normal conversation. My boyfriend finds it fascinating how my perception of blood's flavor changes from person to person. Not sure if I'm unique, but I do know it's not the same for all vamps. Glim, for example, gets to 'enjoy' the normal flavor of blood. Blech. Dalton described his experience as reminding him of steak every time.

Whatever.

For the next hour or so, I forget about all the supernatural weirdness in my life and become a girl out on a date.

Hunter happens to be into older music. He likes many of the same bands my father does, like Metallica, Iron Maiden, Anthrax and so on. Sure, he listens to newer stuff, too, but doesn't like it as much. So weird to me. His father is a complete jerk, yet the music the dude always played around the house is the music Hunter likes. Maybe he finds it difficult to despise the man in spite of the abuse. I'm so lucky to have awesome 'rents. Hunter's mom is fine, if a bit timid. The only really bad thing she ever did to him and Ronan was tolerate the dad's presence longer than she should have. Can't really blame her *too* much for that. It's not easy for some women to escape relationships like that. Lucky for her,

I sent the guy on his way for good. No, didn't kill him. Just gave him a mental poke never to return.

Yeah, that's me. Sarah Wright, vampire marriage counselor. Or should I say 'vampire divorce attorney'?

Once the show ends, we move with the crowd out of the concert hall. The sun had been up when we got here, but it's dark now. Works for me. Kind of a long show for a cover band, really, at three-and-a-half hours. The small bands always seem to work the hardest, right? Wonder how it works for a cover band with licensing and stuff. Do they have to pay royalties to the actual Iron Maiden?

Hand-in-hand, I walk with Hunter down the street to the parking garage we used, which is a few blocks from the venue. We chat about what to do with the rest of our night, or at least the part of it he can remain awake for. I encourage him not to stay up too late for my benefit. The guy has to obey his alarm clock, after all. We keep jokingly talking about going off to make love out in the woods somewhere, but it's not totally serious. Even though I could make anyone who catches us forget the sight, it's still embarrassing to think about. Being stuck outside naked post-morgue was bad enough, but it had been both innocent and not my fault. Having sex outdoors is totally different. Not innocent, definitely my fault... though it could be fun. Some people *do* get a thrill out of breaking rules.

Alas, I am not one of those people.

My superhero identity is Follows Rules Girl.

How much of a dork am I? Even bringing Hunter home and making love in my bedroom feels like I'm doing something wrong. Sure, I'm of legal age now and the 'rents tolerate it. Can't say my mother is too fond of the idea of me having sex in the house. Neither is Dad, but to him, I'm still his little girl. I'm sure he hates the idea of me being grown up. Weird how parents do that. They can't stand the thought of their kid being grown up and having sex, but the instant grandbabies exist, you'd think it was the parents' idea.

I'd say it's impossible for me to give them a grandbaby but it isn't. It's impossible for me to get pregnant. That's technically not the same as 'giving them a grandbaby'. It's fully possible for me to adopt or just 'acquire' a baby if I ever wanted to. My powers of mind control are quite effective. No, I'm not going to take someone else's kid. For one thing, I am in no way ready to be responsible for an infant. For another, it's a really awful thing to do. There's also no need for it. My parents have three other chances to be grands. If I had to guess, I'd say Sophia is going to be the first one of my siblings to start a family. Of course, that means reality is going to be the exact opposite. Watch it be Sierra. She ought to be at the point to start noticing boys soon if she isn't there already, but so far has never mentioned it. Sophia's commented on a few of the boys in her class being cute, though it seems innocent still. Sam, being ten, probably still thinks of girls as icky, though he's never talked about them.

My internal debate as to which of the Littles will be the first to offer up a grandchild on the altar of parental adoration grinds to a stop under the weight of a stare. My senses snap back to my immediate surroundings. The conversation I'd been having on autopilot with Hunter also stops. I become aware the crowd has thinned around us. Apparently, more people at the concert parked in some other garage than the one we used and veered off a cross street or two back.

The weighty stare is coming from a youngish black woman lurking at the mouth of an alley at the middle of the block we're on. She's young but not *too* young, likely midway through her twenties and model pretty, almost like she's ready to do a photo shoot for her clingy black sweater, tights, and 'trendy boots' like the popular girls at school would buy and wear for a month at most before considering them passe. The way she's looking at us tells me she's either about to pull a knife and charge or start telling us about how being vegan changed her life. Her attention falls mostly on Hunter. A few seconds after I notice she has striking gold eyes, it occurs to me she's a vampire.

Yeah, we can recognize each other pretty much on sight with a few exceptions. Me being one such exception. Innocents are so lifelike we can fool other vampires into mistaking us for mortal. Sounds cool, but this won't be the first time another vampire sized me up for a meal. My guess is she's planning to derp me and pull Hunter into the alley for some quality feeding time. This woman appears fairly normal, but she's no Innocent. Being one doesn't let me spot others of my kind as such. I'd mistake them for ordinary humans, too.

My friend Michelle often talks about how the world is stacked against her, specifically black people, and she's generally right. Even vampirism is sorta unfair to them. I mean, the natural state of undeath is corpse pale. That doesn't quite work out too well for people with African ancestry. They tend to turn grey, similar to Shadows, if they don't concentrate on maintaining a lifelike appearance. A vampire like Aurélie can be lazy and not bother. She prefers to be snow white since it saves a bunch of money on makeup. As a mortal, she used to paint herself white for some reason. Silly rich French people, right? Alas, laziness is not an option for anyone who's supposed to have actual color to their skin —at least if they want to fool anyone into thinking they're not a vampire. They'd end up appearing obviously dead, so they have to either stay in hiding or expend the effort to 'warm up.' I don't honestly know how taxing it is to do since 'life mode' is constantly on for me. Maybe it's trivial and not really anything to complain about.

As I expected, once we get closer, the woman stares at me with intent. No weird sensations affect my mind, and her expression rapidly goes from stern to WTF, then 'oh wow.'

"Sorry. Didn't realize you were one of us." She nods toward him. "I'll find someone else."

"Not a problem," I say in a low voice. "He's not my meal. He's my boyfriend."

She raises both eyebrows. "Say what? Boyfriend?"

"Yep." I put an arm around him. "It's cool. He knows about things."

Hunter glances back and forth between us. "Friend of yours?"

"Never met her before. We're in the same, umm, class." I offer a hand. "Sarah Wright."

The woman somewhat hesitantly takes my hand, staring at him, her voice distracted and elsewhere. "Tilloa Winters. He is your, whatever they call it?"

"Boyfriend?" I smile.

"No... you empower him as a servant?" asks Tilloa.

"Oh. Thrall? Nah." I shake my head.

"Sarah charmed me from the moment I first saw her." Hunter brushes the back of his hand over my cheek. "Don't believe her. She had magic powers even before she went vampire."

It takes me more than a little effort not to laugh, both at him being cheesy cute and the almost truth of what he said. Sophia *does* have magical abilities. She always did, just couldn't use them before. Sam, too. Stands to reason it's something running in our family, so hey... maybe I *did* have magic. No idea if dying killed it. Great, now I'm going to spend the next fifty years wondering if my lineage played a role in the wheel of fate selecting Innocent for me.

Tilloa fires such a glare at him, it makes me brace for a fight. Oh, shit. Is this girl a Fury? Rather than throw herself at us, she spins away with an almost despondent scowl of 'oh F the world' and storms off down the alley. It's the sort of facial expression one would expect to see on a vampire right before they threw themselves into the sun. Ugh.

"Sec," I whisper to Hunter, then follow her.

The click of her heeled boots on the pavement echoes in the concrete canyon between buildings. A pigeon or two startles into flight somewhere overhead, faintly louder than the near continuous hiss of cars passing behind me on a rain-wet road. She shoots a look back over her shoulder at the scuff of my sneakers. Hmm. This is one of those moments where I really ought to be second guessing my curiosity and instinct to help people. Seems more often than not whenever I try to do someone a nice favor, it ends up going about as wrong as possible. It would probably be better off for my family and friends if I kept my head down and stopped involving myself in other peoples'—and ghosts'—problems.

But... I'm me. Can't help it.

"What?" snaps Tilloa.

"You okay?" I ask.

Hunter follows us into the alley.

She makes a face like she's torn between walking away again without another word, biting my head off—metaphorically—or talking.

"Sorry. Just... something seems wrong here. You looked really upset and it kinda bothered me." I hold my hands up in a disarming manner and take a step back. "Don't want to intrude."

She lets out a long sigh. "You serious? He's your boo?"

"I'm not a ghost yet..." Hunter winks.

Ugh. He's been around Dad too long.

Tilloa appears wholly unimpressed at his pun.

"Yeah. He's my boo." I manage a weak smile. "Totally normal... as much as it can be."

"Interesting. So, he's mortal, you're not, and you two are making it work?" She gives him epic side eye. Suspicion in her expression gives way to shock and hope.

Uh oh. I think I know why she's so upset. Most vampires cut all ties with their mortal families and friends upon receiving the Transference. This isn't usually a problem since the majority of us go into the process with both eyes open, fully expecting to leave the old world behind. More new vampires than one might expect are already loners cut off from any family or close friends. Tilloa could be like me... had it dropped on her out of the blue. I bet she misses someone.

"Yeah, more or less," I say. "We're making it work."

I don't say the 'for now' that's on my mind... and also on Hunter's mind. He's cool with the idea of growing old at my side despite me always looking like I'm eighteen going on fifteen. Yes, that will get pretty damn creepy after a decade or three. Of course, he also expects not to live that long. Either I'm going to make him into a vampire or my crazy unlife is going to get him killed before people start looking at us like father and daughter instead of a dating couple.

Grr.

He sincerely loves me *so* much, but maybe it would be better for me to disappear from his life. I can't do it though. His little brother and my little brother are best friends. Hunter's become part of the family. As cliché as it seems, he's probably going to end up becoming a vampire at some point. Our realistic options are pretty much limited to either that or breaking up. I've peeked into the heads of a few older guys, and it's kinda strange how their perceptions change. The normal ones look at me and see a child. They look at women I think of as 'old' and consider them hot. If nothing happens to Hunter's mind, he will most likely eventually start seeing me as 'too young to be romantic with' and I'll become 'kid sister' or even daughter instead of girlfriend. Love does not *have* to be sexual, but wow... talk about twisting up his head.

Ugh. I am the queen of untenable situations.

"She read my mind, didn't she?" asks Hunter.

I make a 'possibly' face at him.

Tilloa quirks an eyebrow at him. "Curious. Well, thanks."

Before I can ask 'for what,' she walks off at the speed of mission. It's obvious she has no further interest in talking to us. She's definitely heading somewhere specific to do something specific. My guess is she's going to try making contact with someone who thinks she died. Given her fixation on Hunter, probably a boyfriend or maybe even husband. I decide *not* to further involve myself in whatever mess is coming. I'm not a vampire superhero out to help everyone in Seattle fix their life's problems, even if I can't help myself sometimes.

Ever have one of those moments when you think you just set something bad in motion without intending to? Yeah. I'm having one of those right now as I watch Tilloa whisk away into the night. Can't help but feel like I just tried unsuccessfully to steal the golden idol, and somewhere out there a big-ass *Indiana Jones* type boulder is rolling down a hill toward me.

Hopefully, I'll see the giant rock coming before it makes Sarah pizza.

2

A MINOR ERROR IN JUDGMENT

They say there is a fine line between courage and denial.

Or, maybe someone said it. Whatever. I just thought of it. Dad probably deserves some kind of recognition for his ability to adapt to crazy. His eldest daughter is a vampire. His youngest daughter has magic. His son has a few pet demons—not the frogs, actual demons—and his middle daughter is only twelve but she's already defeated a substance addiction and is obsessed with swords. We've had dead people in the house, ghosts, imps, and even a couple of government agents.

No, Sierra didn't touch drugs. So what if the 'substance' in question is vampire blood, it counts.

What does my father do in the face of all this chaos?

He whips out movies.

It's Thursday night, and much like large American water fowl, my family's habits have migratory patterns based on the season. During school months, movie night usually happens on Friday or sometimes Saturday. In the summer, accommodations are made in case we want to do something with friends, so movie night shifts to Thursday. The 'rents are surprisingly lax when it comes to enforcing the rule of bedtime during the summer. I'm going to fall short of calling them 'permissive,' but they won't give the Littles a hard time if they stay up a bit late. Makes sense. Mom's more concerned with us getting enough sleep for school... not an issue now in July.

We gather in the living room in our usual spots. I'm on the sofa, as are Mom, Sophia, and Sierra. Sam's sprawled on the floor next to Ronan who is sleeping over tonight. Blix, the imp, perches like a gargoyle on the back of the sofa where he can see the screen. Klepto's floating in the air, orbiting Sophia's head like a tiny, grey, fuzzy blimp. No, the kitten isn't fat. I mean 'blimp' purely in the sense of a flying object in no hurry to be anywhere.

Everyone except for Sophia and I are rocking some form of a shorts-and-T-shirt ensemble. Sophia's doing her usual pink dress thing. Me? Sweat pants. Hey, they're comfy and I don't overheat in the summer anymore. Besides, this *is* Washington after all. Doesn't exactly get scorching here too often.

"Okay, so..." Dad whirls away from his shelf of Eighties cheese, holding up two DVDs: *Red Dawn* and *Ladyhawke*. "These two tied for most votes."

Mom couldn't care less which movie goes on, so she remains quiet while the Littles plus Ronan point at one or the other and shout the movie's title. It's somewhat difficult to tell which movie is winning given the complete disorder of the process. Doesn't help that Blix is completely unintelligible to most people. His babbling chipmunk voice makes sense only to Sam, who thus far hasn't translated for us. Not that he really has to. Once I look at the little daemon, it's obvious he's choosing *Ladyhawke* by pointing both fingers and his tail at it.

"Here's an idea," says Dad while raising a conspiratorial eyebrow. "Let's watch both?"

All the kids except for Sophia cheer. I'm including Blix in that. Klepto rotates upside down and continues gliding in a lazy circle around Sophia's head. The kitten is trying to cheer her up. My youngest sister is seriously on edge. Thankfully, the giant anxiety goblin sitting on her shoulder has nothing to do with magic or supernatural craziness. By the way, I am being metaphorical. I don't mean a literal goblin—seems I need to specify these things lately the way my unlife is going.

Mom gives Dad a 'you shouldn't encourage them' sort of mild disapproving look. Watching both movies will keep the kids up until after midnight—assuming they stay awake. Again, not a big deal during the summer. If they fall asleep down here, either Dad or I will carry them up to their beds. It'll be an excuse for Dad to re-screen the movie they missed half of.

My father puts both DVD cases behind his back, shuffles them around, and looks at Mom. "Left hand or right hand."

"Left," says Mom.

Dad pulls *Red Dawn* out from behind his back. "Okay. This one first."

"Popcorn?" asks Sierra.

Sam pushes himself up to kneel. "I'll get—"

Klepto vanishes in a faint flicker of purple light.

Mom face-palms. "Sophia, we need to talk about your larcenous feline companion."

"Aww, Mom." Sophia squishes her toes together, looking down at her lap. "She means well. And she doesn't steal anything important or valuable."

My entire family stares at her in 'massive ruby.'

"Well, okay. Only once. But that was important." Sophia fidgets.

Klepto reappears, dangling between two *massive* paper sacks of movie theater popcorn on the coffee table.

"Awesome," says Sam, his voice more a breath than sound.

Ronan cracks up into laugh-giggles.

"Whoa." Sierra takes one sack. "She got the good stuff. Heart attack city. There's more salt in this bag than there is in the comment section of YouTube videos about *Fallout 76*."

"Such a tragedy." Dad puts a hand over his heart.

"Your cat stole from a movie theater?" Mom shakes her head.

Dad holds up a finger. "Considering what they charge for snacks, I'll call this fair turnabout."

"Come here, oh Robin Hood of popcorn." Sophia squish-hugs Klepto.

"Mew," says Klepto before purring.

Sam yoinks the second bag, moving it to the floor between him and Ronan. Dad looks around like 'hey, where's my popcorn.' Mom defuses the situation by going to get some bowls and portioning out the enormous paper sacks— seriously, they're almost as big as grocery bags—into relatively even amounts for all, except me. I pass this time. Though my bloodline allows me to eat and enjoy the taste of ordinary food, it passes straight through me unchanged beyond what my teeth do to it. I imagine the sensation of insanely greasy chewed-up popcorn grit leaving my body will be... unpleasant. Like, somewhere on the scale of uncomfortable between a job interview with a fifty-year-old sweaty guy who sits a little too close while insisting on calling me 'sweetie' and having to fill out all that paperwork at a new dentist's office.

The movie starts.

Sophia isn't really looking at the screen nor touching the buttery feast. This is not guilt over purloined popcorn. Even *she* wouldn't really care too much about stealing like eighty cents worth of popcorn, especially when the theater charges eight bucks for it.

I nudge her and whisper, "You okay?"

She fidgets again "I dunno."

The kid is throwing off so much fear and nervousness you'd think she'd been scheduled to be burned at the stake tomorrow for witchcraft. Know what's really screwed up? I'm half tempted to say if in some bizarre alternate reality the police really had sentenced her to death by burning, she'd be too afraid to run away because she'd get in *more* trouble for it. I'm still shocked at her non-reaction to the kitten taking that ruby. This is a girl who tried to return a pen she found on the floor at school in third grade because keeping it made her feel too guilty.

Sierra is totally aware of Sophia being Follows Rules Girl's sidekick. She also knows Sophia stole something huge in order to protect her life. I think the two of them have bonded more closely, but it's really difficult to tell. Sierra isn't the most outwardly emotional sort of person unless the emotion in question is rage. Wouldn't call her an overly angry kid, more that she tends to mask every emotion she considers 'embarrassing' under fake rage. I think we made some progress on that, though. Her confidence is growing since Sophia enchanted her. And the magic is pretty darn impressive. The kid's able to mostly keep up with me when we spar out in the yard at night.

This is so weird. Sierra's less worried about a school shooter now because she's terrified vampires are going to invade our house and try to kill us. Is that an improvement or not? I mean, she's *still* afraid to the point of feeling nauseous all day at school someone's going to show up with a gun, but it's no longer her greatest fear.

"You don't *have* to go," I whisper to Sophia.

She peers up at me, making a face like she just broke

something of Mom's by accident. "But I promised. And it's already paid for."

Mom slips an arm around her and squeezes. "I think it will be good for you to experience camp at least once, but you aren't being forced to go."

"Weird you actually wanted to." Sierra leans forward to peer past me at her, seeming concerned.

"I know." Sophia sighs. "Nicole and Priya kinda talked me into it. I'm trying not to be such a scaredy cat. Magic ought to give me *some* confidence, right? I mean... dance recitals don't make me wanna puke anymore. How bad can camping be?"

Blix face-palms and makes a squeaky little "oy!" noise.

"Ack." Sam shakes his head. "*Never* ask that."

"What?" Sierra scoffs. "It's not like some random monster is going to come out of the woods and try to eat you while you are hours away from cell phone reception, internet, or the outside world."

Sophia stares at her, emerald green eyes as big as an anime girl's. Sierra smiles to herself, proud at the successful teasing. Ordinarily, I'd call her a bitch for that, but I wonder if she's trying to frighten Sophia out of going so she stays home. Sierra would probably never admit to wanting her sister to stay close, but she'd definitely do something like this: scare her into staying.

"Sierra, stop traumatizing your sister," deadpans Dad.

"Sorry," mutters Sierra.

"Hey, relax." I ruffle Sophia's hair. "You're not exactly going to some old-world forest in Ireland where brownies will tie you to a tree for three hours."

She rolls her eyes.

"She got teased by girl scouts?" asks Ronan.

"No, actual brownies."

The face the boy makes cracks me up too much to explain I don't mean little chocolate cakes.

Sophia scrunches her hands into her dress, kneading the fabric. "Perhaps I have made an error."

Mom squeezes her again. "You'll be just fine, honey. I went to Girl Scout camp every year until I outgrew it."

"It's not *really* camping, anyway." Sierra waves dismissively. "Girl Scout camping is camping the way being in the Air Force is being in the military. You're just going to sit around all day doing bullcrap arts and crafts stuff... only out in the woods instead of in a nice building."

Mom laughs. "You'd be surprised, dear. It's closer to real camping than you think. Hiking, canoeing, all sorts of fun stuff."

Sophia stares into space, still kneading her dress in her lap. I can practically see the battle between bravery and cowardice going on behind her eyes. Poor kid is not quite 'terrified' but she's definitely a few inches short of throwing up from anxiety.

Hey, I whisper mentally. *The camp is two hours by car and only because the roads are twisty. I can fly there in like twenty minutes. If you get too freaked out, send Klepto and I'll zoom out there and either fly you home or hang out until you feel better.*

Sophia manages a weak smile and clings to my arm while leaning against Mom. "Okay."

Oh, weird. This movie is about a bunch of teenagers stopping Russia from invading the USA. Wow, people were crazy in the Eighties.

3

TROUBLE BREATHING

S
am awoke in the middle of the night with a strong suspicion *something* was wrong.

The feeling of all not being as it should be didn't come from knowing Sophia would be going to camp in the morning. That, in and of itself, represented a radical shift in the paradigm of the universe capable of realigning energies from here to the Andes Mountains. Whatever potential disaster might arise from his sister acting so against her nature remained a future effect he should not be sensing now.

His immediate notion of there being something really quite wrong about the here and now came mostly from the presence of a weight on his chest. Though it felt as heavy as if Dad stood on top of him, it didn't hurt, nor crush his ribs.

Sam opened his eyes and came face to face with a small, green-skinned creature roughly ten inches tall with a head the approximate size and dimensions of a huge tomato. It wore a miniature leather tunic and dingy cloth pants like some manner of rogue or goblin from D&D. The creature even carried a tiny sword on its belt, not quite a full three inches in length.

The most curious aspect of the critter, other than it pressing him down into the mattress as though it weighed more than a hundred pounds, was the expression of complete baffled frustration on its demonically cherubic face. If not for the malevolent glint in its yellow eyes, it might've been considered cute. The goblin waved its three-fingered hands at Sam's face in a manner like a deep sea fisherman hauling in a net, almost as if it tried to pull the most epic snot cord in the world out of Sam's nose.

Other than the heaviness on his chest, he didn't feel anything odd.

Ronan, in a sleeping bag on the floor near the bed, wheezed.

Sam tried to sit up, but couldn't.

Moving his arms proved difficult, as if he had lead gloves on, though not impossible. As soon as he started to reach for the goblin, it gave a wail of alarm like a mortician watching his client sit up. It scrambled off, running directly away from Sam's face, which had the unfortunate side effect of it planting a foot in a highly sensitive spot.

Sam let out an *oof* and sat up fast, managing to grab the creature and pin it to the bed before the pain set in and paralyzed him. Groaning, he squished the little goober into the blanket as hard as he could while weathering the wave of nauseating agony as bad as if he'd caught a little league line drive in the crotch. His bent over, face-in-the-mattress pose gave him a good view of Blix seated on the floor and engrossed in the PlayStation, oblivious to the goings-on thanks to headphones and a short attention span. The bedroom flickered and flashed in blues and purples from the TV screen's rendition of an alien space station.

"Blix…" squeaked Sam.

He really rather wanted to punch the goblin in the nose for stepping on his balls, even accidentally, but couldn't quite move yet. The little fiend snarled and thrashed to get away. For no reason that made sense to him, it no longer had the weight of a grown adult, making it as easy to contain as if he held down a panicky guinea pig.

Despite there being no rational way for the imp to hear him, Blix twisted his head around 180 degrees to look. Upon noticing the situation, he tossed the headphones and controller aside, then leapt at the goblin perched on Ronan's chest.

The smaller boy appeared to be struggling to breathe. Luminous threads of white vapor streamed from his mouth and nose, gathering around the creature's hands like wisps of ghostly cotton candy.

As soon as Sam processed these creatures appeared to be trying to *kill* him and his best friend, pain vanished. He grabbed the goblin around the neck in both hands, throttling it while Blix tackled the other one. It shrieked in a voice like a balloon leaking air, losing its 'grip' on Ronan's breath as soon as imp claws and fangs pierced its skin. The glowing vaporous cord snapped back into the boy's face at the speed of an overextended rubber band breaking.

Ronan abruptly woke in the midst of a severe choking fit.

Sam pinned the goblin to the bed under his left hand while proceeding to punch it repeatedly in the face. Pale green blood splattered from its nostrils after three hits. Before he could slug it a fourth time, the creature yanked the little sword off its belt and stabbed it into his wrist.

"Ow!" yelled Sam, instinctively recoiling—and losing his grip on the goblin.

Blix and the second creature rolled around the carpet like

sped up video of two alley cats brawling. Small leathery wings flapped around too fast to make sense of who had the upper hand. Sam clasped a hand over a tiny bleeding hole. The goblin pointed the sword at him, made an angry, threatening face, then leapt straight from the bed to the windowsill and jumped outside to the backyard.

"Damn!" Sam crawled off the foot end of the bed, banged his knee on the 'chest of cool stuff,' and hopped to the window in time to watch the little monster zoom across the yard into the woods behind the house.

Splat.

"Whoa…" Ronan coughed. "What the heck is that?"

Sam twisted to look behind him.

Blix stood victorious over a puddle of clearish-green slime and tiny bones.

"Uh, oh." Sam cringed. "Mom's gonna be mad if that doesn't come out of the carpet."

Blix smirked, then snapped his fingers. The mess leapt from the floor into the wastebasket by the desk, leaving the rug perfectly clean.

"Awesome." Sam grabbed his nearest pair of jeans and pulled them on over his boxers. "You okay, Ro?"

"Uhh." Ronan rubbed his chest. "Really sore. What happened?"

"Dunno yet. Some little monsters tried to kill us. One got away. I'm going after it."

Blix flew up to hover in Sam's face, shaking his head. "No. Too much danger now. Not at dark."

Sam flailed his arms. "But it's getting away!"

"Many friends. Too many." Blix reached for him, stopped to stare at his bare chest, then snapped his fingers. As soon as a T-shirt appeared on Sam, he grabbed two handfuls of fabric and pulled, pleadingly. "No go now. They hurt you."

"Grr." Sam sighed. "Too dangerous for Mel?"

Blix shook his head. "No, but don't need Mel. Save for important. In day, you beat goblins easy. I find."

Grumbling, Sam paced around. The imp made a good point. True, the succubus had offered to help Sam as often as he needed, but he still shouldn't take advantage. Calling her in to deal with... goblins probably amounted to a villager in a roleplaying game wanting a level twenty character to go beat up kobolds. It sounded as though the goblins gained power in the dark. If he went after them now, he'd be in danger. Tomorrow, they'd have no problem.

"Okay. Fine... but." Sam grabbed his Nerf gun and hurried into the hall. "Gotta make sure the girls are okay."

Blix nodded.

Another goblin appeared to be struggling at Sophia's bedroom door, unable to get it to open. Sam took aim with the Nerf gun, but before he could fire, the creature spotted him. It jumped back from the door, emitting a gasp of shock while making a face similar to the way Sarah reacted if he unexpectedly entered her bedroom while she had Hunter visiting.

Sam fired a Nerf dart, which the creature easily avoided. Frowning, he pointed at it.

Giving off a mood of 'with pleasure,' Blix launched himself from Sam's shoulder like a less-feathery attack eagle. Screaming in the voice of an electrified chipmunk, the goblin fled down the hallway toward the upstairs bathroom. Seconds after it and Blix vanished through the doorway, a gooey splatter brought silence.

Sam glanced at Sierra's room. The door sat ajar, easily wide enough for a goblin to get in. He darted over, pushing it the rest of the way open. Goblin number four stood on top of Sierra's chest. A thin, glowing white cord connected its hands to her nose, but it appeared to lack the strength to pull any more than a few inches of it out of her. Frustrated, the goblin had even stepped on her cheek, pulling the vapor cord over its shoulder for extra leverage—and *still* couldn't move it. Sierra gave a mild cough in her sleep, evidently oblivious to the creature's presence.

Sam shot a Nerf dart into the goblin.

The foam projectile bounced away harmlessly, proving the creature had no connection to demons. He still didn't understand how Nerf guns or other toys could cause serious harm to demons when *he* used them, but they worked.

At the *boink* of the dart bouncing off its forehead, the goblin paused in its struggle to steal Sierra's life energy and stared at Sam with an angry, threatening snarl. It didn't appear the least bit afraid of him. Unsurprising, as these creatures apparently preyed on children for food. Dad wouldn't be afraid of a pizza giving him a hard stare. Never mind pizzas tended not to stare at anything—unless they'd been in the fridge for a week.

"Get off my sister, you little creep," muttered Sam.

The goblin let go of Sierra's energy, which promptly snapped back into her. She barely stirred in response. Emitting a gibbering cry part way between roaring and hissing, the goblin drew its tiny sword and rushed at Sam, moving *way* faster than anything with such tiny legs ought to. Its impossible speed caught Sam off guard, startling him into flinching.

Rather than attack, the goblin simply dashed around him and ran off down the hall.

Sam chased it back into his room, unable to catch up before the little fiend jumped out his window into the back yard. Without even thinking, he dove headfirst out the window after it, summoning his conjured demon wings.

They snapped out to full width, giving off a sharp *fwoof* like a spring-loaded umbrella made of soft leather. Alas, they shredded the T-shirt right off him. From the second-story window, he didn't have time to truly fly, though the wings acted as a parachute, slowing him enough to land on his feet in the damp grass without hurting himself.

"Sam, no!" shouted Blix from the window above and behind.

Snarling under his breath, Sam forced himself to resist the urge to chase the tiny monster into the trees. He trusted Blix. Imps tended to know things, after all. That's what Blix did, after all: he played video games, and knew things. There had to be enough goblins out there to pose a serious threat to him if he chased them alone into the woods at night. Problem being, whatever the creatures' nature, they weren't demonic. Thus, he had no more power over them than any ordinary ten-year-old. Of course, ten-inch-tall goobers didn't scare him much.

He glanced at the smear of green on his knuckles, turning his hand to examine the blood in the moonlight. "Not gonna need magic to beat them."

Ordinarily, the idea of hunting down something alive and killing it would've been repulsive. However, they tried to kill his sister and best friend, not to mention him. At least he and Sierra appeared to have some kind of resistance to the attack, so perhaps they hadn't been in *too* much danger from a single goblin. Ronan, on the other hand, likely came close to suffocating in his sleep. Fuming mad, Sam flapped his conjured wings and fly-leapt back up to his bedroom window, wanting to check on his friend.

Ronan sat up in the sleeping bag, hand pressed to his chest.

"Still hurt?" Sam slipped into the room, walked over, and sat next to him.

"My chest." Ronan patted himself. "Feels like I breathed out real hard, then couldn't breathe back in for a while."

"Yeah." Sam decided his friend would be okay, then smiled and unsummoned the wings.

"What was that thing?" wheezed Ronan.

"Goblin." Blix nodded once. "Or breathweaver to be specific. There are tons of goblins, all different kinds."

"Umm." Sam scratched his head.

Blix mimicked the creatures' 'reeling in a net' gesture. "They steal breath from sleeping innocents. Take back to their dark faerie overlords. Make dresses, robes, and stuff out of it. Powerful enchanted armor for netherfae sorcerers."

"What's he babbling about?" asked Ronan.

Sam translated.

"You really believe that?" Ronan scrunched his nose. "It's like old stories people used to make up to explain why babies sometimes don't wake up because they didn't know medicine."

"Ro..." Sam gestured at Blix using both hands like a game show hostess indicating the new car. "You are sitting right next to an imp. I can conjure wings. My sister is a vampire. Do you really think these are all just stories?"

"Uhh." Ronan swallowed hard. "Guess not. So *every* kid who dies in their sleep was attacked by one of these things?"

Blix shrugs. "Not all. Some, yes."

"Great. Now I'm never going to be able to sleep again." Ronan huffed.

"Strange." Blix rubbed his chin, tiny black claws gleaming in the moonlight. "You too old. Breathweavers don't attack past eight or nine."

Sam grinned mischievously. "Ronan does kinda look like a little kid. Maybe they got confused."

Ronan slugged him on the shoulder. "Dork."

Sam laughed, as did Ronan.

"Doubt." Blix shook his head. "On purpose try hurt."

"Yeah, well…" Sam narrowed his eyes. "Tomorrow, I'm on purpose gonna try to hurt them back."

Blix gave a thumbs-up.

"Yeah." Ronan punched a fist into his other hand. "Me too."

4

SEPARATION ANXIETY IS A THING

The morning started off bad.

Sophia didn't sleep much the previous night, having stared at the ceiling despite Klepto's purr engine running on full blast against her neck. She would have been happy to spend infinity in bed dreading the dawn, but somehow, she managed to pass out and sunrise snuck up on her. Finally, she understood how Sierra felt, not wanting to get out of bed and go to school. Since Sophia *enjoyed* school, she never had trouble getting going in the morning —until now.

This makes no sense. She slipped her arms out from under the blanket and stared at her hands. *I've made time stop for a bit. I shouldn't be scared of camping. Nicole and Priya are gonna be there, and they'll be sad if I chicken out.*

She cast a sideways glance at the two small bags she'd packed, both of which sat on the floor by her dresser. She brought two normal outfits, dresses, but likely wouldn't wear them much given camp policy requiring the uniform. Her bags contained underwear, socks, pajamas, a spare blanket, four sets of Girl Scout shirts and skirts, and two stuffed animals. Maybe Sierra had a point. Going 'camping' in a skirt didn't really sound smart. It probably wouldn't end up being much different than being at the hall, except for not having electricity and spending a whole week there.

Mom poked her head in the door. "Good, you're awake. If you still want to go, you should get moving."

"Yeah," replied Sophia without thinking.

Mom adding the 'if' made her feel better. Attending the Girl Scout camp remained her choice. Grandma had apparently forced it on Mom, though she didn't mind going. Three years ago, Mom suggested Sierra go to the camp. Sophia had been a little too young. Sierra wanted nothing to do with camping, mostly because it meant a complete lack of video games for a week. She also thought Girl Scouts were 'lame.' Two years ago, Mom suggested Sophia *and* Sierra go to camp. Sierra remained uninterested, and Sophia had been too scared.

Dad's road trips mildly freaked her out, but at least the entire family went along so she didn't have to miss them as well as missing home. Sleeping in strange new places didn't work well. If she spent a week at the Girl Scout camp, she might be able to fall asleep at night by the fourth day.

I have magic. I don't need to be scared.

Jaw clenched in determination, Sophia pushed the blanket aside and got out of bed.

HUGGING EVERYONE GOODBYE TOOK A WHILE.

Sophia couldn't *not* do it, even knowing it made her feel worse. Dad almost changed his mind and made the decision for her to stay home when she had difficulty letting go of her cling hug.

"Why are you wearing the uniform already?" Sierra scrunched her nose.

"Umm, because I'm going to Girl Scout camp?"

Sierra shook her head. "It makes you look like a dork."

"I am at peace with my dorkiness." Sophia brushed her hand down the uniform shirt.

"Yeah, well…" Sierra put on a look of fake disgust. "It's ridiculous."

Sophia laughed. If the world ever came to an end and Sierra decided to go to camp, she'd totally go in a T-shirt and jeans, only changing into a uniform *at* the camp, and only after someone threatened her with punishment for not doing so.

"Think of it like a game." Sophia poked her badge sash. "Collecting achievements."

Sierra raspberried.

"Come on, Soph!" yelled Mom from outside. "You're going to miss the bus."

A glimmer of hope flickered across Sophia's brain. If she missed the bus, she could stay home and have an excuse her friends might accept.

Meh. No they won't. They'll know I missed it on purpose. Grr.

Despite Sarah being asleep at this hour, she raced down to the basement and crept into the bedroom for a 'see you in a week' hug. Her older sister looked fairly creepy while sleeping… way too pale with sunken features, almost like a well-preserved mummy. She didn't appear *so* dead it frightened her, more like someone made a life-sized realistic silicone doll but didn't get the coloration right.

Sarah didn't react whatsoever to having her arm squeezed.

Though she tolerated the odd appearance of her eldest sister, Sophia didn't spend too much time holding the limp, rubbery arm. She slipped out of the room, shut the door, and raced upstairs to meet Mom outside by the Yukon.

"Where are your things?" asked Mom.

"Oops!"

Sophia darted back into the house, scrambled upstairs, and grabbed her bags. She slung the backpack over her shoulder and carried the larger bag in front. The brown canvas bumped repeatedly at her chin as she hurried down the stairs. Dad pulled the front door out of her way.

"Have fun, sweetie!" called Dad as she zoomed by.

Sophia almost replied with an 'I won't' but decided to say, "Okay" instead.

She tossed her bags in the back seat and climbed in up front, clutching an invisible Klepto close like a stuffed animal. The camp didn't allow pets, so she couldn't openly bring the kitten with her. She doubted the camp would make an exception for an 'emotional support enchanted feline familiar.' However, her kitten didn't play by the normal rules of reality. Nervousness plus the sleepiness of a restless night made the relatively short ride to the parking lot of the nearby Safeway pass in mere seconds.

As soon as Sophia spotted the three yellow school buses standing in a line, her heart raced. Her body tensed up like a field mouse sensing the eagle coming. Five or six different Girl Scout troops from this region met here for the buses to camp. A whole bunch of different troops would come together at the campground from multiple regions in Washington State and even farther away. Seeing dozens of unfamiliar kids didn't help. It didn't hurt, either. She didn't dread meeting new people, nor did she thrive on it. Blending in came easy for her. Perhaps she had more shyness than she admitted to herself, since she preferred to not draw attention to herself. Still, unless she did something unusual, other kids didn't bother her. Being skinny and—according to Sarah, a nerd disguised as the popular cheerleader—protected her from most teasing. The only time anyone at school got on her case had been fourth grade when Brian Menke tormented her for being *too* skinny. Most people told her he only did it because he liked her, but Sophia ignored them. A boy who liked a girl wouldn't make her feel awful.

Mom pulled into a parking space and cut the engine. "Wow. So many. Good turnout this year."

"Yeah…" Sophia squeezed the kitten harder. "They said twenty-four different troops are gonna be there. One's even coming from like Minnesota or something."

"Are you sure you want to go, hon? You look terrified."

Sophia glanced over at her mother. She almost blurted 'no, let's go home' but caught sight of Nicole and Priya waving at her. Her friends stood with their troop, a bunch of other girls she sorta knew but didn't really consider friends since she only saw them at scouts.

Crap. They've seen me. They'll be sad if I don't go… and I promised.

She took a deep breath, spent a few seconds unsuccessfully trying to understand what about camping gave her such anxiety, then sighed. The idea of going right home and hiding in her bed sounded amazing. She'd give almost anything to be able to get out of her obligation—self-imposed as it was—to attend camp if she could do so without disappointing her friends, parents, and the scout leaders. They, almost more than her parents, had been shocked when she signed up for it.

Despite the increasingly weird feeling in the pit of her stomach, Sophia reached for the door handle. "I'm okay. I told Nicole and Priya I'd go with them, so… it's only a week, right?"

"You shouldn't feel silly about being nervous." Mom smiled reassuringly. "Camping is much less dangerous and crazy than half the things that go on in our lives now, but it doesn't mean social anxiety is any less real."

Sophia frowned. "I don't think I'm *socially* anxious. It's not being around people I don't know that's freaking me out."

"What is bothering you?"

"I don't know." Sophia exhaled hard. "If I could figure it out, I'd be able to fix it."

Mew, said Klepto, mentally—so Mom didn't notice her.

Sophia resisted the urge to pat the invisible kitten clinging to her neck like a purring scarf.

"Well, all right. If you're sure," said Mom.

"I'm not sure, but I'll do it." Sophia opened the door. "I don't care if you get out and hug me. I'm not Sierra. I'm incapable of being embarrassed by public displays of parental affection."

Mom laughed.

Sophia slipped out of the Yukon, jumping to the ground seemingly a full story below. It made sense why the 'rents got such a big vehicle, having four kids... but they could've picked one that didn't require a ladder to get into.

While she gathered her bags from the back, Mom got out and walked around to the passenger side for one last farewell hug. If any of the other kids watching thought it stupid or childish, none said anything or laughed at her, not that Sophia would care.

"Try to have fun. You'll be home before you know it." Mom gave her a squeeze.

"Fun. Right. Outside with the bugs and stuff is supposed to be fun." Sophia slung her backpack over one shoulder.

"You can't spend all summer inside reading. Some air is good for you."

Sophia chuckled. "Tell that to the school. Did you see the

size of the summer reading list? A lesser mortal would be stuck inside *all summer* long to finish it."

"So, about a week for you then?" Mom winked.

"I'm done already," deadpanned Sophia.

Mom laughed so loud all the girl scouts and leaders stared at her.

"What?" Sophia playfully flailed her arms. "I like to read." She fidgeted, then muttered, "Much more than being covered in bugs and nature."

"Soph!" yelled Nicole. "Come on! We're leaving in like five minutes."

She sighed. "Gotta go, I guess."

"You'll be fine." Mom kissed her atop the head. "Remember to have fun."

Yeah, right. Sophia bit her lip, turned, and walked over to her two friends and the other fourteen girls in her troop plus Mrs. Whitaker and Mrs. Brewer, two moms who ended up as their troop's scout leaders. Shante, the eleven-year-old daughter of Mrs. Brewer, had a slightly more enthusiastic attitude toward Girl Scouts than Sierra. She only participated due to her mother being one of the troop leaders, though didn't complain about it. McKenzie Whitaker, also eleven, embodied the exact opposite attitude. One would think the girl invented Girl Scouts. Her mother only became a scout leader after incessant begging.

Sophia paused at the thought. If Mom could go to the camp as a leader, the idea of spending a week away from home wouldn't be anywhere near as unpleasant.

Ugh. I guess I have separation anxiety.

She glanced back at her mother briefly. The woman offered a comforting smile and waved. Sighing, Sophia advanced over to stand with her friends. Soon, random conversation took her mind off the impending horror of being dragged off into the middle of nowhere. Before she knew it, she found herself sitting inside one of the school buses by the window, Nicole and Priya to her right. A *whump* from the bus door sounded as final as the gates of a prison closing on a life-without-parole inmate's first day. She could no longer get up and run off the bus if she wanted to. Overcome by fear, she tuned out everything around her and stared at her lap, daydreaming about her nice, safe, and awesome bedroom. When she finally looked up, the realization they'd already started driving spiked her anxiety as bad as if a vampire came out of nowhere and abducted her.

Chill out. Nothing to be scared of.

She hugged Klepto, earning an odd look from Nicole.

"Something wrong with your neck?"

"No." Sophia smiled.

Klepto briefly revealed herself, then went invisible again.

Nicole and Priya burst into giggles.

Conversation over the next twenty minutes involved the smuggling of pets where pets weren't allowed. Sophia defended herself using the logic of Klepto not being a pet as much as a friend. Also, the kitten didn't exactly count as an ordinary cat.

Her anxiety goblin took a nap for most of the two-ish hours of the ride. It woke up and roared when she looked out the window at a small dirt road and trees everywhere. They'd gone well afar from civilization. She lost track of the conversation, the voices of her friends and all the other girls blurred into a noise as meaningless as the rumble of a school cafeteria and stared fixedly out the window, consumed by worry at being so far away from home. The oddity of being so scared didn't even register. She and Sarah had previously been magi-napped to London, which according to most people with a certain degree of education, is considered farther away from home than a campground two hours southeast of Seattle.

Granted, for most of the time they spent in London, they worked to go home. Now, she *chose* to go somewhere and would not be focused on going back as soon as possible. She grimaced upon noticing how much her hands sweat—and trembled, but worry had her too solidly in its grip for any sense of foolishness to displace fear. She'd made a huge mistake. Mom gave chance after chance to abort the mission and stay home, and she stupidly missed them all.

Sophia shifted her gaze from the window to the back of the bus driver's head. A little magic might convince the woman to turn around and take her home. She focused on her desire to plant such an idea. Her shaking hands slipped from the magic worse than if she attempted to hold onto a slimy, struggling fish trying to jump back to the water.

Being too scared-slash-freaked-out to use magic proved she had made a mistake.

Tears gathered in her eyes. She covered her mouth and nose in both hands, trying to breathe slow and deep in search of calm. The bus hit a few bumps in the road, making girls in the back seats squeal and laugh as they caught a few inches of air. Sophia kept her eyes closed, trying to tell herself going camping wasn't a big deal. Only a week. It didn't matter if anyone saw her hugging Mom, but being caught crying for nothing *would* get her teased. She'd already told her friends she couldn't sleep last night, so pretending to have dozed off now worked. No one could hear the quiver in her voice if she didn't say anything. If they noticed how wet her eyes had become, she could blame it on yawn tears.

Concentrating on her mother's comforting expression helped. In a few minutes, Sophia no longer felt like jumping out the window of the bus and running home. She may or may not have calmed herself enough to use magic, but decided against it. Not only would it be rude to everyone else on the bus who wanted to go camping, it might attract undesirable attention as the authorities tried to determine *why* the bus driver did it. Even if the Persons In Black didn't catch her for bending the laws of reality, she didn't want to be responsible for the poor woman ending up in trouble.

Sophia lowered her hands from her face and stared into her lap for a blurry few minutes until the bouncing and jostling lessened. The winding dirt road ended at a 'gate' made of telephone poles and a large wooden sign reading 'Lake Easton Girl Scout Camp'. Someone near the front of the bus chattered about getting to ride in a canoe on the Yakima River. Sophia cringed, hoping the scout leaders might let her skip it. Who knows what manner of unspeakable horrors lived in the depths? Sarah had been attacked by skeletons months ago at the bottom of the ocean.

Thoughts of nightmarish creatures emerging from the water to capsize their canoe and drag her to a watery demise gave way to quiet. Sophia opened her eyes to find herself on an empty bus. All the kids and counselors milled around about thirty feet away in a grassy field. Past them, a small complex of 'cabins' more or less filled a clearing in the woods. They didn't look terribly authentic, being mostly modern structures designed to vaguely resemble something between Native American architecture and log cabins.

Why did they even bother? Those aren't fooling anyone.

Sophia glanced down at her bag between her feet. Sitting alone on the bus didn't really help, but it represented being one step closer to going home. Maybe she could just sit there and wait until the driver came back. Even if the bus returned to a company lot, it would be easier to walk home from there than from the campground... assuming, of course, the driver didn't work for the Girl Scouts and planned to stay here the whole week, too.

The idea of hiding out on the bus all week seemed momentarily plausible and even a good idea. Somehow, no one had noticed her fail to get up and exit the bus. Maybe they wouldn't notice her at all. Desire to go home more than anything spilled out of her eyes and ran down her cheeks. Klepto purred harder, rubbing her head against Sophia's chin.

Yeah. I'll just sit here until it takes me home.

"Mew," said Klepto.

"I know," whispered Sophia. "I'm being stupid and childish. Gonna need food and stuff."

"Soph?" called Nicole from the front. "You awake?"

Darn. Guess I'm not gonna be able to sit here waiting for the ride home.

"Yeah." She overacted a yawn while stretching, then reluctantly stood, gathered her bags, and made her way off the bus. After one final longing sigh at the door, she jumped down to the grass and trudged along behind Nicole to where her troop clustered.

SOPHIA TOLERATED THE PROCESS OF BEING ASSIGNED TO A bunk cabin and 'oriented' with the basics of the campground. This took up most of the time between arrival and dinner. She ended up sharing sleeping quarters with seven other girls, which thankfully included her friends Nicole and Priya. Each tiny cabin had four bunk beds, but no toilet, sink, running water, or electricity. Sleeping cabins formed a row along a dirt trail that led back to the main campsite. The closest 'large' structure to the bunks contained the bathrooms and showers. If anyone ended up having to pee in the middle of the night, they'd face a long, annoying hike in the dark.

Being an 'experienced' camper, she'd completely forgotten to bring any sort of flashlight. If she ended up needing the bathroom after bedtime, she'd either make a magical glow or ask Klepto to borrow a flashlight.

Meals would be served in a cafeteria fairly similar to the one at school except for two major differences: no electricity and all the cooking happened out back behind the building over charcoal fires. Exposed khaki-painted wooden beams in the ceiling covered in cobwebs further made Sophia feel as if she'd gone to the edge of civilization. The place gave off vibes more like 'pre-electrical Amish village' than camping. No tents anywhere in sight. All reasonably solid—if basic —buildings.

She mostly followed her friends without talking much, clinging to Klepto and dividing her time between regretting her decision to go and trying to make time move faster. They spent about forty-five minutes after the orientation sitting in a huge group with all the attending girl scouts, various troop leaders, and some camp counselors. The camp director, an upbeat, blonde middle-aged woman named Verna, spoke, welcoming them here then introduced a few of the people in charge plus the nurse on staff. Apparently, the rest of today, Friday, would consist of relatively unstructured time so everyone could settle in and get used to being at the camp. Scout leaders cautioned the girls not to wander out of the camp's grounds without an adult, and not to go anywhere alone.

Thus began a fifteen-minute presentation about the 'buddy system.'

Sophia sat on the floor among her troop and friends, staring at her flip-flops and wanting to go home. She wondered what Sierra, Sam, or Sarah were doing right now. Certainly, they'd be having fun or something much more than her. Being away from her family *sucked*. She pined as if she'd been sold off as a political wife to a foreign prince and would never see home again.

Too late now. She frowned to herself. *Sarah said she'd come get me if I wanted to go home, but everyone here will freak out if I disappear.* A long, slow breath leaked out her nose. *I gotta handle this. Not gonna do this again, but I'm already here now.*

The assembly ended with an announcement for everyone to proceed to the 'mess hall.' Sophia scrunched her nose. Before she could ask why the camp had a place specifically to make messes, her anxiety-riddled brain relaxed enough for her to understand they meant the cafeteria. She smirked, thinking it silly to use 'military' terms here. Except for the lack of electrical power, they didn't exactly 'rough it' in the woods. Of course, to some of the girls, not having cell phone access was more horrifically primitive than being a contestant on *Naked and Afraid,* stranded in the woods with nothing at all.

Sophia took no delight in other girls' complaining about the horribleness of being cut off from the internet, but hearing them whine about something so trivial made her feel a little better. An eleven-year-old shouldn't be this messed up at being away from her family, even if her family had become something quite different from normal.

Sighing to herself, she followed the crowd. It finally occurred to her she hadn't eaten breakfast *or* lunch today, being too wound up and anxious. By the time she entered the mess hall, the scent of hamburgers and hot dogs grilling made her realize how hungry she'd become.

HOMESICKNESS KEPT SOPHIA QUIET AND SUBDUED ENOUGH for her friends to notice something wrong. For whatever stupid reason, she didn't admit to why she came off as distracted, sad, and worried, blaming it on not sleeping well. Priya mistook her inability to sleep for her being excited over camping, but Nicole figured it out. She knew Sophia longer and also knew she'd purposefully skipped going to camp last year and hadn't even wanted to talk about the idea back then. Alas, Nicole had Mom's attitude. She didn't feel guilty for twisting Sophia's arm into going and kept saying stuff like 'you'll see how fun it is' or 'give it a chance.'

At the moment, playing chicken with a void octopus sounded more appealing than spending another hour away from home. She'd successfully opened a portal across the country to get the stuff necessary to enchant Sierra. Opening a doorway home—a mere two hours' ride distance—ought to be easy enough.

She took three steps away from the group, intending to fake sickness and go see the nurse. Once inside the big cabin, she could find a closet suitable for a portal. Alas, after a fourth step, she stopped and stared down at her flip-flops, two small pieces of pink proof at her unpreparedness for camping. The documentation the troop sent home wanted her to bring hiking shoes or trail boots. She'd 'forgotten' to mention it to Mom, hoping not having rugged footwear might disqualify her from camping and get her sent home.

Again, she thought of her friends panicking if she 'disappeared.' The adults would go nuts, too, and probably get the police involved, maybe even the National Guard to search the area with helicopters. No one would even jokingly entertain the idea she teleported home. They'd all think she wandered off into the woods and got lost.

The combination of wanting to go home so bad it hurt, plus guilt over the chaos she'd cause if she did so knocked Sophia to her knees. She retched once, but stopped short of throwing up.

Nicole zoomed over and crouched next to her. "You okay?"

A tingle in her eyes warned of imminent tears. Sophia wiped her mouth on the back of her arm, then whispered, "I wanna go home."

"Aww." Nicole patted her on the back. "You really look freaked out. Hey... I didn't know it was like a real thing for you. I probably shouldn't have nagged you about going so much. I thought it would be fun for you."

"I'm being a wimp." Sophia closed her eyes, fighting her need to cry with every ounce of willpower she had.

"Nah. You had some stuff to deal with."

Sophia pressed a hand to her stomach, trying to hold back the increasing urge to throw up for real. Klepto snuggled against the side of her neck, purring loud. As soon as she noticed a bunch of other girls all staring at her, Sophia forced herself to stand and tried to hide her face, certain she'd broken out in a severe blush.

They're gonna make fun of me for being a baby.

"If you need to go home, tell Mrs. Whitaker or Mrs. Brewer," said Nicole.

Sophia took a few deep breaths. "They're just gonna tell me to 'buck up' or something lame."

"Because they don't know it's like a real mental thing."

"I dunno." Sophia glanced at her friend. Seeing genuine concern in Nicole's eyes rather than the plastic, insincere 'go team go' attitude the scout leaders tended to give off helped. "I should at least try not to freak out."

Nicole squeezed her hand. "Give it a day or two. I'm sure you'll be okay. If you're still upset by Monday, I'll nag the hell out of Mrs. Brewer until they call your parents to come get you. And, sorry."

"You don't have to apologize."

"I kinda guilted you into doing something you really are

terrified of." Nicole kicked at the dirt. "Not really a good friend. I honestly thought you might like camping once you actually tried it."

"Sure you are. Just… you failed to comprehend the depths of my personal insecurities," said Sophia in a faux-serious tone.

Nicole smiled. "C'mon. We gotta catch up. Our troop's going somewhere."

Sophia looked over. Mrs. Whitaker and Mrs. Brewer plus the girls from their troop moved off together, heading for one of the larger buildings. "Okay… I'll give it a day or two." She nervously swallowed the urge to puke, clung to Klepto, and followed Nicole back to their group.

5

THE WIZARD OF ODD

Sam decided to call in reinforcements of the not-fully-demonic kind.

Even the usually perceptive 'rents failed to notice his battle preparations thanks to the chaos of Sophia's departure for Girl Scout camp. He'd thought of talking to her about the goblins since she had been studying magic and strange stuff, but decided not to because she looked so upset. As much as she denied it, Mom, too, had been upset. She basically absorbed Sophia's stress. Her daughter being so crazy scared affected her as well. Except for Dad making a joke about there must be something wrong with Sam for a boy to be awake this early on a summer Friday, he largely escaped notice.

Reinforcements took the form of his friends Darryl and Jordan. They, too, had been abducted by vampires trying to get at Sarah, though only Ronan remembered the event. Sarah and Dalton rewired the other boys' brains. The existence of goblins didn't seem as important to keep quiet as vampires. If the boys saw tiny green creatures and talked about it later, most people hearing them would assume they made up stories. Not wanting to be laughed at and thought childish ought to be enough to keep them quiet without needing to ask Sarah to erase their minds.

Since whatever unusual ability Sam had to harm demons didn't work on these goblins, he prepared appropriately. No Nerf gun or foam sword this time—he brought the trail knife his grandfather gave him for his ninth birthday. Grandpa Wright had hopes of Sam joining the Boy Scouts and going all wilderness explorer, perhaps enlisting in some branch of the military when he became old enough given his fascination with military jets. Sam didn't have much interest in the scouts or camping. Playing with jets sounded cool, so the Air Force remained a distant possibility.

Despite it being fairly early on a Friday afternoon, Sam brought a flashlight and a small backpack of important, helpful items: rope, matches, a few cans of Red Bull, several Twinkies, a Ziploc bag of peanuts, two permanent markers, and one pair of clean underpants. Those didn't make much sense when he thought about it, so perhaps Dad's comment about always having a clean pair of underwear handy had been a joke.

Given the comparatively small size of the woods behind the house, an 'island' of trees surrounded by suburbia, he didn't worry about tents, sleeping bags, real food, or toilet paper. It would take serious effort to get lost for days in an area of forest roughly a quarter mile across. No, the goblins must have a lair of some kind dangerously close to the house.

Sam still didn't really like the idea of setting out to kill something. However, these goblins represented a serious threat, not only to him and his family but to any kids in the area. They also didn't really count as 'living things' since they didn't belong in this world. According to Blix, they came from another plane, almost a dream world. This explained why they burst into slime stains and bones upon death. As soon as the energy allowing them to take solid form in this world dissipated, they melted.

The boys assembled on the deck behind the house. Darryl and Jordan both brought baseball bats. Sam decided to be honest with his friends and told them about the goblin, even showing them the skull and bones of the two Blix destroyed. He didn't mention Blix, though. Even though he'd known Darryl and Jordan longer than Ronan, they remained outside the 'circle of secrets' regarding supernatural stuff, mostly for their protection. Also, telling too many people risked the family. Since Ronan's older brother dated Sarah, knew about vampires already, and seemed likely to stay with her for a really long time, he basically counted as family... which meant so did Ronan. Much harder to keep secrets from family.

Still, he'd spilled about the goblins to both of his long-time friends, trusting they would be too afraid of teasing to tell anyone else. Last Sam checked, goblins and other critters didn't have influence over mortal law, finance, and politics... so no one would really care if a bunch of kids started telling stories about them being real.

Heck, the boys could probably talk about vampires, too, and no one would take them seriously—except for the vampires.

"You guys ready?" asked Sam.

Darryl smirked. "Yeah. Goblins? Really?"

Ronan rubbed his chest. "Really."

"Let's go." Jordan grinned. It remained unclear if he believed Sam, humored him, or assumed it a game.

Blix, invisible to all but Sam—and probably Ronan—led the way across the backyard into the trees. They'd gone into the forest here countless times. Any adult neighbor would think them having another fantasy adventure, like LARP-ing only without actual enemies to get into foam sword fights with. If Mom knew the truth of their mission, she'd certainly tell Sam not to run off and battle supernatural bogey men without an adult along. Dad, undoubtedly, would insist on coming with them. Under normal circumstances, this wouldn't be a problem and Sam would honestly like having him there. Problem being, breathweavers—according to Blix —could sense adults coming and disappear. If they brought Dad with them, they'd never find the goblins. The imp couldn't come up with a firm answer about how old a kid needed to be before this particular type of goblin couldn't hurt them anymore. His estimate suggested around nine or so, but it could vary depending on personality. An older kid like Sophia who despite being eleven remained afraid of the dark and easily scared could still be vulnerable to them while an overly mature nine-year-old who stopped believing in stuff like goblins earlier than their friends wouldn't be as appealing.

While something about Sam, perhaps his magical affinity for demons, protected him from a single goblin, Blix felt sure he'd not be able to resist a small army of them. In the twenty minutes or so after the attack last night before Sam fell asleep again, they'd discussed the idea of an open gate being out in the woods somewhere. Even if they didn't manage to find goblins, closing the gate would be good enough.

The trek into the forest felt much the same as any other time the boys went on an 'adventure.' They made their way past the small creek, over the rickety footbridge someone made years ago. It seemed kinda dumb to build a bridge over a stream so small even a kid Sam's age could simply step over it without getting wet.

"What are we looking for?" asked Darryl.

"Goblins," said Sam in a matter-of-fact tone. "They're kinda small."

Jordan laughed. "Ronan is 'kinda small.' These things are *tiny.*"

Ronan shrugged.

"You're one to talk." Darryl nudged Jordan. "You two could be twins."

"Nah, he's prettier than me." Jordan fluffed at his shoulder-length blond hair.

"Bite me," muttered Ronan, who had even longer blond hair.

Darryl and Sam laughed.

Kids at school teased Ronan for being girly, but he didn't care. To him, long hair equaled fantasy hero. Considering the boy's short, skinny stature, he gave off more elven warrior vibes than Conan the Barbarian. Sam had quietly let his hair go as well. Surprisingly, Mom hadn't said anything even though it had reached his shoulders. Uncle Hank always complained about 'the long hairs,' and Mom's parents spent years insisting they constantly cut Sam's hair really short. He'd never really cared about it before, but once he expressed a preference to letting it grow a bit, the 'rents said 'it's his hair. His choice.' The grandparents didn't seem pleased, but also didn't complain too much.

"Goblins…" Darryl glanced around. "Here? We never saw them before."

"I know." Sam continued walking somewhat fast, following Blix. "They haven't always been here. There's a gate or something we gotta find."

Darryl and Jordan exchanged a glance, shrugged, then followed.

Ronan clutched a hockey stick in both hands, warily eyeing the trees as if expecting a goblin to come flying at his face at any second.

The imp glided into a tree, clinging to the trunk at head

level while peering around it. He looked back over his wing at Sam. "Found it. Ahead. Cave."

Sam knew the cave. The boys frequently played there, pretending it to be everything from a bunker, to castle, to spaceship. At the approximate center of the wooded area stood an odd, misshapen hill, a house-sized massive dirt clod jutting up from the ground. It sloped only on one side, the other three being sheer cliffs. The face opposite the slope had an opening concealed behind a tangle of old, dried roots that led to a smallish one-chamber cave.

Familiarity bred confidence.

The boys approached the tall end of the hill, going straight to the cave with no hesitation. Sam pulled the roots aside and ducked into the cool stone passage. Being surrounded by civilization didn't necessarily guarantee a bear hadn't moved back in. He didn't doubt bears often made a home of the cave many years ago before humans took over. People spotted the occasional bear in town, so perhaps one might've found its way in after all.

No big deal. Blix can scare a bear off.

Expecting goblins, Sam pulled his trail knife out of the sheath on his belt before proceeding deeper.

The first six or so feet of cave descended at a relatively steep angle before leveling off into a hollow approximately the size of the living room back home, only with a shorter ceiling. Darryl's hair touched the stone above them. He kept grumbling and swatting at dangling roots. One fact about the cave having only a single chamber: quite easy to tell they'd found an empty cave.

No goblins.

"You sure this is it?" asked Sam.

Blix emitted a confused grumbly noise.

"How should I know?" asked Jordan.

"Umm… no idea." Ronan shrugged.

"Who are you talking to?" Darryl nudged Sam.

"The voice in his head." Jordan twirled a finger around his right ear.

They didn't know he had an invisible imp following him pretty much all the time.

Sam grinned and jokingly puffed out his chest. "To have a conversation with my equal, I'm forced to talk to myself."

The obvious humor in his voice—and poor attempt at an Irish accent—made the other three boys laugh.

"Well, there's nothing here." Darryl poked the wall with his baseball bat. "If your goblins came out of this cave, they're gone."

Blix prowled around, exploring and sniffing.

"Hang on." Sam re-sheathed his knife. "Give me a second to concentrate."

"Don't concentrate too hard." Jordan laughed. "You'll hurt yourself."

"Naw, he's not Kelly Miller," said Darryl.

Sam focused on Blix, tuning out his friends making fun of this girl Kelly at school who everyone basically considered the world's dumbest person. After a few minutes, Blix gave up, looked at him, and shrugged.

"Nothing?" asked Sam.

"Energy here. Can smell, but no find." Blix fanned his right wing, sniffing at the air. "Maybe gate closed already. Maybe gate somewhere else, close. Not cave. Top of hill?"

Sam spun toward his friends. "Let's look on top of the hill. Might not be in the cave."

"Okay." Ronan planted the end of his hockey stick in the ground like a wizard's staff.

Darryl took the lead on the way out, followed by Jordan. Sam, Blix perched on his back, went next, with Ronan at the rear.

"Whoa…" Darryl stopped at the cave mouth. "What the hell?"

Jordan squeezed forward to peer out. "Holy shcrap."

"Schrap?" asked Ronan. "What's that?"

"That's him not getting in trouble with his parents," deadpanned Sam.

"Duuuude." Darryl turned, grabbed Sam by his shirt, and pulled him forward, pointing at something in the distance. "Explain."

Sam squished into the cave mouth between the other boys, peering out at forest. The trees seemed somehow different, but he couldn't quite grasp what exactly had changed. Certainly nothing drastic enough for his friends to stop short and gawk. "What?"

Darryl grabbed Sam's head and twisted it to the left, directing his gaze at a long multi-wheeled truck painted in reddish-brown-green camouflage that should not be there. It certainly hadn't been there moments ago. The thing had so many wheels it looked like the vehicle version of a centipede. An enormous tube big enough for a grown man to stand inside without ducking ran the entire length of the vehicle, its conical point extended past the cabin at the front, splitting it into two separate small windshields. He counted eight axles, the front two pairs and back two pairs of tires turned slightly as if it had died in the middle of making a turn. Considering the weeds growing around it plus the general look of abandonment, he assumed it had been sitting there for quite a long time.

"Holy crap," whispered Darryl as he exited the cave. "That looks Russian."

"Oh, shit," muttered Sam.

The other three boys stared at him. Jordan cringed. His parents had a tendency to get angry at foul language. Darryl finally looked worried. Sam didn't swear much at all, but a nuclear missile carrier definitely warranted at least a 'shit.' It probably would've excused an f-bomb, but he didn't feel like teasing the universe just yet. And really, if the tube didn't contain a live missile, the f-bomb would be an overreaction. Who would abandon an actual nuke in the woods? Truck, sure, but a weapon?

"What?" whispered Ronan.

Sam approached the truck, noting the presence of red writing on the side, *definitely* not in English—or even normal letters. He had to look *up* at the top of the tires. "I think this is an ICBM carrier."

"Seriously? How did someone sneak a missile truck into Cottage Lake?" Jordan whistled. "And how the hell did we not notice it before?"

"No one snuck it into Cottage Lake." Sam kicked at the weeds growing out from between the two front steering wheels. "This thing has been here for a long time. Probably since the Eighties."

"Is there still a missile inside it?" asked Darryl.

"How should I know?" asked Sam.

"You sometimes just know stuff." Jordan snickered.

Sam peered back at Blix, who perched on his right shoulder.

The imp nodded.

"Crap. Yeah. There's probably still a missile in there. Whoever operated this thing just abandoned it." Sam backed away from the truck. "We definitely shouldn't mess with this. Probably want to get the hell away from it."

"What's the worst that could happen?" Darryl opened the cabin door.

"Worst? We start World War III by accidentally launching a nuclear missile at the USA." Sam pulled his friend back. "Second worst, this thing is radioactive and we all die. Third worst is it explodes and vaporizes us."

"How is being radioactive worse than exploding?" Darryl made a face at him.

"Because," replied Sam in a matter-of-fact tone. "Radiation is a long, slow, horrible death. If it exploded, we wouldn't feel anything."

"Radioactive?" Jordan backpedaled fast. "You think?"

"They left a nuke abandoned in the woods for forty years?" Sam pulled Darryl back even farther. "Dad says the Russians do that all the time. Just leave stuff around."

Darryl rolled his eyes. "Russians? Are you serious? How did they get to Cottage Lake?"

Sam shook his head. "They didn't. We aren't in Kansas anymore."

"We never were. We're in Washington State." Darryl sighed.

"No, dorkus." Sam playfully shoved his shoulder. "It's a saying. You know, from *Wizard of Oz*. We somehow went... elsewhere."

Jordan stared around at the trees. "Where are we?"

Sam flapped his arms. "No idea. Somewhere with Russian military stuff. Probably Russia. Maybe somewhere else like Czechoslovakia or Poland. I dunno. Not even really sure it's Russian. Kinda looks it."

"How did we get here?" asked Ronan, his voice somewhat shaky. "I wanna go home."

"I'd ask if you're making fun of Sophia, but I kinda want to go home too... like fast." Jordan backed up even more from the truck, and stood next to Ronan. "Before that thing explodes."

Sam shrugged. "I don't think it's going to explode. If it's going to hurt us, it'll be a slow, painful death to radiation poisoning."

All three of his friends stared at him.

"What? I'm being logical. Nukes don't just randomly explode. They get old, leak, and—"

"Stop," shouted Darryl. "Let's go back into the cave. It has to be something with the cave. Maybe the CIA has some kind of warp gate or something that lets them sneak into Russia whenever they want."

"Yeah, sure they do." Jordan whistled. "This is messed up to the next level."

Sam turned in place, scanning the woods for any sign of goblins. "Maybe the goblins' nest isn't in Cottage Lake. They might've gone through the cave, too."

"Possible." Blix looked around. "This place have lots woods. I think breathweavers from here. Use cave to get to us."

"Don't care." Jordan took a step back toward the cave. "I'm not supposed to go too far away from home. I think Russia is past my limit. If my parents catch me here, I'm *so* grounded."

"Okay." Sam faced the cave. "Let's go into the cave and see if it sends us back."

A little girl's terrified scream came from the left, not too far away.

Sam stopped, staring in the direction the frightened shout came from. Despite being a kid himself, the screaming girl sounded younger than him. Either a bear snuck up on some random child or she fell into a hole. He had to help her. Or... perhaps the goblins chased a little girl. "Think we found the goblins. C'mon."

"Uhh," whispered Darryl.

Without waiting for any further response, Sam sprinted in the direction the shriek came from.

6

ANOTHER TASK LIKELY TO GO HORRIBLY WRONG

I wake up feeling strange.

It's not a 'day after eating overly spicy chicken nuggets' strange, nor something deeper like an existential crisis. This feeling is a combination of being overly aware I have nowhere to be and nothing specific to do mixed with the mild thrill of a teenager on summer break from school and a mind-twisting notion I'm going to feel exactly like this for the rest of my existence. One of the worst parts of adulthood—other than needing a day job—is how summer stops being awesome. Or at least, it feels *less* awesome. Those silly day jobs don't go on hiatus for three months like school does.

Sure, I could be one of those crazy, damaged individuals who take classes over the summer but... why? I'm neither addicted to education nor struggling to finish a degree as fast as possible for any reason. Honestly, a notion of 'if' has crept into my college life. The more involved I become with Wolent and the vampire world of Seattle, the more obvious it becomes having a college degree won't significantly alter the course of my future.

The 'rents both say it won't bother them if I decide not to continue going to school. Of course, what they say and what they mean aren't exactly on the same page. It would be one thing if time worked the same way for me as everyone else. Can't really call it *wasting* the 'best years of my life' doing college purely for someone else's benefit when I'm going to be this age forever. So, yeah... I'll probably stick it out. I already feel lazy enough not having a summer job.

However, it's still summer, which means I don't have classes right now. Ashley, Michelle, and Hunter are all doing the job thing. Of the three, only Michelle doesn't really need the money. She's doing it in hopes of getting herself known at the law firm, thus having an easier time getting in the door once she passes the bar exam in... however many years it takes. After normal college, she goes to law school. I probably won't see much of her for a while. Sigh. At least she thrives on being inhumanly busy.

Ash would go nuts. She tends to stress out fairly easy, but if someone else is in trouble, she's like the queen of handling things. As a vet, it would be some animal or pet owner having a bad time of it, so she'll be fine. She'd totally rock handling a crazy day at a clinic as long as it's not *her* pet in crisis.

This feeling of being free of all responsibility simultaneously relaxes me and puts me on edge. I'm quite sure the Universe isn't done messing with me yet. *Something* crazy is going to happen soon, I just sense it in the air, like that prickly, tingly electric breath of dread anxiety that wraps around the back of your neck the instant you make eye contact with a forty-year-old soccer mom standing on a street corner at a traffic light with a donation can for her kid's sports team.

Also in the air: weird paranormal energy. Oh, wonderful. What manner of nonsense invaded our house this time?

Hmm. Sniff. Not too much doom to it. Sniff. Malevolence? Yeah, but weak like tiny Australian wildlife, the critters that *want* to kill you but can't. As paranormal residues go, this is similar to the little bit of foot funk left on the rug two days after Uncle Ricky kicks his boots off at the front door. You know it's there and it's not terribly pleasant, but unless you pay attention, it's easy enough to ignore it. Something tells me getting *this* out of the house is going to be more involved than renting a carpet steamer.

Whatever it is, gotta be something minor. Can't even call it scary. I had more anxiety as a twelve-year-old babysitting the Littles, wondering if a door was open or why Sam didn't make more noise. Wouldn't be surprised if it's a leftover from Sophia playing around with magic. Maybe she tried to cast a spell in search of a way to avoid going to Girl Scout camp that wouldn't disappoint her friends. Good grief, I hope she didn't summon a changeling and sent it to camp in her place.

Given the silence in the house, I'm guessing either her spell failed or the energy didn't come from wayward magic. Really should go upstairs and check her room to make sure she's not camping out in her closet. It's been a while since a tentacle slapped me in the face. And wow, I'll take 'phrases I'd never thought I'd say seriously' for $400.

Right. Time to get up.

I don't feel like dealing with the sun just yet, so I trudge to the downstairs mini-bathroom for a shower. The relatively cramped space still kinda smells like Hunter, so I stand there for a few minutes in the warm water pretending he's here… at least until an explosion shakes the house.

Before I can freak out, Dad yells, "Please turn that down!"

"Sorry!" shouts Sierra.

Oh, whew. Merely the PlayStation.

Have I ever mentioned my father is really into movies?

This made him buy an overly elaborate sound system, which he hooked up to the living room television. Pretty sure his subwoofer could shake the plaster off the walls given the right soundtrack.

Anyway, showering is quick. I never have to shave my legs anymore. Got lucky... well, I suppose 'lucky' is kind of a strange thing to say about the day I was murdered. Shaved earlier that morning. Vampire anatomy freezes at the moment of transference. Our ability to regenerate resets us to the exact moment of death, with a few tiny exceptions—like gaping wounds. If someone gets shot, or like me, stabbed in the heart, the wound will close. Trivial stuff like hair length, fingernail length, and so on become permanent. If Sophia cuts my hair in the middle of the night, my body would consider it 'damage' and regrow it out to length. So, yeah. I never need to shave my legs again... or anywhere else. Gee, thanks Scott for insisting I get a wax. Sigh. Why did I keep listening to him about shit like that? Why did I do stuff to myself out of fear he wouldn't like it if I didn't? Our relationship probably counted as abusive more than I admitted to myself. Makes no sense to me. Nothing about my family or home life explains why I tolerated his attitude or craved his approval. The first time he told me to go fix him a sandwich and didn't mean it as a joke, I should've dumped him. He probably would've told me to do his laundry, too, if his mother didn't do it for him.

Whatever. Blood under the bridge, so to speak.

After drying off and throwing on a nice top and jean shorts, I head upstairs. For a summer Friday, the house is—PlayStation notwithstanding—quiet. I don't hear anyone upstairs. Dad's in his office typing away. No one else is making any sort of detectable noise downstairs. Yeah, I'm offline thanks to the stupid sun, but my hearing is still good enough to pick up the Littles. They aren't exactly the quietest critters on the face of the Earth. You'd think Sophia would be, but she can't read without constant emotional noises in reaction to whatever happens in the book.

"Hey," I mutter, leaning across the back of the sofa above Sierra.

"Hey," she replies without looking.

Sierra could be my younger twin at the moment, except for her hair being much lighter brown. She's also wearing jean shorts and a loose top. Another difference: purple-pink toenail polish. My toenails are presently unadorned. *Sierra* painting her toenails is about as uncommon as an honest person surviving more than six months in politics. Wait, no... Sierra wearing polish actually happened. I can only infer she and Sophia had a moment last night. Soph's been anxious as hell for the past week over going to Girl Scout camp. Sierra probably had a 'girly session' with her in hopes of helping ease her nerves.

At the moment, my twelve-year-old sister is fixated on the giant TV screen, quietly giving off vibes of 'say a word about the purple and you will die' vibes. Or maybe I'm misinterpreting simple concentration. Her aversion to being perceived as girly seems to be lessening somewhat. Guess whatever Sophia did to her magically has given her confidence. I mean, why would she be worried about being teased? If *Sam* wore pink toenail polish to school, he'd get teased. Not Sierra. Besides, she doesn't wear open-toed shoes or flops to school. No one would even see the paint.

Right. In addition to not using my powers of mind reading on my family, another thing I shouldn't do is play therapist to close relatives.

"So quiet today," I say.

"Yeah."

"Sophia okay?"

"No." Sierra shakes her head. "She's probably trying to

climb out the window on the bus right now. Wouldn't surprise me if she ends up walking home by herself."

I chuckle. "If she really has a panic attack and needs to come home, I told her to send Klepto to let me know and I'll go pick her up."

"Cool." Sierra pauses the game, looking down at the controller. "I feel guilty."

"Why?" I climb over the sofa back and sit cross-legged on the cushions behind her.

"I should've gone to camp with her, but I'm not in the Girl Scouts anymore, and I didn't wanna join up again just to go to camp *once* and then have them expect me to put on that dorky uniform and do dorky stuff all the time." She flicks her thumbnail at the buttons on the controller. "Now I feel guilty for letting her go alone."

Dad, who can obviously overhear us—since he always does—wisely chooses not to make a joking comment about preserving the moment Sierra admitted to guilt.

"It's Girl Scout camp, not the Trial of Seven Flames," I say, referring to a tedious gauntlet we had to deal with in one of Dad's D&D campaigns. "Nicole and Priya are with her, so it's not like she's all alone with people she doesn't know."

Sierra sighs, then twists around to look up at me. "Yeah, but can either one of them punch a vampire in the face?"

I chuckle. "Yeah, they could. Wouldn't do much, but they *could* punch one on the face."

She frowns. "You know what I mean."

"What makes you think a vampire is going to be a threat to her at Girl Scout camp?"

"Not there specifically." She exhales hard. "Just in general. She's far enough away to be outside Aurélie's protection."

If it hadn't been strange to watch my kid sister be so consumed with dread over school shootings, seeing her talk about elder vampire's protection and politics is equally weird. "Her protection applies to the family. We haven't moved away. If there are any vampires around the area of the camp, they wouldn't know who we are or care enough to target her. Any vamp from here running all the way out there to mess with Soph would still have to deal with Aurélie being furious… not to mention what I'd do to them."

She grins. "Got a feeling they'd be more afraid of her."

"Yeah, well…" I lean back. "Give me a few centuries. So, she really went?"

Sierra resumes playing her game. "Yeah. Shocked me, too."

Wow. That's going to end in one of two ways. Either she'll be traumatized and never want to do it again, or she'll get over her fear. Doesn't necessarily mean she'd want to go to camp next year, though. If I know Sophia, she's going to remember the two weeks of dread leading up to today more than anything that happens at camp. Even if being away from home for a week doesn't turn out to be the worst torture to ever happen to her, I doubt she will want to do it again.

"No Sam?" I ask.

"He's at Darryl's, I think."

"You think?"

"The boys came over, hung out for like five minutes, and ran outside." She shrugs. "I don't hear them screaming in the yard, so they probably went to Darryl's to go swimming."

Dad pokes his head in from the hallway leading to his mini office. "You planning to sit there playing video games all day?"

"Yeah," replies Sierra matter-of-factly. "Everyone's gone. You want me to—" She coughs a few times. "Go outside and stand there throwing a Frisbee at trees?"

"Hmm." Dad's mouth shifts left into his 'thinking expression.' Uh oh. Good chance this ends with either the house on fire, Sierra mortified, or both.

"You feeling okay?" I lean forward.

"Yeah." She pats herself on the chest. "Just woke up kinda sore."

"Overextend yourself at the sword place?" I ask.

"No." Sierra takes a few deep breaths. "My chest kinda hurts. It's not that bad. Feels like the time I got kicked at Taekwondo. Butthead."

Now there's a memory with a complex emotional reaction. Not sure whether to laugh or cringe. Third time she went to Taekwondo class—and a big part of why she initially quit doing it—they paired her off with a pudgy boy who was also fairly new. The kids weren't supposed to actually spar with each other. One wore hand pads, the other tried to kick the hand pads. This chubby kid either missed or did it on purpose, but he planted a side-kick straight into Sierra's chest that knocked her off her feet. It took her a few minutes to regain the ability to breathe, but once she got back up, she went after him with murder in her eyes. The instructor had to hold her back. Kid initially claimed he missed the pad, but when challenged, said he kicked her on purpose because she made fun of him for being fat.

I hadn't been there. Dad confirmed Sierra didn't say a word to the kid before the kick. Maybe she made a face at him because they paired her with a boy. She's totally not the type to pick on anyone. I can see her giving him a 'you gotta be kidding me' face, expecting a boy his size to throw a scrawny kid like her around even kicking the hand pad. Sierra has a funny way of making fear look like anger or scorn.

Whatever.

She rubs her chest. "Did Sam put a bowling ball on my chest when I was asleep?"

"I don't think we have a bowling ball in the house." I raise an eyebrow.

"We don't," calls Dad from his office.

"Maybe Klepto slept on your chest? Kittens can seem abnormally heavy under the right circumstances." I flash a cheesy smile.

She exhales again.

"Need a doctor visit?"

"Nah. I'm fine. Just a little sore." She resumes playing.

I stretch out on the sofa, watching her play for a while, relaxing. No real point fixing myself breakfast, tempting as pancakes are. One nice thing about immortality, it takes the urgency out of things. Sitting around doing nothing doesn't feel like I'm wasting time anymore. Any minute now, Dad might suggest the three of us do something like a board game... but those are kinda 'meh' with only three people. It's still Friday afternoon, meaning he ought to be working, so maybe not.

Hmm. It's July already and he hasn't said anything about a family road trip. This is unusual since he usually starts talking about it in late May. Admittedly, I thought of the trip to the caverns a year ago as our 'last family road trip.' Didn't expect to be correct, though. Mostly, I figured it would be *my* last road trip. Had my life gone according to plan, I'd have been living in Southern California attending USC... and may or may not have come home for the summer. Ever since I can remember, Dad's packed us up and taken some manner of trip every year.

Grr. Now I feel guilty. Did he give up on a family tradition because my existence as a vampire makes it a little tricky to swing a road trip? It's not like I'd object to going. Sigh. Also, the Littles aren't all surly teenagers complaining about being dragged off... yet. We've still got a year or three before that starts. Can't see Sophia complaining. Sierra already does. Sam... probably wouldn't. He can be obliging sometimes. And, he's curious. Whatever mental condition

Dad has that makes him adore going to see new places, Sam has, too.

My phone rings.

Caller ID says 'Shogun West.'

Weird. That's the Japanese restaurant we went to a while back. I have questions. Like, how did they get my number and why are they calling me? It's probably some robo-dialer with a sales promotion, a total coincidence we happened to eat there a month or two ago. I mute the call and toss the phone on the sofa beside me.

"Who was it?" asks Sierra, while guiding her on-screen character down a narrow underground shaft full of pipes and proximity mines.

"Marketing call probably."

"Ugh."

I roll my eyes. "Seriously."

The phone is quiet for a few seconds before ringing again. Same Caller ID. Okay, robot dialers don't usually redial the same number right away after no one answers. A live person is most likely on the other end. This still doesn't explain why a hibachi restaurant is calling me. Only one way to find out.

I answer. "Hello?"

"Sarah?" asks a fairly average sounding man.

"Umm. Who is this?"

"My name is Mark Allard. I am an associate of our mutual friend, Arthur Wolent."

I blink. "Oh... uhh..." That's right. Pretty sure someone told me he like owns the restaurant my parents like. Or at least, he owns a company that owns it—or something convoluted like that. "Yeah. This is Sarah."

"Great. If you aren't terribly busy, there is a matter we'd like to discuss with you. Mr. Wolent requests your assistance with a matter of mild importance."

There it is. I gaze up at the ceiling. While I'm not claiming to be precognitive or psychic, this does certainly explain the strange feeling from earlier when I woke up. Calm before the storm type thing. My sense of enjoying summer vacation and simultaneously feeling awkward about having no obligations while enjoying the idleness takes on a sudden clarity. Did I sense imminent badness? This better not end up with a sword where it doesn't belong. It's been two whole weeks without me bleeding from open wounds. I'm kinda getting used to it.

After a silent sigh is done sliding out of my nostrils, I force a smile. "Sure, no problem. What does he need me to do?"

It's not that I don't want to take the job or help Wolent out… I just know this is going to hurt.

"Would you be able to stop by the restaurant so we can explain in more detail?"

Right. Phone bad. Whether or not there's any truth to the stories the government listens in on all telephone conversations, vampires—especially men like Wolent—don't take the chance. There's also his age. He's totally from an era before phones went mainstream. Many elder vampires still regard phone conversations as less than polite, like we're disrespecting them to talk electronically rather than show up in person. My suspicion is they enjoy being able to read our minds, which they can't do over a phone. I ran into a vampire at the last soiree who still couldn't believe televisions caught on. Dude was around when they first appeared and thought only rich people would bother with them and the 'fad' of TV would die out fast. Note to self: don't trust that guy's stock advice.

"Urgency level?"

"Pardon?" asks Mark.

"Is this a can wait for the fiery ball of nope to go to sleep or should I drive?"

"Ahh." Mark chuckles. "Mr. Wolent is hoping your particular talents might turn a somewhat complicated situation into a triviality."

Ugh. Yeah, that means he wants to exploit my truce with the sun. It also means some other vampire or vampires have pissed him off and he thinks they'll be defenseless against me during the day. You know, if 'firebombing a giant nest of vampires' before age nineteen helped one's career prospects, I'd have a... 'killer' resume. Sometimes, I feel like *La Femme Nikita* or something, but honestly... reality is more *Hit Girl.* I still look like a kid to most adults. Thank the Universe I'm not abnormally short or people *would* think I'm a pre-teen.

Le Sigh.

That's French exasperation, by the way. From anywhere other than the Perrier region of France, it's technically 'sparkling frustration.'

"All right. I'll be there as soon as I can."

"Thank you, Sarah. I will be here."

We hang up.

Great. Guess I have a summer job after all. Wait, no... it's just a job. Not a summer job. This is going to stick with me all year round. Yay for undeath fast-tracking me into a career. Go me: Sarah Wright, minion of the undead mafia. Mom would be *so* disappointed. Heh. I tease. Wolent's organization merely resembles the mafia in some respects. Can't really say it's organized 'crime' or even all that organized. Honestly, it's closer to medieval baronies than the mob. They—we—don't generally do bad or illegal things. Just... political things in vampiric interest. About the worst activity I can think of Wolent's involved with is making money off arms trading somewhere overseas. I don't know who his people are selling weapons to, or what kind of weapons they are... or even *if* that rumor is true. If he *is* doing something like that, his motivation is mostly to get influence rather than profit. Don't get me wrong, he loves the profit part, too... but influence is more valuable.

Anyway... got stuff to do now.

"Uh oh," says Sierra. "What happened?"

"Got called in to work." I pretend frown.

"You have a job?" Sierra gawks at me. "At a Japanese restaurant?"

"Hah, no. It's Wolent's guy."

At the mention of 'vampire stuff,' Sierra instantly pauses the game and gives me her full attention. "Need help with something?"

"Dunno yet. They didn't tell me much over the phone." I scoot forward on the sofa, about to stand. "Pretty sure it's *not* going to be something I'm inclined to drag you into."

"You don't have to shelter me like I'm a little kid." Sophia eyes the hallway to Dad's office, then makes an intense face at me as if to remind me she's been 'enchanted.' "I can keep up."

I stand. "That's what I'm afraid of. You might be capable, but you're still twelve. That means you're overconfident."

"Hardly," she mutters, then whispers, "You know..."

I pat her on the shoulder. Yeah, she's really not confident at all. Honestly, the girl's as frightened as Sophia about some things, merely hides it well—usually behind fake anger. "I just want you to be safe."

She gives me this annoyed stare like I'm patronizing her.

"Someone's gotta stay here and protect Dad, right?" I crouch next to her and whisper, "Felt something weird in the air when I woke up today. Did Soph do magic last night?"

"I dunno. Nothing blew up, caught fire, or screamed, so I don't think so." Sierra gazes up at the ceiling. "Still feel it?"

"A little. But only when I think to look for it. Maybe another ghost came by to visit. Whatever it is, stay alert. I'll be back as soon as I can."

"Okay." She holds up a fist. "Call me if you need assistance."

"Will do." I bump fists.

Hmm. Do I go in shorts and a T-shirt or should I dress professionally? Bleh. Something tells me what they're going to ask me to do isn't compatible with a skirt suit and heels. I really need to get some kind of outfit made that's resistant to vampire claws and swords. Chuckling to myself, I mutter, "No Capes!" as I head downstairs to throw on a cleaner shirt, one approved for going outside.

7

GRR!

Sierra mowed down alien troopers one after the next, barely taking any hits.

Omicron 4 had pretty graphics and a decent story, but the enemy AI didn't offer a noticeable challenge. She couldn't criticize it *too* much. After spending so many dozens of hours playing *Call of Duty* against human opponents, any computer-controlled bad guys seemed dull by comparison. Game developers hadn't yet come up with 'real' AI. The only way they had to infuse challenge into a game was to make the computer literally cheat. Opponents went from trivial to ridiculous with no middle ground. Since she didn't feel like getting punished for screaming curses at the television, she left it on the 'hard' difficulty instead of turning it up to 'nightmare'.

In addition to offering a nice change of scenery, this game also didn't come with idiots cursing her out over the voice chat. The PlayStation CPU didn't care if she killed its minions and wouldn't subject her to streams of accusations of hacking, foreign cursing, or some idiot threatening to send a SWAT team to her house.

Much like her developing skills with a sword, Sierra didn't want to let herself get rusty at *Call of Duty*, so she'd go back to it soon. A break, however, proved relaxing. The dull pain in her chest had lessened quite a bit since she woke up. Sam denied messing with her in the middle of the night. Sure felt as if he'd been kneeling on top of her. His pranks tended to take the form of jump scares. Sneaking into her room at night and sitting on her didn't even remotely sound like anything he'd do, so she didn't insist on interrogating him. This meant something *else* happened. A little worry it might be a side effect of the enchantment kept her fidgeting.

At the end of a spaceship hallway, Sierra paused the game to look around at the living room. The repetitive clicking of Dad's keyboard accompanied the soft tones of subtle science-fiction background music from the PlayStation. Nothing sounded or felt strange, but she couldn't help but dwell on what Sarah said before going out the door.

Her older sister had sensed something weird in the house. Could an outside force have tried to hurt her last night?

Sierra pursed her lips and stared at her glittery pink-purple toenails. Sarah noticed them but said nothing, like a girl painting her toenails was totally normal. Dad made a big, embarrassing deal about it, as if her wearing polish came as more of a shock than Sam putting on one of Sophia's frilly dresses to spite Uncle Hank. Of course, everyone—except Uncle Hank—knew exactly why Sam did that, and it wasn't because he liked wearing dresses. Someone looking at Sierra would assume she enjoyed girly nail polish. That she didn't really hate it as much as she made everyone believe bothered her. Sophia loved the chance to paint her nails for her and definitely needed the distraction.

I could maybe sneak into the Girl Scout camp. Not like they'd notice.

There remained the small problem of how a twelve-year-old could get herself to a destination so far away from home when no public transportation went there and she didn't have money or a credit card for an Uber. Logistics of travel presented slightly less of a problem than having to suffer wearing a Girl Scout uniform. Maybe it didn't bother anyone there because *everyone* had to wear the stupid things. Same logic as one of those naked beach places. *One* person streaking is embarrassing, but if everyone is… they somehow aren't embarrassed.

She squirmed at the thought. Unlike one of those beaches, if she happened to be at a scout camp as the only kid in a T-shirt and jeans while everyone else had to wear the dorky uniform, she wouldn't feel singled out, she'd feel like she escaped having to do something stupid while everyone else suffered. If someone saw her in a Girl Scout uniform, they'd instantly *know* she was a nerd.

That by all reasonable estimations, she happened to qualify as a nerd only made her snarl more.

Dad once tried to point out a subtle difference between 'nerd' and 'geek.' He claimed their family counted as geeks due to their obsession with comics, science fiction, and such things. True nerds finished college by age twelve and designed world-changing technology before they turned twenty. Since Sierra could reasonably fake being a normal human with passable social skills, Dad said she didn't count as a 'nerd.'

Still didn't make her feel better. When Dad was a kid, other kids teased him for liking *Dungeons & Dragons*, fantasy movies, and video games. Sierra had never been made fun of for any of that. Video games and even *D&D* had become more or less mainstream compared to the prior epoch when Dad was in grade school.

Sierra looked at her fist.

Something in the house.

Nervousness crept into her mind. Specifically, fear regarding the enchantment Sophia cast on her. How long would it last? Taking a sip of vampire blood made her stronger and faster, but only for a few days. She kept expecting to wake up as a normal kid again, helpless if vampires tried to hurt them. Thus far, it had been about two weeks since they scummed the bathtub in powdered ruby dust, and nothing changed. She hadn't become weak or slow. Two nights ago, she and Sarah fought with stick swords in the backyard for practice, and she had no difficulty keeping up with her vampire sister. Admittedly, Sarah appeared to be going easy on her.

Sierra set the controller on the rug beside herself, scrambled to her feet, and ran upstairs to her bedroom. Once safely away from sudden parental observation, she squatted by the end of her bed and tried to lift it using one hand. Much to her relief, her bed rose off the ground about as easily as if she tried to lift an empty footlocker.

Whew. Still got it.

She finally relaxed, then opened her closet to check herself out in the full-length mirror. Doing martial-arts type stuff while staring at her reflection didn't help much since the motions never appeared unusually fast to her. She could catch Nerf darts out of the air when Sam fired them at her face. At school, she could yoink things off other kids' desks so fast they didn't see her move—and put them back just as fast. She didn't want to steal, merely test her speed and reaction time.

In her daydream nightmare, a blurry, indistinct figure in camouflage stepped through the door of a classroom, raising a rifle. She would totally be out of her seat and on the guy before he could pull the trigger. Ms. Butler told the class to make themselves as chaotic and annoying as possible. This terrified Sierra. The teachers basically told the kids 'some of you will die and there's nothing we can do about it but make it more difficult on the crazy person.' No… the crazy person would never expect Sierra. Not in a million years would they ever think a scrawny twelve-year-old could punch them so hard their jaw exploded into a thousand pieces. It didn't matter who saw what. Sierra would *not* hold back if her worst nightmare ever happened. Either Sarah or the Persons-in-Black could clean it up. No one would believe scrawny, quiet, antisocial Sierra Wright could possibly beat a grown man senseless.

Maybe they'd call it one of those super adrenaline situations like a mom ripping the door off a burning car to get her baby out.

Standing there alone in her bedroom in a mostly silent house filled Sierra with the impending fear something bad hurtled toward her and she couldn't get away from it. As if she found herself in a plummeting elevator with nothing to do except wait for the crash, she clenched her hands into fists and tried to breathe evenly.

Nothing to be scared of. It's light out. No vampires, no monsters come out during the day.

She again lifted the bed a few inches and put it down.

Still strong. I don't have to be scared. Stop being such a wimp.

An odd warbling noise echoed out in the hall, similar to the quiet babble Blix sometimes gave off when confused by a piece of technology he'd never seen before. Since Sam went to Darryl's, Blix shouldn't be in the house. The boy and his imp had become inseparable. This meant one of two things: either the noises came from some other little creature aside from Blix, or something strange happened to Sam.

Sierra crept to her door and peeked out into the hall.

The inhuman almost chipmunk-like muttering continued, sounding as though it came from Sophia's room. She steeled herself to be jump scared, then advanced, creeping up on her sister's door. An olive-drab T-shirt and jean shorts left most of her arms and legs exposed and vulnerable to tiny claws, but she didn't have time to change. Also, the source of the noises might not even be dangerous. Perhaps Sophia summoned something cute and harmless.

She nudged the door open, gazing around at the pinksplosion the room had become. When they shared it, they'd always battled over décor. Sophia gave off a Zerg creep of cute. Like the alien bugs in the *Warcraft* game, pink frilly crap seemingly spread like a kudzu invasion across the room, encroaching on Sierra's relatively ordinary space. Sam's bedroom clearly said 'young boy' thanks to various models of spaceships, fighter jets, and the selection of toys littered around. Any stranger looking at Sierra's bedroom would probably not be able to tell if it belonged to a boy or girl unless they rummaged the closet and found the handful of dresses stashed way in the back.

But Sophia's room? No doubt whatsoever a girly-girl slept there.

Pink walls. Frilly white bedclothes. Giant dollhouse. Unicorn crap everywhere. Stuffed animals flowed like a waterfall off the bed. Closet full of fluffiness.

Sierra exhaled at the extra-ness of it. She wouldn't tease Sophia about it, but seeing it filled her with a squirmy, uncomfortable awkwardness like watching a Will Ferrell movie. Didn't help they all knew Mom wanted a girly-girl. The unspoken joke in the family went something like Sarah wasn't quite girly enough. Once the 'rents realized this, they tried again. Sierra went in the wrong direction away from girly, so they had Sophia... then some passing aliens dropped Sam off.

Mom never complained about Sierra not being frilly, at least. Some of the moms from Sophia's dance class sounded like real terrors. She smiled to herself, thankful for at least the one aspect of her luck that worked out awesome: good parents.

The grumbly high-pitched whispering happened again, coming from the space between the giant dollhouse and the big pink toy chest.

Sierra crept over, stunned to find what she thought to be a stuffed animal moving like a tiny person. It stood about ten inches tall, generally human shaped insofar as it had a head, body, two arms, and two legs. Its head looked oversized for the rest of it, being almost as wide as its shoulders. The little critter wore a brown leather hood and tunic, even a miniature sword in a scabbard. It clutched a glowing pink crystal in slightly chubby, three-fingered hands, turning it over and over while staring in rapt awe as a thread of energy seeped from the tip of the crystal into the creature's mouth.

Whatever it was, it appeared to be trying to steal from Sophia. It didn't seem likely Mom would approve of glowing crystals in the house. Either she hadn't found it yet or surprisingly tolerated a stash of magical stuff.

"What are you?" whispered Sierra.

The creature gave a yelp of shock, nearly fumbled the crystal, then spun around to glare at her, breathing hard. Bright yellow eyes in its greenish-brown face narrowed. Rounded cheeks and a button nose might've made it appear cute, if not for the palpable malevolence radiating from it.

After a second of staring, it flailed its arms at her and gave off a shriek like six rats being electrocuted.

Sierra leaned back, raising an eyebrow. "Is that you trying to be scary? Try harder."

The small creature sneered and started to glower at her, then eyed the crystal. It shifted its gaze back and forth from crystal to Sierra a few times before flashing a sinister grin. She folded her arms, not the least bit threatened.

"*Ghat ooru naam!*" The goblin pointed the crystal at her.

A flash of light burst from the pointy end, followed a split second later by an explosion of olive drab fabric covering Sierra. After a brief sensation of falling, she found herself sprawled on the floor, pinned down by a burdensomely heavy pile of cloth. Diminutive chipmunk laughter somewhere in front of her deepened and deepened until it sounded like a grown man making fun of her for falling down the stairs.

Ooh! You little turd. You're gonna get it now.

Growling, Sierra grabbed at the rug to drag herself forward—but paused at the realization the carpet fibers had become the size of ropes. Worry and panic increased exponentially. In a frenzy, she fought the cotton-polyester blend tomb trapping her until she got her head and both arms free of the cumbersome weight pressing down on her. Not far from where she emerged, the creature continued cradling the glowing crystal, sniffing at it. Only, it now appeared to be closer to ten *feet* tall. The pink toy chest had become the size of a five-story building, the dresser next to it, a skyscraper.

"Oh, shit," whispered Sierra, not at all caring about her language. Dad would never hear her.

Too furious to think about where the massive pile of fabric came from, she grabbed two fistfuls of carpet fiber and pulled herself out from under whatever the stupid creature dropped on top of her. No sooner did she get to her feet than the now-giant monster spotted her. It shifted to face her, protectively hiding the crystal behind its back and drawing its sword—which looked full size and quite deadly.

"Put me back to normal or I'm gonna kick your ass!" shouted Sierra.

Unimpressed, the goblin raised its sword and attacked.

Sierra rushed toward it, roaring as much of a war cry as her lungs could produce. The creature didn't intimidate her at all. Size wise, he felt like sparring Jim, the tall bearded dude from her sword class who couldn't take girls—especially scrawny tweens—seriously as fighters. Granted, Jim didn't exactly stand ten feet tall. Sierra hadn't yet had the pleasure of sparring him after Sophia enchanted her. As much as she wanted to kick his ass for being patronizing, doing so would only invite the sort of scrutiny the Persons-in-Black tended to frown upon.

One major difference with Jim at sword class—this creature legitimately wanted to kill her, not simply tease her for being a 'weak girl.' It also broke into her home... and seriously pissed her off. She had zero doubt of its intention based on the look in its eyes. The reckless charging slash trying to take her head off also provided a less-than-subtle clue of its feelings toward her.

Sierra ducked a crossing slash at neck level, then sprang upward into an extended right hook, having to rise up on her toes to reach its chin. The creature's jaw cracked on contact with her knuckles, crunching under its rubbery skin. Emitting a *blart* like a stepped-on chicken, the goblin staggered backward, dazed. Consumed by fury, Sierra pressed her attack, unaware of anything more than the little monster in front of her. She slugged it in the gut, knocking an *oof* out of it. The creature staggered to the side, twisting around as it whipped the blade upward at her face again. It moved almost in slow motion—slightly faster than an ordinary mortal, but nowhere near as fast as Sarah—thanks to the magic Sophia infused her with. Sierra ducked. The weight of its sword hitting nothing pulled the creature into a spin. She maneuvered around mostly behind it and kicked it in the back of the knee. The goblin's leg snapped, dumping it face-down on the floor.

Growling, too furious to think, she pounced on it, hammering her fist into its head over and over until the creature stopped moving. Upon realizing her right arm had a coating of slimy green blood on it up to the elbow, she regained control of herself, got up off the monster, and stepped back, breathing hard.

A few seconds after the goblin disintegrated into a puddle of slime and bones, Sierra finally noticed she didn't have anything on. She peered down at herself, disgusted at the green splats of goblin blood all over, then glanced behind her at the massive pile of fabric she'd been trapped under. The goblin hadn't summoned a strange avalanche of random material. She'd shrunk right out of her clothes.

Sierra gasped, face hot with blush in an instant. At least she happened to be in a bedroom upstairs with some privacy. However, she couldn't exactly put on a pair of shorts the size of a galleon's main sail. She also didn't have any interest in roaming the house bare-assed. No way could she let Dad find her like this. She'd prefer Sarah or Sophia helped her, but Soph wouldn't be back for a whole week. It wouldn't be a big deal if Sam spotted her. He wouldn't make fun of her or laugh, and would sincerely try to help. The bigger problem with Sam discovering her at the moment is lately, he *always* had Ronan with him. Or worse, Darryl and Jordan. Under no circumstances did she want the boys to see her with nothing on, even if she'd been reduced to the size of an action figure.

"Shit!" she shouted, probably no louder than a mouse squeaking. "This is totally not fair!"

After spite-kicking a goblin bone one last time, she looked around at her situation. Standing there panicking was a Sophia move. She couldn't do that. Embarrassment, no matter how severe, could never hurt her. Malicious green-skinned creatures, on the other hand, could. For a few seconds, she closed her eyes and sent 'thank yous' into the Universe to Sophia. Without the enchantment, the monster would've totally killed her.

The giant—now colossal—doll house caught her eye.
"Hmm. Maybe."

Sierra stumble-ran across the carpet, feeling as if she
trudged half a city block through shin-deep snow to the
front door, which thanks to her becoming smaller now
appeared relatively normal in terms of size. A good sign. She
pulled the door open and went inside, searching for a doll
she could mug for its clothing. Her sister's Barbies all had
dresses, most of which looked like Disney princess ball
gowns, ridiculously frilly and extra. Other than being
strangely proportioned and not at all realistic, the dolls
looked about as tall as Mom, meaning Sierra had been
shrunk to roughly the same scale, being about as tall as a
twelve-year-old version of Barbie. Mom's clothes fit her a
little big, but she could already get away with borrowing
some stuff.

Finally, on the third floor of the dollhouse, she found one
wearing a gown that *didn't* look like it got rejected from
Bjork's dressing room for being too over-the-top. Alas, it was
pink. Still, compared to her other options, the fairly plain
garment would have to do. She stared at it, cringing at the
overwhelming pinkness.

Bad enough I'm stuck having to put a dress on. Why does it
have *to be pink!?*

Even worse than a Girl Scout uniform, it would almost be
more embarrassing to be seen wearing a pink dress than
nothing at all. Sierra stood there for a few seconds gazing
back and forth between the doll in a pink shift dress and her
birthday suit, trying to decide which one would be more
mortifying. Faeries didn't have clothes, and no one made fun
of them. She also didn't happen to be a faerie. The idea lasted
all of two seconds before she blushed and gave in.

She hauled the doll off the plastic sofa, dumping it face-
down on the floor, then gathered the long blonde hair out of

the way of the awkwardly large zipper on the back of the dress. After stripping the doll, she held the garment up to examine. The fabric seemed strangely thick, likely a byproduct of it being so small. She stepped into it, pulled it up, and proceeded to experiment in transcendental acrobatic yoga to reach the zipper. Getting the dress zipped felt like more of a workout than killing the murderous goblin thing, but she prevailed.

Slightly out of breath, she stood there, appraising the dress. On the doll, the dress fit like a miniskirt. On her, the hem came within two inches of her knees. Totally safe. Dad would not give her a hard time for wearing it any more than he'd make a joke about *her* wearing a dress. The zipper, many times larger than it ought to be thanks to the dress being mini, felt like she had a metal potato stuck to her back, but she couldn't exactly do anything about it. She ignored the doll's plastic shoes. Not only were they too small for her—the dolls had unrealistic tiny feet—they looked incredibly uncomfortable.

Ugh. He's going to make a joke about me in a dress, like me being six inches tall is totally normal.

She screamed an F-bomb for good measure. If anything warranted such an extreme, being miniaturized by a goblin certainly counted. Surrounded by Barbie dolls in elaborate princess gowns, fake pink curtains, and plastic furniture, she fumed, trying to figure out what to do. She absolutely did *not* want to spend all week like this until Sophia came back. Realizing she literally *couldn't* use a PlayStation controller at her size almost made her cry. Maybe the goblin's curse would wear off on its own? Probably not. Her luck didn't work that well. Of course, her PlayStation Portable would look as big as the massive TV at Aurélie's place.

Another high-pitched warbling grumble came from the hallway. Evidently, the house had more than one invader.

Snarling under her breath, Sierra stomped down the stairs of the dollhouse to the ground level, kicked the front door out of her way, and stormed over to the puddle of slime and bones to pick up the goblin's sword.

It weighed a little more than the sword Dad gave her for Christmas, but certainly didn't feel heavy thanks to her magically augmented strength. She swished it around a few times to get a feel for its balance, then glared down at the pink dress circumstance had forced her into wearing.

"Asses are going to be kicked for this." She narrowed her eyes. "*Severely* kicked."

8

REALLY OUGHT TO KNOW BETTER

T hey say with age comes wisdom.

Not sure who exactly said it, but someone must have. Problem is, I don't have much age *or* wisdom yet, so I've been relying on youth and impulsiveness. If the old adage is true, then one can assume old people seldom make errors, and by extension, elder vampires who have been around for centuries *never* make errors. Somehow, I doubt that. Seems unlikely, or there wouldn't be so much competition-slash-rivalry going on among them. Obviously, then, age is not the be-all-end-all measure of wisdom.

Take Arthur Wolent for example. He's old—not ancient, mind you, but old—yet he's also a Fury. No matter what he wants to do, if someone pokes him in just the right way, he'll explode into a fit of rage and do something rash. Call me hyper critical, but to me, that's the exact opposite of wisdom. Can't blame him for it, really. I'm sure he doesn't *want* to surrender his rational thought to an explosion of uncontrollable fury Could be worse. He's not a Beast. At least Furies only go off if something 'lights the fuse' so to speak. They have to experience something that would ordinarily annoy someone… only they take 'annoyed' to new levels. Beasts? They can go from total calm to murderous rampage completely at random, even if nothing provokes it.

Not such a big deal for vampire secrecy in 1490, but nowadays? Yeah… it can be a problem.

Know what else is weird? Like ten minutes after I started driving, this inexplicable sense of worry came over me like I left the kettle on. Can't imagine Dad and Sierra will get into much trouble. Unless I blacked out, there shouldn't be any kettles, microwaves, ovens, or stoves turned on unattended. Never even went to the kitchen before hopping in the Sentra and heading to the city.

The first traffic light I hit on the red gives me a chance to shoot a quick text to Dad.

<Feels like I forgot something dangerous. Kettle? Can you look around?>

A few seconds after the light goes green, my phone tweeps with his reply. Alas, I am offline at the moment so I don't bother trying to read his response while driving. Yeah, I might be undead, but that's not an excuse to be reckless.

The traffic lights are part of a conspiracy of annoyance. Every single one of them is green the rest of the way to Shogun West, thus preventing me from looking at the phone. It's about a half hour after my text message before I have a chance to come to a full stop in the parking lot. Dad's reply is a simple 'ok.'

This means he didn't bother getting up from his chair and simply listened and sniffed for anything out of the ordinary. By now, he's probably gotten up to go look. I must have caught him in the middle of a groove. It's how he programs. Whenever he hits his flow and everything's coming together, it's pretty damn hard to get him off the computer. Of course, it's his job and around forty percent of the reason we have a house, clothing, and food, so yeah... no one complains. However, we definitely understand where Sierra got her ability to sit on the PlayStation all damn day.

I grumble, stuff the phone in my purse, and stare over the steering wheel at the sleek, black building. It's like the set designers for *Blade Runner* and *Tron* got drunk together and went to Japan. Lots of shiny onyx and silver trim, Japanese style roofs. Random small trees everywhere. There's a huge circle on the front door containing a gold silhouette of a dragon. Thanks to my geeky father, I can't help but think it looks like the icon for House Kurita from the BattleTech universe. It's not an exact match, but similar enough to make me think of it.

The world is full of lies. Most of them come from marketing executives.

Who would ever expect a Japanese Restaurant is really owned by a rich white vampire? Or owned by a company owned by another company owned by a rich white vampire. I hate this stuff. Corporate accounting gives me a headache. I'd rather do something simple, like calculus. At least math makes logical sense and has rules. Don't care about power or wealth. I'm just here to be a good little vampireling and not piss anyone off. Doing a favor here and there for the big guys is a small price to pay for security. Yeah, sure, I *could* ignore it all like the Lost Ones do... but knowing my luck, something bigger than me would eventually decide to eat my lunch. It's nice to have friends with some clout.

I still have no idea what endeared me to Aurélie. Not complaining at all. Maybe it's the backswing of karma from the horrible luck of my ex-boyfriend killing me. Bleh. Whatever. Some questions shouldn't be asked.

The place doesn't look to be open yet, no surprise. Some

restaurants like this open for lunch, then close for a few hours before dinner service. Being in such an empty parking lot makes me feel like a stripper showing up at the club before it opens. This, of course, causes my stupid brain to run off on a tangent contemplating the crazy kinds of money a vampire could make at such a job. Charm powers, eternal youth, transience... a girl could spend a few decades stripping across the country and end up on the Fortune 500.

Except... stripping. No thanks. How weird is it for me to recoil from the idea as being worse than charming a bank executive to handing over cash? I mean, I wouldn't do that either... but in the grand scheme of things, mind-controlling a random person in a big bank to give me $10,000 cash bothers me less than the idea of going stripper... which is sleazy but honest money. It's not stealing.

Sigh.

I'm anxious and thinking about nonsense. Okay, doesn't help there *is* an adult club within sight of the sushi restaurant. Pretty sure a windowless purple-and-grey building called 'Daphne's Den' with neon legs in fishnet stockings on the wall is a 'certain kind of establishment.'

Part of me really hopes Wolent has nothing to do with the adult club. However, it seems that for most people, vampires and sex are like peaches and cream: always together. Mmm. Now I want to soak in a bath bomb, wash these embarrassing thoughts out of my head.

Right. Job to do.

I shove the door of the Sentra closed with a *whump*, sling my purse over one shoulder, and head across the lot. A T-shirt, jean shorts, and sneakers is definitely underdressed for this place. Shogun West just exudes a feeling like one needs to dress on the upper end of nice to get in. Don't care. It's outside normal hours and it's not like I'm here for dinner. Besides, when my family came here to eat, only the 'rents kinda-sorta dressed up. No one from the restaurant gave me or the Littles dirty looks.

Surprisingly, the door is open. I walk into a small foyer with red tile floor and one of those artificial waterfall setups on the right. Another version of the dragon-head-in-a-circle is on the left wall, easily six feet tall, partially concealed behind fake bamboo plants. The interior glass doors are, however, locked. Signs on the window indicate they don't open for dinner service until 6:00 p.m.

At me rattling the aluminum, two people inside peer up from a podium nearby: a black-haired woman in a dark blue kimono and a man in a black suit. Neither is Japanese. Both give me 'can't you read the hours?' stares.

Sigh.

I take my phone out and hit redial. It rings a few times before someone answers, but doesn't say anything.

"Mark?" I ask after listening to silence for three seconds.

"Ahh. Sarah. Yes. What can I do for you?"

I smirk at the people giving me 'go away' stares. "I'm at the front door. It's locked. Some woman and a guy are glaring at me like I just parked a Ferrari across two handicapped spaces."

He clears his throat. "Terribly sorry about that. One moment."

The plastic rattle of a standard phone handset echoes in the background over the line. One button clicks. A phone on the podium rings.

Kimono woman answers, then eyes me again. "I... don't know. Some random kid."

I hold up my iPhone as if she might make the connection that it's me on the line with Mark. The woman waves at the guy next to her in a 'go ahead' manner while muttering, "Yes, right away" into the phone.

Suit Man approaches the interior door, wearing an

expression like he can't believe 'the organization' is desperate enough to hire a kid. You'd think if this guy is at all aware of vampire stuff, he'd know the outside isn't any guarantee of age or power. If—fate forbid—Sophia became a vampire tomorrow, 200 years from now she'd still appear cute, innocent, and harmless... but would be terrifyingly powerful. Oh, maybe *that's* why vampires in general disapprove of giving the Transference to children. It might not have anything to do with it being 'wrong' or 'sad' to do to an innocent kid and all about creating a being with the powers of a vampire and the temperament of a child. Professor Heath, Glim, and even Aurélie have told me my personality and attitude are pretty much frozen as they were at the moment of my death. I will forever have the outlook of a teenager. I'm not going to 'grow up' any more than I already have. Thankfully, I'm kind of a mature eighteen-year-old already. But geeze... imagine a spoiled little brat being able to throw cars across the street when he doesn't get what he wants?

Eek.

Suit Man flips the deadbolt and opens the door. At least up close, he gets a better sense of how tall I am and his confused disdain lessens somewhat. "You're Sarah?"

"All my life." I fake smile at him.

No, I'm not *tall*. I'm just not child-sized. Much. Sigh. I should really stop being annoyed by this and consider it an advantage. Depending on the bagginess of my clothing and how much I slouch, I can be taken for anywhere from twelve to seventeen. If not for a little thing called personal dignity, I could totally exploit the hell out of seeming harmless when needed.

He looks me up and down... and there it is. That note of pity that 'someone so young' died. So many vampires make fun of the emos who 'miss the sun' and cry about being cursed with unlife. Why do they pity me? Either they think vampirism is awesome or a curse. Can't make fun of the emos, then pity a vampire for being a vampire. Ugh. Guess even the undead are full of contradictions. Then again, he might not know what I am. Maybe he thinks I'm a thrall since it's the middle of the afternoon. If Wolent went around telling *everyone* about me, he couldn't use me as a secret weapon.

"Where can I find Mark?" I drop my iPhone back in my purse.

"C'mon. I'll show you to his office." Suit Man re-locks the deadbolt once I'm inside, then whisks off across the seating area, heading for a back hallway.

A tapestry-like cloth hangs in the doorway, black with a gold version of the encircled dragon on it. We go past it into a corridor. Bathrooms on the left and right, around a corner, storage closets… offices. Aha!

The door at the end, right next to a fire exit, appears to be the manager's office.

Mark, or at least a man I assume to be Mark, sits behind a shockingly ordinary desk. His chair is not so ordinary. It looks super fancy, like someone ripped it out of a Lamborghini or some other car more expensive than a reasonable house. Seriously, this guy's office chair belongs in a futuristic spacecraft. Guess he has ergonomic issues.

It is, however, the *only* thing about the room to stand out. Everything else looks like a slice of grey-cubicle-farm corporate America, completely divorced from the faux-Asian aesthetic of the rest of the restaurant. Only a katana/wakizashi sword set on a shelf to the left gives any sort of thematic nod to where we are. Considering this restaurant is a front of sorts for Arthur Wolent, those blades are probably real and there for more than show.

Being offline, I can't tell anything about the guy from

simply looking at him. No more so than any ordinary person could. His being awake and functional in a sunlit room is pretty good proof he isn't a vampire... or if so, another Innocent. That, I find unlikely, both due to our rarity and Wolent wanting *me* to do this favor. Chances are, this guy is either a well-paid mortal or a thrall. Not that I'm terribly wise in the ways of business, but he looks a bit young to be the manager of a place like Shogun West— unless his parents own it. Yeah, he's gotta be a thrall, late twenties on the outside, probably closer to fifty or more inside.

As soon as he looks away from the computer screen at me, he almost chuckles, but contains himself while standing and offering a shake. "Well, you certainly aren't what I expected."

"What were you expecting?" I raise an eyebrow as we shake hands. "One of Wolent's glamorous deadly redheads?"

"From what he said about the assistance you provided at the graveyard, I'd been thinking more 'bond girl.' Less..." He waves his hand in a small circle, searching for a way to call me his friend's kid sister and not be insulting about it. "Normal."

Huh? Wow. Did not expect that. *Normal* is what I've been trying to pull off ever since my death. Yeah, this dude's definitely older than he looks. A refreshing change from everyone in the vampire world thinking I'm fourteen. Sierra has a shirt with a slogan on it something like 'I'm staying inside, the world is too peopley.' Yeah, kiddo. I feel you.

I shrug one shoulder. "Think that's kind of the point why Mr. Wolent picks me for some jobs. The Forces of Evil™ don't expect much from me by appearances."

He chuckles. "Well, in this case, it's your unusual schedule. They tell me you're, how to say... 'fully invested?' Not merely a borrower?"

Assuming he's asking me if I'm really a vampire and not a thrall like him, I nod. "Yeah."

"Amazing. You don't even appear uncomfortable, or sluggish."

I wag my eyebrows. "You haven't seen me right when the alarm clock goes off."

"Now *there* is something I'm rather looking forward to when the day comes." He gazes off into the distance, smiling to himself. "Can't come fast enough. Though..." He gives me side eye. "I do sometimes wonder if I'll have regrets once the, umm, contract is signed. Did you?"

"Deals with the devil never end well for the mortal. I never signed any contract."

He rolls his eyes.

"Seriously. It just kinda happened." I idly scratch behind my right ear, wondering how far he wants to take the evasive language. Is this guy afraid of eavesdroppers or bugs? "But no. Not really. No direct regrets at all. It's quite amazing, to be honest. Can't say for absolute certain it's something I would have chosen, but I'm happy at how things turned out."

Mark grins, seeming relieved.

I fold my arms. A mild sensation something at home demands my attention nags at me, making me fidget. "So, what's the McGuffin this time?"

He blinks. "Pardon?"

"I assume you are going to ask me to deliver, acquire, protect, or locate some item Wolent is interested in. What's the significant object that's going to make my unlife chaotic for the immediate future, put my family in danger yet again, drive me crazy... you know... the *item* upon which all the insanity relies. Like, if my life was a book or something, what would this installment be titled?—assuming of course, the person writing it didn't try to be slick and *not* title the story after the important object."

"Wow." Mark whistles. "You've done this before, haven't you?"

I make a pinchy gesture. "Few times. So, what is it? Locating, transporting, or stealing?"

"A bit of all three." He spins the computer screen on his desk around so I can see a picture of a relatively plain sword lying on a black desk. "This."

I move in for a closer look, sitting one butt cheek on the desk. The blade doesn't appear remarkable, ornate, or expensive. It does, however, seem old and *real*. Like, it's got a certain solidity and workmanship suggesting someone probably made it back in the day when people legit carried swords all the time. The blade is straight and double-edged with a deep fuller down the middle. It's about twenty inches from point to hilt. Basically, a short sword. Can't place the style, but it doesn't look English. It's incredibly plain, in fact the only decorative element to it is on the pommel, which is ever so slightly shaped to hint at a crown.

"Museum piece? Looks like a real blade." I fold my arms. "Not a movie prop or a fancy show sword. Is it historically significant?"

"Yes, but not terribly famous." He sits again in his ridiculous chair. "This blade belongs to Mr. Wolent but has recently been stolen. Your objective is to recover and return it."

"I'm guessing there's a reason he wants me to do it instead of hiring well-paid mortals." I stare at the photo on the screen, trying to memorize it. The weapon is so... unremarkable it would be easy to miss. Good thing swords as a general rule aren't too common these days. "I'm not terribly good at stealing stuff."

Mark smiles. "The sword has already been stolen. You wouldn't be stealing it. And yes, there is a reason your name came up. This blade formerly belonged to a man by the name of Vlad Tepes."

I blink. Sounds familiar in an 'oh give me a break' sort of way. "Why do I think I ought to recognize that name?"

"Vlad the Impaler? Dracula, if you believe in that sort of thing."

Ugh. I gaze at the ceiling. There's no possible way 'Dracula' is real. Maybe a guy once existed and people made up stories about him, but I have to believe Wolent is not crazy enough to send *me* to go mess with a vampire from a thousand years ago... or however long ago the dude lived. With all the weird crap I've seen since becoming a vampire, it wouldn't shock me too much if the guy *is* real. I'm just not about to piss off a vampire who's old enough to slap Aurélie around like a child.

At least, I assume.

Still don't know if vampires reach a plateau after a time or if they just keep getting more and more powerful.

"Relax. The actual Vlad has nothing to do with this other than having been the sword's former master." Mark clicks the mouse, changing the photo on the screen to a late-thirties white guy who looks like he's spent more than a few years in prison. "This man broke into one of Mr. Wolent's properties. He bypassed several other more obviously valuable items to take this sword. We believe he was hired specifically to obtain it by others who could not operate during the day. Those others also did not fully understand the situation."

"Situation?" I raise an eyebrow. "What, that Wolent would come after them?"

"No." Mark purses his lips. "They attempted to avoid direct conflict by making use of a thrall. Unfortunately, or perhaps fortunately for us, they didn't understand the nature of this particular blade."

I shift to add my other butt cheek to the desk. Take that,

decorum. "This is the part where you tell me how he messed up and what not to do?"

"Correct." Mark leans back. The amazingly elaborate—and likely expensive Lamborghini chair doesn't even creak. "Mortals, even thralls, who touch this sword usually end up becoming possessed by it and going on killing sprees."

"Oh, so no major problems then."

He tilts his hand in a so-so gesture. "You have, of course, heard of Jack the Ripper?"

"Who hasn't?" I chuckle.

"One of the reasons that case has proven so elusive to solve is the likelihood multiple individuals were involved, not a single killer... and not a killer who anyone would suspect to be prone to such horrific violence." He clicks the mouse again, going back to the sword picture. "This blade is the culprit, via multiple mortals' hands."

I point at the screen. "So, the dude who took it—"

"Is already dead. The blade possessed him and the police later killed him."

Cringe. "Lovely..."

"The last known location of the sword is Olympia. Our sources have not yet picked up on any unusual goings on, so we believe the weapon may still be located in the police station."

I point at him. "Wait a sec. If this thing possesses any mortal who touches it, wouldn't the cop carrying it to the evidence room go nuts, too?"

"A distinct possibility." Mark nods. "Artifacts such as this can often be difficult to predict. Nitrile gloves or indirect handling *might* protect a person. It also depends on how long they are in contact with it. I suspect—and this is purely *my* guess—the more a person wishes to possess the sword, the faster it will take their mind. A police officer merely transporting it with no interest in taking it for him or herself might escape danger if they don't remain in direct contact with it for too long."

"Here's hoping." I exhale out my nose. "So, basically, Wolent wants me to go break into the Olympia PD and steal something out of their evidence locker."

"Yes. Should be a simple matter for one such as yourself." He raises an eyebrow.

"At night? Sure."

He winces. "At night, those who sent"—he clicks the mouse to go back to the man's mugshot—"this poor fool to his death will surely be doing the same thing. You will need to go there before they can, preferably during the day."

I shift my jaw side to side. Great. Normal, offline me is not equipped to do this. I'm going to need to be creative. Worst-case scenario, I get arrested and have to wait until dark to get myself out of jail and make everyone there forget me. Police stations must have closets or interrogation rooms without windows. I don't need sunset, just the absence of sunlight.

Oh, boy, Sarah. Follows Rules Girl is screaming.

"You may wish to hurry," says Mark. "I suspect the blade will not remain there for long. St. Ives has people looking for it, too."

I groan. "*How* did I know she'd be involved?"

"We don't believe she is responsible for the theft." Mark leans back a little more in the ridicu-chair. "However, she's become aware of it and feels it's fair game for the taking as long as it is not in Wolent's possession."

Face-palm time. "Please tell me this woman isn't so dumb as to think she can take it from him without there being *some* kind of consequence?"

"Oh, I imagine she will gladly return it to him and claim a favor owed." Mark frowns. "Mr. Wolent would prefer not to owe her a favor."

"Yeah. Good plan."

A sincere smile shows off Mark's teeth. "You do have the advantage of more hours in a day."

"Yay me." I slide off the desk to my feet. "Might as well get started then. I'm sure this is gonna be... fun."

9

AN ALTERNATE SET OF RULES

I t's not that Arthur Wolent takes pleasure in giving me stress attacks, it's more he's stuck in the previous century—to a point.

Considering his age, he's really progressive. He doesn't treat women like objects or helpless creatures meant only to decorate a man's arm. What I mean by last century is the general attitude of people. Look at World War II. Back then, they had all this rationing and general hardship going on, and the average person buckled down and dealt with it for the good of the country as a whole. The way people are today, if something like that happened, no doubt there'd be whiny protests from people upset they couldn't just eat as much McDonalds as they wanted. People are so selfish, flighty, or generally cynical anymore there's little concern beyond immediate personal need. Ask some people to mildly inconvenience themselves for another person's life, they'd get as pissed off as if you tried to steal their baby.

Wolent expects me to simply do what needs to be done and doesn't really consider how my Gen-Z butt feels about the danger it puts my family in. Or could potentially put my family in. Like society was during his mortal days, he's figuring we'll all cope as best we can. Also, he's not being totally callous with me or my family's safety. The sword in question is dangerous. Based on what Mark told me before I left his office, Wolent doesn't want it recovered out of greed or ego or pride. He kept it in a warehouse, theoretically secure, as opposed to on display at his home, in order to protect the world from it.

This is why I didn't hunt for a way to weasel out of the task.

If he asked me to risk my unlife to recover some lost pretty thing so he could brag about having it to his elder vampire buddies, I'd have been *far* more likely to look for a way out. Having him as an ally is a huge help, but it's not worth putting my family at risk over superficial nonsense. A rich guy losing an expensive toy is hardly a crisis. However, this is a matter of public safety. With the sword of Vlad Tepes (supposedly) out in the world, we are on course to see a reenactment of the Jack the Ripper murders.

Or at least an attempt. Police have come a long way since those days. It's not quite as easy for a killer to go undetected. Problem being, no detective in their right mind would *ever* blame the sword. They'd arrest whatever poor fool got possessed, then be baffled as soon as a 'copycat' killer does it again. Maybe after a few killings they'd notice the same murder weapon was involved each time, but even if they suspected something strange, they wouldn't take it seriously. Sure, cops are superstitious and they'd talk about it, but the instant one of them tried to legit suggest an 'evil sword' made the killers do it, they'd be on paid administrative leave and a psychiatrist's couch.

The world is not ready to handle the existence of supernatural phenomenon.

The world wasn't ready for reality television either, but I

suppose there's no putting *that* genie back in its bottle. Sigh. Fight the battles we can win, right?

So, yeah. Here I am in the Sentra driving to Olympia on the spur of the moment. I texted Dad an update, mentioning an 'errand.' No reply yet. He also didn't respond with any new information about my earlier request to check the house for something not being right. Had it been dark, I'd have flown home real quick to check. Unfortunately, I'm stuck obeying mortal laws for the time being, which means driving. Four minutes to zip home and look around is doable. Forty, not so much, especially when I'm now racing against sunset to beat St. Ives' minions to a police station in Olympia.

Or the minions of whoever originally stole the blade.

I wouldn't necessarily put it past one of the local elders to take it from him only to 'find' it and give it back as a gesture of good faith. St. Ives can be a bitch, but she's not interested enough in political leverage to initiate the theft. My guess is, she learned of the blade going for a walkabout and got the itch to study it. She is, after all, an Academic. They come in three types: mystics (super rare), driven scientists-slash-scholars, and the utterly obsessed type of scientist like the ones responsible for *Jurassic Park*. Guess which category she falls into. Yeah. She'll do or study anything without much care for the resulting damage it causes.

So, while she would probably return the sword to Wolent —eventually—there's no telling what will happen as a result of her having it. Then again, swords capable of possessing people aren't exactly 'science.' I'm fairly certain this thing counts as 'mystical.' She might very well look at it, be baffled, and toss it to Wolent in frustration.

Still, he doesn't want to owe her the favor, nor take the chance of her accidentally unleashing some sort of badness on the world. We already have Kardashians, *Duck Dynasty,* and endless Hollywood remakes of mediocre movies to deal with. The country doesn't need *more* misery. It's like there's a hidden cabal of evil masterminds working to make us all dumber.

A cop follows me for a few minutes, before thankfully deciding not to pull me over. He changes lanes and zooms off ahead.

It's mildly gloomy today, and my hair is still in 'not leaving the house' mode—which means I look like a Maine Coon with severe static electricity issues—so he probably can't see my face too well. There's no reason for him to single me out of traffic. I tend to drive fairly sheepishly, so any interest he has in me is not from anything I'm actively doing. When cops pull me over, it's always because they think I'm too young to be on the road. And yes, it's annoying as hell. This cop might've only been coincidentally behind me for a while. Grr. I'm already paranoid. Doesn't help I'm about to go mess with the police. Yeah. Guilty conscience.

Really, I'm not going to mess with cops. They aren't equipped to deal with paranormal nonsense like a cursed sword. Gotta think about it like I'm doing them a favor, making their lives easier. No need for Follows Rules Girl to be so nervous.

This sounds all good in theory... right up until I park the Sentra in downtown Olympia, walk a few blocks, and enter the police station via the front door like any ordinary citizen. The instant I take in the scenery, dread punches me in the gut. For a few seconds, I'm no longer a vampire operating outside mortal rules, but some stupid kid who just messed up big time and is about to get in a ton of trouble. It's not against the law to enter the lobby of a police station. The overactive fear of getting in trouble that's haunted me ever since my first day of kindergarten roars. Wanna know how sad and pathetic it can get? I was the kid who cried in third grade because a preprinted test form said 'use black ink only' and all I had was a blue pen. Thought I would get detention if I wrote on the paper with blue ink.

Sigh.

Chill out, Sarah. Relax. Even if this goes as wrong as possible, I'll be fine as soon as the sun goes down. Vampires do not get arrested. I'm still Follows Rules Girl... only the rules have changed. Maybe I'll convince myself of it after a few more decades. Wolent finds my difficulty being deceitful cute. To him, a vampire who struggles with lying is about as hilarious as a lawyer who can't bend the truth without looking guilty as hell. There's an art to it I lack. Mom's a pro. She never lies, but she can say almost anything and be technically truthful while conveying a nearly opposite meaning. Whether or not corporate law is more morally pure than being a criminal defender is up for debate, but blargh. I'm sure my mother wouldn't help them do something horrible. Then again, she works for Boeing... not some shady chemical company or nuclear waste handling outfit.

Right. Police station. Cursed sword. Me about to throw up all over the place.

The woman at the front desk giving me the 'are you lost, sweetie' stare isn't helping. I'm here to flagrantly ignore the law and do whatever I want, yet this officer is looking at me like she's worried about my welfare. Wow, so this is what it's like to be a politician. Chill out, Sarah. I'm helping the cops, even if they don't know it.

This lobby has far too much sunlight. I need to find a way to go from here to wherever they keep evidence. Bad enough they won't let me walk around looking for it, I have no idea where to even start. Gotta come up with a way to get inside that doesn't involve vampire powers. Unfortunately, I am not a spy, not a thief, haven't done any of the 'planning stuff' they show in heist movies (like looking at blueprints), and would never pass for a cop. Even if I somehow got a realistic uniform, they'd all think me a kid dressed up for Halloween. Thanks, face. Sigh.

Also, I'm pretty sure breaking into a place unnoticed does *not* start with step one: walk right in the front door. Grr. Well, I'm kind of committed now since Desk Woman is still staring at me. Guessing she thinks my fearful hesitation is something much worse than it is. To her, I probably look like some kind of victim who found the courage to go to the police station and is getting a bad case of cold feet at the last second, about to turn around and leave.

To be fair, I *am* contemplating turning around and leaving, but it isn't because I'm scared of what some mysterious man will do to me if I tell the cops about him. However, this woman gives me an idea. Trying to ham it up will only make me look (more) ridiculous, so I decide to coast on my already ample reserves of anxiety instead of overacting like I'm afraid for my life.

Desk Woman appears to relax a little as soon as I start approaching her. Bet she'd have come after me if I walked out to ask what's wrong and try to talk me into going through with whatever I'd come here to do. As annoying as it can be to be constantly patronized for looking young, it's definitely better than everyone always thinking I'm up to no good or dangerous. Gotta use the advantages fate gave me.

"Umm, excuse me," I say, letting my natural nervousness shine through in my voice. "Can I maybe talk to someone in like private or something?"

"Are you okay, hon?" asks the woman.

I force a weak smile. "I guess. Kinda."

"What do you need to talk about?"

The best way not to come off as a liar is not to lie. Truth doesn't necessarily need to be applicable to the here and now to work for me. I think about Scott stabbing me to death. Up until that moment, he'd never been physically abusive to me, just mentally. Still, plunging a knife into my chest counts as violence.

I look down. "My boyfriend—umm, *ex* boyfriend... he, umm..." I fidget. "Do I really have to talk about it out here where he might be watching?"

Hey, his ghost might be out there somewhere watching.

She puts on a comforting expression. "Of course not, hon. Hold on, let me see if one of the detectives can make time for you."

"Thanks." I mutter at my sneakers.

Desk Woman types away on the computer for a moment, then looks back at me. "Detective Espinoza will be right out."

I nod... and stand there squirming for a minute or two until a slender Hispanic woman in a grey pant suit emerges from a door on the left side of the lobby, one of those badge-access ones labeled 'authorized personnel only.' Desk Woman indicates me with a glance. Not like she has to. I'm throwing off more awkwardness than Charlie Brown trying to sing at a school talent show.

"Hello. I'm Detective Alissa Espinoza," says the woman after approaching me. "You can call me Alissa, Detective, or Ms. Espinoza if you like. Whatever helps you feel at ease."

"Thanks." I offer a flimsy smile, then eye the windows behind me. "Can we maybe talk somewhere else? Maybe somewhere without any windows in case he's following me?"

The detective's eyebrows go up. "You think he's here?"

I fidget. Dammit. Don't want to cause a scene. "I dunno. He said he'd know if I went to the cops. Figure he's just looking at the phone, yanno. So I came here."

"All right." She stares at the windows for a moment, then waves for me to follow as she returns to the door she came in from.

"Thanks," I whisper to Desk Woman before scurrying after the detective.

She leads me down a white hallway full of doors and little silver signs with names of people or various departments. Uniformed officers and plain-clothes cops mill around here and there. A few look at me out of curiosity or concern, though given I'm following a detective already, none of them intrude on our space.

Detective Espinoza shows me to a small, windowless interview room. It's only a little bigger than a closet and contains two beige cushioned chairs and a tiny round Ikea table. At least, I assume it's Ikea. They're big on the naked wood look. I enter the room first, already feeling the stress melt away from the absence of direct sunlight. Oh, that explains my nervousness. I'm always on edge while offline. Still don't know how permanent it would be if something hurt me during the day. Not convinced it's reassuring to think breaking the law *isn't* why I felt like throwing up. Don't want to get too casual about it or I'll stop being who I am.

A faint tingle washes over me as I go online, a second or two before the detective pulls the door closed behind her. She hesitates, perhaps picking up on the subtle tint of red light on the wall in front of me for the brief instant my eyes flared. Or maybe she's perceptive enough to sense the complete reversal in my demeanor. Even though I have absolutely zero intention to harm this woman, there's no arguing she followed a timid little victim into a room and is now in the presence of a higher order predator. Some deep, long-buried part of the human psyche is still able to sense things like that, even if the ability for our thinking brain to properly interpret the information is many generations gone.

I turn to face her, smiling as reassuringly as possible. The change in my attitude is more obvious than intended, causing her to stop short and stare at me with a 'is this some sort of prank' expression.

She doesn't say anything before I dive into her thoughts. Walking into this place while offline made me feel about as vulnerable as a soldier showing up for combat in their underwear. In this small bit of shelter from the sun, I have my confidence—and vampiric armor-back.

Well, points for my acting ability. The detective believed I'd been abused by my ex-boyfriend. Technically true, though the issue is long since resolved and not her problem. I alter her memory of me slightly so she won't recognize me once I'm gone. She'll think she spoke to some other girl about a stalker boyfriend. Next, I implant a time-delay compulsion. First time doing that, so here's hoping it works. Two days from now, she'll remember scaring the nonexistent idiot boyfriend away for good, but no one wanted to press charges. Detective Espinoza can be happy about protecting Mystery Girl, even if nothing goes into the legal system over it.

That done, I give her a strong urge to escort me to the evidence room. While doing this, I discover it's in the basement. Awesome! Once we go down there, I'll be free from the sun and able to control the situation at will. Perfect. Wow, okay. This is turning out to be much easier than expected. Compelling a detective to do my job for me *is* a bit of a... 'cop out,' but I'm not above it. Or above bad puns. Thanks, Dad.

Crap. I shouldn't have called this easy. Just jinxed myself.

Here goes.

Detective Espinoza's eyes flutter as she comes out of the mental fog and reaches for the doorknob. "C'mon. This way."

I cringe as the sunlight hits me. Back to being nervous and vulnerable. All I can do now is follow the detective and act like we aren't doing something strange. Easier said than done, but my face is my biggest enemy whenever I try to break the rules. If I keep my head down, my hair comes to the rescue, hiding the guilt radiating from my eyes. The worst part is, I'm not one of those people who is motivated entirely by fear of getting in trouble. Yes, I am afraid of getting in trouble, but it genuinely makes me feel bad to do bad things, so my subconscious mind makes sure I get punished since it thinks I deserve to.

Doing good deeds. This isn't as bad as it looks. I'm protecting the cops.

I mentally chant these words to myself repeatedly while following the detective down the hall to a stairway. The instant we round the corner of the switchback, I'm back online and feeling confident. Good thing, too. Thanks to me having mental powers, seven people down here aren't going to remember seeing me. Plus, I doubt a detective's say-so is going to convince whoever is in charge of the evidence room to allow a civilian to go inside at all, much less take something out.

The station has more than one evidence room with varying degrees of security. Evidence like files for cold cases or boring financial stuff is in one room protected only by a locked door. Other things like bloody clothing from crime scenes, rape kits, murder weapons, bullet fragments, and so forth are in other rooms behind increasing layers of security up to a check-in desk staffed 24/7 where an oldish guy in a police uniform needs to buzz people in and out of the room containing all the important, dangerous, or valuable stuff. Poor man looks like he's spent the better part of the last fifteen years down here as the Guardian of Evidence. He's probably close to retiring, and I'm sure he doesn't mind the peace and quiet. Beats getting shot or yelled at all day long.

It doesn't take me much effort to charm my way past the guy with his finger on the magic button. No, not *that* magic button. I mean the one connected to the magnetic lock on the door of the room where they keep the sensitive stuff. You know, guys often get a bad reputation for not being able to find *the* magic button. Hunter had no trouble. Considering I'm the first girl he's ever been with, I'm not sure how to take it. Either conventional wisdom about 'guy kind' is woefully exaggerated, or he spent entirely too much time on the internet doing 'research'.

Don't need to think about that now.

My current McGuffin is, according to these cops, a sword used to kill someone held by a man who the police later shot to death when he attacked them. Conflict. Would they put it in the most secure room or not? It *is* a weapon, but not a gun. It had been used in a murder, but there's no trial needed since the guy's dead already. It doesn't look valuable, so they might not consider it at high risk for being stolen. Grumbling to myself, I walk up to the older cop at the check in desk, offer a pleasant, "Hello," and poke him in the brain.

"Where did you put the sword?" I ask, while sending him a mental image of the blade.

"C-2." The man indicates the somewhat less-high security room on the left, not the one directly behind the desk.

"Thanks. Mind opening it?" I glance at Detective Espinoza and give her a minor compulsion to follow me in. Assuming this is going to show up on video, my cover story is 'curious kid who's thinking of becoming a cop getting a tour.'

Desk Cop reaches under the counter. A soft buzz comes from the door on the left. Perfect.

I step into a room of plain white cinder block walls and grey steel shelves packed with nondescript white cardboard boxes. A standing wall of nasty psychic energy slaps me in the face hard enough to make me flinch, even worse than the stink of blood, chemicals, and basement. Something tells me the 'chemicals' I smell are a vampire's nose reacting to drugs. They probably put confiscated narcotics in here for however long it takes to go to trial and/or be stolen. Kidding. Movies always have corrupt cops stealing the drugs out of evidence and selling them on the side. No idea if that happens in real life, but I doubt it. Then again, I'm the good girl who trusts cops.

Regardless, I know for a *fact* objects in here are murder weapons. The psychic darkness hanging over the room is oppressive. Thankfully, there are no visible spirits loitering around. What I'm picking up on is more than likely the latent emotional energy trapped in items used to murder people. This is all pretty new to me, so I can't tell by potency if there are a handful or a ton of bad items around me. For all I know, *one* hatchet responsible for killing one person could throw off this much ick. I'm probably on the sensitive side to it since I'm so 'squishy' as Dad calls it.

Also, the complete lack of any other distractions in here intensifies the mental energy. No windows, sounds, motion... purely a bunch of creepy boxes, each one labeled only with a case number. Grr. This isn't helpful. Gonna take hours to open each one and peek.

I poke my head out into the foyer and lock stares with Desk Cop. "What's the case number for the sword?"

He mechanically recites it.

Gotta give the man credit. The evidence room is well organized. In only a few minutes, I've made my way among the shelves in case number order to a large white box bearing the number du jour. I pull it off the shelf, set it on the floor, and open the lid. Inside are a bunch of plastic baggies holding blood-soaked clothing. It's disconcerting to rummage it, but what choice is there? I'm simultaneously relieved and annoyed. Good: none of the clothing items look like they belonged to a kid. Bad: there is no sword in this box.

After putting everything back where it belongs, I walk out into the foyer and approach the desk again. "Excuse me" —hey, doing mind control doesn't mean I need to be rude— "the sword's missing."

"Yes, I know."

I blink. "You know? Why didn't you tell me?"

"Because you asked for the case number, not where the sword is."

Good thing I am not Sierra. She'd probably punch him for saying that. I merely growl—at myself. He's halfway to Derptown thanks to vampiric mind control, so he's basically on truth serum. The man presently lacks the capacity to lie to me or be a wiseass on purpose. Plain literal truth can often sound like being patronized. That's the downside to overriding a person's willpower. They don't add any intelligence to their responses. It's like computer programming. The machine does only what it's told to do.

"Figures. I should have known." Sigh. "No McGuffin is ever obtained this easily."

"What?" asks Detective Espinoza.

"Nothing." I wave my hand past her face. "Forget I said that."

Yes, I'm a geek. No, the 'Jedi mind trick wave' doesn't help. Oh, holy crap. I can totally 'these aren't the droids you're looking for' people for real. Heh. Awesome.

I lean on the counter, peering past the metal mesh at Desk Cop. "Do you know what happened to the sword?"

"Yes."

Ugh, the literalness. "Tell me what happened to the sword and why it isn't here."

Desk Cop types on his computer for a few seconds,

glancing at the screen. "Detective Warner signed it out yesterday."

"Jake?" asks Detective Espinoza.

"You know of any *other* Warners up there?" Desk Cop chuckles.

"Odd. Jake didn't show up for work this morning." Espinoza partially breaks away from my control, so she must have strong feelings for this Jake Warner guy. Her look of worry about him—and complete disregard to me, a civilian, standing in the secure evidence room—confirms it. He's like a brother to her.

Yeah. Shit.

This is bad. This is *really* bad.

I derp Desk Cop into forgetting our conversation, then face Espinoza. "Where does Detective Warner live?"

10

DAD WOULD LOVE THIS

S am ran through the woods toward the sound of a kid screaming in terror.

While only a kid himself, he had a Blix. If some girl fell in a hole or had a problem with wolves, it shouldn't be too big a problem to help. Darryl, Jordan, and Ronan followed with varying degrees of hesitance. Mostly, he suspected they didn't want to split up and get lost alone.

He ran for a little less than a minute before a man shouted in not-English as if barking commands. At this, Sam slowed to a stealthier fast walk, trying to make as little noise as possible while still advancing.

A child whimpered, "Mama."

At the sight of camouflage green in the woods ahead, Sam slowed even more and crept over to hide behind a tree, peering around it at a group of soldiers standing by a military style truck clearly not American in origin. Two had black, furry hats. All carried AK-47 rifles, but didn't point them at anything in particular.

Curious, Sam sank into a crouch and crept even closer, huddling down behind a fallen log.

Six men in camo waited by the truck while another two confronted a woman a bit younger than Mom and a little brown-haired girl somewhere around eight, give or take a year. The woman and daughter looked fairly poor, in shabby —though intact—clothing. It occurred to Sam at last the air had become noticeably chillier than it ought to be. Not exactly *cold* but more like early autumn than summer.

A small house, almost a cabin, not far behind the civilians had the look of a place abandoned for twenty years.

The girl clung to the woman, staring fearfully up at the nearest soldier, who appeared to be yelling at the woman as if she'd done something wrong. Though he couldn't understand a word of what he said—or what the woman offered in protest—their exchange made him think of a scene out of a movie where someone accidentally strayed into restricted space. It didn't seem as if the soldiers intended to harm either the woman or the child, merely chase them away. Sam suspected the little girl probably screamed when soldiers surprised her, possibly pointing rifles at them. The woman gestured insistently at the cabin while repeating the same short phrase multiple times.

Ronan and Jordan scooted up on either side, also peering over the log.

"Whoa," whispered Ronan. "What's going on? Are they gonna shoot her?"

Sam peered at Blix. "I dunno."

"They tell woman she can't be here." Blix tilted his head, listening. "She say she found the house, so it's hers now. Man tell her to go away. This bad place people shouldn't be."

Sam looked back at the heated conversation. The woman seemingly tried to argue with the men, at least until one of them gestured at the kid and shouted. Whatever he said made the girl burst into tears and shut the mother up in an instant.

"What'd he say?" whispered Jordan.

"How should I know?" Ronan shrugged. "Something bad."

"Guys!" whispered Darryl, still a short distance behind them at the tree.

"He say if don't leave, they take woman to jail. Kid not have mom for many years. Kid be alone in forest and probably starve." Blix scratched at his chin.

Sam didn't think the soldiers would just leave the kid all alone out in the woods. The men still made no move to do anything violent, so he kept hiding. If, in fact, the woman trespassed into a military zone people didn't belong in, he couldn't do much to help. Of course, it also meant he and his friends probably shouldn't be seen here, either.

The sound of an approaching engine emerged from the woods. Taking opportunity from the distraction, the woman picked up her daughter and hurried off to the left. None of the soldiers made a move to stop her, evidently happy they'd succeeded in chasing her off. A moment later, a tall black van trundled into view along a dirt road. It didn't look like any car belonging in America, though had a huge Mercedes symbol in the front grill. The long black-and-white license plate further proved they'd gone somewhere else.

Sam, Ronan, and Jordan hunkered down behind the rotting log, watching. The smell of wet wood and earth flooded Sam's nose. Normal enough. Not much different than the way nature smelled back home.

We're probably still on Earth... just another part of it. We have to get home before Jord's mom finds out we went to Europe. She'll freak.

Two muscular men in nice black suits exited the van and approached the man who'd been yelling at the woman. He appeared to be the oldest of the soldiers, with the most stuff on his uniform. Probably the sergeant or whatever. Two additional men hopped out and opened the van's back doors.

One soldier got out of the military truck's cab carrying a metal briefcase, which he rushed over to the sergeant, who opened the briefcase and showed the contents to the two men in suits.

The bald guy on the left nodded once, then took the briefcase from the sergeant. "Dobro. Iskrcajte ga[1]."

Numerous soldiers hurried over to the van and began unloading green cases from the back, which they lugged over to put in the military truck.

"What's going on?" whispered Ronan.

Sam shrugged. "They're selling stuff."

"Probably bad guys doing a deal. Could be drugs." Jordan buried his face in his elbow to stop himself from sneezing.

"Or weapons." Sam stared at one of the long crates going by. It seemed a bit small for shoulder-launched missiles, but rifles would fit in it. Or drugs. Maybe explosives, or even chemical weapons. The scene playing out in front of them reminded him so much of corrupt soldiers dealing with generic 'organized crime' guys from a movie, he started to look around for cameras. "Stay down and don't make any noise."

"Why would the military buy weapons? It's gotta be drugs," whispered Jordan.

"Guys!" rasped Daryl.

Sam didn't react, trying not to move or draw attention. A few seconds after Darryl whisper-shouted, ground debris crunched rather loudly behind him. Annoyed, he twisted around to shush his friend, but froze upon noticing two soldiers standing right behind the three boys. They carried their rifles sideways, their expressions somewhat amused.

"Šta ti radiš ovde[2]?" asked the dark haired soldier, his rifle not *quite* pointed at Sam.

Darryl, too far back for the men to have spotted, made a

'you idiots, I was trying to warn you' face before he ducked out of sight behind the tree.

"Eep!" whispered Ronan.

The light-haired soldier gestured in the direction the woman ran off. "Je li to tvoja majka tamo?[3]"

"Umm." Sam exhaled. "Sorry. We're kinda lost. Made a wrong turn at Albuquerque."

Both men exchanged a glance.

Dark hair asked, "Da li je to Engleski[4]?"

"Mislim da je tako[5]." The man leaned closer to the boys, narrowing his eyes in suspicion. "Američki špijuni[6]?"

"Hah." Dark hair laughed. "Amerikanci bi uradili sve, ali su deca. Mislim da nisu Amerikanci. Nemaju višak kilograma[7]."

Light hair laughed.

Darryl stepped out from behind the tree with his hands up. A third soldier walked behind him, prodding him along at rifle point.

The first two peered back, startled but more confused at having missed Darryl.

Dark hair pointed at the truck. When the boys just stood there, he pointed his rifle at them, then at the truck.

"I think he wants us to go to the truck," whispered Ronan. "Should we?"

Sam eased himself to his feet, keeping his hands up. "Yeah."

"Are you serious?" Jordan's voice came out as more of a squeak. "You don't know what they're gonna do to us."

Sam grabbed his friend's arm and pulled him to his feet. "What do you think they're going to do to us if we don't listen?"

Jordan stared pointedly at the AK-47s. "Umm. Right."

Darryl made a 'we are so screwed' face at Sam.

"Chill out." Sam walked around the log, making his way

toward the military truck. "We really aren't doing anything wrong."

"We saw their deal thing." Ronan shivered. "What if they want to kill us for being witnesses?"

"Dude, shut up," muttered Darryl.

"I don't think they will." Sam shook his head. "But we're not going to sit around waiting to see what happens."

The two soldiers who found them stood by guarding the boys as the rest of their crew continued unloading the crates. Whatever they contained, the soldiers made no effort to conceal the exchange. Perhaps they didn't really do anything illegal, or maybe they figured the boys had already seen enough to render further efforts of concealment pointless. Ronan stared at Sam making a 'c'mon, do something' face. Jordan looked about ready to faint from fear. Darryl glanced around, his expression about halfway between dread and 'this is cool.'

Upon noticing the boys, the sergeant walked over and got into a conversation with the other soldiers. Sam picked out a word that probably translated to 'American' a few times. Blix, still perched on Sam's back, didn't react much to the conversation, suggesting little need to worry.

Soon after the soldiers loaded the last case, the sergeant pointed at the back of the military truck. "Go in."

Sam contemplated asking Mel for help then and there, but two things stopped him. One: a bunch of guys with automatic rifles would probably not have a great reaction to a demon appearing out of nowhere, even if the demon looked like a beautiful woman. His friends might get hurt in the crossfire. Two: the soldiers didn't hurt that mother and daughter and could have easily done so with less effort than yelling at her until she ran away from the deal site. They probably wouldn't hurt a bunch of kids for stumbling across their supposedly secret and probably nefarious meeting in the woods. Even if they *did* change their mind later about being nice to the boys, he planned to escape as soon as guys with rifles stopped paying total attention to them. At best, they'd be brought back to the camp and talk to someone who spoke English, then sent somewhere like an embassy. At worst, they'd be locked in a room for a while until the bad guys decided to get rid of them. Both scenarios ought to provide ample time for escape.

Sam didn't like being an unknown kid in an unknown country. The soldiers could easily kill all four of them and no one would ever know what happened. They didn't have anyone around here who would report them missing, and no one back home would have the first clue where to even start looking. He really didn't like the idea of going home as a ghost to tell Sophia the truth. Asking Mel to incinerate living people—who so far hadn't been too mean to him—felt wrong. Forcing Sophia to deal with him as a ghost felt even wronger, but not as wrong as the word 'wronger.'

He faced the truck, surprised to find himself only eye-level with the back bumper. Before he could figure out how best to climb, one of the soldiers grabbed him from behind and half-threw him up inside. Sam stumbled into the stacked-up cases, catching himself before falling over. Though the boxes likely filled the Mercedes van, the military truck still had plenty of room around the pile to access the bench seats on both sides and at the end near the front.

Not wanting to be thrown, the other boys hastily climbed in on their own.

Soldiers herded them to the deepest end of the truck's cargo area, directing them to sit in a row with their backs against the wall of the driver's cabin. One soldier sat to the left and right on the same bench, the rest filling in down the sides all the way to the tailgate. In order to run away at this point, they'd either have to climb over a half dozen armed men or a pile of cases containing mysterious cargo purchased from even more mysterious people in a black van.

Sam decided now would not be the best time to attempt fleeing. While the men appeared to be reasonably polite to that woman and her kid, they didn't seem to trust Sam and his friends at all. Being thrown into the back of a truck like a criminal both annoyed him and kept his guard up.

The low rumble of a diesel engine roared to life, making the poorly padded bench vibrate. None of the men spoke as the truck got underway, jostling them around thanks to the rough dirt road. Blix sat on Sam's shoulders, draped over the top of his head, chin propped up on one hand, bony little elbow poking into Sam's skull. The thin tail wrapped around his neck felt too much like the collar of a formal dress shirt for comfort, but also like a pet snake, so he tolerated it.

A few minutes into the ride, Darryl nudged Sam. "How are you so calm?"

"I'm thinking."

"Yeah, me too," muttered Jordan. "I'm thinking we're in deep crap."

"Thinking..." Darryl gawked. "We went into the same cave we always use for a base, only this time, when we come out, we're somewhere else. Now, we get kidnapped by Russians who are taking us... somewhere."

Jordan appeared to be fighting super hard not to cry.

Ronan continued to stare pleadingly at Sam, as if he trusted him to fix this. He had been allowed to remember vampires, demons, and weird stuff, so didn't have the same level of 'we are completely screwed' as the other two.

Sam tapped his foot, torn between wanting to reassure his friends the situation was far from as bleak as it appeared and needing to keep certain secrets. For now, he hoped his outward calm would be enough. If either Darryl or Jordan started to come apart mentally, he'd ask Blix to show himself.

The cave somehow teleporting them across the planet counted as weird enough he'd probably ask Sarah to make them forget. Adding a little imp-ness to the memory deletion wouldn't be a big deal.

The truck drove for an exceedingly long almost-hour. Sitting in the back behind a pile of cases didn't offer much of a view of the surroundings, merely a blur of green going by. Trees eventually disappeared to open sky. Soon after they passed through some manner of gate in a huge chain link fence, the truck came to a stop. Soldiers shuffled out except for one, who sat there watching the boys while the rest of the men unloaded the cases.

"How do you say 'I gotta pee' in whatever language they're using?" whispered Ronan.

"Dunno." Sam shrugged. "Just do the pee dance when they let us out of the truck. They should know what you mean."

Ronan blushed.

"This is bad." Darryl fidgeted. "They're acting weird for soldiers. Army guys don't deal with creeps in the middle of the forest like that. Think they're like Cobra or something?"

Sam shrugged. "Whatever's going on, I think we can agree it's far from normal."

His friends all stared at him.

"We left normal behind at the cave," said Jordan.

"Oh, maybe this is a top-secret project." Darryl swallowed. "The Russians are making like a wormhole to invade America. Like *Stranger Things*."

Jordan snickered. "Dork."

Sam frowned. "I dunno. Just... don't freak out, okay?"

Once the soldiers finished unloading the crates, one motioned for the boys to leave the truck. Sam got up, walked to the back end, and lowered himself over the edge. After jumping from the back bumper to the ground, he turned in place, surveying a concrete tarmac containing multiple

Quonset-style huts, a few brick buildings, and a scattering of various military vehicles including two attack helicopters. All of it had a general Eastern European run-down vibe to it, though he couldn't place the exact country.

His friends climbed down one after the next.

Two men escorted them across the tarmac to a grey brick building, inside, and down a hall to a medium-sized office. A fortyish man in a field uniform looked up at the boys, making about the same face he'd expect to see on Dad if a clown randomly walked into the house. His confusion gave way to annoyance as the men who escorted them in here evidently explained things. This guy had to be a higher-ranked commander than the man who gave away the briefcase, probably an actual officer.

"Ko ste i odakle ste[8]?" barked the officer.

"I don't understand what you're saying," replied Sam, calm as anything.

"Nije trenutak da se igraš, dečko[9]." The man sounded annoyed and threatening, narrowing his eyes as he spoke.

Sam raised his arms out to either side and let them flap against his body. "I'm sorry, but I have no idea what you're saying."

The officer grabbed a fistful of Sam's shirt, pulling him up on tiptoe. "Govoriti[10]."

"Komandante, mislim da su Amerikanci[11]." The escort soldier raised a hand.

For a moment, the officer continued holding Sam up off his heels. Finally, he let go and glanced at the lower-ranking man. "Šta, pobogu, rade Američka deca u našoj zoni bezbednosti?[12]"

"What's he saying?" whispered Darryl. "He sounds like a robot shorting out."

"Shh!" Jordan nudged him.

The officer and soldier exchanged a rapid back-and-forth

conversation before the soldier hurried out. Apparently, they didn't feel too threatened by a bunch of kids that leaving them alone with the base commander (probably) became an issue. The man threw off a ton of irritation, frowning at them for the next several minutes until the same soldier returned with another, somewhat younger man who immediately snapped to salute.

"Otkrijte ko su i zašto su ovde[13]." The commander, staring at the new arrival, gestured harshly at the boys.

"Hello," said the young man, in a thick accent. He looked about Hunter's age or a year older. Not twenty yet. "The commander wishes to know who you are."

"I'm Sam. These are my friends, Darryl, Jordan, and Ronan."

"You are Americans?" The young soldier blinked in shock.

"Yeah." Sam nodded.

"What are you doing in the restricted zone? No one is allowed in there."

Sam offered a blasé one-shoulder shrug. "Sorry. We're on vacation and got separated from the tour group. We couldn't find the bus. I think they left without us. We've been wandering in the woods trying to find a road or something."

The younger soldier they brought in to translate spoke to the commander, intermittently gesturing at the boys, then shrugged. His body language appeared to say 'I don't believe him either, but do you really think the Americans would send kids as spies?'

"What tour group were you with?" asked the translator.

"I dunno." Sam scratched at the back of his head. "The one my parents used. I'm only ten."

The translator reached toward him expectantly. "Let me see your papers."

"Papers?" Sam blinked. *Wow, we really are in a movie.*

"Umm... I don't have anything. My mom's carrying all of it. I'm just a kid."

The soldier and the officer conversed again.

Blix leaned over to Sam's ear and whispered, "They not believe you, but also not have better idea. Old man thinks CIA might try using kids, but doubts. He's trying to figure out what to do with you. I smell fear. He doesn't want be caught. He doing stuff he should not be doing. Do not trust."

Sam smirked. "I don't."

"Hmm?" The young solder glanced at him. "You don't what?"

"Know where we are." Sam considered taking his phone out to check a map, but decided against it out of fear the men would steal it. "Sorry if we entered a restricted area. We didn't mean to."

The commander waved dismissively at the two soldiers, barking another order in not-English.

"Follow me," said the younger man. "The commander wishes to make sure you are telling the truth and not spies. Do not do anything suspicious and we will send you home as soon as possible."

Sam chuckled. "Spies? Really? We're kids."

"Americans are sneaky. Your government would exploit children for political gain whenever it could." The man started for the door. "Follow."

Sam sighed, but decided to comply for now and wait for a better chance to escape—like as soon as they ended up locked in a room somewhere. Once the bad guys stopped paying attention to what the boys did, it gave them the advantage. They definitely wouldn't expect demons coming to Sam's assistance. Barring the extremely unlikely event the bad guys possessed powerful magical locks, they couldn't confine them anywhere Blix couldn't get them out of.

If Dad's movies taught him anything, he and his friends

would end up trapped somewhere while Arnold Schwarzenegger ran around blowing crap up until he found them. Alas, they didn't have an Arnold coming to get them. Olmaz could easily fill the role of a huge, muscular badass and tear the place to bits... but Sam didn't know for sure if the demon *would* do something like that. Might be too obvious a breach of secrecy. Of course, he could appear human. Still, these soldiers hadn't done worse yet than lightly threaten to shoot him if he didn't do what they said. While scary, soldiers in a restricted area would likely treat everyone the same way. Honestly, if Sam and his friends had been old enough to be mistaken for adults, the soldiers probably would've just shot them before trying to talk.

As much as seemed possible for bad guys to be, the men appeared to be reasonably nice—so he didn't want to set a demon loose to kill everyone here. If something crazy bad happened like the soldiers lying to them and bringing the boys out for a firing squad, he'd have no choice but to summon Olmaz or Mel and hit the ground. Nervous, but trusting that patience would prevail, Sam squeezed his fists and kept calm.

The English-speaking man led them out of the commander's office, down another hall, and down a flight of stairs to a basement room containing a couple folding cafeteria style tables and four tall metal cabinets. Two other soldiers met them in the room, evidently expecting them. The muscular one had a shaved head and a scar under his left eye, the other seemed too skinny to be a soldier, with shifty eyes like the bad guy in movies who always runs away and abandons his buddies.

These men didn't have rifles on them, only handguns in belt holsters. Both stared at the boys the same way cops might stare at kids caught spray painting graffiti. Even though Sam didn't do anything wrong, he started to worry about being in serious trouble. He and his friends weren't in the USA anymore. These men didn't have to obey any sort of laws, rules, or whatever like back home. Worse, not only had they ended up in some scary Eastern Bloc country, no record of travel existed and none of the boys had any sort of ID on them. As soon as the commander realized the boys couldn't be traced anywhere, he'd probably have them 'disposed of.' Considering he almost certainly broke the law in some way, he wouldn't want to do anything to bring unusual notice to his base, like report discovering four American children who seemingly came out of thin air.

"All of you," said the young soldier. "Empty your pockets on the table. Then remove your clothes except for... what is word... briefs? You keep those on."

Darryl's face reddened. "Uhh... are you serious?"

"That's messed up," whispered Jordan.

"Why?" asked Darryl.

"We make sure you not have wire. Listening devices. Cameras." The soldier gestured impatiently at the table.

Sam shifted his gaze to Blix. *Hide our phones.* "Guys, just do it. We didn't do anything wrong and... this isn't home. These guys aren't cops."

His friends' eyes widened as the implication of pointing out the soldiers weren't police sank in.

The imp nodded, then promptly relieved all four boys of their smartphones. None of the soldiers seemed to notice the devices emerging from pockets and vanishing. Sam begrudgingly emptied his pockets onto the table: couple hard candies, a few dollars, house keys, and some lint for good measure. After, he stripped down to his underwear, putting everything on the table beside his stuff. The concrete floor surprised him at being so cold in the summer. Still, they'd probably gone a bit farther north than Washington State, plus being in a basement.

His friends emptied their pockets, all clearly surprised at the absence of their phones… though none of them said a word about it.

The soldier with the facial scar gave Sam a brief visual inspection, looking him over for any signs of concealed weapons or listening devices. Sam braced for an embarrassing pat-down, but the man didn't touch him. Seeming satisfied, the big guy pointed at a spot a short distance away from the tables as if telling him to go wait over there.

"I'm not wearing a wire, or a bug," muttered Sam as he plodded over to the indicated spot.

One by one, his friends joined him, forming a line.

"Is this what it's like to be arrested?" whispered Ronan, arms folded and shivering.

"How should I know?" Sam shrugged.

The three soldiers picked through the boys' clothing, squeezing each garment repetitively as if searching for electronic devices or wiring sewn into the fabric like something out of a James Bond movie. The skinny guy made a sour face and almost gagged while examining Daryl's socks and sneakers, which set all four boys off chuckling.

After an annoyingly chilly twenty-ish minutes, the English speaker waved the boys back over to the table. "All right. Take your things back. Get dressed."

Sam and his friends wasted no time grabbing their clothes.

"See? Told you." Sam pulled his T-shirt on. "We aren't spies. No bugs."

"Yes, yes… but we must be sure you do not have weapons," said the man.

The three men waited impatiently as the boys dressed and restuffed their pockets.

"This way." The young soldier crossed the room to a plain steel door at the back.

Sam followed him to the doorway, but hesitated briefly upon seeing what waited on the other side: jail cells. Ronan gasped. Jordan lost his composure and succumbed to sniffling. Darryl's facial expression dropped a silent F-bomb. Unafraid of ordinary locks, Sam steeled himself and marched over to where the English speaking man stood gesturing at an open cell. It looked a bit smaller than he expected a prison cell to be, with a single cot, tiny sink, and a corroded metal toilet in the corner. The hall had three other cells, all empty.

"We didn't do anything," muttered Sam. "It's really lame to put us in jail."

"Then you have nothing to fear." The man pushed him into the cell. "We can't have you running around unsupervised and no one has time to babysit. You will wait here until the commander decides what to do."

Ronan darted in behind Sam before the other soldiers could shove him. Darryl and Jordan didn't enter until 'helped'. As soon as the cell door shut with an echoing crash of steel, Jordan fell seated on the cot and cried into his hands. The three soldiers walked off, closing the solid door at the end of the hall with an echoing *boom.*

"Chill." Sam folded his arms. "We're not gonna be here long."

"I think that's what he's afraid of." Darryl paced. "These are bad guys. They aren't going to take the time to figure out who we are and where we came from. Bad guys deal with questions by getting rid of the questions. They're gonna take us into the woods and—"

"Stop." Sam sighed at him. "If they were gonna shoot us in the woods, they'd have done it while we were already in the woods."

"This is bad." Jordan sniffled. "Any place with prison cells is not a good place."

"Yeah." Sam held out his hand as Blix set the stack of smartphones in it. "Exactly why we are leaving. Heh. It's like we're in one of Dad's movies."

Darryl shook his head. "Unbelievable." He blinked. "Hey! How'd you get our ph—"

Sam clamped a hand over his friend's mouth, then whispered, "Shh. I figured they'd steal 'em."

His friends all slumped in relief as they took their phones.

"Damn, no signal." Jordan sighed. "It's like they're being jammed."

"Probably because they are jamming them." Sam stuffed his phone in his pocket without bothering to try using it.

"Dude." Darryl shook his head. "I still don't get how you're so calm. We somehow ended up in another country and got kidnapped by corrupt soldiers."

"How do you know they're corrupt?" Ronan scrunched his nose.

Darryl lowered his voice. "Because normal soldiers don't buy stuff with a briefcase full of cash from dudes who look like mobsters in the middle of the woods."

"I'm calm because this is less scary than being kidnapped by vampires." Sam grinned. "We're basically in one of my dad's movies. Probably not a good idea for us to try and take on the bad guys, but we can definitely escape."

Ronan snickered.

"Vampires..." Jordan rolled his eyes. "Come back to reality. We are in big trouble."

"No, we're not." Sam stuck his head between the bars to scope out the now-empty hallway. "We have a Blix."

11

A SMALL HOME INVASION

S ierra stood there fuming, shin-deep in the plush beige carpet.

For at least the past three years, she'd been terrified a crazy person would show up at her school trying to kill her. Not *her* specifically, rather any kid they could hurt. That *something* had finally tried to kill her and it ended up being a ridiculously small goblin infuriated her. Well, being shrunk down to the size of a Barbie doll's adolescent daughter didn't help her anger situation much. Dealing with these goblins would have been trivial at normal size. Making her tiny turned it into more of a challenge, but they still didn't scare her too much. Thanks to Sophia, she could keep up with vampires in a sword fight. Giant goblins—who still moved only as fast as ordinary people—wouldn't be a serious threat unless they outnumbered her.

She looked around for the glowing pink crystal the creature had been holding when she surprised it, certain it had something to do with her severe case of smallness. The way the creature reacted to it made her believe it absorbed power from it or somehow used it like a magic wand.

Shrinking people did not feel like one of the creatures' normal abilities. Unfortunately, the crystal had vanished, likely yoinked by another goblin.

This sucks. Sierra gazed around at the enormous pink bedroom.

Part of her shied away from needing to ask for help. Normally, she'd sit there being quiet and trying not to appear outwardly upset at a situation. Taking a D on a math test rather than admitting to her teacher or Dad she needed a little extra help felt like a more dignified outcome. Only, she *had* confessed to Sarah about wanting help. Sophia, too. Not with math, but her ability to remain alive in the face of this supernatural stuff. Asking for help hadn't gotten her made fun of or treated like a helpless little girl.

Being six inches tall embarrassed her.

Being stuck in an incredibly pink dress embarrassed her.

Except for there being no food or water in the dollhouse, hiding in there until Sophia returned from camp sounded like a decent idea. Of course, her family would freak the hell out once they couldn't find her. The 'rents would probably assume something 'normal bad' happened and call the police to report her missing. No, she couldn't hide from this problem.

The normally awesome soft carpet that felt like walking on a cloud had become markedly less awesome. At her present size, it amounted to a field covered in eight inches of snow, only without the cold or hidden rocks to step on.

I have to go tell Dad what happened.

While psyching herself up for the inevitable reaction of having Dad laugh at her, she briefly considered trying to scale the four-story-high toy chest and rummage for something different to wear. At least *one* of Sophia's dolls had to have jeans or something *not* pink. Alas, climbing a mostly sheer plastic wall looked impossible. Even Sierra couldn't justify risking a deadly fall purely out of her desire not to be seen in a pink dress. Going downstairs to find Dad would be dangerous enough.

Sighing, she trudged across the room.

Despite the extra endurance given to her by Sophia's magic, by the time she reached the door, she needed to lean against the doorjamb to catch her breath. She'd basically walked the equivalent of four football fields' distance in heavy snow.

"Wow. This totally sucks. No wonder faeries have wings."

Goblin muttering came from the left, closer to the bathroom, Sam's room, and the 'rents' bedroom. An itch for revenge almost made her go hunting, but she ignored it and went to the right. The hallway carpeting had about half the awesomeness of the bedroom carpet, meaning it wasn't as soft and cloud-like. Her feet only sank up to the ankles in the stiffer pile, making it easier to walk on at her present shortness.

The walls stretched impossibly high over her head. She felt like an adventurer exploring the Hall of Titans from Dad's D&D game. Really being so small compared to a normal person made the idea of a fantasy character killing a titan with a teeny sword ludicrous. The goblin blade she carried couldn't possibly pose a threat to a person's life unless she climbed all the way up their body and slit open their carotid artery.

It took her a few minutes to walk a third of the way to the stairs.

The door to her bedroom, Sarah's old one, on the left swung inward at a slow creak. She froze, staring at the widening gap... until another goblin raced out of the room and came charging at her.

Sierra dropped into a fighting stance, raising her sword in a defensive posture.

Snarling, the goblin skidded to a stop two paces away, pointing its sword at her. "You kill one of us. Now you be punish."

She lunged forward and stabbed it in the face. "Punish *this.*"

The shocked goblin stared at her for an instant before its skin, eyeballs, and muscles liquefied into a translucent green slime that fell with its bones to the floor. The oddly wide and oval-shaped skull remained in place, impaled on her sword.

"Disgusting." Sierra let the skull's weight pull her blade down to the carpet. Grimacing, she braced one bare foot on the slime-covered bone to hold it down, then wrenched the sword out. "Seriously disgusting."

After wiping her foot on a dry patch of rug, Sierra stormed toward the stairs, expecting more goblins to attack at any second.

"Gah!" yelled Dad from downstairs, sounding startled— his deep, thundering voice reminiscent of a 4,000 pound dragon stubbing its toe.

"Dad?" shouted Sierra. "Duh. He's not going to hear me squeaking."

She fumed again. Another thing to be embarrassed about. Talking sounded normal to her, but to anyone who hadn't been miniaturized, she'd chirp like a chipmunk. Scowling, she stomped on down the hall for what seemed like an hour. At long last, she reached the top of the stairs... and suffered a moment of vertigo at the sight of a veritable canyon as deep as a massive skyscraper.

"Whoa..." She bit her lip, momentarily unsure how to proceed or even *if* she could go downstairs.

Each step amounted to roughly a one-story fall. If she stood on her toes, the tips of her fingers wouldn't reach the top of the previous step. Down appeared possible, if dangerous. Up would have been out of the question... if her increased strength didn't allow her to jump higher than a normal kid.

"Oh. Duh." She looked down at her scrawny self. "I am boosted. I can do this."

Scaling a giant staircase while carrying a sword probably ranked somewhere between running with scissors and sticking a fork in an electrical socket for bad idea. It could be said that soldiers running around carrying loaded rifles was *more* dangerous than running with scissors, but they needed to do it due to the demands of their job. At present, she needed the sword. The house had a goblin problem, and neither mousetraps nor roach bait would help with this infestation. Also, as far as she knew, they didn't *have* mousetraps or roach bait handy.

Sierra tossed the sword to the first step. Next, she turned her back to the stairwell, crouched at the edge, lowered herself to hang by her grip on the upper hallway rug, then let go. Dropping a few feet didn't bother her at all. She picked up the sword and repeated the process twice more before getting bolder. On the third step, she tossed the blade first, moved a few paces to the side, then jumped without dangling first.

Dropping a distance roughly one and a half times her height probably should have been ankle-spraining, or at least quite uncomfortable. It didn't bother her at all. Feeling like a superhero, she stood out of the crouch she landed in, grinning from ear to ear.

"Sweet."

Sierra picked up the sword and moved to the edge. This time, she just jumped, holding the blade. Finding it manageable, she kept doing it... making decent time going from step to step until she finally reached the square of linoleum at the bottom by the front door, Mom's 'shoe permitted' zone. Her sneakers looked as big as rowboats and wouldn't do her any good right now. The thought Mom would be more upset at her for stomping across the living room carpet wearing shoes than at her being shrunk offered a welcome chuckle. Her mother wouldn't seriously think that, but they liked to tease her for being overly protective of the rugs.

"You little bastard!" yelled Dad—his voice sounding normal, not deafening, deep, and slow like a titan.

Sierra blinked. "Oh... shit."

She ran as fast as she could move in the deep carpeting past the back of the sofa, heading for the hallway to the kitchen. Going from the space by the front door to the dining room amounted to running four or five city blocks, though it surprisingly didn't tire her out too much. Goblins rushed out from under the dining room table, charging at her. Fortunately, the creatures had the tactical acumen of Black Friday shoppers at Walmart, coming in in blindly and in mostly single file.

Sierra maneuvered around their attacks, cutting them down in one or two strikes each. She soon realized the goblin blade worked much better as a thrusting weapon and gave up trying to slice them. Each goblin she killed appeared to enrage the others more and more, making it even easier to beat them. She focused on their weapons, well aware that despite the creatures being comparatively slow, they remained a lethal threat. She ducked a goblin leaping at her, spun out from under the sword of a second one slashing at her face, and thrust her weapon into the chest of a third, killing it instantly. Its disintegrating goopy remains melted to the floor. She lunged at the jumper, stabbing it in the back of the head before it could get up.

A war cry announced another goblin running up behind her.

With her sword still stuck up to the hilt in a goblin skull,

Sierra ducked under the creature's crossing slash while stomp-kicking to the rear. Due to her comparative size, her foot squished into its lower belly rather than the middle of its chest. Her kick knocked the proverbial stuffing out of the creature and threw it off its feet. It seemed to hang horizontally in midair for a second before dropping straight down, crashing chest-first on the floor, gasping for air and making a noise like a balloon gradually losing air.

Sierra gave a grunt of exertion mixed with a bit of war shout as she yanked her blade free of the dead goblin's skull, swinging it around in time to parry the attack of yet another goblin before stabbing the winded one in the back. Chest shots spared her the worry of the blade ending up stuck in a non-disintegrating skull. The creature obligingly melted into a puddle of jelly and bones, freeing her sword so she could defend herself.

Fighting three goblins advancing on her at once, Sierra backpedaled, weaving side to side to avoid stabbing strikes, focusing on caution, waiting for the best opportunity to counterattack. Each time she evaded a sluggish, though enraged goblin, she wanted to grab Sophia and hug her until she squeaked. In a single afternoon, she'd already almost died a dozen times if not for the enchantment.

Somehow, slicing through these goblins didn't feel entirely real. Not like she *killed* things. More like a video game. Perhaps because they melted so fast into goop or didn't really look like people. More likely, her adrenaline level refused to let her think deep thoughts about morality at the same time green-skinned monsters tried to chop her head off.

The transition from gym sparring with blunt metal swords to a serious fight ended up being surprisingly easy. Not once did she automatically pull a swing and fail to kill a goblin. Hopefully, next time she went to the training class, she wouldn't hammer someone at full strength without thinking.

Eventually, the swarm of goblins ran out.

Sierra found herself standing alone under the dining room table, surrounded by a veritable ocean of boogery slime and small bones. Since she already stood up to her ankles in ooze, it didn't much matter if she stepped in more of it. Cringing at the nauseating sensation of snot squishing between her toes, she held her arms out for balance and made her way across the mess toward the kitchen.

It's ectoplasm or something. Not booger. This stuff did not come out of anyone's nose.

Grunting, banging, and repetitive thumping from up ahead announced more problems.

Once clear of the slime, Sierra ran the rest of the way across the living room to the archway where carpet gave way to tile. The instant her feet met the smooth surface, they shot out from under her, thanks to a lubricating coating of goblin guts. She landed on her butt, gawking at her father engaged in a wrestling match with a single goblin. His T-shirt, sweat pants, and flip-flops lay abandoned by the fridge, so huge they appeared to be an alternate landscape. Mercifully, he'd fashioned a skirt like garment out of one of Mom's cleaning rags from the under-sink cabinet.

He looked like a gladiator from that Russel Crowe movie struggling to stay alive in the arena. He also looked like a Ken doll having a fight with a groundhog. The goblin had three or so inches of height on him, plus about twice the width— mostly pudge. Athleticism had never been one of Dad's gifts. His genes were largely responsible for Sierra and her siblings being so scrawny. However, the Nerd That Roared had one big advantage: stubbornness. Dad never gave up on anything, even when everyone told him to... like trying to fix plumbing himself. Or that one time he thought he could replace the master fuse box in the garage with a circuit-breaker box. He'd been shocked to discover the task above his skill level.

At least momentary unconsciousness after the rather electrifying experience convinced him to call a real electrician.

Sierra doubted Google would help her locate a professional goblin removal service. In fact, the closest thing the world *had* to such a service happened to be sitting there in a doll's pink dress. Good chance no other living human on Earth right now had killed as many goblins as Sierra. At least if they had, they wisely kept quiet about it. Stories like that tended to get people put in mental hospitals.

She scrambled upright and rushed over at the maximum speed her slime-coated feet allowed. With each step, traction improved as the gunk wiped off on the floor. By the time she made it halfway to Dad, she had enough confidence in her footing to break into a legit run. Unlike the stupid goblins, she did *not* give a war cry. The goblin never noticed her coming until after she rammed her sword into its side, then kicked it in the head to fling the body off Dad before it melted into nastiness.

Dad lay there on his back, gawking up at her, breathing hard.

"You okay," asked Sierra, trying to play it casual.

"Holy cow. You're wearing a dress." Dad blinked.

"Grr. I knew you were going to do that." She scowled off to the side, then yelled, "We're the size of Barbie dolls and you're shocked at me in a dress?"

"Yes." Dad nodded once, his face completely serious. "Seeing you in a dress is more unusual than being eight inches tall. Or closer to six in your case."

Sierra frowned at him.

Dad held up a finger. "Also unusual is your clothes shrank, but mine didn't."

"Mine didn't either. This is one of Sophia's dolls' dresses."

"Ahh, that explains." He smiled. "You look adorable... in a vaguely homicidal way."

Sierra looked down. "Why do you think I hate dresses so much? Everyone always freaks out when I wear them. I don't like having everyone staring at me."

Dad sat up. "I was more shocked you found one the right size. Sorry, I didn't appreciate how much it really bothers you. Not trying to tease. You know you can wear whatever you like... as long as it covers enough. Speaking of which"—he eyed the rag around his waist—"is there anything up there I could fit in?"

She exhaled. "There's plenty of doll clothes up there, but they're all stupid extra and frilly, except this one."

"Dolls. Right." He tightened the knot holding the rag around his waist. "Might be worth going upstairs if I can figure out a way to do it."

Sierra quirked an eyebrow. "You'd seriously wear a ball gown?"

"Instead of this rag? Yes. I think I'd rather *rock* a Disney princess gown, don't you think?"

She smirked, fully aware he tried to throw himself on the sword of embarrassment to spare her feelings about his earlier comment. "Yeah. Totally."

Dad stood and pulled her into a hug. "Are you okay?"

"More or less. Just pissed off."

He patted her on the back, then released the squeeze. "So... this creature said something about us having to be punished for what we did... know anything about that?"

She fidgeted. "I might've killed one."

"One?" He chuckled.

"Okay, like twenty. But the first one tried to cut my head off!" She thrust her arms out to either side. "Soon as it saw

me, it went crazy and attacked. I beat the snot out of it...
literally."

Dad glanced sideways at the puddle of goop and bones.
"Any idea where they came from?"

"Nope. First one I saw was rummaging around Soph's
room. It grabbed a glowing crystal like it was going to
steal it."

"That crystal?" Dad pointed.

Sierra twisted around. Roughly in the middle of the
kitchen, the glowing crystal lay on the floor next to another
goblin sword. "Yeah. That's it. I think it's got something to do
with us being small. Not sure why, but shrinking doesn't feel
like it should be one of those goblins' special abilities."

Dad chuckled. "I'd love to have a *real* monster manual so
we know what we're dealing with."

"There kinda is one. The mystics have this giant book
they're afraid to touch." Sierra padded over to the crystal and
picked it up. At her present smallness, the glowing artifact
was about the size of a thermos. "Wonder if this thing can
fix us?"

"I have no idea." Dad approached, peering at it. "Never
suspected my daughter would be hiding crystal in her
bedroom."

"Dad..." Sierra rolled her eyes. "Not funny."

He pretended to act serious. "We need to determine the
proper crystal method... and undo this."

She groaned. *Ugh. How can he be laughing about this? We're
in big trouble.* "What are we going to do?"

"I have two thoughts." Dad rubbed his chin. "We can
either try climbing up to my work desk where my phone is
and call Darren Anderson, or we find a safe place to avoid
goblins and wait for Sarah or your mother to come home."

Sierra shifted her jaw side to side, thinking. "If I'm wrong
and the goblins don't need this crystal to shrink people,

they're going to do the same thing to Sarah or Mom. Climbing to your desk sounds dangerous. Do you have any other ideas?"

Dad raised both eyebrows. "I suppose we could run."

"Run?" Sierra tilted her head.

Dad pointed over her shoulder.

She twisted around.

Dozens of goblins massed at the archway connecting the kitchen to the dining room, seeming seconds away from a bloodthirsty charge. The sight of a literal army of murderous, blade-wielding giants nearly made her lose control of her bladder. It also nearly made her yell 'Daddy!' and grab him, but she didn't do that either. Her weird mixed-up brain once again translated terror into looking furious. She ended up glaring at them as they spilled into the kitchen, fanning out into a wider and wider battle line. Beady glowing yellow eyes narrowed in hateful anticipation. Blades glinted in the feeble daylight coming in from the glass sliding door out to the deck. The creatures didn't seem terribly happy about being in direct sunlight, even on an overcast day, as if they had to force themselves to advance step by step. She couldn't really think of them as tiny annoyances at the moment, since they towered over her.

Dad grasped her shoulder. "We should probably run."

Sierra gave him side eye. "Yeah, but run where?"

12

ON EDGE

I f things keep up like this, my alter ego is going to develop a drinking problem.

Here I am in my car, driving to the home address of an Olympia Police detective after essentially breaking into their evidence storage room *and* their computer network. To be technical, I didn't hack anything, merely compelled Detective Espinoza to give me Detective Warner's address before making her and Desk Guy remember me as a completely different girl. They think a twelve-year-old on a school project interviewed them for a tour around the station. Probably not a good idea to make Espinoza think she ran into two different young women. The confusion might cause the memory tinkering to unravel, but it also might have the reverse effect and prevent her from remembering the real truth.

Nothing blew up, no one got hurt, and I didn't take anything. There shouldn't be any reason someone pores over surveillance video to find me. Still, I've illegally obtained the home address of a cop and am going there. Follows Rules

Girl is alternating between curling up in a ball and anxiety vomiting in the corner.

I am adjusting to my new reality a little, though. My hands aren't shaking because I'm terrified of getting in trouble. They're shaking because I'm anxious at a problem getting away from me and my not being able to stop it. This is a horrible situation, and not even the tiniest piece of it is my fault. For once in my unlife, the mess dropped in my lap to clean up isn't one of my creation. Sophia didn't even do this.

Remember that movie *Pulp Fiction*? I feel like The Wolf, on the way to clean up a problem.

Maybe wolf cub.

Okay, I'm more like a fluffy Husky puppy.

Whatever.

Point being, there is zero guilt weighing me down, only the dread I'm not going to be good enough to fix things. In my favor, Warner only took the sword last night. It's possible he ran out the door of the police station and psychotically murdered some random person in an alley ten minutes later. However, Detective Espinoza didn't know about any unexplained violent murders between last night and now, especially ones involving a cop. My hope is that Jake Warner has strong willpower and he's still at home trying to fight off whatever demons—literal or metaphorical—plague his mind.

Mark the Thrall didn't have time to go into the specifics of it, but he seemed quite convinced vampires are not vulnerable to being possessed by this sword. Conventional wisdom—as much as anything involving the undead could be called conventional—doesn't include Innocents. We are so rare (and considered weak and unimportant) most other vamps don't even care to study us. A chance exists I could be affected by it while offline. It might require the full potency of my immortal powers to resist it. Hmm. Wonder if it's like how I can sometimes use superhuman strength during the day at the expense of burning myself a little. Divert power from shields to weapons, so to speak? Few things in this world are stronger than a vampire's subconscious urge to survive. Anyone who thinks Karens are pushy has never tried to come between a vampire and a dark place when the sun's about to come up.

As frustrating as it is, I force myself to drive like a normal person. Being offline means I can't send a cop on their way to avoid a speeding ticket, and the few minutes driving like a crazy person might save me will more than be lost if I get pulled over. Besides, it's not like Detective Warner's house is on fire. He's had the sword in his possession since yesterday evening. I'd say a few more minutes won't change much, but don't want to jinx myself.

Shit. Does thinking it without saying it count?

What the hell am I doing? The only experience I have rushing somewhere to throw water on a crisis fire is putting Ashley back together after whoever she's dating breaks up with her or a pet dies. Pretty sure it's going to take more than a box of ice cream and a movie marathon to make Warner feel better.

Guy lives a bit out of the city, near Evergreen State College. He's a bit north of Goldcrest in this tiny cluster of houses embedded in forest. Makes finding it fairly easy. According to my phone, I just need to take Aztec Drive until it dead ends.

An unexpected bonus surprises me soon after I find Cooper Point Road: bad weather. The sky goes from dreary to straight up gloomy in a seeming instant. It's so dark out, my vampiric side comes online. In my head, a little cartoon plays out where an overly cute version of me (Follows Rules Girl) is clinging to a stuffed panda on the Anxiety Couch™ when a more teenaged version of me in dark clothing with glowing red eyes barges in the door. FRG flings the stuffed panda over her head, screams 'You deal with this!' and storms off. Vampire Me looks at the camera, blinks once, then shrugs, making this 'what the heck did I just walk in on' face.

My phone guides me to the address. Maybe a bad idea to use it. Someone, somewhere who is far more tech savvy than I will no doubt be able to determine I used an app to look up Warner's address. Yeah, it's serious needle-in-a-haystack type stuff and probably won't even be discovered unless someone is already investigating *me*. Can't worry about every little thing or I'll drive myself crazy. Not sure if it's reassuring or scary how much of what we think of as the normal, modern world has been infiltrated by vampires. It's not as if they're keeping humans as feed stock, but they've got their fingers on enough levers of control to ensure people remain in the dark about our existence. Well, 'society,' really. *People* sometimes learn about us. As long as it's only a handful, they can easily be dismissed as crazy. Anyway, I have the address of a police detective.

And, here I am.

It's probably dumb to park my car anywhere near Warner's house in case a curious neighbor hears strange noises and starts taking video. It's dark enough. Screw it. I pull off the side of 28th Ave and leave the Sentra on a narrow strip of grass. This road isn't really two lanes. There's no paint on it. Yeah, it's wide enough for two cars to pass going in opposite directions, but the drivers could trade Grey Poupon as they pass.

Not far in front of where I stopped, a partially paved driveway leads up to the left to a house perched on a shallow hill. It's not Warner's place, but I stare at it for a moment to make sure no one is watching me. Once satisfied at being unnoticed, I cut the engine, get out, and jump into the air.

Flying will never stop being amazing.

It's crazy how much the real world looks like Google Maps from the air. This whole area is full of trees. Great for privacy, nature lovers, and slasher movies. Within seconds of me swooping in for a landing beside the detective's house, the scent of blood floods my nostrils. It smells like actual blood, not some crazy food translation, which means it's been outside a body long enough to lose its *vitae essentia,* basically life energy. Older vampires tend to use Latin phrasing for things when they want to sound like archaic pretentious douchebags.

A common misconception about vampires is we drink blood.

Well, we do... what I mean is the blood itself isn't really what we're consuming to sustain ourselves. Blood in a living person contains spiritual energy. Said energy only stays in the blood for like a minute or two after it's no longer inside a person if nothing is done to preserve it. You know that old joke about vampires and blood banks? Yeah, doesn't work. There's no life in it.

And... shit.

Smelling blood outside the house of a guy who took an overgrown knife known to possess people and turn them into killers is a not a good sign. The pit of my stomach gets heavy like I just looked out the window to see who rang the doorbell, and it's a pair of LL Bean rejects holding copies of The Watchtower. Unfortunately, I don't have the option of simply not opening the door—or answering it naked. Supposedly, they go away and leave you alone for years if you do that. Never had the balls to do it before, but if a pair of Witnesses happen to bother me when I'm home alone—no 'rents or Littles there to see—I just might answer the door wearing only a pentacle necklace. I could even make it better... get Blix to illusion himself as a black cat and hiss at them.

Nah. Sending a pair of idiots on their way is one thing. Putting them in a mental health hospital is a bit over the line.

Okay, Sarah. Stop distracting yourself. Bad shit happened here. Time to ignore rules for a little while. I'm expecting to find a bloodbath, a dead guy, and no sword. Can't imagine other vampires beat me here, but knowing my luck, I'm going to be stuck breadcrumbing after this stupid sword all damn day into the night.

The front door is locked, so I head around to the back, flying over the fence to land on the deck by a sliding glass door similar to the one at home. It's starting to rain a little, but far short of the monsoon type downpour the angry sky appears intent on delivering. Blood's smeared on the floor and cabinets. Shit. Shit. Shit. I pull my T-shirt up a bit and use it to avoid direct contact with the door handle. Problem of being overly lifelike as an Innocent. There's a good chance I *will* leave fingerprints. Don't want to risk it.

This door is locked, too, but the mechanism is no match for my strength. It's easy to snap the little hook thing and pull the door aside. Blood scent overpowers the ghost of microwaved chicken nuggets, probably cooked long enough ago a normal person couldn't smell them anymore. Raspy, labored breathing comes from one of two doors leading out of the kitchen, straight ahead. Guessing the one on my right connects to the garage.

It's a man wheezing, so hopefully, I've found Detective Warner and not some random guy his wife cheated on him with... assuming he's married. Yeah, I also smell a woman's presence here... and kids.

Before my brain can run off with worst-case scenarios, I rush to the doorway.

A dude who looks like a somewhat older version of one

of the swim team jocks from my former high school lays on his side, curled up in a fetal position beside the dining room table. Bloody handprints on the wall reveal the path he staggered in from before collapsing. He's as pale as a vampire with spiky brown hair. If not for his bulging eyes and manic 'want to kill everything that moves' glare, he'd be fairly cute.

I'm stunned to see the sword still in his hand. Like, legit shocked so much I freeze in awe. No one got here before me and ran off with it. Okay, Universe. Listen up. I would rather chase this stupid sword for the next ten years than find a dead kid somewhere in this house. So... if you want to send some minions in here to grab the thing before I can get to it, now's the time.

Nothing happens other than Jake Warner wheezing while clutching what appears to be a gunshot wound in his left side. All the grunting and groaning coming from him sounds like he's trying to get back up but his body's not having it. I haven't heard this much futile straining since Dad tried to carry our sofa into the house by himself a couple years ago.

I move closer, careful to step on his wrist and pin the arm holding the sword to the floor. He looks up at me, half confused, half murderous. Mother Nature misses an opportunity here—no dramatic thunderclap the instant our stares meet. I squat, push him over flat on his back and concentrate on forcing my way into his head.

My mental influence crashes against rubbery resistance. Feels as though I've run full speed into an enormous cube of Jell-O. It's not a wall, but the possessing entity has a pretty deep hold on his brain. Wherever I push forward, it fills in elsewhere like I'm attempting to dig a hole in a bowl of soup. Snarling, I hold him down and get into a mental boxing match with the thing—whatever it is—trying to force it out. Rapid camera-flashes of memory jump out at me. I see a terrified little girl screaming. A boy almost the same age running away from me (Warner) and a blonde woman screaming, flailing around, blood flying all over the place.

Dammit. Would Wolent be pissed at me if I dropped this sword into an active volcano? Seriously. Screw this evil piece of shit. Anger gives me a boost of mental strength to shove at the entity inside this guy's head. Feels like I've pushed a dark cloud out of his skull, but it's still clinging by two little claws to the back end of his brain. The shadow snaps back inside an instant before Warner rolls to his right, ramming a knee into my side and throwing me to the floor.

I may have supernatural strength, but I'm no Aziz. Doesn't take a huge guy to throw me around. Warner springs to his feet, somehow ignoring the pain of his gunshot wound, and stabs at me. I throw myself forward, literally flying out of a push-up position. The sword whistles over my head close enough to shorten a few of my hairs. I pivot upright, hovering behind him. Warner recovers his balance way faster than seems reasonable for a police detective. His stance and posture tells me exactly where the sword is going. There's no way in hell Jake Warner is a sword fighter. Someone or something else is in charge right now.

My dodge is not perfect, but effective. He thrusts the blade for my heart, but ends up putting it in the gap between my arm and my side. Strange energy wafting from the sword gives off a sense of hunger, as if the blade itself seriously wants my blood. Whatever entity is inside it and possessing people is major furious, like 'Sierra dying more times than she gets kills in a *Call of Duty* match' raging. Big angry.

He tries to snap the blade up and slice my armpit. Backflip to the rescue. Hooray for being online and seriously fast. Jake might be possessed, but he's still an ordinary human, not even anyone's thrall. There's a reason vampire hunters love crossbows. If we get close enough to hit with swords and knives, a normal human is pretty much screwed unless they have some paranormal trick allowing them to keep up with us. Not too many vampire hunters these days use magic. Might've been more common back in the day.

Jake slashes at me again, the tip of the blade missing my chest by about a finger's width. It's hard not to giggle at him. Really... what's he think a sword is going to do to me other than cause some temporary pain? Oh, duh. He doesn't know I'm a vampire. He's expecting me to play by the normal rules and die if stabbed in the heart.

For the record, that's one rule my alter ego is happy not to follow.

He spends about a minute slicing and slashing at me. I tease him a little for no particular reason, letting the blade come within millimeters of hitting me but never allowing contact. If I had a sword in my hand right now, I'd totally disarm him. This guy is surprisingly good, whoever he is, but he's not fast to me. If my superhuman agility didn't give me a massive speed advantage, he'd probably kick my ass.

Finally Jake, or the entity possessing him, accepts it's completely futile trying to kill me. He swipes at my face as a distraction, then bolts, running toward the interior hall. Sorry pal. Can't let you run off and do murder. Time for a Supergirl maneuver. My haste to catch him imparts perhaps too much speed to my flight. I hit Warner in the back of the knees so hard it knocks him into a reverse somersault over my back. Fortunately, I manage to stop before having an intimate encounter with the wall.

After flipping vertical, I whirl, then land on my feet facing him. He's already standing, sword poised. However, he's hesitating. Not an unusual reaction to watching a girl fly. Warner, however, doesn't look freaked out or confused by it. His expression is completely one of 'oh shit.' Hmm, did someone realize I'm not mortal?

He hauls ass for the kitchen.

"Mommy! Wake up! Noooo! Mommy! Please wake up!" cry-screams a small child upstairs.

FML. Seriously. FML.

Wait, no. FMU. Unlife.

Growling, and remembering the deal I made with the Universe, I zoom for the living room instead of chasing Warner out the back door. He can wait. Not gonna be able to live with myself if some kid bleeds to death because of my impatience at chasing a sword all over the city.

Screaming and crying leads me to the end of the upstairs hall, likely a bathroom. The door has multiple holes in it from both a sword and bullets. The sword holes have traces of blood around them. Sounds like two kids bawling their eyes out on the inside.

Predictably, the door is locked.

I punch a hand through it—making both children shriek —fumble at the interior knob, and unlock it. Both children shriek again when I pull the door open.

The blonde woman I saw in Warner's mind lays slumped on the floor, stabbed and slashed on her chest and arms. A Glock handgun dangles limply from her fingers. A boy and a girl kneel on either side of her head, crying and begging her to wake up. The boy appears slightly older than his sister, maybe seven or eight.

Sorry, Mom, but this scene in front of me deserves it. Fuck...

I'm about to yell another F-bomb instead of merely thinking it, but notice the woman is still breathing. Not deeply, but she hasn't died yet. I mentally derp both kids and pounce on her. While the children stare into the fifth dimension, I rip the woman's shirt off to expose the wounds. Not sure how much it will help, but I do the only thing I can... extend my fangs and ever so slightly bite near each bloody spot to 'magically charge' it, which allows my postfeeding ability to seal the wounds. Yeah, she's still ripped up internally, but I can stop her from losing even more blood.

Once I have the biggest injuries closed, I palm the boy's head and make him look me in the eye, giving him a compulsion to run to the nearest phone and call 911. He's going to tell the dispatcher a 'strange man' broke into the house and attacked his mommy. As he sprints out, I dive into the girl's head, modifying her memory of Daddy chasing them around the house by filling in an indistinct, shadowy form. She's going to think her father was at work when someone else attacked them.

I'll do the same to the boy when he comes back.

The woman opens her eyes, staring up at me. She's too weak to talk, but the 'who the hell are you' look in her eyes doesn't need words.

"I'm no one important. Look, Mrs. Warner, your husband didn't do this."

She exhales. "Not… him. I… know. Something happened. Not… Jake."

Say what? She knows about weird stuff? I peek into her head. Oh. She's thinking he cracked and lost his mind. A 'not my Jake' in the sense of thinking he's suffering a serious mental problem and she doesn't really blame him for being out of control. Let me help that denial along. She, too, soon thinks an unknown man in a black ski mask did it while her husband was at work. Normally, I wouldn't cover like this for a psycho husband, but it's really not the guy's fault.

The boy walks back in holding a cordless phone to his ear. He looks at his mother and mutters, "Yeah," into the phone.

I go into his head again, cementing the idea of an unknown shadowy figure instead of his father doing this. The kid already thinks I'm some kind of angel or ghost—not a real girl—here to help, so whatever. Let's run with that, too.

The woman wheezes.

"Hang on. You're gonna be okay." I squeeze her hand.

"They always tell people that." She emits a really scary sounding breath, almost a death rattle. "I'm not gonna make it."

Thanks to my mental tinkering, the children are still in too much of a fog to process what their mother said and don't erupt in tears.

I gaze around at the room. This woman has lost a ton of blood. Can't tell if it's too much, though. Shit. Here it is. The moment I'd been dreading—sorta. I mean, it's not one of my siblings or parents, but I'm right next to someone who's about to die. Should I do it? Give her the Transference if her heart stops? I could probably do it now and it would take. She's lost enough blood for that. I don't *have* to do it before death, but there's only like a minute-long window afterward. I'm a screw up and a dork, but not so much of one that I'm going to set a *Sefil* loose on Washington State.

What happens if I make this woman a vampire? Will she inherent the Innocent bloodline? What if she doesn't? How will her family react? Will the vampires of the area demand she cut ties with them? Hell, even if I *do* give it to her, she's going to appear to die for like three days. Ask me how I know this. I won't pull a Dalton and 'forget' to steal her body from the morgue in time before she wakes up.

But Jake and the kids are going to think she died. It'll be on the news. Crap.

Ooh. Idea. I stare at her. "Do not die."

Mental commands have been known to do crazy things before and defy the laws of reality. For example, I could compel a vegan to eat a cheeseburger, Sierra to put on a frilly dress, or even force my father to call a real plumber. If those are possible, I have to be able to give this woman enough drive to fight off death for a few more minutes.

Another idea. Transference is about intent, right?

I extend my fangs again and nip myself on the wrist. Concentrating *hard* on my desire *not* to make her into a vampire, but instead empower her like a thrall, I dribble a little blood into her half-open mouth. Three drops ought to be enough to do something. Probably won't give her too much superhuman speed or strength.

The woman licks at the blood, closes her mouth, swallows.

I make the kids forget seeing this, then lick my wrist to close the wound.

Sirens pierce the distant silence of a peaceful woodland community.

Mrs. Warren stares at me, renewed strength in her eyes.

"Trust me. You're gonna make it." I wink.

The siren gets really loud and really close before cutting out. Automotive doors open and slam. Metal rattles… likely a stretcher.

"Yeah. I hear sirens," says the boy into the phone. "They're outside."

A woman on the other end tells him to go open the door for the police.

"Okay." The boy walks out, far too calm.

My fault. He's still in a compulsion haze, so his emotions are muted. Not a problem. They'll either praise him for his bravery or blame it on shock.

"Paramedics are here," I say. "Time for me to go."

Taking a bit of inspiration from Glim, I make the woman believe I simply disappeared into thin air like a ghost. My friend creates actual illusions. I'm stuck tweaking memories. Not as flashy, but it works. At the clamor of a bunch of people scrambling up the stairs starts in the hall behind me, I go out the bathroom window and pull up fast, gliding over the roof to stay out of sight. Flashing lights from an ambulance and two police cars flood the front yard in a shimmering red-blue haze. Any neighbors in the area are going to be distracted by the commotion down there. It's also raining a little harder now.

Makes it easy for me to fly away unnoticed.

Crouched on the roof of the Warner house like a gargoyle, I stare at the backyard until Jake's trample path in the grass becomes apparent. A streak of blood in the rain running down the back fence tells me where he climbed it.

Gotcha.

Well, I am a higher-order predator. Suppose it's time I hunted like one.

13

STEALER OF SOLES

S ophia liked arts and crafts, but could do that stuff at home. She liked swimming, but in pools—not rivers or lakes. She could also go swimming back home. She didn't really care for hiking but could tolerate it. That, too, she could do at home. From a logical standpoint, Sophia couldn't come up with any good reason to go way off to a camp. Not like they lived in Los Angeles or New York or somewhere full of concrete. They didn't need to escape a big city. Home had plenty of green forest. Heck, directly behind their house was a patch of untamed woodland. Sam and his friends always ran around there. It even had a small cave the boys often used as a pretend base, fort, command center, or whatever depending on their mood.

Sophia had never gone with them, but she knew those woods covered a decent amount of ground, enough to make getting lost a possibility. Fortunately, getting lost in those woods only ended up being annoying, not dangerous. Suburbia surrounded it. If the boys kept walking in the same direction long enough, they'd eventually find houses and sidewalks. The woods around the Girl Scout Camp, however, stretched for miles. Out here, she *could* get lost bad enough to run into serious problems.

The girls had been divided among small one-room cabins containing four bunk beds apiece. Sophia's troop took up three adjacent cabins, with one unused bed in cabin three. While the girls transferred their stuff from bags and backpacks to the footlockers by each bed, Mrs. Brewer finally noticed the acute lack of outdoors-capable shoes among Sophia's belongings. She ended up being the only kid wearing flip-flops among roughly 200 Girl Scouts.

Sophia stood there, hands clasped in front of herself, gaze downcast, weathering a lecture about being irresponsible and unprepared. Normally, getting in trouble of any kind made her want to cry. Two reasons kept her from being upset over this particular chewing out. One: she'd omitted telling her parents she needed proper shoes for the outdoors on purpose, so felt she deserved the scolding. Two: she still didn't really want to be at the camp and couldn't care less what Mrs. Brewer thought of her capability as an outdoorsperson. Yelling at Sophia for being bad at camping was like yelling at the sky for appearing blue. A total 'no duh' moment.

"Mew," said Sophia's backpack.

Mrs. Brewer stopped short, frozen in mid-diatribe. "Sophia Wright, did you smuggle a cat into camp? You know pets aren't allowed." She pointed at the purple backpack. "Open it."

"Probably a stuffed animal with a sound chip," whispered Hadley.

A few other girls giggled.

Trusting Klepto would be invisible, Sophia tugged her bag open without hesitation. The fuzzy grey kitten 'smiled' up at her, teal eyes aglow, sitting next to a brand-new pair of chocolate-brown hiking shoes.

"Oh," said Mrs. Brewer, not reacting whatsoever to the presence of the kitten. "Why didn't you say you had proper shoes in there? You let me rant at you thinking you'd only brought flops. Dear, you are too polite sometimes."

Sophia swallowed, nursing a swirl of guilt swimming around in her gut. She hadn't said or done anything, yet still felt as though she'd lied. Considering the 'new shoe smell' wafting from the gift Klepto brought, the kitten had likely yoinked them from a store. Stealing shoes bothered her more than taking a giant ruby. As soon as she got home, she'd send Klepto back to wherever she obtained the shoes from to deliver enough of her allowance money to cover them.

Mrs. Brewer drifted off, checking on the other girls as they unpacked.

Sophia sat on the edge of the lower bed. Nicole would be sleeping above her, Priya on the adjacent one. At least she had two friends here. While she generally knew the rest of the girls in her troop, she wouldn't call any of them real friends. They got along well enough, though. Some of them avoided her because they liked to do things they believed she'd immediately tell on them for—likely true. Sophia had a reputation among her troop for being the 'good girl' and a bit of a chicken. Given the truth of it, she didn't let it bother her. Her lack of snooping around to find stuff she could tell on them for, being content to let them exclude her when needed, spared her teasing or retaliation. She didn't need to 'play cop,' merely did not want to be involved personally in anything bad. Their troop had McKenzie Whitaker to be the tattletale already. It didn't need two.

Having a multipurpose kitten of acquisition came in super handy, even if random long-distance shoplifting bothered her. Once she finished transferring her stuff into the footlocker, she curled up on the bed with her back to the room, cuddling Klepto so no one could see.

"You okay?" asked Nicole a few minutes later.

"Yeah. Just bored."

"Gonna just lie there until camp is over?"

"Tempting." Sophia rolled her eyes at herself. She'd been ready to sit on the bus and wait for it to leave. "I'd probably get in trouble, though."

Nicole nudged her. "They can't *force* you to do anything."

"Something's bothering me." Sophia rolled flat on her back, staring up at the underside of the upper bunk.

"No kidding." Nicole laughed. "Thank you, Captain Obvious."

Sophia chuckled. "No, I mean... more than being homesick. Feels like I left a candle burning in my room and my house might burn down."

"Whoa." Nicole blinked. "Did you?"

"No. Haven't lit candles lately. Just saying it's what I feel. Like something's a little bit wrong right now and it might turn into a big problem."

"Wow." Nicole whistled. "Sucks we have no cell phone reception out here. Can't call home to check."

A sick heaviness welled up in the pit of Sophia's gut at being reminded of how cut off she was from her family. It's like the Girl Scouts went out of their way to make sure she couldn't communicate with the outside world. No phones, no internet, no electricity—absolutely zero way for her to talk to anyone outside the camp. For a few brief seconds, she felt as though she'd been kidnapped and taken to a remote prison camp. Any minute now, the girls would all end up in chains, dragged to the mines where they would be forced to labor away digging Thin Mints out of the walls. The melodrama waned after a breath or two.

I'm like Sarah. We play outside the rules, now.

Sophia held Klepto up over her head in both hands, staring into the kitten's glowing eyes, not particularly concerned if anyone thought her weird for 'pretending' to hold an animal. "Can you go look around, make sure it's okay?"

"Mew," said Klepto—right before she vanished in a purple flash.

Nicole narrowed her eyes. "What's up?"

"Just worried," whispered Sophia. "Asked her to go home and make sure everything's okay. It's probably just my anxiety making me think about home so much."

Mrs. Whitaker breezed back in the cabin door. "All right, girls. Gather up." She clapped twice. "We'll be going to the pavilion to do some projects." The woman's overly cheerful voice made her sound like the mother on a 1950s-era sitcom.

"Ugh," muttered Nicole. "She is way too happy to be camping."

Sophia kicked off her flip-flops, put on the new hiking shoes, and stood. "Yeah. She sure is."

SITTING IN A LARGE-ISH ROOM AMONG A FEW HUNDRED KIDS AT cafeteria-style tables doing arts and crafts somehow lacked a true sense of 'roughing it' at camp. Sophia didn't mind. Getting crafty and messy offered a welcome distraction from thoughts of home. The scout leaders of various troops plus camp counselors patrolled the aisles between tables, ready to answer questions, distribute supplies, or offer help where needed. Mrs. Brewer randomly talked about 'all the fun stuff' they'd be doing in the coming days. This being 'arrival day,' it wouldn't involve doing too much beyond settling in and this arts & crafts session.

Sophia busied herself making a picture of Klepto by cutting out tiny bits of multicolored construction paper and gluing them onto a bigger sheet of white paper. Eventually, it came time to eat. Gathering up in lines to go from the art room to the actual cafeteria once again made Sophia feel like she'd been sent to some kind of detention camp. Of course, the negative feelings came entirely from homesickness... so she did her best to ignore them and not act the sad sack. All the way to the 'mess hall,' she kept staring off into the woods, debating how scary or dangerous it really would be to try running away and going home.

AFTER DINNER, SOPHIA AND HER TROOP COLLECTED AROUND A pit outside for a quick workshop on building a campfire. One of the counselors, an auburn haired twentysomething named Kayleigh, sat with them and went over fire safety before showing them how to get a campfire going when no one had a match. Klepto hadn't come back yet, which worried her. When she tried to establish a mental link with her familiar, she got the vague sense something really had gone wrong back home... but also that the kitten felt capable of dealing with it. Due to the distance between them, communication ended up being limited to vague notions instead of telepathy or seeing through the kitten's eyes. Sophia forced herself to remain calm. A problem at home freaked her out, but if Klepto felt confident in her ability to handle it by herself, it couldn't be anything *too* serious.

Predictably, once the sun went down, the presence of a campfire resulted in two absolute truths coming to pass: marshmallows on sticks and scary stories.

"Tell us a spooky story," said Andrea, reigning cookie sales champion of the troop.

"Yeah!" chorused a few others.

Sophia winced. *Great. I'm scared enough already.*

Kayleigh cleared her throat. "They say the woods around

here are haunted by the vengeful spirit of a wild forest hermit, Crazy Coleman."

Nicole snickered. "Coleman? Really? That's a lantern."

"It is." Kayleigh nodded at her. "But it's also a name. Some stories claim Crazy Coleman lived around here like 200 years ago. He hated people and wanted to be alone. Anyone who trespassed on his land, he'd hunt them down and"—she made a throat slicing gesture—"kill them in the night." She shared a series of quick stories about a farmer who went looking for a lost goat and never returned, a pair of young lovers who snuck off into the woods to kiss—and never came back. "Now, he haunts this forest... his ghost is still out there, killing everyone he thinks doesn't belong here... which is pretty much everyone." Her eyes caught the firelight, gleaming with pretend evil. "He especially hates kids and anyone who looks happy or innocent."

Again, the girls gave a collective gasp of worry. Nicole sat there with a 'you have to be kidding me' expression of bored suspicion. She whispered to Sophia about how the counselors told this 'Coleman' story every year, and no one had yet been murdered here. Priya appeared about as frightened as Sophia felt, shivering where she sat. No one spoke for a moment.

Grinning, Kayleigh continued, leaning closer to the fire so her face seemed to glow orange. "There used to be a small village not far down the river. At first, they blamed all the disappearances on wild animals, until one day a young girl he tried to kill got away from him. She told her daddy about it and the whole town set off to hunt the killer. It took them all night to catch him. They didn't even try to arrest him, just cut his head off where they found him because he killed like a dozen of the townspeople who went out to hunt him."

Sophia squirmed. The other girls all stared at her in

horrified awe, except for Nicole who appeared to be fighting super hard not to roll her eyes.

Kayleigh gestured around. "They say in the hour before the sun comes up, you can hear the shouts of the townspeople hunting the woods. All the ones who died trying to catch Crazy Coleman are trapped here, too. They won't hurt you... but he will."

"Ghosts can't hurt the living," said Nicole.

"You'd think." Kayleigh nodded. "But like forty years ago, before the Girl Scouts bought this land we're sitting on right now, a bunch of college students came out here to camp by the lake for a weekend. They disappeared without a trace. When the search parties went looking for them, they heard screaming but never found anyone—not even a body."

Some of the girls gasped.

Sophia shivered. Sure, it sounded like the plot of all the scary movies Dad liked—meaning completely cheesy—but it still unsettled her. From the instant the young camp counselor said 'Crazy Coleman,' the mood in the air darkened. It sure felt as though *something* out beyond the light of the campfire in the forest watched them.

Kayleigh flared her eyebrows. "I did some research after my first time camping here. A guy named Coleman *did* really live around here a long time ago. No one knew much about him since he lived alone in the woods. He hated people when he was alive, and it got worse now that he's dead. He comes back from the grave to attack anyone who dares set foot in 'his' forest."

The char-sweet scent of scorched marshmallow mixed with the fragrance of wood smoke and the smell of damp leaves. Judging by the overall quiet, other troop leaders also told their clusters of girls spooky stories. Sophia tried not to pay attention to Kayleigh's continuing horror stories about all the people Coleman killed. She stared at the melty remains of marshmallow on the stick in her hand, debating if she could stomach a second one. The ghost apparently got his first kill this year: her appetite.

A faint pale-green glow manifested in the trees a fair distance off to the left, well away from the light of eight campfires. Sophia tensed, too terrified to look but also too terrified *not* to.

It's probably moonlight reflecting on something. Maybe a faerie.

Reluctantly, she glanced away from the stick toward the spot where a faint glow seemed to hover between a pair of thick trees. An amorphous cloud of teal-green light roughly the size of a man's torso floated there. While it didn't appear to be anything more threatening than a cloud, it gave off a strong sense of being aware.

Sophia stared, trying to figure out what she looked at. Spirit energy? Will-o-Wisp? Faerie lights?

The cloud shifted, stretching vertically. Two wisps of fog coiled to the ground forming legs. In seconds, it took on the shape of a semitransparent man in a tattered green coat, shaggy pants, and floppy fur hat. He looked older than Dad but not *old*. Greyish-brown hair jutted out from his head and face in a frazzled spray of wildness. In his left hand, he held a raised lantern containing a flickering ghostly white flame. He clutched an axe in his other hand, the ancient blade smeared in a dark substance. The spirit appeared to be watching the camp of girl scouts, a manic glint of desperation in his eyes... until he noticed Sophia looking right at him. The instant their gazes met, his eyes grew even wider, fixated on her.

The spirit had obviously noticed she could see him... and took a step closer.

Sophia did the only thing her brain allowed... and screamed in terror.

14

THE KITTEN OF INEFFABLE GLORY

Part of Sierra wanted to hide behind Dad.

Goblins filled the only accessible means of leaving the kitchen, swarming in like a slow, menacing lava spill in serious need of dental care. She and Dad couldn't make it to the dining room due to a hundred goblins. Going to the basement would only trap them underground. Besides, the door at the top of the stairs was closed, and neither one of them could reach the knob. The gap under it didn't have enough room for even a kid as skinny as Sierra to slip through. Despite offering the hope of the outside world, the patio door proved an equally impassable barrier.

Dad backed away from the approaching goblin horde, tugging Sierra with him.

Having a Sophia meltdown and screaming for help wouldn't do anyone any good. As much as her childish side wanted to, Sierra didn't jump and cling to her father for protection. It didn't seem at all likely she'd walk away from the fight ahead of her, but it's not as if she had the option of running away. 'Taking as many of them with her as possible' sounded all badass and cool, but Sierra didn't want to die. She couldn't even stare death in the face without flinching yet. Wanting the ability to survive a fight against something like a vampire did *not* mean she wanted to get into fights.

The moment of her death wasn't anything like she imagined it would be.

For years, she'd had nightmares of dying while screaming and cowering under a desk at school. She'd wake up pissed at herself for being such a chicken, then proceed to spend hours arguing with herself if she'd bravely give the shooter the finger before he ended her life or if she'd surrender to fear and beg to be spared.

The moment arrived in front of her and she did neither. Perhaps because the agent of her demise didn't turn out to be a disaffected, crazy man with rage issues but a hundred annoying, ugly, irritating, stupid, damned goblins. Little pus-filled snotlings no bigger than Sophia's stuffed animals had the audacity to break into her home and try to kill her. Yeah, they appeared to be giants, almost twice her height, but she thought of them as infuriating little goobers.

Sierra grew furious all over again. She leaned forward in an aggressive, ready stance, prepared to end the first little bastard to come close enough. Worries of surviving or not surviving leaked out of her mind. No thoughts other than the next tactical move she'd have to make remained in her consciousness. Six minutes from now no longer mattered, only six seconds, and the next six seconds after that.

Cool glass touched her back as Dad pulled her up against the patio door. The latch and handle hung something like seven or eight stories above them, well out of reach. Goblins swarmed in on all sides, trapping them against the patio door. A small D-shaped area of open floor around them gradually shrank. The goblins seemed to take delight in drawing it out, jeering and chattering at them.

Dad glanced at his borrowed sword, then at Sierra. "Damn."

"What's wrong?" She didn't take her eyes off the goblins.

"We forgot headbands."

Sierra shook her head, unable to come up with anything to say back.

A flash of purple light went off in front of them.

She flinched at the unexpected glare, then stared dumbfounded at Klepto's butt—which happened to be perfectly at face level. Sierra really didn't appreciate having such an up-close and personal view of the kitten's exhaust port, but seeing this particular kitten here meant Sophia either was—or soon would be—aware of the problem at home.

Klepto hissed.

Shockingly, the entire goblin army recoiled, leaning away from the horse-sized kitten like vampires cringing from the sun.

Klepto stepped forward, emitting a meowing growl, then spitting.

Given her size compared to Sierra, the 'kitten' sounded like an angry tiger.

The goblins scrambled back in unison, opening about five feet of floor between their front line and the glass door.

"Whatever these things are," whispered Dad. "I think they're morbidly afraid of cats."

"Klepto!" yelled Sierra. "Tell Soph to get home right now!"

Dad raised an eyebrow. "Is that wise? The Void Octopus of Eternity will likely slap her all the way to Scotland."

"Mew," said Klepto.

Sierra growled. "Well, she should try. She got us to—"

"What's that?" Dad glanced at her.

Head hung, Sierra stared at her slimy toes. "Can Soph and

me getting in trouble wait until after we're no longer about to be torn apart by an army of goblins?"

"All right." Dad nodded once. "If we aren't brutally killed in the next few minutes, I expect a complete explanation."

"Deal," muttered Sierra.

The kitten hissed again, making the goblins cringe.

"Klepto, can you open the door?" Sierra pointed her sword up.

"Mew!" The kitten twisted around to peer up at the mechanism.

A sharp *snap* came from the lock and the patio door slid a few inches open by itself, letting in a cool 'rainy summer day' breeze.

"Awesome!" Sierra held up the glowing crystal. "Give this to Soph! The goblins want it."

Klepto nodded.

Sierra tossed the crystal, waited for the kitten to catch it in her mouth, then jumped out onto the deck. Dad hurried after her. A few goblins emerged from under the deck furniture and chased them across. Sierra leapt over the gaps between boards, the openings presently big enough to swallow her foot and give her a broken ankle. She ran toward the stairs, swerved away when six goblins pulled themselves up into view, their swords in their teeth like pirates climbing sails.

The goblins hemmed her and Dad in, forcing them to the edge of the deck, beneath the railing. Sierra peered over, wondering how far the enchantment would go in terms of toughness. Could she survive a six-or-seven story fall into grass? As soon as she spotted a flowerpot full of water, she decided to risk it and jumped.

She dropped feet-first straight down. Air flooded up under the doll dress, cold, but nowhere near as frigid as the water she landed in. Her shriek filled a thousand bubbles before she surfaced in the muddy rainwater and clung to the side of the pot. No sooner did she slump over it and spit out dirt-flavored liquid, Dad crashed into the 'pool' behind her. Goblins overhead probably cursed them out while angrily waving their swords, though she didn't understand their chittering.

Sierra pulled herself up over the flowerpot edge, which hadn't really been made for a tiny person to perch on. Rather than spill face-first into the grass, she swung her legs around and allowed gravity to make her fall to a fairly soft landing. Dad jumped down next to her, surprisingly not landing flat on his back like her.

"Wow. Nice dismount." Sierra sat up. "When did you take gymnastics?"

"I didn't." Dad flexed. "I got my varsity letter in fence jumping from sixth grade through sophomore year."

"Fence jumping?" She stood.

"Yes. Jocks are much less inclined to chase down and beat up the smart kid when they have to run across nine backyards, jumping fences along the way to catch him." Dad brushed mud from his arm. "It's a question of effort versus payoff. Make it too much work, they go bother someone else."

She laughed. "My father's a nerd."

"As if this is any great secret." He beamed with pride.

Goblins emerged from Mom's flowerbed, surrounding them.

"Uh oh," muttered Sierra. "We're not out of the woods yet."

Dad raised his sword. "Technically, we're not in the woods. We're in the tulips."

"Dad..." Sierra sighed, pointing her sword at a goblin. "This way. We can fight our way through."

Klepto reappeared in a violet flash. At her sudden

appearance, all the goblins jumped back. Several screamed. The kitten crouched low as if inviting Sierra to hop on her back.

"Wild," whispered Dad... right before he jumped on the kitten. "Like Battle Cat."

"What?" Sierra decided not to question and climbed up to sit in front of him.

Klepto stood, hissed again, and charged away from the deck at the goblins in the yard—who all broke and ran for it. Sierra clung to the kitten's neck as the now-not-so-little furball zigzagged across a lawn so abnormally huge it had become an untamed expanse of wild jungle.

"*He Man?*" asked Dad. "The tiger?"

"Oh. Yeah. I guess." Sierra slashed at a fleeing goblin as they rode by.

Dad stabbed at one on the other side, slicing it on the arm. "You didn't watch it? I have all the episodes recorded."

"I know," deadpanned Sierra while face-stabbing a goblin trying to smack her. "It's kinda lame."

"Blasphemy, I say." Dad gasped, faking upset. "*He Man* was one of my favorite shows when I was like eight."

Sierra rolled her eyes and ducked flat against Klepto's fur to avoid another overly brave goblin slashing at her. A metal-on-metal *clank* came from behind her as its sword bounced off Dad's. Klepto hissed at it, but didn't slow down. The goblin shrieked in terror and ran.

"Have you watched it since you were eight?" Sierra smirked to herself.

"Well... no, not really."

"It's basically a twenty-minute commercial for toys that takes up a half hour because they interrupt it with commercials for *other* toys." Sierra pushed herself upright.

"Okay, I'll concede you that." Dad smiled.

"Nice parry, by the way." Sierra blocked a goblin stabbing

at her from the left, effortlessly maneuvering her blade around its and stabbing it in the face.

Wailing, the goblin fell over backward and melted into a puddle of slime and bones.

"Thanks. Also, it's a *cool* twenty-minute commercial for toys." Dad hacked at a goblin on the right, slicing its face and some of its chest open. The gurgling creature collapsed. "Just about every kids' cartoon back then ended up being a commercial for toys. Kids had to do *something* before everyone had a Nintendo."

Sierra clutched a handful of fur and held on as tight as she could with her legs. Riding a cat—kitten—proved significantly more difficult than any cartoon or movie implied it ought to be. For a glorious minute or two, the reality around her became so patently absurd she lost herself in the fantasy of being a warrior princess from one of Dad's movies, valiantly slashing her way through a goblin army from the back of her enchanted war-cat. At their present size, the yard had become a vast, almost alien landscape. Grass blades as big as floorboards rushed by on both sides as the kitten ran in a seemingly random, frenetic dash away from the house.

It occurred to her no goblins had taken a swing for at least ten seconds, so she figured they must've finally outrun them. Klepto barreled headlong into a thick tangle of forest. It took Sierra a few seconds to realize what she assumed to be a magnificently huge, twisted fantasy woodland with titanic trees was likely just the row of hedges bordering the yard. A flying bug as big as a golden retriever zoomed by.

The thick 'forest' passed completely in three seconds, giving way to even taller grass she couldn't see over. An area of relatively untamed underbrush encircled the houses on her cul-de-sac, not technically belonging to any of the residents... so no one bothered mowing it. Since she couldn't tell where the heck the kitten took them, she focused completely on not being thrown.

Out of nowhere, a huge pillar of plaid fabric appeared in front of them.

With zero time to react, Klepto crashed into the strange tower. Sierra flew face-first into the fabric, briefly squished between it and the kitten. Dad careened off to the left. Sierra bounced away from the strange monolith and landed next to him. Her sword went flying somewhere into the thick grass. Klepto flipped back to her feet, gave them a 'wait here, I got this' sort of look, and vanished in a purple flash.

A tremendously loud bellowing roar came from far in the sky above them.

Sierra, still flat on her back, gazed up past the wall of grass surrounding her landing spot at the sky. The massive face of Mr. Niedermeyer crept into view, glaring down at her. He looked as tall as a six-story building—and he'd already spotted them.

"Don't move," said Dad, his voice shaking in a way that could have been barely suppressed laughter or crying. "Pretend to be an action figure."

"Again?" bellowed Niedermeyer. "Damn kids."

His deep, epic voice sounded like the wrath of an angry elder god. Sierra stiffened herself and tried to put on as vacant an expression as she could manage, thinking of this girl Bethany Walters from school—her generation's version of Bree Swanson.

Mr. Niedermeyer reached down and grabbed Sierra, his hand only slightly smaller than her bed. Hopefully, he wouldn't notice she had body heat or lacked the rigidity of plastic. The irony that wearing a doll dress might actually help her pretend to be a toy almost made her giggle despite the relatively terrifying situation.

If he figures out we aren't toys, he'd probably just have a heart attack and drop dead.

"The heck?" Mr. Niedermeyer held Dad up in his other hand. "Bimbo doll and some Chinese knock-off of Conan? *Robinson Crusoe on Mars?* Huh. Didn't think they made toys for that."

Bimbo! You jerk. Ooooh! Sierra fumed.

Fortunately, he didn't spend too much time studying them before stuffing Sierra and Dad together in the pocket of his bathrobe. Unfortunately, he put Sierra in first, so Dad kinda landed on her.

"Oof," she grunted.

"Sorry," whispered Dad.

She squirmed out from under him.

"Careful. Don't move too much." Dad turned his head to look up at the opening. "If he thinks he's got a mouse in his pocket, he might smash us."

Given what the neighborhood kids thought of Mr. Niedermeyer, Sierra totally believed he'd have no problem killing a harmless little mouse—or spitefully destroying toys 'trespassing' on his property if he thought the kids who left them there did so on purpose to antagonize him.

Is he gonna throw us in the garbage?

Ending up trapped in a trashcan the size of a five-story building, unable to climb the plastic walls, amounted to a nightmare scenario regardless of any potentially disgusting rotten food. If the goblin curse responsible for shrinking them didn't wear off on its own, she and Dad would be stuck there and either starve to death or be crushed inside a garbage truck days from now. She clenched her jaw, determined not to let him throw her in the trash. If he tried, she'd stop pretending to be a doll and freak out as much as possible.

Hopefully, he'd only have a heart attack and fall over instead of panic-smashing her.

The pocket swayed back and forth, bumping her rhythmically against Mr. Niedermeyer's leg as he walked. Sierra squeezed Dad's hand and tried to keep herself calm and still. Her father managed to keep hold of one of the goblin swords. Somehow, their mean old neighbor hadn't realized the 'toy' had a sharp weapon. Stranger still, neither Sierra nor Dad *felt* like plastic dolls. She figured he got so irrationally angry at the mere idea children *might* have been in his yard he didn't think straight or really take a good look at the 'toys.' He should have recognized them. Other than becoming small, they still looked like themselves.

Sarah said something about how people tended to subconsciously ignore paranormal things. Maybe Niedermeyer *did* recognize them, *did* suspect he'd found something more than dolls… but his brain refused to accept it and continued on in denial.

Sierra's mental debate came to an abrupt end when a massive hand plunged into the pocket, squishing her into Dad forcefully enough to bring a tear to her eye… though no bones broke. Squeezed too hard to breathe, face mashed against Dad's stomach, she did her best not to surrender to panic. Her heartbeat pounded in her head. Seconds felt like minutes.

Finally, the hand opened.

Free fall.

Sierra landed face-down on top of a baseball, draped over it like a discarded banana peel. The crash knocked all the air out of her chest. Stunned, she could only stare at dancing lights flickering in front of her face. When they stopped, she peered down the curved slope of scuffed, dirty white leather between her splayed arms at where Dad went headfirst into a mass of GI Joe figures and a Boba Fett, about a story and a half down from the baseball.

Next to Dad, the action figures appeared too small to be real adults, but shockingly large for toys... about as big as Sam. A baseball the size of a tool shed didn't make for the softest cushion, but surprisingly stung much less than doing a belly-flop into a pool. This pain had a duller, more persistent quality. Niedermeyer had likely dropped her from as high up as the roof of a two-story house. She considered herself lucky not to end up seriously injured. Maybe physics worked differently at this size. A bug didn't die if she flicked it off a table to the floor, after all.

Dad groaned, favoring his side. "I am tempted to ask Blix to enact a mild degree of revenge."

Sierra merely stared at him. Being spread eagle over the top of a massive baseball, unable to breathe, move, or speak embarrassed and scared her at the sense of helplessness. While Dad pushed at the figures surrounding him to test the toy pile's stability, Sierra focused on convincing her body to start breathing again. Gradually, the shock of impact wore off and she took in her surroundings more and more. She and Dad had been unceremoniously dumped onto a pile of confiscated stuff, surrounded by walls of bare plywood. Baseballs, a football, several Frisbees, action figures, plastic spaceships, and a few other dolls sprawled out around her. She couldn't come up with any explanation for how Barbies might have ended up in Niedermeyer's place.

Girls wouldn't randomly go into a stranger's yard to play. Most likely, annoying little brothers stole the dolls and threw them there to prank the old man. It really didn't make much sense for the GI Joes, toy spaceships and such to be here either. Little boys might be more prone to go where they didn't belong, but they probably wouldn't bring toys.

Frisbees, baseballs, and the football made sense. Those could go stray and end up in the wrong yard by accident.

Some of the stuff looked pretty old, like they'd been here since Dad was small enough to play with them.

Whoa... did Niedermeyer have kids?

"Dammit." Dad sat up.

Sierra wheezed. "Ow." She puffed a blast of air out of the side of her mouth, chasing a strand of hair away from her eyes.

"Are you hurt, hon?" Dad braced a hand on the side of the giant box, one foot on Boba Fett's helmet, the other lost somewhere in Chewbacca's nether regions. With a grunt, he managed to stand upright on the shifting pile of plastic toys.

"Not really. Couldn't breathe before, but I think I'm okay now." She un-draped herself from the baseball and maneuvered around to sit on it, gazing up at the rim of the wooden box. "We're in some kind of toy chest."

Dad set his hands on his hips. "Yep."

"Is that why you said dammit?"

"Not exactly. All these action figures are plastic. Can't swipe their fatigues." Dad re-tightened the knot in his rag skirt.

"Some Barbies down there. Take a dress." Sierra pointed, grinning.

Dad made his way across the action figures, ducked under an old X-wing toy, and squeezed between two tennis balls to where a tangle of Barbies sat wedged in the bottom corner. After examining the dolls for a few minutes, he turned to climb back up, shaking his head. "I would, but... unlike her, I *have* a waist."

"You do?" She fake gasped.

He stuck his tongue out at her.

Sierra gazed up the toy mountain at the top of the wooden enclosure. Beyond it, a dim, plain white wall suggested the box occupied a little-used room within the house. Better than the basement or attic, but still a bad situation. Not as bad as the garbage can, though. At least she didn't have to worry about being crushed to death inside a compactor truck.

Her mind raced among various horrible situations. Sitting there forgotten until they both starved topped the list of bad. Trying to escape the box, falling, and breaking her neck came in close second. The curse wearing off and her growing back to full size—destroying the doll dress in the process—then being caught inside Mr. Niedermeyer's house with no clothes came next. Wait, no. *That* ranked number one. She'd rather starve in a heap of toys. Even if she could get outside without him seeing her, she'd still have to run two-thirds of the way around their cul-de-sac naked. *Someone* would see her. Trying to steal a towel from Mr. Niedermeyer before leaving the house could be an option, but it also increased the odds of him finding her.

Is this how Sarah felt when she woke up in the morgue? She had to run across the whole town bare-butt.

All of a sudden, a glaringly pink dress didn't feel quite so embarrassing after all.

Every possible outcome of their being stuck in the toy chest stank.

"Ugh." She exhaled hard. "This sucks."

15

A TRUE EIGHTIES MOVIE

Sam walked over to the nasty little toilet, cringing inside.

The more he looked at it, the less he wanted to spend another minute here.

"What are you doing?" asked Jordan.

"Standing here stunned in horrified disgust," said Sam.

"I'm not watching." Jordan hesitated. "Please tell me you're not going to bomb us out when we're locked in here?"

Darryl and Ronan laughed.

"No. We're not going to be here long enough to need the toilet." Sam poked at the corroded green handle. The ancient bowl didn't seem *capable* of flushing.

"I already need it," whispered Ronan.

His friends joked about how much it would suck if one of them had to take a dump. Not only did the cell lack toilet paper, they wouldn't be able to escape the smell. Sam suspected the stink would be epic since the toilet also didn't seem to have working water.

These guys probably don't lock people up too often. No one's been in here for a long time.

Darryl seemed to be taking the situation in relative stride, mostly because he questioned the reality of it. Any rational person would have doubts regarding instantaneous transport halfway around the world. Ronan, though arguably the least brave of his friends, held it together reasonably well thanks to his awareness of Blix and 'weird stuff.' Jordan, on the other hand, teetered on the verge of crying.

Sam had to play it careful. Normal human bad guys with guns concerned him much more than the annoying demons responsible for the attack at Darryl's house. Except for what he could ask his infernal friends to do, he had no direct ability to affect ordinary people. If a demon tried to hurt him, he could kill it with a Nerf gun or a plastic fork. No way could he fight a grown man. Sure, if he got a hold of a gun, he could... but the idea of really shooting someone freaked him out. He might be able to do it if absolutely necessary to save one of his friends' lives, but best to avoid it entirely.

No, they wouldn't fight their way out. Sneaky all the way.

For the same reason, he didn't want to invoke Mel or Olmaz. Also, the nature of their friendship remained something of a mystery to him. They might be happily willing to help him as often as needed for anything. Or, he might have a limited number of times they'd listen to him. He had yet to find a copy of *Demonology for Dummies* to explain how it all worked. Considering the imps and demons showed up and latched onto him without the use of any sort of rituals, candles, or even effort on his part, whatever magic he'd inherited likely didn't follow any 'traditional' paths.

Even if the demons' favors *were* unlimited, he didn't want to abuse their help.

Blix can get the door open. We go out of the cell to the big room where they searched us. If those guys are still there, that's gonna be a problem. Blix will have to mess with them. Get past those guys, go upstairs. Probably out the first window. Find a Jeep or something and get back to the cave.

Sam spun to face his friends, who all had their backs turned, expecting him to use the toilet. Ronan squirmed like he really had to go.

"Ro. All yours if you dare." Sam walked over to the guys. "That thing's nasty. I think I got tetanus just from looking at it."

Ronan crept up to the toilet. "You didn't flush."

"I didn't use it. Besides, I don't think it *can* flush." Sam whistled. "If you're gonna go, just go. And hurry up. We're about to leave."

It took about three seconds for Ronan's biological need to overpower the awkwardness of using a toilet in front of an audience. He rushed over and opened his fly.

Blix folded his arms, nodding once.

Sam crouched in front of the imp, as close to eye level as he could get. "Can you go check the room? See if those guys are still there? If they are, please get rid of them."

Blix blinked, seeming shocked.

"No, dork. Not *get rid of* them. I mean, make them leave the room or distract them so they don't notice us leaving." Sam biffed himself in the forehead. "You've been watching too many crime movies."

"I tease you." Blix snickered. "I know you not mean kill. Back soon."

"Who are you talking to?" asked Darryl.

Sam sighed. While he didn't want to break secrecy, telling the guys about Blix would probably provide more benefit than problem, especially for Jordan. Confidence they had more chance of success than mere ordinary kids could make the difference. "Guys, I have an imp."

"We all do," muttered Jordan. "But we don't talk to ours."

Darryl snickered.

"No, dork." Sam playfully punched Jordan in the shoulder. "You know, like from D&D? A minor daemon."

Darryl raised both eyebrows. "Your sister's here?"

"Ha. Ha." Sam shook his head.

He almost said 'I wish,' but stopped himself. While any of the girls *could* make things easier, Sierra would end up wanting to kick the ass of everyone who kidnapped them, and Sophia would probably sneeze in the middle of opening a gateway and end up sending them to Mars. Also, Sierra had a thing about guys with guns, so he didn't want her to experience this. Sarah wouldn't be able to do much until sunset, and they likely didn't have time.

"You're right. It won't flush," muttered Ronan before scrunching up his nose in disgust. "It's gonna start to smell soon."

Men shouted in not-English from down the hall. Though he couldn't understand a word of what they said, the startled tone of the yelling conveyed a sense like they'd seen a giant rat running around. All the lightbulbs in the ceiling fluttered in time with an electrical buzzing noise and a strained, stuttering scream like a man trying to shout past a clenched jaw.

Sam gazed up at the faltering bulb in their cell. "Shocking."

A heavy *thud* with a hollow metallic resonance boomed from the hall. He pictured a guy running headfirst into one of those tall, metal cabinets. Soon after, silence. The lights stopped wavering. Darryl, Jordan, and Ronan exchanged glances.

"What's going on? Are the aliens here?" Darryl pointed at the lights.

"No." Sam walked over to the cell door and grabbed the rusting, paint-flaked bars. "Blix is dealing with the bad guys."

"Blix?" asked Jordan.

"The imp."

"Dude, you named it?" Darryl whistled.

"No. He had a name already."

Darryl's grin melted. "Whatever's wrong with you isn't something small."

"Guys, just deal, okay?" Sam glanced back over his shoulder at his friends. "You can't tell anyone about him or it'll be a total *Stranger Things* deal. The government will be all over us."

"Dude. You're getting creepy now." Jordan leaned back. "Are we really here? I wanna go home."

Darryl tried to do an Arnold Schwarzenegger voice. "You whine like Sophia."

"Knock it off, man." Sam shot him a look. "Don't pick on my sister."

"He won't pick on Sierra." Ronan grinned. "She'd kick his butt."

"Sure she would." Darryl rolled his eyes.

Sam didn't feel the need to correct him... or point out that Sierra 2.0 could probably kick the ass of these soldiers, at least in a one-on-one.

The door at the end of the hall opened. Blix, triumphant, marched down the corridor in front of the prison cells like a twelve-inch-tall microgeneral, chin held high, wings tucked back like a cape, gazing side to side as if appraising troop formations. When he reached the cell containing the boys, he turned on his heel to face them.

Sam saluted.

Blix returned the salute, then snapped his fingers.

A *clank* came from the cell door as the lock mechanism opened itself.

Sam pulled the door to the left. "It's go time. Stay quiet."

"How did you do that?" Darryl stared in awe.

"Shh." Sam stepped into the hall. "I didn't. Blix did."

"Oh, right. Your imp." Darryl sighed.

Blix pounced on Darryl, grabbed his shirt, and pulled himself up nose-to-nose with the boy, revealing himself. All the color drained out of Darryl's face. Jordan looked ready to faint. Ronan clamped a hand over his mouth to stop from laughing.

"Holy crap!" whispered Jordan. "It's alive."

"That's what she said," muttered Sam.

"Who is she?" asked Ronan. "And why is she saying stuff?"

"Forget it." Sam shushed his friends. "It's a stupid dad joke. I don't understand it either."

The boys exchanged confused glances. Sam shrugged. Dad thought the phrase funny for some reason.

"It's got wings." Darryl gawked at the imp.

"I hope she didn't say that." Blix wagged his eyebrows.

"What did it say?" asked Jordan.

"He. And another dad joke I think." Sam grabbed the doorjamb and peeked into the big room.

The soldier with the facial scar slumped on the floor next to a water cooler under a cloud of smoke. A light switch on the wall behind the cooler smoldered, on fire. The man didn't look dead, merely unconscious. Sam grimaced. Helpful as he was, Blix remained an imp, which meant his pranks often went a bit past 'playful' and into 'painful.'

The other man lay on the floor with his face against the door of a tall metal cabinet exactly as Sam imagined. Based on the dent above him, he'd gone flying into the thing and likely knocked himself cold. Darryl crept over to him, reaching for the handgun on his belt.

"Don't." Sam waved him off. "We're sneaking out. If we pick up guns, they're really going to think we're spies and shoot us."

"Ack." Darryl recoiled from the unconscious man. "Okay."

Sam opened the other door and hurried up the stairs to

the ground floor. Sounds of activity echoed in both directions. Blix pointed left, so Sam went that way, walking in a slight crouch as if 'video game stealth pose' might actually help keep him hidden. He ducked while passing an office so the men talking inside wouldn't see him through the window in the door. His friends followed suit.

The building began to shake.

For an instant, Sam almost threw caution to the wind and ran for it, but hesitated long enough for the loud rumble and vibration to resolve into the recognizable throbbing *whud-whud-whud* of a big helicopter outside—not an earthquake or attack.

However, the noise gave them cover.

Sam waved for his friends to follow and sprinted down the corridor. No one could possibly hear them running over the sound of a giant attack helicopter landing nearby. The fourth room on the right offered the perfect opportunity of an empty conference room with big windows. Even better, the windows looked out on a junk-strewn alley between two buildings, out of sight from the tarmac. He skidded to a stop in the doorway, waited for his friends to race by, then pulled the door shut.

Mildly winded from the short, but intense run, the boys stared at him making 'holy crap' faces.

Blix waved both arms upward as if lifting something. The middle of the three windows opened by itself, intensifying the helicopter roar. Sam vaulted the windowsill, jumping straight to the concrete outside. Darryl pushed Ronan to go next, standing back as if he'd be able to actually do something if a soldier came in and found them. Ronan scrambled out the window, dropping to the ground on all fours. Jordan practically landed on top of him in his haste to get out. Darryl jumped down last.

Sam glanced left and right. Both directions appeared

about the same. Swirls of dirt and small bits of forest debris swirled in a half dozen mini-cyclones of wind thrown off by a gigantic helicopter coming in for a landing on the other side of the buildings. Thirty or so feet of alley opened at each end to military base. Random pipes, slabs of sheet metal, hoses, and drums had been dumped here, offering plenty of—albeit dangerous—hiding places. Between rust, sharp edges, potentially dangerous chemicals, and rats, it didn't look like an awesome place to be for long.

The helicopter noise shifted to a higher-pitched whine, the engines in the process of shutting down. Since it sounded louder on the left, Sam headed the other way. His friends followed in single file. Blix jumped, flapped his wings once, and glided to land on his shoulder.

A pair of large, blue plastic drums near the end of the alley provided something to hide behind, a place from which Sam could survey the area ahead. Multiple vehicles from smallish trucks to six-wheeled troop transports sat around at various distances. Perhaps 200 yards from where he hid, a tall chain-link fence separated the base from the surrounding meadow. Multiple crates stacked behind them contained tall, metal canisters similar to the ones used to contain welding gas. One tank had a scrap of red fabric tied around the neck, perhaps intended as a 'danger' flag.

"Now what?" whispered Jordan. "If they catch us out of the cell, we're gonna be in trouble."

"Easy." Sam pointed at the nearest, most ordinary looking vehicle, similar to one of the land rovers they always used in African safari movies. Big, boxy, and definitely nothing available in the USA. However, unlike most of the military vehicles in sight, it came closest to being an ordinary car. Meaning, it most likely had pedals and a steering wheel... not some weird levers or whatever. "We take that thing."

"Umm. Keys?" asked Darryl. "Since when do you know how to hotwire a car?"

Sam pointed his thumb at Blix. "I don't need to know how to hotwire a car. Or unlock the doors. Blix has us covered."

The imp grinned.

"Okay..." Darryl put a hand against his forehead. "Let's pretend you can magically get into and start the truck. Do you know how to drive it?"

"I have vast experience at driving games on the PlayStation." Sam smiled. "How hard can it be?"

"Oy." Blix face-palmed.

Ronan and Jordan exchanged worried stares.

"It's that or walking." Sam sighed. "Do any of you know how to drive a real car?"

After a long, awkward silence, Darryl sheepishly said, "I drove my dad's car once when he had too much beer. If you guys tell anyone, I'm *so* dead."

The boys all raised their hands, swearing to secrecy.

Sam pointed at Darryl. "Okay. You drive then."

"Where are we?" asked Jordan.

"Eastern Europe somewhere." Sam scratched his head. "Russia, Czechoslovakia, Bosnia, Serbia, one of those places, probably. Not sure which one."

"Dork." Jordan shook his head. "I meant like... where are we compared to the stupid cave?"

"Oh, umm..." Sam fidgeted. Being stuffed at the innermost end of a giant military cargo truck behind a stack of suspicious cases didn't give them much of a view. He'd only seen a bunch of trees, and then no trees after a while. "We might have a problem."

Blix shook his head so rapidly his ears made leathery flapping noises. "I point. You not be lost."

"Cooool," said Jordan in a drawn out, whispery voice while staring at Blix. "What did he say?"

"He can lead us to the cave. We won't get lost. One problem left." Sam turned to look over the drums at the tarmac. Somewhere between ten and twenty people, mostly men, in military uniforms walked around or loitered by vehicles and small buildings. "The truck is pretty far away. We're definitely gonna get seen if we run for it. Need a distraction."

Blix wagged his eyebrows, did 'weasel hands,' then disappeared.

"Ack!" Jordan blinked. "Where'd he go?"

"Didn't you hear Sam? The imp's gonna go make a distraction." Darryl crept up to the drums, crouching like a sprinter waiting for the starter pistol to go off. "Get ready to run."

"When?" asked Ronan.

Sam chuckled. "It should be obvious when."

He ripped the red rag off the canister of volatile gas. It seemed intact enough to suit his purpose, and not *too* grimy. Smiling to himself, Sam put it on.

"What are you doing?" asked Jordan.

"Red headbands are a matter of vital importance for times like this," said Sam, matter-of-factly. "My dad would insist."

"Get a load of *Rambo* over here. You are such a dork." Darryl rolled his eyes.

Sam shrugged. "At what point have I ever claimed not to be one?"

Something exploded to the left and behind, powerful enough to feel the *thud* in the ground and jostle the collection of welding gas tanks. Alarms went off and a PA system began blaring some manner of Eastern Bloc power metal music. Another explosion went off, then a whistle and rapid crackle like fireworks. Men shouted.

Most everyone in sight from Sam's hiding place sprinted toward the main part of the base, heading to the left of the building they hid behind and leaving the tarmac ahead wide open. Figuring it as good a time as any to go, Sam leapt over the drums and sprinted hard for the dingy grey land rover. The commotion going on in the background concealed the clapping of sneakers on concrete. Sam barreled into the side of the weird Jeep-like thing and tried the door. Surprisingly, it opened.

He jumped in, crawling across the single front bench seat to the passenger side. Ronan and Jordan got in back. Darryl scrambled in behind the wheel. Despite being the biggest and oldest of the boys (he'd be turning eleven in two days, assuming they didn't get themselves shot here) the oversized steering wheel and generally large truck made him look like a little boy.

Darryl stared at the shockingly plain dashboard. It had only two old-school gauges, one for fuel and a speedometer, plus a switch for headlights. "Where's the damn start button?"

"I dunno." Sam looked around, then pointed at a socket on the side of the steering wheel column. "Key."

"Which we don't have." Darryl banged his fist on the console. "Piece of crap."

Another explosion went off. Jordan and Ronan both ducked.

Blix reappeared in the middle of the front seat.

"Start it!" yelled Sam. "Please."

As soon as the imp licked his finger and touched the key socket, the engine came to life.

"Go!" shouted Sam.

Darryl threw the truck in drive and stomped on the gas. The vehicle lurched forward, giving off a labored whirring of gears. He steered right, aiming for the gate in the big fence, and kept accelerating. Two soldiers rushed out of a tiny guard shack, waving at them to stop.

Blix snapped his fingers and the big chain link gate activated, sliding open despite there being no one in the control shack to hit the button.

Darryl didn't slow down. He leaned forward, clinging to the wheel. "Brace for impact!"

Realizing the boys had no intention of stopping, the soldiers raised their AK-47s.

Blix snapped his fingers again. Both rifles fell apart into loose pieces.

Sam and his friends laughed. The men dove to either side, narrowly missing being run over a second before the truck smashed a red-and-white striped security bar. At a 'breakneck' fifty-two miles per hour, Darryl followed the sorta-paved road leading away from the military base purely because they already happened to be on it.

"Wait." Sam rubbed his chin. "This wouldn't be a true Eighties movie unless that whole stash of drugs, weapons, or whatever the bad guys bought blows up as we're fleeing the compound."

"This isn't a movie!" yelled Jordan.

Sam raised an eyebrow. "Blix?"

The imp winked and vanished.

Darryl glanced over at Sam. "It also wouldn't be a proper Eighties movie unless we get chased by one of those big ass attack helicopters the Russians always have, shooting rockets at us."

"Or a whole bunch of bad guys chasing us into the jungle," said Ronan.

"Ack!" Sam spun around to look behind them. No sign of a helicopter yet, but the bad guys definitely had one. "You're right... crap! Drive!"

"I *am* driving. This piece of junk won't go any faster,"

shouted Darryl while stomping at the pedal as if to prove he'd already pushed it as far down as it would go. "Where are we going, anyway? Why did you send the imp away?"

A massive fireball leapt into the air from the base, painting the grassy field around it orange. Seconds later, a tremendous *boom* shook the land rover. Black spots darkened out of the rising fireball, soon recognizable as smoldering cases tumbling back to earth.

"Whoa," chorused Jordan and Ronan at the same time. "That's awesome."

Blix reappeared and pointed to the right, off the road into the field.

"Hold on!" shouted Darryl.

"Wait, no!" yelled Sam. "Slow down a bit. Don't go off road at full speed."

"We gotta get out of here before the helicopter comes." Ronan banged his hands atop the front seat. "Fast is good."

Sam nodded. "Yeah. Fast is good. Rolling over and exploding is not."

Darryl braked a little too hard, flinging Sam against the dashboard and the other two boys to the floor in back. Blix flew from the seat, hit the windshield upside down, then flopped onto the console. The truck bounced onto the field. Darryl sped back up once he got it going in a straight line again.

"Heh, whoa." He laughed. "This thing isn't fast, but I can still do top speed on grass."

Sam picked himself up off the floor and peered over the metal dashboard out the windshield. A wide line of trees waited for them a few miles away, the edge of a huge forest. The cave had to be in there somewhere. Unfortunately, driving a big wheeled box across a meadow made for a highly obvious target. As soon as the two gate guards told the commander about the truck leaving, there'd be a chase.

Maybe we shouldn't have blown up the stuff. It's gonna make him angrier. Sam shrugged. *Nah. Pretty sure he was gonna do something bad to us, anyway.*

"Faster." Sam pointed at the trees. "We need to make it to the forest before the helicopter's on us."

"Uhh, Sam," said Jordan in a squeaky voice. "We're not gonna get there fast enough."

Sam twisted his head to look out the window on his right. A big, light brown helicopter just like the one in *Red Dawn* floated up from the base, already pointing at them. The pilot *had* to see them already. At least the wings didn't have rocket pods on them. Good chance the gun under the nose had bullets. Thanks to Dad's old movies and a bunch of video games, Sam knew exactly what he stared at: a Mi-24 Hind model D. This proved two things.

One: whatever country they went to used Russian military scraps, many years obsolete.

Two: they found themselves in deep poop.

The helicopter tilted forward, gaining speed.

Sam gazed back and forth from the woods to the attack helicopter, doing some quick mental math. He didn't like the answer, but also didn't have a choice. The bad guys in Dad's movies never seemed to be able to hit the good guys. As much as this all felt like he and his friends had been pulled into a movie, he doubted the real world played by the same rules. As soon as the helicopter got in range, they would have serious problems of the gatling gun kind.

"Just keep driving," Sam muttered. "Don't stop for anything."

"What about trees?" squeaked Ronan.

"Okay, fine." Sam exhaled hard. "Stop for trees. I don't want to crash."

"Road. There." Blix pointed. "Follow."

Darryl veered left a second before a line of dirt puffs

burst up from the ground on their right. As the soil plumes began to settle, a distant, loud grinding buzz came from the air behind them.

All four boys screamed.

"Uhh…" Ronan half dove over the seatback to grab Sam. "Did they miss or was that a warning?"

Sam didn't know what to say. It could've been either. He looked down at his hand. It wouldn't take much effort on his part to summon Mel and ask her to knock the helicopter out of the air. Well, she couldn't do much to the helicopter, but she could definitely take out the guy flying it… which would cause the helicopter to no longer be in the air. Doing so would make him a killer. He couldn't cross that line yet… until he looked up and saw Ronan's terrified green eyes, wet with tears.

If he *had* to kill some bad soldiers to save his friends' lives, so be it.

Come on, Darryl. Drive. Sam clenched his hand into a fist, staring out the rear window at the approaching helicopter, fixated on the gun bubble under the nose. No matter what happened, he'd probably regret it for the rest of his life, even if the 'rest of his life' only lasted for a few more seconds.

16

THE RELIQUARY OF FORGOTTEN TOYS

S ierra sat in the cockpit of an X-wing fighter toy, staring at the fake controls.

The hard plastic seat left much to be desired in terms of comfort; however, it beat trying to balance on a shifting mountain of dolls, action figures, and balls. Mr. Niedermeyer existed as a thunderstorm in the distance, loud enough to chase away thoughts of trying to escape for what felt like hours. The man likely didn't really do anything overly energetic or violent, merely his size making it seem as if his mere existence could shake the world.

She'd lost track of Dad. Knowing him, he probably crawled around among the toys, having nostalgic moments whenever he found something he remembered playing with as a kid. None of this stuff could possibly have belonged to him. He didn't grow up in this area. He and Mom bought the house they presently lived in a year before they had Sarah. Whenever he muttered something like 'Ooh, original Lando figure… I had one of them. Probably worth a lot now if it wasn't so beat up' she scowled to herself.

How can he be so calm? We've been shrunk, almost killed, and now we're caught and imprisoned by the enemy. Sierra gazed up at the white ceiling far, far overhead above the box. *I rode a damned kitten into battle. This is* not *normal!*

An even bigger problem came to mind than being six inches tall: she really had to pee. Also, they'd missed lunch and it had to be getting close to dinner time already. Some of the plastic 'doll food' at the bottom of the chest started to look tempting. As a general rule, neither dolls nor action figures ever needed to use the bathroom, so their toy vehicles and furniture suffered a conspicuous lack of plumbing.

"Dad," called Sierra.

"Yeah?" replied her father, his voice coming from almost directly beneath her.

"I'm done waiting for the curse to wear off. Don't think it's gonna go away on its own." She squirmed. "Really gotta pee."

Dad made a sort of grunting sigh of defeat. Without uttering a single actual word, she understood he agreed with her fully—and also needed to go to the bathroom. They had, after all, been stuck there for at least two or three hours.

Sitting down any longer would result in an accident, so she stood inside the toy cockpit, trying to take the pressure off. The odds of finding a toilet of appropriate size seemed slim, but she had to go so badly that embarrassment no longer factored into her decision making process. The instant they made it outside, she'd do what needed to be done. This, of course, required escape first.

Dad grasped the side of the X-wing cockpit and pulled himself up to stand next to it. He'd traded the rag skirt for a slightly oversized old school Army uniform that made him look like a Vietnam-era soldier, save for being barefoot and armed only with a goblin sword in a plastic back-sheath he'd probably taken from a different action figure. "I think you're right about the curse. Question is, do we shelter in the yard until your mother gets home, try to retake the house, or sneak back in to use my phone."

She squirmed. "I can't think about anything right now except how bad I gotta pee."

"Didn't see any bottles in here." He peered down to the left.

That she didn't react by gasping and blushing worried her. Not once in her life ever before had she needed to go this bad. Then again, she also hadn't been miniaturized and trapped in a box for hours before, either. The closest she'd ever been to stuck in a confined space away from a toilet for any extended period of time happened on the family road trips—except for last year. The RV had a bathroom.

She sighed out her nose. Thinking the most awesome part of the vacation had been the ability to use the bathroom whenever she needed without begging Dad to stop somewhere probably meant something. She didn't bother debating exactly what.

"We are leaving." Sierra stepped on the back of the plastic seat, then climbed over it to stand atop the X-wing in front of the R2-D2 dome. "I think we can climb out of here."

"Yeah, probably." Dad gazed around. "I always heard kids around here call this guy a dick, but I never truly appreciated the extent of his bad attitude until seeing this box."

"Could be worse." She walked down the plastic spaceship's body, jumped to the wing, and crept to the end. "He could've dropped us in the garbage."

"True." Dad carefully followed her over the X-wing.

The wing she stood on dropped about a foot as the plastic spacecraft shifted under his weight. Sierra yelped, waving her arms for balance. A patch of gummy residue where a sticker had been years ago gave her enough traction to avoid slipping and falling into the pile below. Not trusting the X-wing to be stable for much longer, she jumped from the wingtip to the underside of an upside-down green helicopter, also seemingly life sized to her. Her bare feet got along quite smoothly with the plastic hull. Too smoothly. So smoothly, in fact, they shot out from under her. She landed on her rear end and slid over the side, but managed to grab the strut connecting the landing skids to the body to stop herself from plummeting down into a legion of mangled Barbie dolls.

Sierra looked down past her legs at the pit of despair below, certain she'd be having a nightmare of this moment where all the dolls staring up at her came to life as plastic zombies. Grunting, she pulled herself up and braced a foot on a giant white button attached to the side of the helicopter.

Dad stopped at the edge of the spaceship's wing. "Oh, wow. I used to have one of those. The heck was it called?"

"I don't care," muttered Sierra.

"Dragonfly!" Dad snapped his fingers, then pointed at her. "That white button under your foot... if you push it back and forth, it makes the rotors spin."

"Don't care," repeated Sierra somewhat louder in an almost singsong tone. After a momentary waking nightmare of being forever stuck six-inches tall and Sam stuffing her into similar toys as a living action figure passed, she finished climbing back to stand atop the belly of the Dragonfly. "Guess those goblins, or whatever they are, gave up on us."

"They're probably afraid of Niedermeyer." Dad stepped from the X-wing to the helicopter.

"Hah. Yeah. I can see him chasing them around his backyard with a pitchfork." Sierra balance-beam-walked down the tail boom, then jumped to the windshield of a pink-and-blue plastic van wedged on end against the wall of the box. It wasn't to scale, being only about the size of a huge refrigerator to her. Still, it appeared to be a reasonably secure platform.

"Where's Klepto?" Dad heel-to-toed it to the end of the helicopter's tail, waving his arms around in a constant battle to avoid falling over.

"Probably went back to Sophia."

The Dragonfly shifted as the dolls and Frisbees under it settled. Dad started to topple over to the left, but Sierra lunged and grabbed his hand. He fell, swinging by her grip on his arm, and cashed against the side of the pink van. Sierra snarled at the extreme discomfort of an overly full bladder as she hauled him up onto the plastic grille. Dad stared at her, processing the last few seconds, specifically how his wisp of a daughter managed to catch, hold, and pull him up.

"Something's not quite right here," said Dad.

"What was your first clue?" Sierra pulled at the doll dress. "We're tiny? Goblins invaded our house? *I'm* wearing a dress, or we've been stuck for hours in a box of toys?"

"All of the above." Dad smiled, then test-squeezed her bicep. "You've been working out."

"Had a little help," she deadpanned. "Relax. I'm not a vampire."

"Sophia's doing?"

Sierra nodded. "Yeah. Umm. Remember the night the microwave zapped you?"

He winced. "How could I forget? I still can't get the taste of pizza rolls out of my mouth."

"It's safe. I think." Sierra looked down at herself, then shrugged. "Haven't sprouted any tentacles yet."

"Hah." He peered up at the rim of the box. "Almost there. So, you think the kitten went back to Sophia?"

"She's at camp and probably scared out of her mind. Needs a soft, warm, fuzzy thing to hold on to." Sierra leaned against him.

He put an arm around her. "You know, needing a soft, warm, fuzzy thing to hold onto isn't a bad thing."

She gave a silent sigh, surprised, thrilled, and grateful he didn't tease her for admitting to being a bit scared herself. Not that she expected it from him, of all people, merely in general. Perhaps Sarah had been right. She *did* take herself too seriously. Occasionally looking foolish or seeming frightened wouldn't be the end of the world. So what if someone laughed at her? She could physically keep up with vampires—at least new ones. Nothing another kid said to her really mattered.

"Climb?" asked Sierra.

Dad peered up. "That's about fourteen feet of blank plywood. We're going to need a ladder."

"Or a rope. I can probably make this jump." She bit her lip, contemplating the rim above her. "Then pull you up."

"Physics, hon. You might be oddly strong, but you're still only sixty pounds. If you jumped off, you'd end up hanging on the rope, not pulling me up."

She pretend scoffed. "Yeah, well, you're only eighty pounds."

Dad chuckled. "Gah. I haven't climbed a rope since high school."

"Idea." Sierra threaded her fingers together, making a step out of her hands. "I'll try to toss you up."

"This is too bizarre to think about."

"As if being this size is normal?" She blinked at him. "I'm wearing a Barbie dress and I'm about six seconds away from peeing myself. Stop thinking. Start doing."

"All right." Dad braced his hands against the wall and rested his foot on her hands. "Don't want you to hurt yourself."

"I won't."

It took him an annoyingly long few seconds before he

attempted to put his weight into her grasp and stand. She didn't complain at him too much. The idea of a grown man expecting a girl her size to support him *was* ridiculous. When his foot didn't instantly force her hands apart or shove her to the ground, he whistled in awe.

Sierra clenched her jaw. Holding Dad's entire weight up took some effort, though proved easier than she expected. She bent at the knees, then sprang up, flinging him into the air as hard as she could manage. Dad crashed over the box rim at chest level, barking like a kicked goose. Fortunately, he got enough of a grip not to fall back down, though clung to the plywood for a moment to catch his breath.

"You good?" asked Sierra.

"Not really. More mischievous."

"Ha. Ha. I'm about to climb you. Gonna fall?"

"Nope. I'm good. C'mon up."

Sierra leapt up, grabbed his leg, and pulled herself up to perch on the box edge next to him. "Uh oh."

"What?" Dad threw a leg over and sat astride the plywood wall.

"We're basically on top of a five story building. How the heck are we going to get down?"

Dad rubbed his chin. "I think one of the GI Joes down there hanging out with Han and Luke has a parachute."

"Good to know *now*." She rolled her eyes.

"Hmm." He glanced around, then pointed at the wall behind the box. "There. We can climb down the curtains."

Sierra raised an eyebrow at floor-length fancy curtains. They certainly didn't look like anything an old man living alone would choose. *Oh, wow. There must have been a Mrs. Niedermeyer... wonder if she died or left him.* Sierra stood. Despite consisting of a single slab of plywood, at her present size, the rim of the box appeared to be about a foot wide, more than doable to walk on. Still, traversing a narrow path five stories in the air without railings stirred a queasy feeling in the pit of her stomach. Trying not to look down, she walked to the corner, turned left, and proceeded to the end where the toy chest almost touched the wall.

Dad edged past her. He gave off an air of being petrified, though somehow didn't hesitate to reach for the massive curtain. Sierra felt as if she stood on the edge of the Hoover Dam, gazing down at the water far below. The fabric 'waterfall' didn't appear terribly easy to climb. Having never needed to slide down fifty feet of curtain before, she had no idea how to go about doing it.

"Here goes. Just… hold on as best you can." Dad smiled at her. "Remember. Down is easy. Let gravity do the work."

"Right. That's what I'm afraid of."

He jumped onto the curtain, clung for a few seconds, then slipped down a few feet before clinging again. Sierra spent a few seconds trying to convince herself Sophia's enchantment made her resilient enough to survive a five-story fall without too much damage. If she did screw up, it wouldn't seriously hurt her—or so she made herself believe. Also, the room had carpeting. Ordinary plush carpeting amounted to a ten-inch-tall cushion.

Sierra took a breath, steeled herself, and jumped for the curtain. Screaming, she plummeted down an engulfing fabric tunnel for *way* too long before finding a grip. The curtain folded in around her, making it impossible to see how much farther down she had to go. Still, not being able to see the floor got rid of her fear of heights. She found it quite possible to support her entire bodyweight on one arm's grip. Hand-over-hand, she lowered herself until her feet sank into the carpet.

"Dad?" whispered Sierra, pushing at the fabric surrounding her.

"Right here." He pulled the curtain apart. "We made it."

"Cool." Sierra started for the door, *way* on the other side of a room as big as a suburban neighborhood. She no longer cared if Niedermeyer saw her moving. If she suddenly burst up to normal size and Incredible Hulked her way out of the Barbie dress, it wouldn't even bother her. The only thing she cared about was getting to a toilet—or flowerbed—as fast as possible.

Dad hurried after her.

Trudging across the carpet sucked in ways she couldn't describe without ending up grounded for language, so she kept her mouth shut. Thankfully, the corridor outside had a much shallower rug. Going from deep pile carpeting to essentially walking on sponge made travel much easier. Thunderous voices came from the right, but still sounded boring. Mr. Niedermeyer appeared to be watching television, some manner of talk show where grown-ups rambled on, discussing grown-up stuff she couldn't care less about. With any luck, the exceedingly dry conversation about stock market prices already put the guy to sleep.

She ran—as much as she could without having an accident—down the hall to the kitchen. There, she stopped in the middle of the room and looked for any way out of the house. The door closed too securely for them to fit under. Even if they could reach the knob, neither she nor Dad could turn it without an intricate system of cables and pulleys they didn't have. Upon noticing a breeze, she faced into it and stared up at a window above the sink.

"Ugh. Climbing up there is going to suck, but I don't see any other way out." Sierra pointed.

"Dishtowel." Dad ran across the kitchen to where a towel hung from the knob of the cabinet below the sink.

Sierra went up first, climbing the damp, stinky towel to the giant porcelain knob. "Hang on, Dad. Wait."

"What are you thinking?"

"I dunno yet. Just wait there a sec. You aren't going to be able to do this..." She eyed the decorative facing of the cabinet, zeroed in on the upper edge of a fake drawer front, and jumped.

Somewhat like a flea, Sierra leapt several times her height straight up. She caught the top of the faux drawer panel and pulled herself up to stand on it. From here, another—much shorter—jump got her to the edge of the countertop. Alas, the edge stuck out a half-inch from the cabinet face, which to her amounted about a foot. Sierra dangled from her fingertips above a ten-story fall to linoleum. Enchantment or not, she'd probably go splat. Fortunately, she didn't look down or waste any time thinking about danger. She hauled herself up onto the countertop, rolling onto her back to catch her breath.

Her bladder *seriously* objected.

It occurred to her she lay inches from a sink. As tempting as an open drain was, she couldn't get past the utter wrongness of it being a sink. Even while this small, the thought disgusted her. Holding it hurt so much, she damn near cried.

"Hon?" called Dad. "You okay?"

"Not really." She forced herself to stand up, gasping at the discomfort. "But I'm not hurt."

"Got a plan yet?"

"Working on it!" yelled Sierra.

She scurried across the counter to the coffee maker, standing up on her toes to reach an electrical plug the size of a suitcase. With one foot braced against the wall, she pulled the cord from the outlet, then lugged it to the counter edge, tossing it over. The wire dangled at about the level where the towel met the cabinet knob.

"Genius." Dad grinned up at her, then climbed the dishtowel.

Once he stepped from the cabinet knob to the cord, Sierra tried to reel him in. Unfortunately, her feet kept sliding on the counter. She dragged herself forward rather than pulled him up. With nothing at the counter edge to brace against, she forced herself to simply watch as her father inchwormed up the power cable. Thankfully, at the size of a Ken doll, he didn't weigh enough to drag the entire coffee maker off the counter to the floor.

As soon as she could reach him, she got down flat on her chest, grabbed his arm, and helped him up. Mr. Niedermeyer would definitely notice the wire moved. She didn't really care if he found it after they left. She got back up, darted around the sink, and climbed a liquid soap dispenser to the windowsill. Dad followed, nearly out of breath by the time they stood in the window by the screen, enjoying an early evening breeze.

"Cut it?" asked Sierra.

Dad pulled the goblin sword off his back and sliced a hole in the screen big enough for them to squeeze through to the brick ledge outside.

Sierra stepped up to the edge of the warm bricks, curling her toes over it. The fall from the toy chest seemed laughable compared to the distance between exterior windowsill and ground. Their only salvation appeared to be another water-filled flowerpot. People around here—her parents included—had a weird habit of collecting flowerpots but never using them.

If I jump in that, I'm not going to need a toilet anymore. She cringed. *Eww. Dad's gonna jump in it too.*

"We're out." Dad eyed the pool waiting for them at the bottom. "Looks doable. Still quite a drop. Make sure you go in feet-first or you could break a bone."

The totality of her present situation crashed down on Sierra in one overwhelming moment of 'oh screw it.' She jumped. A second later, she plunged into lukewarm water, which rapidly turned opaque brown thanks to her splashdown disturbing the soil at the bottom. She swam to the top, pulled herself out, and flopped to the grass.

Dad fell into the water with a splash big enough to knock water over the edge on top of her.

"Okay. Ouch. This is not waiting anymore," grumbled Sierra. "Dad, don't look."

"Copy," replied Dad from inside the flowerpot.

Sierra hid behind the tree-sized stem of a bush. Nature had gone past calling to demanding and making threats.

A few minutes later, she felt awesome—except for still being six inches tall, and seriously hungry. Dad probably did the same thing on the other side of the flowerpot. She didn't want to know about it.

Careful not to look anywhere he might be, Sierra walked out from the bushes to the lawn. Dad soon appeared beside her. They'd both ended up muddy and soaked, but they'd successfully escaped Mr. Niedermeyer's toy graveyard.

"Here." Dad offered her the sword. "You're a little better with this than I am. In case there are more goblins."

She took it. "Thanks."

They trekked across a wilderness of grass taller than Dad. Apparently, Mr. Niedermeyer didn't take terribly good care of his backyard lawn. Like a jungle explorer, she occasionally hacked at the titanic grass blades to make passage easier. Finally, they reached the hedgerow at the edge of the yard where the going got easier. After traversing the gnarled mini-forest, they set out across the utterly massive expanse of grass between the houses on their cul-de-sac and the woods. At normal size, the trip would've been about as long as four-and-a-half backyards.

Presently, it felt like a five-mile hike.

Dad seemed ready to pass out by the time they reached

the edge of their yard. Sierra prepared herself to deal with goblins. For everything she just went through, she'd definitely enjoy kicking a few more green butts.

Her jaw dropped open as soon as she emerged from the thick shrubbery wall surrounding her backyard. At least fifteen stray cats lounged here and there on the deck, in the yard, by Sophia's old play house, and on the little sidewalk going around toward the front of the house. Not a single goblin appeared to be anywhere in sight.

"Umm... Dad?" Sierra pointed. "Look."

"What the heck?" He ran a hand up through his hair, then scratched at the back of his head while making a face of disbelief. "Cats?"

"Yeah. Are they gonna eat us?" She bit her lip. Tigers could be quite scary when not behind a wall at a zoo, but these *housecats* had to be double or even triple the size of a tiger to her at the moment. She felt as small as a starling compared to them.

Dad moved his hand around to rub his chin. "I have questions."

"No kidding." Sierra gave him side eye. "What, specifically about this situation *now* bothers you?"

"Where is Max?"

Sierra blinked. Her brother's hellhound friend hadn't done anything about the goblins, nor did he appear to have a problem with a bunch of cats. Maybe he only *looked* like a dog and didn't possess the same propensity to chase smaller creatures. "Uhh... probably here somewhere. Maybe we're too small for him to notice, or he didn't think the goblins are a serious enough problem to get involved. Sam *did* ask him to try and stay hidden."

"Oh, Max," called Dad. "If you can hear us... please don't let these cats have us for dinner."

A heavy rumble came from the back corner of the yard.

Every cat in sight jumped to look in that direction, a few arching their backs.

"Think that means 'no problem.'" Sierra shrugged and ran for the deck.

The cats took notice of her and Dad, though made no move to come after them. They almost gave off the sense of having expected them to return. Sierra made the laborious climb up the deck stairs, then crossed to the still-open patio door, careful not to let her feet slip down in the gaps between floorboards. The sight of Mom standing in the kitchen looking around in confusion almost made Sierra burst into tears. A massive weight fell from her shoulders. Dignity or not, having Mom there to help her was *awesome*.

"Mom!" shouted Sierra.

Her mother glanced around.

"Moooooom!" yelled Sierra louder.

"Oh, drat," boomed Mom. "That's the last thing we need. Someone left the door open and we have mice."

"Allie?" yelled Dad. "Down here."

Mom looked everywhere but down at floor level.

Growling, Sierra ran across the kitchen and started jumping up and down, waving her arms (and sword) back and forth.

Mom finally spotted her, jumped back, and screamed, half falling into a seated position on the table and pulling her legs up.

"I'm not a mouse!" shouted Sierra.

"What...?" Mom stared at her for a few seconds before her brain switched gears. 'Screaming at mice face' melted into a momentary expression of confusion before morphing into a glare of 'who did what to my baby?'

Dad walked up to stand next to her.

Mom slid off the table, crouched, and scooped them up in her hands. "What happened?"

"Sorry, honey." Dad faked a sad sigh. "I've been downsized."

Mom groaned.

"Mrow," said a calico cat, prancing in from the hall.

Another cat, somewhere inside the kitchen cabinets, trilled like a pigeon.

"Jonathan... you're in the palm of my hand and making bad puns?"

"Is there such a thing as a *good* pun?" asked Sierra.

"The child has a point." Dad chuckled. "And hon, I've always been in the palm of your hand. It's... just a bit more literal at the moment."

"Eww. Get a room." Sierra cringed.

"Are you wearing a dress?" Mom stared.

"Ugh. Why do you guys make such a big deal about it?"

Mom held them up closer to her face. "I'm not trying to make a big deal about it, sweetie. It's just unusual enough to make me ask why. Are you starting to date?"

"No." Sierra blushed. "It's from one of Sophia's dolls. I shrank, my clothes didn't. Extreme measures needed to be taken."

"Why did you shrink?"

"Goblins," said Sierra and Dad simultaneously.

The calico purred while winding between Mom's legs, rubbing against her.

"Why is our house full of cats?" asked Mom.

"Got me there." Dad peered over the side of the giant hand they sat on.

Sierra blinked as realization hit. "Klepto! The goblins were scared of her, and she's just a kitten... so she brought reinforcements. If one kitten freaked those little green bastards out, an army of full grown alley-cats probably made them shit where they stood."

"Dear, language," whispered Mom.

"I'm six inches tall." Sierra folded her arms. "Consider it a miracle that's the worst thing I said."

"Honestly, Jonathan..." Mom sank to sit in one of the kitchen chairs, then gently put Sierra and Dad down on the table. "I don't know how much more of this weird I can handle. Our house is full of cats."

Dad wagged his eyebrows. "The mews are upon us."

Mom stared at him. "Ugh. I'm half tempted to put you in Sam's old hamster habitat for that one."

He laughed. "Hon, would you please grab my phone from my desk and call Darren Anderson?"

Sierra leaned back against the pepper shaker, one hand pressed to her stomach. The scary part appeared to be over with. Only the embarrassing and annoying parts remained. If she ended up being stuck at this size for a week until Sophia came home, she'd... probably end up doing nothing but complaining a lot. Six more days without being able to play video games would truly suck, but at least it wouldn't kill her.

Mom stood. "Okay. Be right back. Anything else?"

"What's for dinner?" asked Sierra. "We kinda missed lunch."

GHOST STORIES

Sophia shivered under the blankets, too terrified to sleep.

The creepy ghost figure staring at her from the trees hadn't come much closer, but she couldn't help but notice him following the girls the quarter mile or so from the camp center down the trail to the little cabins as a distinct spectral glow off in the trees. At night, they had only flashlights and two gas lanterns—carried by the scout leaders—to see by. Bad enough darkness made this part of the Girl Scout camp look like the setting for one of those scary movies she couldn't bear to watch, a real spirit wanted to kill them.

She would have spent most of the night lying there awake, staring at the underside of the top bunk, but couldn't since she'd pulled the covers completely up over her head. Due to being in an unfamiliar place, she'd have been up most of the night anyway, but having the heck scared out of her by a ghost story—then seeing an actual ghost who looked quite crazy and sinister—made sleep truly impossible.

Learning magic and dealing with supernatural stuff *had*

given her a little confidence. Enough to be stupid and think she could handle going away to summer camp for a week. Not enough to actually do it. Fortunately, Klepto had returned. The kitten curled up in a little donut of fur atop her chest.

Goblins got loose in the house and pranked Sierra and Dad. Klepto dealt with the situation, having called in some reinforcements. Unfortunately, the kitten lost track of Sierra and Dad after they'd gone into Niedermeyer's yard. Being given a perfect excuse to go home while being too terrified to leave this bed frustrated her to the point of tears. It didn't make sense to her what interest the goblins had in the crystal. Mr. Anderson loaned it to her to practice with, claiming it came from Tibet or somewhere exotic and held a reserve of spiritual energy. He'd purposefully not told her much about it because her 'lesson' involved divining its nature and purpose. She hadn't yet managed to do it.

Worse, she couldn't tell the scout leaders or camp counselors she had to rush home to undo some magical calamity. They'd either think she told a childish lie as a weak excuse or that she'd gone nuts. Going home to check on her family made sense. She wouldn't get in trouble from her parents for it, but she'd have to return to the camp before anyone there noticed her missing.

Of course, going home required her to do two things she couldn't. One: leave the safety of bed. Two: walk a quarter mile in the woods at night to find a building with a suitable closet. Technically, any door could work. She *could* try summoning a portal using the bunkhouse—essentially a huge closet—but didn't know what would happen to any people inside it. The little cabins were one big open room, without even a toilet closet. If she used it as a host for a gate, it might launch the other seven girls somewhere unexpected... or dissolve them entirely.

She dreaded having to pee in the middle of the night. No way could she walk to the outhouse in the dark by herself. Even without an angry ghost in the area, she'd never dare. Any second now, the spirit would get her. In fact, he might already be standing next to the bed, glaring at the lump she made in the blanket.

Sophia shivered harder, cringing in anticipation of being grabbed by icy claws at any second.

Even if she found the courage to get out of bed, then the courage to make her way back to the main camp, she doubted she could concentrate well enough on portal magic to successfully open a doorway home.

Minutes crawled by as she lay there curled up in a ball, crying quietly to herself. Every aspect of going to camp had been a huge mistake. She most likely wouldn't survive the night. The angry ghost knew she saw him. He'd probably thrust his hand into her chest and freeze her heart as soon as she closed her eyes. Her parents would never know what really happened to her. At the funeral, everyone would whisper, asking why no one stopped her from going to camp. She'd been so homesick, her heart stopped.

"What's wrong with you?" asked McKenzie. "Why aren't you rowing?"

Sophia jumped, startled to find herself sitting in a canoe, holding a paddle. It appeared to be late morning on a mildly cloudy day. They floated along a small river, the last canoe in a procession of twenty or so. Likely, they fell behind due to Sophia not helping paddle. A low-hanging fog clung to the water's surface, seeping out of the trees on either bank. Nicole sat in the front-most seat, grunting from the effort she put into trying to catch up to the other canoes.

McKenzie Whitaker, eleven-year-old daughter of Mrs. Whitaker, sat behind Sophia at the rear of the canoe. She continued paddling while lecturing Sophia on the importance of teamwork and how all three of them had to put in a fair share of the work to get anywhere. The girl often acted like her mother being one of the scout leaders gave her some special rank or something over the other kids. Somehow, she never came off as mean or overly bossy, though she frequently pulled a 'Hermione' and talked down to everyone like they didn't know as much as her.

Sophia thought it strange she'd gone canoeing in her nightgown.

She thought it even more strange McKenzie and Nicole didn't appear to notice or care. The girls in her bunk house last night certainly laughed at the pink nightdress. They'd all brought tank tops and pajama pants to sleep in. Like flip-flops, her nightie didn't really belong at camp. She'd have to ask Klepto to pop home again and borrow some of Sierra's PJs.

"Come on, Soph. You can't just sit there," said McKenzie. "We're never gonna catch up. Do you want to get lost and never see anyone again?"

"The river's a straight line," deadpanned Nicole without looking back. "We literally *can't* get lost. We are, however, late."

Disregarding the oddity of how she got from bed to canoe, or how no one seemed to care about the nightgown, Sophia leaned to one side and attempted to paddle. The instant her oar broke the foggy surface of the water, a rotting, grey hand thrust upward and grabbed her around the wrist in a rubbery, clammy grip.

More zombie hands burst from the river, grasping the canoe on all sides, rapidly pulling it underwater.

Sophia screamed—and lurched upright in bed, gasping for air in a pitch-black bunkhouse. The little cabin had no electric lights and only four small windows, barely visible as slightly glowing dark blue squares.

"Knock it off," muttered a girl too groggy and whispery to recognize.

"That had to be Sophia," said another drowsy voice.

"Go back to sleep," groaned a third.

The bed above her creaked. She assumed Nicole peered over the side to look at her.

"What happened?" whispered Nicole. "Bug, frog, or nightmare?"

Sophia buried her face in both hands, unable to stop crying.

"Sounds like nightmare…" Nicole grunted as she climbed down. A hollow metallic *bonk* accompanied her drawing in a sharp breath. "Grr. Ow. Knee."

A few other girls chuckled.

"Aww, sweetie having a nightmare?" whispered someone.

"Knock it off, Lynn," snapped Nicole.

"Hah. If she's so scared of camping, she should've stayed home." Lynn yawned. "We're trying to sleep here."

Nicole sat on the edge of the lower bunk. "Sorry your home sucks so much you can't wait to get away from it. Not everyone has that problem."

A few girls chorused, "oooh!"

"Shh!" hissed Priya from the next bed over. "We'll get in trouble if they catch us awake."

Nicole put an arm around Sophia's back. "Hey. Just a ghost story. Nothing to be scared of."

Sniffling, Sophia leaned against her friend, still shaking. Nicole, being the same age and size, didn't offer the same feeling of protection she got from her parents or Sarah, but helped far more than she expected. After a few minutes of sitting in silence, she managed to stop crying. To distract herself from the horrible dream, she thought about confronting the jar entity. The mystics taught her how to banish bad spirits. Why the heck did she freak out over seeing a creepy ghost staring at her from the forest?

"I'm being stupid," whispered Sophia.

"Maybe a little." Nicole nudged her. "Just a ghost story."

"Not really. I saw him."

A few random gasps came from around the room.

"No way," muttered Lynn.

Three flashlights turned on; aimed at the ceiling, they effectively lit the room enough to see the other seven girls all awake and staring at her. Apparently, she must have looked seriously freaked out since they all appeared more concerned than ready to tease her.

"Saw him?" asked McKenzie, shivering a little. "Are you serious?"

"Yeah," whispered Sophia. "When Miss Thorpe was telling us about Crazy Coleman, this glowing man appeared in the forest watching us. He looked exactly the way she described him, a homeless guy who lives in the woods. Crazy hair, beard, wearing a poncho or raincoat… he was watching us. Seemed angry, like this camp being here really made him mad."

"Bull," muttered Hadley Ross, though her voice shook a bit. "You're just saying that to mess with us."

Nicole bit her lip. "I think it's true. Soph's like a medium or something. She can see ghosts. There used to be one in her house."

"Is he gonna hurt us?" asked McKenzie in a whispery, high-pitched voice.

"You guys are so stupid." Andrea laughed. "I can't believe you're letting Sophia scare you. Just stupid stories. There's no such thing as Crazy Coleman."

The cabin door flew open and slammed against the wall.

All eight girls screamed at the same time, Sophia's voice the highest-pitched and longest lasting before she ran out of air. Two of three active flashlights fell to the floor. Nicole grabbed Sophia and clung, treating her like a giant teddy bear. Shante Whitaker clutched the only remaining active flashlight not on the floor, her eyes huge in an 'oh hell no with the ghosts' expression.

Sophia stared at the empty doorway. What little moonlight made it through the branches overhead illuminated the faintest hint of trees. It had become too dark out to see the cabin across the trail, or even the trail. The girls sat in shocked silence, as if the first one to move or make a sound would be the one the monster chose to eat.

A *long* minute later, Hadley leaned over the side of her bed to pick up the flashlight she dropped, and pointed it out the door. "Just the wind. There's nothing there."

Three seconds later, eerie teal-green mist manifested in a glowing cloud a few paces away from the cabin, right above the spot Hadley's flashlight illuminated. The spectral mass expanded vertically, ethereal spirals stretching out into arms and legs as it took on the shape of a ghostly, frazzled man.

Crazy Coleman stared at Sophia, eyes manic, and raised his right arm to point at her.

"Just the wind," repeated Hadley, evidently unable to see the ghost.

"No," whispered Sophia. "He's here."

HAUNTED

So much for my big advantage of being able to go out during the day.

It gave me a head start, but nothing more. Gloomy weather and rain allow me to go online before official sunset. Other vampires are still stuck snoozing no matter how thick the clouds are. Unfortunately, by the time I catch up to Detective Warner, it's dark out. Legit dark, I mean. 'Other vampires are now awake' dark.

Sure, life isn't a video game. As vexing as my luck is sometimes, 'bad guys' aren't simply going to spawn in nearby because I ran out of time. St. Ives' people won't magically know where we are. At least... I don't think they will. No, they'll do the same thing I did: track Warner into the surrounding area like a hunting dog following a wounded deer. It ended up being shockingly easy for me. Between heightened vampire eyesight allowing me to notice disturbed branches, footprints, blood smears, and my nose picking up the man's scent trace, it's almost like I'm playing *Skyrim* or something and following a glowing light trail to a mission objective.

Yeah, I know. Vampires are predators. Hunting people is as easy for us as breathing is for mortals. My worry is the people St. Ives are sending after us are better at it than me. I am not what one would call a 'vicious creature of the night.' It's not like modern day vampires routinely chase terrified peasants into the forest—as much as Ladonna Winter might adore such a pastime—but more experienced vampires, especially those lacking my regard for mortal life—could find Warner much faster than me.

Great. Why did I randomly think about Ladonna? Bad enough Mark the Thrall said this sword belonged to Vlad Tepes. I've never been one of those goth girls who's obsessed with morbid crap, so it's not like I have an encyclopedic knowledge of Dracula. What little I've heard about him is pretty scary stuff. I bet he was an Oblivare—if he existed at all. Just because vampires are real doesn't mean every story about vampires is based on truth. Impaling thousands of people? That's like the exact opposite of subtle. Oh, wait. Back in the 1400s or whenever he supposedly lived, vampires didn't care about subtle.

Gee. I really hope he's not still out there somewhere and *he's* the one who sent people to get the sword back from Wolent. Bad enough I've gotta deal with a crazy, possessed detective who almost murdered his wife. The last thing I need is a vampiric Viggo the Carpathian rampaging around Seattle. Something tells me it's going to take more than upbeat music and the Statue of Liberty to make him go away.

Right, back to my present problem: Detective Jake Warner.

This area on the western outskirts of Olympia is mostly woods. Specifically, little pockets of suburban houses surrounded by a crapton of trees. Finding an idling car with an open driver door and a glowing Domino's Pizza thing on the roof—plus no sign of a pizza guy—right where Warner's trail leads is not a great sign. Screaming and crashing in the woods past the houses is an even worse sign.

I fly toward the commotion and spot Warner up ahead in only a few seconds. He's chasing a dark-haired girl about my age, who's sprinting like mad into the woods. My hunt turns into an episode of Tom & Jerry written by Alfred Hitchcock. I chase him while he chases the pizza delivery girl. She's clearly aware her life's in danger. There are only two things in this world capable of making people flee so fast: psychopathic killers with giant knives coming for them, and tween-age kids in sports (or Girl Scout) uniforms standing outside a supermarket asking for donations.

Jake Warner's a bit old for Little League or Girl Scouts, so I feel safe in assuming he's shown her the sword.

It's almost comical to me since he keeps tripping on roots and crashing into trees while the girl's zooming like a legit forest nymph. No, she's fully dressed... I mean nymph in the sense she's become one with the woods, flowing among the branches with ease in complete defiance of all horror movies ever made. Maybe the reason she hasn't helplessly tripped and been killed already is she's not blonde. The brunette always lives. Points for team brown, I guess. Though, her hair is closer to black than mine.

Relieved to see the detective hasn't managed to hurt anyone else, I toss my anxiety goblin into the trees and dive after Warner. He can't quite seem to catch this girl and doesn't appear to be the least bit likely to give up any time soon—without help.

I plow into him from behind, giving a hard shove, then hover there watching him go down in a chin slide, then tumble butt over head a few times before sliding to a stop in the underbrush. Ooh. Talk about the opposite of graceful. I drop out of my hover and walk up to him. Jake leaps to his feet and raises the blade as if about to charge—then recognizes me. As he starts to turn away in relative slow motion, I rush forward, grabbing him by the throat and right wrist. It would be fairly easy to crush the bones in his arm and force him to drop the blade, but he's not a vampire—and not at fault for what he's doing.

Jake gurgles and flails as I throw him around. He's not too big nor is he stronger than me, but containing him is still a bit of a challenge due to my not wanting to hurt him. Whatever the sword did to him, it hasn't given him any supernatural abilities beyond bloodlust. We lock stares in the midst of our improvised slam dance routine. Trying to derp him doesn't work, so I focus on disarming him first.

Ramming Jake into a tree a few times finally dislodges the blade from his grip—and maybe dislocates his shoulder. Sorry, man. I'm trying here. The blade flies into the underbrush, landing with a *thump* in the dirt. I yank him off his feet like a kid power-bombing their little brother after watching too much wrestling on TV. Drilling him into the ground flat on his back knocks the wind out of him long enough for me to jump on top of him and pin his arms on either side of his head.

"Holy shit," whispers a young woman. "What the fuck is going on?"

I peer up through a curtain of my hair at the pizza girl. She's way out of breath, clinging to a tree about ten paces away, staring at me. Pretty sure if she let go of the tree, she'd fall over. As soon as we make eye contact, I dive into her brain. She ran back thinking some other girl needed help, hoping the two of us might be able to fight off one psycho. When she saw little me throwing this dude back and forth like a giant rag doll, her mind kinda shut down.

Oops.

To Derpville with you for now. I'll fix later.

I redirect my attention to Jake. He's just about recovered

from the body slam. Before he can throw me off, I hammer him in the cerebellum as hard as I can, using my emotional reaction to the bloody bathroom scene back at his house for extra oomph.

I'm in! But it kinda feels like I smashed a window with my face, only without the shredding of razor sharp glass bits. My nose hurts. The resistance shell around his brain shatters. Aha! Good guess on my part about the sword. When he's not touching it, it's *much* easier to fix his brain. Well, the difference is not so much 'easier' as it is 'possible.' It takes me a few minutes to erase the urge to kill from his mind and let his actual personality come back to the surface.

There's a surprise waiting for me below the shadowy malice in Jake Warner's mind: a vampire's compulsion. I catch a flash of a young twentysomething guy with short, spiky snow-white hair come out of nowhere. His eyes glow red for an instant, and the next thing Jake knows, he's in the evidence room picking up the sword. Whoever this vampire is, he compelled Jake to obtain the sword from the secure storage room.

He most likely expected to pick it up from Jake's house after dark, or if he understood what the sword could do to people, follow the trail of destruction. Strange. Why didn't he simply visit the police station himself at night and mind control his way in? It's not like the buildings become inaccessible after dark. Maybe using a detective offered a layer of separation from discovery? Or perhaps they wanted a cop to go on a murder spree. Only reasons I can think of.

"What... what's going on?" mutters Jake, struggling to reach up and grab his face.

"It's hard to explain." I sigh, grab two fistfuls of his shirt, and pull him up to a seated position. "Feel more like yourself now?"

He makes a series of increasingly confused faces, then horrified ones. Crap. He remembers everything he did.

Rustling in the weeds to my left makes me look. Two guys in punk style clothing rummage around the forest floor not far from where I'm sitting on top of Jake. One has short white hair in a brush cut. He also stands up out of the foliage holding the cursed sword.

Son of a bitch.

"One sec." I let go of Jake's shirt and stand.

White Hair Guy taps the sword to his head as if saluting me, then takes a small gun from the pocket of his denim vest and tosses it to Pizza Girl. "Shoot yourself in the head."

Motherf—

Both vampires leap into the air, White Hair Guy giving me this smug 'thanks for doing my work for me' smile. Grr. Dammit! No time to think. I fly-leap at Pizza Girl instead of chasing the assholes, grabbing her wrist before she can put the little handgun to the side of her head. I'm about to drill into her mind to erase the compulsion when it occurs to me she's holding a squirt gun.

Plastic toy.

Grumbling, I release her and let out an exasperated sigh-growl at the ponderous grey clouds hanging over us.

Spritz.

Pizza Girl stares at me, utterly baffled why she just squirted herself, or where a water pistol came from. Two guys' laughter echoes from above, the night sky the only thing left in the world that appears dark to me. I honestly don't know whether to laugh or cry. They set Jake loose knowing he could go psycho killer, but tossed a *fake* gun to this girl to slow me down from chasing them.

Vampires: the original pre-internet trolls.

Still, I can't leave Jake in this condition or Pizza Girl here after witnessing dudes fly into the air and me manhandle a guy bigger than me. She probably also saw me fly at her when I thought her about to off herself.

My unlife. Sigh.

Go recover this sword, he said. It'll be easy, he said. Do it when no other vampires are awake, he said. Yeah, sure. Argh!

It doesn't take me long to make Pizza Girl (Danae, by the way) forget mostly everything. She will remember some guy in a black hooded sweatshirt trying to rob her, but she outran him. By some odd coincidence, Danae *is* my age—nineteen. I need to do a little more reinforcement of the memory alteration to explain why she didn't kick Jake's ass. The girl's former varsity track and field, plus a black belt and amateur kickboxer. An ordinary mugger with a knife, she'd have stomped his face in. Jake gave off some seriously creepy supernatural vibes, enough to terrify her into fleeing. Also, even a black belt will say it's a better idea to run away from a guy with a sword when you're unarmed.

Fixed.

A highly confused, guilty, and distraught Jake sits where I left him, making little sound while I finish up with Danae and send her back to her car. Some poor family is getting free pizza tonight. Pretty sure she's not gonna make the delivery in thirty minutes. Is that still a thing?

After she's out of earshot, I sit on the ground next to him. "Your wife is not dead and your kids don't remember you did anything."

He wipes at blood on his palm. "I couldn't control... something..."

"Possessed you. Yeah. I know." I rest my hand on his arm. "No need to convince me. I understand the situation more than you think."

Jake peers up at me. "What do you mean my kids don't remember?"

"I mean, they don't remember *you* did anything. They

think some random guy in a ski mask invaded the house. Your wife does, too. While you were at work."

"I don't know what's happening." He rakes his fingers through his hair.

Well, I can try real truth. Deletion is always an option if it doesn't go over well. "Someone hypnotized you into taking a sword out of the evidence room at the station. This sword is evil. It possesses anyone who touches it and turns them into a killer, out of their mind. *You* didn't do anything. It took your body over."

He leaps to his feet, pacing around. "Oh, my God. I killed Christina. Fuck. How the hell am I going to deal with this?" Jake breaks down, sobbing.

"No, you didn't. The sword attacked her."

He stops pacing, stares at me for a second, then scoffs. "Swords don't do things on their own."

I sigh, stand, and grab a fistful of his shirt, lifting him off his feet. "Do girls my size normally lift you with one arm?"

"You kinda have a point," he wheezes.

Yeah, the shirt's squeezing his chest. I set him down.

"Christina's not dead?"

"Nope. She's messed up, but she'll pull through."

Jake stares at the ground. "How do you know that?"

"I did some supernatural stuff. Should be enough to carry her past the worst of it."

"Are you serious?"

"No, I'm Sarah."

He stares at me.

"Sorry. Bad habit." I flash a cheesy grin. "If you want me to make you forget the attack, there's not much point in me explaining anything else to you since you won't remember it."

"I dunno." Jake resumes pacing. "I couldn't stop myself. I

wanted to. I fought so damn hard. The whole day is a blur of crazy thoughts. Just couldn't..."

"Jake." I grab his arm. "I think you *did* stop yourself. Fighting as hard as you did to resist bought her time. Gave her the chance to get the gun, get the kids in the bathroom."

"Gun?" He blinks.

I point at his chest. "Yeah, you're shot."

Jake peers down at the gunshot wound in his side, shocked as if he hadn't even noticed it before. "Oh, crap." He staggers to one side, seemingly about to faint. Wow. Cartoon logic. He's not hurt until he realizes he's been hurt.

Dammit. Dammit. Dammit. I *still* can't chase the sword. If I leave him here, he's probably going to pass out and bleed to death. Without the sword giving him inhuman endurance, shrugging off a bullet in the lung isn't an easy task for a mortal—only slightly easier than making those people stop calling about a car's extended warranty.

Sigh. Okay, Universe. You called my bluff. The kids were alive, so you're making me chase this sword all over the place. I accept the terms of my deal. Doesn't mean I can't grumble a little. And no, I don't honestly think muttering about a deal altered fate, but I'm also superstitious enough not to test a jinx bet.

"Come on." I take his hand. "Let's get you to the hospital. Probably better you remember a guy in a black hoodie, too."

"Huh?"

"Heroic dad. Raced home to protect his family. Suspect got a hold of the gun, shot you, and ran off."

He blinks, confused. "But that's not what happened, is it?"

"No, but it's going to be." I wag my eyebrows at him.

INEDIBLE

Most people with a task to finish go from point A to point B.

Feels like I'm somewhere around point N. I doubt my little 'deal' with the Universe had any bearing on reality, but it's comforting to remind myself I asked for this. Definitely better to chase this stupid sword around than find Detective Warner's kids dead. Yeah, sure, I know… the sword slipping away from me could mean someone else dies. Better some random adult than a little kid. Don't look at me like that. People have been value-judging lives for a long time. Like, that whole 'women and children first' thing from the age of passenger ships.

Society as a whole tends to prioritize the survival of one group over another. Sucks to be a dude and considered expendable. I suppose from a primitive persistence of the species standpoint it makes sense. Women can have babies, so in like a 'playing Civilization' sense, they're more important. Honestly, I think society has advanced beyond worrying if humanity is going to survive the winter, but we still do the value judging thing.

Like, my Dad would totally throw himself in the path of an oncoming car to save my unlife even though it's patently stupid of him. *I'd* get back up... eventually. He wouldn't. Dad would do the same for any of us. He'd probably trade his life for that of some random kid, too.

Again, I get the weirdest feeling of having forgotten something important at home. I also want to find Sophia and hug her thanks to a nagging inkling she is not coping with camp well. Even more strange, an inexplicable sense of worry about Sam comes out of nowhere. That's easy enough to address. It's not *too* late. He should still be awake.

Speaking of late—I'm presently acting inconspicuous and walking away from the hospital where I dropped Jake Warner off. On the ride here, he deliriously explained how he'd been in and out of control all day, fighting the urge to kill. He tried isolating himself in the garage, but his wife popped in to check on him and it set him off. Well, not *him*. The sword. Anyway, he now believes he was on the way to the station in the morning, forgot something, and turned around. Upon returning home, he surprised an unknown man who'd broken into the house and attacked Mrs. Warner.

Yeah, the timeline doesn't add up, but the whole family believes the story so it won't come off like they're lying. Heck, they'd even pass a lie detector test if the police department is suspicious of the story.

I call Sam.

"We're sorry. The cellular subscriber you are trying to reach is not in our coverage area," says a recording.

I blink. Ugh. Did Sam go to Hell again? Or whatever the demons call the other plane? Figures they have AT&T down there and we're on a Verizon family plan. Pretty sure the roaming charges there are pretty severe. Coralie hasn't shown up to warn me in a panic about something bad happening to him, so he's probably fine... or there's no possible way I could get to him in time to matter. Would she warn me about imminent disaster, even if it would be futile to do so?

Grr. Sam. Where are you?

I try again and get the same message.

The parents haven't called me either, so I'm probably overreacting to a weird hormonal imbalance creating random emotions of worry—or something like that. Yes, I am psychic thanks to vampirism, but it's not the crystal ball kind of psychic. Seeing the future or clairvoyance isn't my deal, just telepathy and mind control. Hmm. I wonder if mortals claiming to be psychic are occasionally telling the truth?

Whatever.

I call the number for Wolent.

"Amanda," says a woman who sounds thirtyish.

"No, Sarah."

A sigh comes over the phone. "*I'm* Amanda."

Who the heck answers the phone with their first name like that? "Sorry... think I might've been connected to the wrong place."

"Sarah Wright?" asks Amanda.

"Umm, yeah."

"You're on the correct line. I work for Mr. Wolent."

I stare up at the sky. Being a vampire at night makes me feel like a character in a surrealist landscape painting. Everything around me at ground level appears lit as bright as a moderately gloomy day, yet the celestial canopy looks much the same as it always did after sunset. "Is it safe to talk?"

"It should be. Depends on who might be near you."

Grumble. I turn in place, scanning for potential eavesdroppers. A few people are coming and going from the hospital, probably not close enough to listen in on my conversation unless they happen to be vampires, too. To be extra careful, I walk down the street a bit and duck behind a bank. It's closed, and no one's at the drive-through ATM. I'm alone in the pale glow of a dying orange-tinted light struggling to provide some sense of security for anyone who comes to take money out.

"What's known about our kind in the Olympia area? Need the deets on a dude with spiky white hair. Twenty to twenty-five as far as looks go. Punkish. Think half Billy Idol, half David from *Lost Boys*—without the mullet."

"Who and who?" asks Amanda.

Wow, she's youngish and deprived of an Eighties-obsessed father. "How many vampires can there be around here with punk hair?"

"You'd be surprised. I can do a little asking around, but the individual you describe is not familiar to us." Amanda stops talking as the clicking of computer keys comes over the line. Wow, have I called the Vampire Help Desk? Is she logging notes on my account? "Our friends in Olympia are known to hang out at a club called Blackrose."

I roll my eyes. "Wow. They might as well put up 'vampires here' signs."

Amanda chuckles. "Sometimes, being overly obvious has the opposite effect. Mortals think we are simple mortals obsessed with goth culture. There is another establishment, an upscale bar named Bosch."

"Like the artist?" I ask.

"Artist?"

Sigh. "Yeah, the dude who painted all those really trippy hellscapes with giant eggs eating people and mass demonic orgies?"

"I have no idea what you're talking about."

"Never had an art class?"

"Many years ago."

Heh. That explains it. School is still fresh in my memory. Hmm. Maybe I should take an art history course at SCCC. Should be some easy credits. My art teacher senior year was, how do you say, *overly motivated*. I think Mr. Hawthorn gave us the equivalent of college level material. Heavy on the history and lore, but kinda light on the actual 'how to draw' part. I thought it would be a fun class, but it ended up being tedious. More memorizing facts than creating art.

Bleh.

"Right, so… Blackrose or Bosch?" I sigh. Please tell me they didn't name the bar that because they're trying to recreate the imagery of those paintings. If there's a hedonistic Sybarite orgy of darkness in the basement, they can keep Wolent's damn sword. "Somehow, I doubt a dude in a leather jacket and spiky hair is going to hang out with the elites."

Amanda 'mm-hmms' me.

"Thanks."

"Mr. Wolent is curious why you have not yet returned. He'd expected to wake and find your errand finished already."

What can I say? Shizz got complicated.

Can't respond with that exact phrasing. Something tells me it wouldn't go over well. So, I give her a brief summary of certain unexpected events, specifically that this white-haired punk prompted a detective to take the sword and it happened to be gone before I ever made it to the police station. Technically, the sword went on walkabout before Mark the Thrall even contacted me. In no possible way could it be my fault the Forces of Evil™ stole it. Maybe it *is* my fault the sword is *still* missing, though. If I'd abandoned Mrs. Warner to chase Jake right away, I could've kicked his ass easily and taken the sword.

Except, she'd be dead, two children would be screwed up

for the rest of their lives, and Jake would either be dead, too, or in prison for a long damn time for something he really didn't do. So no, I couldn't really have done that. The sword is still out in the wild because I have a conscience. Maybe it's an overdeveloped, squishy, bleeding-heart conscience, but I own it. And hey, it's not like I'm saying screw it and going home or even trying to make excuses in hopes of being told to go home. I'm still out here looking for the damn sword.

Amanda 'mm-hmms' me again. "I see. What's the status of the blade now?"

"Good question." I whistle. "At least vampires have it now, so it hopefully won't end up destroying any lives in the foreseeable near future. Let me get going. Faster I find this punk, faster I'll be able to track down the sword."

"All right. I will tell Mr. Wolent you've been delayed due to the actions of other vampires."

"Thanks."

I hang up, then sigh. It's fairly important for minions of the boss *not* to hear anything that sounds like complaining. Not particularly scared, just... people who sigh and eye-roll their bosses tend not to keep their jobs for long.

Once off the call, I google the Blackrose club. Ugh. Even thinking the name makes me cringe at the cheesiness. Kids at my old high school used to pick on the emos for taking themselves way too seriously. I admit to finding them a bit pretentious, but never bothered them. It's their life. My opinion of what someone else likes doesn't mean anything... unless that person's likes include screwing with me or my family. But, yeah. Blackrose. Ugh. Come on guys. You're *actual* vampires, not a bunch of high school kids playing a vampire roleplaying game. Have some self-respect.

Shaking my head, I stuff my phone back in my purse. I'm about to jump into the air when the crunch of sneaker soles on pavement alerts me to someone trying to sneak up on me.

I turn, startling a youngish guy in a dark hoodie. A blue bandana covers most of his face. He almost yelps, then hastily tries to pull a little revolver from his sweatshirt pocket, only the hammer snags on the pocket, causing him to fumble and drop the weapon to the sidewalk with a surprisingly loud clatter.

I gesture at it. "You dropped your gun."

The guy stares at me for a second.

I stare back. Dude can't be twenty yet. I'd say he might've even been in my class at high school, only this is Olympia. Don't think the buses run that far. After a momentary standoff, he scrambles to recover the weapon and points the snub-nosed revolver at me. It's not that he's inept at this— much—or even trying to rob someone for the first time. My spin startled him, and he's freaking out that I'm so calm, not running away when he derped the gun to the ground.

"Take out $400 and hand it over."

"Sorry. This isn't my bank. I'm not actually here to use the ATM, just needed some privacy for a phone call."

He blinks. The confusion in his eyes is *epic*.

I tilt my head. "What?"

"Uhh." He raises the gun a little higher. "Doesn't matter what bank you use... you can take money out of any machine."

"Yeah, but the ATM fees are obnoxious. They're the real robbers." I sigh. "Look, why don't you follow me to *my* bank so I only get robbed once tonight?"

"You're out of your freakin' mind," rasps the guy.

I smile. "No. I feel completely sane, but now that you mention it... I *am* a little hungry."

Before he can fully process my words, I lunge forward at vampiric speed, grab the wrist of his gun arm, then swing him into the brick wall beside the ATM. Time to make a withdrawal.

How weird is this? I'm stalking an undead.

Be vewwy vewwy kwiet. We're hunting vampires.

I sent the mugger on his way after feeding. Not sure what effect a compulsion to 'make better life choices' will have on him, but had to try something. Follows Rules Girl demanded I take his gun away... so I grabbed it in a handful of shirt. Damn fingerprints. While flying toward where my phone tells me Club Blackrose is, I drop the revolver on the ground from a few hundred feet in the air, landing it in the grass between street and sidewalk next to a cop. He's got questions now. Like what the hell are the local pigeons up to?

A few minutes later, I'm gliding over downtown Olympia, still chuckling to myself at the mental image of Elmer Fudd, vampire hunter. The nightclub's on the corner next to an auto-body shop. The stark, rectangular grey-and-metal building oozes goth-industrial. Got a feeling the only one in the place over twenty-five is the owner. Maybe the bartender. And by 'over twenty-five' I mean looks/acts like it. Vampires are like boys from affluent families: they never grow up. We could be 300 years old, but mentally, our personality won't change much. Professor Heath and I got into a long circuitous conversation a few months ago about the nature of personality, whether it derives from physio-chemical stuff in the brain or a more-difficult-to-quantify soul. That vampires tend to freeze personality wise where they are at the time of the Transference kinda points the finger at physio-chemical stuff in the brain, since our bodies are preserved exactly as they'd been at the moment of mortal death... refer to my earlier thoughts regarding the length of our body hair and fingernails.

So this white-haired punk I'm hunting is still going to look, act, and think like he did in life. About the only difference would be comparing the attitude of a twentysomething from the 1980s to someone my age now. And yeah, he's gotta have been turned in the Eighties. Why the heck else would he dress like a thrift store Billy Idol?

I land in an alley on the next block and walk the rest of the way to the front door.

Two large-ish guys (tall not muscular) at the door decked out in leather, denim, unnecessary metal bits, and gaudy hair dye both give me 'yeah right' stares when it becomes obvious I'm approaching the club. For once, it's not immediately obvious they think I'm a child. The guy on the left has three metal stars—like an Army general's rank insignia stuck in his forehead. Their hair is so frizzed up it's tempting to look for the electrical socket he's sticking a fork into. There's more shredding going on with their jeans than in Kyle Irving's garage.

Who's that? Just a guy from my school who tried to start a heavy metal band.

These two could be making the faces they're making at me due to my clothes. What kind of square dweeb shows up at a club like this in a 'girl next door' T-shirt and jean shorts with ordinary sneakers? I'd stand out less in this place being topless in a leather skirt with little Xs of electrical tape over my nipples. No idea who that girl was. Saw a poster somewhere, maybe a singer or some such. But, yeah… these two are looking at me like I'm either an idiot or they're being pranked. For some reason, I'm not surprised the place doesn't have a line waiting to get in.

"You got ID?" asks the guy with the stars stuck to his forehead.

"I do." I hold up an empty hand as if showing him something, then make him ignore me.

The other guy tilts his head at my non-ID. "What? This some kinda joke?"

"Not as much as your hair," I mutter to myself, then send the guy to Derpville.

"Hey!" shouts a girl to my left as soon as I walk past the guys and grab the door handle. "Her ID is *obviously* fake! That kid's younger than I am. Why are you letting *her* in? How much did she bribe you?"

Grr. I glance over at a girl with dark azure hair in a reverse bob, black leather miniskirt, tons of bracelets, enormous armored boots, and more eyeshadow than the entire audience at an Evanescence concert. She's probably around seventeen, and she's pissed her fake ID didn't work on the door guys.

Great. Just what I needed tonight, a haunting from the goth faerie of jealousy.

Thankfully, both guys are still tasting colors in the air. My mental baseball bat hasn't worn off yet, so neither one of them notice her throwing a tantrum. Follows Rules Girl gets the better of me. I charm her into silence, then insert a notion to go home and be safe. Sneaking into places alone and getting drunk around strangers is *not* going to end well for a girl her age—or mine, but I can't get drunk anymore.

Her urge to take out a phone and call an Uber bumps its head into the barrier of confusion left behind in the wake of vampire mental tweaking. She'll stand there for a minute or two bewildered, then go home. I slip into the club, but linger inside the doors watching her in case someone happens along and tries to mess with her while she's out of it. The door guys recover from the fog, acting like I'd never been there. A moment later, goth girl pulls out her phone. Her attitude has gone from jealous and demanding to somewhat fearful... as if she needs to get home fast before something happens to her.

Oops. Little too hard. Whatever. If I made her abnormally afraid of being outside alone, it won't last more than a day or two. This is what Mom would call 'erring on the side of caution.'

Yep. That's me. Evil creature of the night stealing free will and compelling young women to... be responsible. Sigh. Tonight's turning into one heck of an event. I can't just fall down the stairs. I have to hit my face on every single step. Bet the punk is already gone or had never been here.

Grumbling, I move away from the door and walk into a standing wall of sound thick enough to almost push me back. It's heavy techno-industrial-metal or something as if Bauhaus, the Cure, and Rammstein merged into a single band, then decided to sing in some indecipherable Slavic-sounding language. It's not a live band, so I can't even lip read.

Night clubs are not my scene.

Night clubs where most people are wearing leather and white face paint are *definitely* not my scene. Wow. Feels like I've jumped into one of Dad's movies and ended up in a James Cameron vision from 1984 of a futuristic techno bar set behind the Iron Curtain in a dystopian East Berlin circa 2050.

I swear, if a terminator shows up to grab this sword, I'm done.

So the mild-mannered suburban girl who never breaks the rules, doesn't wear outlandish clothing, and tends to be responsible walks into a place full of punks and people at the fringe of society. What could go wrong?

People who happen to notice me stare. Mortals tend to react with mockery in their thoughts, thinking of me as some 'cute little girl' who's obviously gone to the wrong place. A few give off pity, as if some boy brought me here without telling me what kind of place it was as a prank, then took off. The handful of vampires I run into regard me mostly in confusion, though it's probably more from their inability to see into my thoughts than my exceptionally ordinary clothing. I feel like the lone killjoy at a renaissance festival who didn't bother dressing in costume. Everyone here would think I'm a narc or something, except narcs at least *try* to blend in among the locals. I'm so *obviously* out of my element, no one suspects me of being a cop... just a dork.

A few people respond to mental pokes of the guy's image. They've seen him here, but can't recall the last time, nor do they know who he is. Damn, this is frustrating.

"Ooh, aren't you cute," says a woman on my left.

"Totally adorable." Another woman appears on my right.

I have about enough time to process they're only a little— visually—older than me, are in full goth regalia, and undoubtedly vampires before they grab my arms and usher me across the club. The 'abduction' isn't terribly forceful or hostile. It's almost as if I'm the awkward new girl with zero social game who just transferred to school, and the popular crowd has decided to adopt me and make their pet project to whip me into shape.

My escorts both have black hair, the one on my left wearing it in a pixie cut, the other waist-length. They're also loaded up with so much steel jewelry—bracelets, bangles, necklaces, earrings, random chains hanging here and there on their clothes, these two walking around jingle more than a shackled prison work detail reenacting Michael Jackson's Thriller. At least, they would if I could hear anything over the music.

They whisk me over to a booth at the left rear corner of the club, a spot for people who want to be social but in smaller doses. A woman with long, straight blonde hair in a punk-goth outfit and black lipstick watches us from the table. She looks a teeny bit older than the two holding my arms, maybe twenty-three or so, but has a youngish doll face. Imagine one of Aurélie's innocent fairy princess dolls going rebel and growing to life size. None of them need white face paint. Like Aurélie, they simply don't bother 'warming up' their skin tone. I swear the modern era is awesome for vampires. Being deathly pale anywhere but Ireland used to get us chased with torches and pitchforks. Now, it's considered cool. I'm sure the medieval Irish would've chased vampires with torches and pitchforks too—if they could have told them apart from the living.

The women deposit me on the bench seat and sit on either side of me. I don't get the feeling they intend to torment or mock me. It's also highly unlikely this initial awkward meeting is going to end with us bonding deeply as friends then going off on a life-changing cross country road trip culminating with someone dead, a building on fire, and our car flying off a cliff.

"Well, look at you," says the blonde. "New around here?"

"Obviously," replies Pixie Cut, half-lidding her sapphire blue eyes at me.

The woman on my right picks at my shirt. "LL Bean or Macy's?"

Blondie and Pixie Cut laugh.

"Walmart, actually." I put on my best unimpressed face. Yeah sure, my parents make decent money... but it doesn't mean we waste it. "Or maybe Marshalls. Kinda don't remember where this came from."

"Fascinating." Pixie Cut leans in, sniffing at the side of my neck. It's neither sensual nor scary. More like a curious cat scoping out a new addition to the family. "You smell like strawberries."

"It's the conditioner," I deadpan.

"Get a room already, Beckah," says Blondie.

"This one's not into girls." The one with long black hair examines her—equally black—fingernails.

She doesn't feel old enough to be able to read my mind, so

I chalk it up to a judgmental comment about my outfit. Girl ain't wrong but... rude.

"Neither am I." Beckah stares at her.

The other brunette smiles at me. "Don't let her fool you. She'll sleep with anyone. Heartbeat optional."

Beckah flips her off. "Suck it, Courtney."

Courtney—the girl with long black hair—grabs Beckah's wrist and starts sucking on the extended middle finger like a popsicle. Beckah rolls her eyes. I get the sense they're not really fighting and doing it to mess with me, so I ignore them.

"So, what's a girl like you doing in a place like this?" asks the blonde.

I fake cringe. "Don't tell me... Heather?"

The other two laugh.

Blondie shakes her head.

"Brittany?"

Beckah snort-laughs. "Oh-em-gee. She totally *does* look like a Brittany."

"Sure, after the cheerleader rose from the dead." Courtney bangs her head against my shoulder twice, still snickering.

Beckah puts a hand on my thigh, a bit too high up to be casual friendly. Before I can process being pawed by a girl, Courtney brushes the back of her hand across my cheek. I grab her wrist.

She leans in as if to kiss me on the lips. "Relax, sweetie. Just let it happen."

"Mmm." Beckah slides her hand even higher up my thigh, her fingertips slipping under the leg of my shorts—and bites me on the neck.

I'm a nanosecond from flipping out on them... but Beckah recoils, making a face like she took a bite out of an unidentified brown substance in the fridge expecting it to be chocolate mousse... but it's liver pate.

She gawks at me, staring open mouthed. Blood—*my* blood—drips off her fangs, over her black lip, and down her porcelain-pale chin. "Shit... you're one of us?"

Generally, vampire blood does not taste pleasant. It doesn't give us nourishment. Too much makes us sick.

Courtney's pawing comes to an abrupt stop. Her expression freezes in a horrified sort of half-cringe as though she'd gotten drunk at a party and didn't realize the boy she'd been making out with for the past five minutes wasn't her boyfriend. Maybe a little more severe, but not quite as horrified as if she'd been kissing her brother in the dark without realizing it. "Umm. Wow, really?"

Now I sense the telltale mental tingle of a failed attempt to read my mind.

"Holy shit. She is." Courtney blinks.

"Wow..." The blonde leans forward, staring at me. "You're really good at that."

Beckah yanks her hand away from my lap. "Uhh, sorry. Just like a feeding thing. I like messing with mortals. Sorry if it made you uncomfortable."

"Just a wee bit." I hold up a pinchy gesture.

Not sure being mistaken for a mortal excuses them getting handsy, but of all the things other vampires have done to me thus far, a grope is mild. I'd rather a hand on my leg than having metal objects rammed through me. Helps she wasn't really intending to like molest me or anything. She did it to confuse and disorient a mortal she prepared to feed from, making it easier to get into their mind.

At least the ladies appear genuinely contrite. Beckah dabs a napkin at my neck. Since her intention when biting me had been feeding, not fighting, the puncture marks seal themselves fairly fast and don't hurt.

"My question takes on a new meaning." Blondie rests her elbows on the table, no longer seeming like an aloof popular girl about to demand tribute from the norms. "What are you doing around here? You're not local, are you?"

"Sorta. Technically Seattle, but I don't live downtown."

"Cool." She offers a hand. "You were way off. Name's Vivica Thorne."

I almost laugh. Bad Sarah. Rude. For her sake, I hope she renamed herself after becoming a vampire. A name like that belongs in one of two places: a character in a Regency Romance, or an adult film actress. The more I look at her, the more she feels older. Not an elder, but definitely has some decades as a vampire. Heck, maybe she really is from the 1800s.

"Sarah Wright." I shake hands.

"You've met my friends, Courtney Moss and Beckah Spurling already." Vivica smiles.

"Yeah. You can say that."

Beckah and Courtney ever so subtly scoot away from me, no longer draped on me like a pair of revved up oversexed Sybarites. Anyone looking at us now would think us a bunch of girl pals hanging out—and they'd probably make fun of my normal clothes.

"She's *so* wholesome." Courtney makes an 'aww' face at me.

"Totally," says Beckah. "Never saw an adult who smelled like a little kid before."

"I know, right?" Courtney sniffs the air near me, careful not to lean intimately close. "What's up with that?"

"You guys bite kids?" I raise an eyebrow. "And seriously, you *are* smelling shampoo."

"Now and then," says Vivica. "Why not? They don't notice. It's like candy. A little bit every so often won't hurt you. Beck's got a bit of a problem, though. She's addicted."

Courtney leans forward to peer past me at Beckah. "Want some Girl Scout cookies, or just the girl scouts?"

"I could totally go for some brownies right now." Beckah rubs her stomach. "Don't wanna get fat, though. I'd eat too many."

Ugh. "Please tell me you guys are teasing. I think you are since we *can't* get fat."

"Chill." Beckah playfully shoves my shoulder. "We don't kill them. Just a sip or two. It's seriously like candy."

"So blood tastes like other food to you guys, too?"

They all nod.

I try to ask them about the white-haired punk, but get derailed by compulsory small talk. Like, everything I say not related to what these girls are already talking about gets ignored. Sigh. C'mon people. There's a ticking clock here. Over the next ten or so minutes, I learn that Vivica is around ninety, and basically the unofficial leader of the Lost Ones in Olympia. This, of course, is kinda funny to me since the big thing with the Lost Ones is rejecting organizational authority. Maybe it's a bit like a roving band of thieves. One among them tends to be considered the leader.

The other two aren't Lost Ones, though... which surprises me. Courtney's a Fury, and she's been a vampire going on forty-one years. Beckah, a Scion, is their 'baby' at a mere fifty-three years of total age, having received the gift at twenty in 1987.

Okay, this explains why they're hanging out with Vivica. People tend to like keeping a certain distance from Furies if they can help it, and wouldn't dare be condescending to them over their associating with a Lost One. Scions... well, they're kind of like the person at work who only got the job because their parents own the company. No one pays attention to what they say or do. As long as they aren't actively causing damage, they are ignored. It's strange to think about another bloodline actually being *less* respected than Innocents... but it's because they are so new. 'My people' have been around for a long time. We're just rare.

When they learn I'm a month over a year as an immortal, they react much the same way three copies of Sophia would to a new kitten.

Ugh. Shoot me now.

Finally, the cooing slows down enough—coincidentally with a lull in the pounding music—for me to shift the conversation to less banal things.

"Hey, so you asked what I'm doing in Olympia before..." I glance among the three. "Trying to find this guy. Young twenties, punkish. White spiky hair?"

"Billy Idol?" asks Beckah.

I cackle. "I thought that, too."

She swoons over the table. "I used to think he was *so* hot. Had a poster of him on my bedroom wall. Mom hated it." Beckah lifts her head off her arm to squint at me. "How the heck do you even know who he is? You're a baby."

"You died in the Eighties. My dad is still mentally stuck in the Eighties." I shrug. "He even listens to Madonna sometimes."

Beckah whistles. "Wow."

"If it's who I'm thinking of..." Vivica shakes her head. "You should avoid him. He's a pigeon-livered ratbag."

All three of us stare at her.

"Umm, what?" I ask.

Vivica leans back, confused by my confusion for a second before she covers her mouth to laugh. "Oh, forgive me. I forget sometimes. I believe you'd call him a scoundrel."

"The word is asshole," says Beckah. "Dieter is a complete asshole."

"Hang on a sec. Dude's name is 'Deeter'?" I blink. "What kind of name is that?"

"D-i-e-t-e-r," says Courtney. "It's German."

The trio nods. Why do I feel like I'm having a meeting with the three sorcerer sisters? Only, instead of standing around a cauldron in a dark creepy forest, I'm hanging out with the modern Tim Burton retelling of Dracula's three brides, though the scene's a lot closer to *Beetlejuice* than Bram Stoker. There's something in the air between these girls. Not romantic love, but definitely love of some kind. Getting the distinct feeling they're almost a singular entity with three distinct personas. Considering how strange my unlife is, I should clarify. It's my opinion of how close a friendship these three have. I don't believe they are actually a greater paranormal entity projecting three reflections of itself in human form. Lately, if I'm talking to Ashley or Michelle and I say someone's 'eyes lit up,' they ask me if I'm being literal—as in talking about glowing eyeballs—or metaphorical in the way anyone else would use the phrase 'their eyes lit up.'

My unlife.

"Yes. He's from Germany." Vivica drums her nails on the table. "Maybe even East Berlin."

"It's not *East* Berlin anymore." Courtney pretends to drink water.

Wow. No wonder he looked like a reject from the cold war underground. He literally is one.

"Whatever. He's still an asshole." Vivica scowls.

I think back to him tossing a water pistol at Danae, the Dominos driver. "Yeah. I kinda got that feeling about him."

PARANORMAL ENCOUNTER OF
THE TOO CLOSE KIND

S ophia stared at the ghost of Crazy Coleman for all of
two seconds before she screamed.

In a panic, she leapt out of bed and ran to the
back of the cabin, jumping face-first into the screen blocking
the back window and crashing through it to the ground
outside, falling in a clattering tangle of flimsy aluminum,
insect screening, and pink nightgown.

Pale green light welled up in the window above her, the
ghost drawing nearer.

She threw the screen to the side, rolled to her feet, and
sprinted into the woods. Within seconds, she crashed into a
tree. Hardly any moonlight made it past the leaves overhead.
Despite not being able to see anything other than the
indistinct greenish glow following her, Sophia continued
fleeing, raising her hands in hopes of detecting trees before
her face found them.

Unseen things scratched at her feet and legs, nipping and
snagging her nightgown. Rocks stabbed her soles, making
her stumble repeatedly. Somewhere behind her, the other
girls shouted for her to stop. Their voices grew faint from

distance but still managed to pull her back from the edge of blind panic enough to consider herself foolish and look over her shoulder.

Crazy Coleman glided toward her, barely ten feet away, reaching for her.

Sophia screamed again. Next thing she knew, she crashed into another tree after a brief attempt to sprint. Her left foot came down on a rock, root, or something painful. She stumbled one step more before a vine or dead branch snagged across the front of her right ankle, trapping her leg. Unable to get her foot under her, she toppled forward, throwing her hands out to soften the landing.

The fall seemed to go on too long, as if the ground stopped existing.

She belly-flopped on a steep downward slope, sliding for several panicky seconds before her shoulder hit something marginally softer than a rock. Her body flipped over it and went into a tumble, then a logroll, then a foot-first slide. She skidded to a stop on flat ground, aching in a dozen different places. Nothing hurt *too* much, so she probably hadn't suffered a broken bone.

Sophia lay there on her back, inhaling the damp earthen flavor of the forest. She couldn't see anything other than the faint hint of moonlight leaking between leaves overhead. The hill she tumbled down could have been four feet tall or forty feet tall. Camp might be in flashlight reach or a mile away. She couldn't even tell which direction she'd gone or which way she'd need to go in order to return to her friends.

No ghostly luminescence disturbed the peaceful darkness. She kept still, hoping she'd gotten away. As long as she didn't move or make any sound, maybe the ghost of the former killer wouldn't be able to find her. Tempting as it was to cradle the sore spots and cry, moving would make noise, so she didn't.

I'm being stupid. She fought the urge to break down into sniffles. *I hate this camp. Why did I agree to go? I'm so upset and homesick, a dumb ghost is scaring me. I know magic to make bad spirits go away. What am I afraid of? It's this camp. I'm acting like a little kid. They're all gonna think I'm a baby now. Screamed and ran away from nothing. They can't see him.*

"Nothing to be scared of," whispered Sophia. "Except being lost."

The ghost of Crazy Coleman appeared out of nowhere, standing over her, staring down into her eyes.

Paralyzed in fear, Sophia couldn't even scream. She almost wet herself in the two seconds it seemed certain her life would end, and probably would have if the ghost didn't do something utterly unexpected.

He crouched beside her. "Y'awright, kiddo? Took quite a spill there."

Stunned, she managed to open her mouth, but couldn't find a voice.

"S'wrong wit' ya? Kin see me, aye?"

She nodded.

"Aw. I get it. Dem camp people tellin' stories ain't true." Coleman waved dismissively. "Ain't nothin' like what they say."

"Umm." Sophia swallowed. "You're not a killer?"

He chuckled. "I am, but not of people. Or was. Can't do much anymore."

"Not of people?" Sophia pushed herself up to sit.

"Naw. You prolly know a thing or two about the *real* world. The world what lurks unner the surface. World what most folks never see, and ignore if they do."

"Yeah." She pulled her knees closer to her chest, wrapping her arms around them. "Did college students really die here?"

"Aye. Tried ta stop it, but damn thing was too strong. Got me. Then got them." Coleman spat to the side. "Made a life huntin' crap like that. Anyone sees too much 'o that stuff, they can't live in polite society no more, so I stayed out here. Like a fool, I got overconfident, and paid for it."

The frazzled old man no longer gave off a sense of dangerous craziness. His wild hair, wilder eyes, and unkempt clothing made him seem more like the nutty old grandpa who let the kids do fun, risky things then suggested they not tell their parents about it. Sophia blushed, firmly convinced she'd been an idiot for panicking. Childish homesickness plus a scary story rattled her so much she didn't think at all, merely freaked out like she would've done before her magic woke up. Horror movies *still* made her cry and hide, but an actual ghost—or dark spirit—she didn't have to fear anymore.

The spectral glow allowed her to see enough of her immediate surroundings to realize she'd fallen down a fairly large hill. Leaves, twigs, and dirt clods covered her. A few scratches on her shins and arms dribbled blood, but none of the cuts looked serious.

"Sorry they tell lies about you. I'm Sophia."

"Hello, Sophia." The spirit mimicked shaking hands, as his fingers possessed no substance. "Coleman Emerson."

"I'm sorry for running away from you."

"You ain't the first one ta run. First ta *see* me when I didn't show m'self, though."

She brushed at her arms and chest, knocking away debris. "I should go back to bed before the whole camp comes looking for me."

Coleman's expression shifted serious. "Child, you must warn them. The evil I failed to stop is back. Damn thing's wakin' up, and when it breaks loose, it's gonna do unspeakable things. You gotta tell 'em to get outta here when they's still capable of it."

Sophia shivered. "What is it?"

"A wendigo." His form blurred, stretching upward from crouch to standing. "Somethin' about you, kid. You bein' here woke it up. Prolly has ta do wit' how you kin see me. Don' much matter now. What's done is done. You gotta get out."

She vaguely remembered a monster in the D&D games they played at home called 'wendigo,' but didn't trust a fantasy game to be accurate at all to real life. The creature had to be dangerous, since it killed Coleman as well as an unknown number of college students years ago. Unfortunately, it would be more likely she could convince Mom to let Sam's hellhound sit on the living room sofa than convince the Girl Scout leaders to abruptly abandon camp and flee from the woods before a scary monster got them.

Even thinking about it in those words made her cringe.

Other girls and their troop leaders totally knew how much she *loved* camping. She'd refused to go for a few years, and hadn't exactly been the image of having a blast all day. They all had to suspect her of being homesick and wanting to leave. No matter the truth of her story, the scout leaders would assume she made up stories to get out of being at camp.

"They're not going to believe me." She sighed.

"Aye. Prolly not. Them kids didn't believe me either. Thought me a kook of an old man." He frowned. "They believed me eventually, too late. Should'a seen the faces their ghosts made at me."

Sophia looked around. "Are they haunting the woods, too?"

"Nah. They moved on ta wherever movin' on goes. I'm stuck here on account o' the wendigo bein' not dead. Can't do nothin' much but try an' scare people away afore it gets 'em. Been doin' reasonable job of it. Damn thing got bored and went ta sleep for years."

"And I woke it up..." She slouched. "Sorry. I knew it was a

bad idea to go camping. Maybe that's why I never wanted to go before."

"Nothin' ta apologize fer, kid. You didn't do nothin' on purpose."

Sophia stood. "My friends might believe me. I can tell them. But the scout leaders aren't going to send everyone home."

"Damn shame." Coleman stared down. "Hard enough on a man's soul watchin' what happened to them college kids. Gon' be worse seein' it happen to a bunch o' children."

The hollow look of incredible sadness... and shame in his eyes frightened Sophia almost to the point of throwing up. Something definitely *bad* stirred in the forest nearby, and would be coming for the Girl Scouts.

"How long," whispered Sophia, "until it wakes up?"

"Already started wakin' up." Coleman glanced off into the trees. "Been sleepin' couple decades now. Take it a while to gather up its power. Wendigo'll be here maybe t'morrah night. Maybe day after."

"Crap." Sophia ground her toes into the dirt, gazing warily around at the dark in every direction.

She had to at least try to come up with *something* to do. The easiest solution would be to call home and tell Sarah to get out here fast and mind-control the counselors. Her sister might think she's being a homesick chicken and simply show up to collect her. It shouldn't take *too* much effort to convince her the wendigo represented a serious threat. However, no one had cell phone reception out here. She'd have to somehow elude the scout leaders and counselors to sneak out of camp, not get lost, and follow a road back to civilization all while avoiding creepy strangers grabbing her or the cops dragging her back here thinking her a simple runaway.

Wait. Stop being dumb. Sophia closed her eyes and breathed a few times. *I can send Klepto with a note.*

Unless her sister happened not to be home. The kitten had an uncanny knack to find objects, but it couldn't just teleport to wherever a person happened to be. Alas, a mental ping from the kitten said she just went home and back... and Sarah hadn't returned yet. Good chance by the time she managed to make contact with Sarah, it would be too late. No, sneaking out wouldn't work. She'd have to do something else. Maybe she could open a gateway home instead of running away like an ordinary kid with separation anxiety from hell. Or, she might be able to use magic to put the wendigo back to sleep.

The idea of confronting it scared her to shaking. Sure, it killed Mr. Emerson and a whole bunch of college students, but none of them had magic. Since no one would possibly believe the truth, and she'd never be able to live with the guilt of running away and leaving everyone to die, she *had* to try doing something herself.

"Sophiiiia?" called a woman, probably Mrs. Whitaker.

Multiple flashlights swept around the woods at the top of the hill.

Uh oh. I'm gonna get in so much trouble.

21

THE CAPITAL THEATER

Wow, a guy who casually let Detective Warner nearly murder his entire family and pulled an unfunny water pistol suicide prank is an asshole. Never would have guessed. I'm sure the Odd Sisters have stories to tell about him, but time isn't on my side.

"I'd love to avoid him, but he kinda took something I need to get back." I glance side to side at the women flanking me. "Any idea where I can find him?"

"Ooh." Vivica leans close. "Sounds interesting. You wish to make his life difficult?"

"I'm in." Beckah thrusts both fists into the air.

Courtney grabs me in a one-armed hug. "He'll never see her coming. This will be awesome."

Heh. "Kind of the point. I hope he doesn't see me coming. But… he's already seen me."

"Dish." Beckah folds her arms on the table. "Spill all the words."

"Agree." Vivica tilts her head forward, staring under her eyebrows at me.

Okay, what other people are into doesn't affect me at all.

My opinion on piercings and such means nothing except to me. Still, I can't help but stare at the horseshoe-shaped silver nose ring dangling from Vivica's face. Every time I see one of those things, all I can think of is a minotaur from D&D. Seriously, though. A dangling snot is super irritating. I can't stand the feeling of something being in my nostril wobbling around. Why would *anyone* want to feel that on purpose all the time? She also—in my meaningless opinion—doesn't have the face for it. A piercing like that looks weird in a cute, button nose like an old timey porcelain doll.

Right. Distracted. Time ticking, Sarah. Stop going off on tangents.

"You guys know who Arthur Wolent is?"

They all nod.

"Cool. Saves me some time." I lean back against the cushioned bench. "Someone stole an old sword from him. I don't know if it was Dieter originally, but he somehow discovered the sword ended up in the police station here and charmed a detective into getting it for him. Almost caught him but got stuck fixing a mess. Dieter grabbed the sword and took off. This thing is really dangerous. Not even a question of value, really. No idea what interest it is to Dieter, but Mr. Wolent wants it back. Can you help me find this guy?"

"Yah, like totally easy. We can do that," says Beckah in a weird accent... maybe 1980s New York?

Vivica makes a shooing gesture at us. "No time like now. This should be delicious."

Courtney slides up in the seat, flips over the back of the booth, and lands on her feet behind it. Amid the flashing lights and loud music, no one notices her pointlessly acrobatic maneuver. I wait for Beckah to get up, then slide out of the booth behind her.

The girls stride across the club, Vivica at the lead like the mother duck leading her offspring. Wait, no. Ducks go single file. We're kind of a vee. The guys outside the front door don't pay us much attention as we exit the building and turn right, heading for a parking lot beside the club. Not a terribly big deal leaving my car where it is. I can always fly back to it.

Vivica approaches a nice grey BMW. The car chirps happily as she opens the door. We get in, Courtney up front in the passenger seat, Beckah and I in back. Nice. These seats are lush. No, I'm not jealous, nor do I develop a sudden need to run out and mind-control a random rich person into buying me a high end Beemer. Doesn't mean I can't appreciate it on a temporary basis.

"Sorry. We gotta drive since Court can't fly." Beckah overacts a sigh of annoyance.

Right. Furies are too angry to outsmart gravity, mostly anyway. It's probably better for the rest of us. Makes it easier to survive if they can't reach us when they fly into an irrational rage.

Courtney gives her the finger. "Go watch Max Headroom again."

Beckah laughs.

"Heh. My dad loves that show," I say.

"I was *in* the show." Beckah beams at me.

"Really?" I gawk at her. Been awhile since Dad insisted I watch it, but she doesn't look at all familiar. "What character?"

"Terrified bystander girl," says Courtney.

Vivica chuckles. "Oh, let her have her eight seconds of fame."

"Isn't it fifteen minutes of fame?" I ask.

"No, she was only visible on the screen for eight seconds." Vivica sighs. "She thought it would be her big break."

Beckah bats her eyelashes at the headrest in front of her.

"Dear, it *was* my big break. Immortality is far better than fame."

I tilt my head at her.

"The one who gave me the Transference followed me home after shooting. He picked me out of the crowd of extras." Beckah smiles to herself.

She clearly adores being a vampire, though it's not obvious if she asked for it. Not going to pry. Too much else on my mind.

The ride lasts only about five minutes before we pull over in front of an office building in downtown Olympia. It's six stories tall and fairly plain looking. No names or anything on the outside other than silver numbers over the door—3202, probably the street address. Vivica turns the engine off, gets out, and walks off toward the entrance, leaving the car door open.

"She not expecting to be here long?" I ask, waiting for Beckah to get out.

"What?" She pauses with one foot on the sidewalk to peer back at me before standing up.

"Left the door open."

Vivica grins back at me. "Saving the cops the trouble later."

"Huh?" I stare.

"This isn't her car," says Beckah.

"What?!" I hold my hands up like a surgeon who just scrubbed, looking around and trying to remember if I touched anything. "You stole it? But... you just got right in like it's your car."

"Aww," says Beckah. "She's precious."

Vivica's laugh echoes down the street.

Courtney leans back into the passenger side up front to stare at me. "What's your problem?"

"Stolen car?" I hold my hands up at them. "Fingerprints?"

"Wow, you must be new." Beckah examines her nails. "We don't leave fingerprints... unless we touch ink or something."

Yeah, maybe *you* don't miss Fully Dead. Sigh. Okay, fine. I'm completely dead, too... just better at faking the opposite. My skin doesn't produce quite as much oil as a real living person, but it still makes some. I think. Haven't exactly tested it, but no point taking a chance. Also pointless: explaining myself to the girls. I laugh it off as a newbie vampire mistake, then use my ability to fly to escape the car without touching it.

Just because it bothers me so much to see, I nudge the driver door shut with my sneaker.

A few minutes of 'aww how cute' type ribbing follows. They'd probably find me 'adorable' for still trying to follow mortal laws as much as possible. Not going to say anything. Don't want to be here all damn night. At least the odd feeling of forgetting the coffee maker on at home has stopped. Hope I don't return to a complete disaster by the time this sword mess is over with. Nagging doubt coming to an end either means it's a nothing burger or whatever bad thing I got a psychic tingle over is done, too late to stop.

Vivica approaches the door, grabs the handle, and peers inside as if trying to figure out if the place is open or not. The girl's blonde, but come on... It's *obviously* closed. Lights are off, no one there. Not sure what—

She pulls the door open and steps into the lobby.

Oh. Duh. I sigh at the clouds. She's a Lost One. There probably aren't too many locks in Olympia she couldn't sweet talk open. Didn't realize their powers worked on car security systems, too. Whatever. What's the saying? In for a penny, in for a pound? Hoping she's keeping us hidden from any sort of CCTV cameras, I follow the Odd Sisters into the lobby.

We go up a stairwell all the way to the top floor. So happy

to be a vampire. Rushing up six flights doesn't make me want to collapse and gasp for air. Vivica leads us down a bland, grey-carpeted hallway past a bunch of small offices like accountants, a lawyer, an IT consulting outfit, and one podiatrist before stopping at an unmarked door with a distinctly 'closet' quality to it.

She stares at the doorknob for two seconds before opening it to reveal a small cinder block room with a ladder leading up. Okay, these ladies are tight friends. Beckah and Vivica could have flown to the roof in four seconds. The only reason we went inside is Courtney.

One plain steel ladder later, we're on the roof. Yanno, I get the weirdest feeling these girls have done this before. Meaning, come to this exact building and made their way to the roof along the same route. After floating up out of the hole in the ceiling—ladders are for mortals... and Furies—I follow them to the edge of the roof opposite the street out front.

All three women lean on the wall, peering over the edge. Mortal me would've noped straight the heck back down into the building. Have I mentioned my fear of heights is gone? Vampire me has no problem walking right up to the chest-high wall and peering over it.

The lot behind the office building contains the crumbling remains of an old theater. A huge dome takes up most of the roof closest to the office building. Thanks to several big holes in it, it's obvious the dome is directly above the stage. Four guys and two women dressed like punk rockers sit around on an array of worn sofas and old recliners. One of the women plucks at a bass while two of the guys fiddle with guitars. They're not playing songs as much as just farting around. Sounds like they *do* know how to play, but never go past a riff or two from any one particular song. The other woman is engrossed in some manner of handheld video game. No sign of Dieter.

When I say 'theater,' I don't mean movies. This is the kind of place where live actors put on plays or terrified tween siblings endure dance recitals. Still amazed Sophia got over her fear of dancing in front of an audience. Can't even say having magic gave her confidence since she kinda beat that fear gremlin before everything went completely crazy. Takes a bit more to scare her now. Not a *lot* more, but it's noticeable.

"Dieter and his people lair here," says Vivica. "In the basement. The theater has a small network of old tunnels, probably used for bootlegging back during Prohibition or some such thing."

"Shanghaiing people, wasn't it?" Beckah scrunches her nose in thought.

"You're thinking of Astoria." Courtney yawns. "These tunnels are far more boring. No spirits, merely a bunch of idiot Scions."

Beckah picks at her eye using her middle finger.

"Not you." Courtney grins. "I mean Scions who are idiots. Not that all Scions are idiots."

A man's laugh echoes up from inside the theater.

White Hair—a.k.a. Dieter Herbert—strolls into view out from one of the aisles between seats. He appears to be on his way in from the street-facing doors at the opposite side of the theater from where we are. To my absolute shock, he's carrying the sword. Dude also looks kinda pissed off. His attitude makes me think he tried to sell it or drop it off to the person who put him up to obtaining it and something went wrong. He jumps up on the stage, crosses it, and vanishes from sight through a curtain near the back. Nine other punkers, all guys, follow. One of the men fiddling around on a guitar strums the 'That's all, folks' riff from Warner Brothers.

Hah.

"Yeah, that's him," I whisper.

"So what's your plan?" Beckah elbow nudges me. "Little thing like you isn't gonna kick all that ass."

"Nope." I grin. "Gonna come back a little later and try to be sneaky."

All three Odd Sisters laugh, though not too loud.

"Good luck, kid," says Vivica.

"Yeah, totally." Courtney shoulder-punches me. "The more like an idiot you make Dieter look, the better."

"Hope it works for you." Beckah pats me on the arm.

"Yeah… me too."

22

THE CAVE OF INEXPLICABLE TRANSLOCATION

U p until the moment a Mi-24 Hind D attack helicopter pointed its nose cannon in his general direction, few things had truly frightened Sam.

It seemed every movie Dad liked where bad guys had heavily armed aircraft used one. They happened to be quite old, totally obsolete at this point. Whatever country they'd landed in looked fairly resource poor. Probably not actual Russia, but some other nation close to it all too happy to soak up the junk the Red Army offered them. These guys might even be mercenaries or criminals and not real soldiers. The land rover Jeep thing also looked thirty years old. This comforted him in one small way since it made it unlikely the cave pushed them across time.

Sam swallowed a bit of saliva. Waiting much longer would be stupid. He didn't know if the rippling plumes of dirt going by from machine gun fire had missed on purpose or due to Darryl unexpectedly swerving. The soldiers may or may not realize four ten-year-old—well, three ten and one soon-to-be-eleven-year-old—boys were in the vehicle. Worse, they might not care. Commander Butthead certainly didn't seem too concerned for their wellbeing. More annoyed. Almost a 'damn, I better make sure no one will miss them before we get rid of them' vibe.

Since he'd recently watched *Red Dawn*, he considered the possibility something in the cave made them sleep and have a shared dream. Imagery of 'evil Russians' featured prominently in the movie—as well as many of Dad's favorites. Another possibility was they'd been sent into a temporary alternate dimension containing a manufactured reality. Essentially VR but from magic rather than computers. This seemed even less probable than time travel. It didn't feel right. The most likely truth said they'd been transported via some manner of wormhole like effect to somewhere else on real Earth in the present day, to a poor Eastern Bloc country using outdated military equipment.

No matter what the truth happened to be, Sam didn't want to take the chance his friends would end up shredded by an antiquated death machine.

"Machine. I am a dork." Sam smacked himself in the forehead.

"What?" shouted Ronan.

Darryl zigzagged back and forth, evidently expecting the helicopter to blow them up at any second.

"A helicopter is a machine." Sam grinned, relieved. He didn't have to kill anyone.

Blix got the message—and vanished.

"No shit, Sherlock," said Jordan. "Aren't you supposed to be like smart or something?"

Sam held a finger up. "My intellect is likely above average. However, this is the first time anyone has pointed a giant machine gun at me. Kinda blanked out."

"So what if it's a machine?" yelled Darryl.

"Blix can mess with it." Sam continued staring at the

helicopter, waiting. "Imps *love* making machines malfunction, especially if explosions are involved."

"Eep!" Ronan ducked down behind the front seats, covering his head with both arms.

Sam chuckled. "Blix is cool. He's not gonna kill them."

"Why not?" yelled Darryl. "They're trying to kill us."

"Because I asked him not to. He's, uhh, not exactly a normal imp." Sam aimed an imaginary rifle at the helicopter and made a soft, *pa-shoo* noise.

The Hind abruptly swerved side to side, tossing a barrage of cannon fire at least a mile off target to the left.

Crap! Sam's eyes bulged. *They really are trying to kill us.*

A bunch of flares burst out of the helicopter's back end. The landing gear extended. Blix had to be in the pilot's lap mashing random buttons. Engine laboring, the massive air beast veered to the side, sliding off to the right while continuing to twist back and forth.

"Hope the pilot packed clean underwear," said Sam.

"Is it gonna crash?" Jordan peered back at him.

Sam tilted his head in a so-so gesture. "Fifty-fifty chance. If it does, it'll hit hard enough to break the helicopter but not kill the guys in it. Blix is really nice for an imp. Most imps, we'd be stupid not to kill. They play mean pranks."

"Mean pranks aren't bad enough to kill someone." Jordan blinked.

"Not mean like when Bobby Carter pantsed Mike in gym class in front of the girls. Worse." Sam paused to watch as the helicopter dropped straight down, but it leveled off before smacking its belly into the grass. "Yeah, they definitely need clean underwear now."

"Uhh." Darryl glanced over at him. "What's worse than having every hot girl in class know you wear Pokémon briefs?"

Sam sighed. "Mean like making traffic lights change

wrong and causing accidents. Making old people fall down stairs and break their necks. *Mean* stuff."

"You mean they kill people." Jordan whistled.

"Umm, they don't really *try* to kill." Sam reflexively ducked as the helicopter rotated to face them again—but it kept spinning without shooting. "It's like they do crazy stuff and if people happen to die because of it, they find it hilarious."

"That's evil." Ronan scowled.

"Yep." Sam nodded. "But, Blix isn't evil."

"Are you sure?" asked Darryl.

"Yep." Sam nodded. "Totally. An evil imp would not help us... and if he did, he'd do it by making the helicopter crash into our Jeep."

"This isn't a Jeep. It's some Russian crapbox." Darryl stomped at the gas pedal. "Stupid thing won't go faster than fifty-five."

Sam looked back at the meadow, clenching his jaw upon spotting a six-wheeled troop transport coming toward them. "Uh oh. BTR."

His friends stared at him.

"What?" asked Ronan.

"BTR. Russian troop transport vehicle." Sam pointed.

His friends continued to stare at him.

"I play a lot of video games." Sam pointed ahead at the forest. "Primary mission objective: avoid detection or capture. Secondary mission objective: locate evac point."

"Dork." Darryl shook his head. "Such a dork."

The helicopter dove and climbed, spun around, slid backward, and generally appeared to be entirely out of control. Watching it made Sam feel a little sick with anxiety for the pilots. Stopping bad guys from killing them was fine, but they didn't deserve to be tortured.

"Hang on!" yelled Darryl.

Sam tore his gaze off the helicopter's drunken aerial ballet and looked out the front. They rapidly approached the start of a narrow dirt road into the forest. A tree knocked the side mirror off the door on Sam's side.

"Little far to the right," deadpanned Sam.

Darryl corrected left a touch. "This thing has zero handling. It's like a drunken cow on roller skates."

Still doing fifty-something, the rickety, giant land rover bounced along the unpaved path with trees whizzing by far too close for comfort. Branches and leaves thwapped at the metal roof. Out in the meadow, the same speed felt as if they'd been creeping.

Sam reached for a seat belt, but the old vehicle didn't have them. *Uh oh. Not good.*

Ronan and Jordan both screamed at the same time. One yelled, "Look out," the other shouted, "Slow down."

"Slow down?" Darryl struggled to keep them centered on the road. "They're coming after us with guns and stuff!"

"Helicopter's not a problem anymore. Even if they get control back, the pilots can't see us in the trees." Sam clung to the door handle. "We're trying to escape, not die in a crash. BTRs are even slower than this thing. They aren't chasing us in a sports car."

"Fine." Darryl eased off the gas.

Forest continued to rush by on both sides. Thankfully, the road didn't twist or curve too much. His friend appeared to be going as fast as he could get away with before Ronan and/or Jordan screamed. Sam had no real idea how far they needed to go. His sense of time from the forced ride to the base felt unreliable. It probably hadn't been *too* long, but even a five-minute trip under armed guard while dreading how much trouble they got into could seem like an hour. It didn't help to think a BTR full of soldiers followed them on the same road. Finding the cave might have to wait until they ditched the bad guys.

Blix appeared out of nowhere, sitting on the dashboard.

"Aaaah!" Darryl jumped and stomped on the brakes.

The truck spun to the right, sliding sideways on the road, mud spraying. All four boys screamed for the three seconds it took to stop—courtesy of some helpful trees after they skidded off a curve. Both windows on the driver's side shattered. A huge crack split the windshield. The crash flung Sam across the bench seat into Darryl. Jordan and Ronan vanished in a flash of blond hair and groaning.

Everyone sat in silence for a few seconds, listening to the distant struggling roar of a faltering helicopter.

Darryl, still clutching the giant steering wheel in both hands, offered a weak smile. "We made it to the forest, but I think we're walking from here."

As if to underline his words, the engine died.

"Most people don't use trees to stop." Ronan's dizzy voice floated up from the back seat.

"Soon as I hit the brakes, we started spinning. I didn't crash on purpose."

Sam scooted over and opened the passenger side door. Two long, squiggly trenches grooved the ground where the tires dug in. The truck had gone twenty or so feet off the road into the woods and bottomed out on the dirt, the wheels deep in soupy mud. "This thing isn't going anywhere. Not worth even trying to get it unstuck. We gotta ditch it and run before those guys catch up." He jumped out of the land rover onto squidgy ground and opened the back door. "C'mon. C'mon!"

Ronan and Jordan lay in a tangle of gangly limbs on the floor behind the driver's seat. The boys groaned again, struggling to pick themselves up and crawl out.

Darryl stumbled out behind him. "Ugh. I think I smacked my head on the window. Kinda dizzy."

At the not-too-distant rumble of a diesel engine growing louder, Ronan and Jordan discovered the motivation to move much faster. Darryl seemed surprisingly less dizzy. Blix leapt on Sam's back, pointing the way. Sam ran a bit slower than sprinting, saving energy for an emergency. It took far less time than he'd have liked before the shouts of men yelling in not-English announced the bad guys had arrived at the crash site.

Time didn't matter. Sam concentrated on not running into trees or tripping on anything. As soon as they made it to the cave, everything would be fine. They'd go home every bit as mysteriously as they got here, leaving the bad guys baffled and searching the woods all night. Their imminent frustration made him grin. A mild punishment for shooting at them, but guys getting stuck tromping around the woods all night wouldn't make him feel bad.

"There," chirped Blix.

The sight of the cave up ahead gave him a burst of energy. Sam picked up to a sprint, zooming over the last fifty yards or so of forest to the rocky opening. His friends caught up a few seconds later, gathering in the smallish one-room chamber, all so out of breath they could barely speak.

"Do the thing," rasped Darryl, doubled over with his hands on his knees.

"I didn't do it before." Sam flailed his arms. "It just happened."

"Well, make it happen again." Jordan flopped on the ground. "I've never run so fast in my life."

Sam gazed around at the ordinary cave. It didn't have any unusual markings, crystals, glowing parts, or anything suggesting it might be a place of great, mysterious power. No odd energy hung in the air. Whatever occurred, it must have been Blix's doing. The boys had been to the cave in the woods behind the house countless times and never ended up being somewhere else when they walked out of it. Only Blix changed. He hadn't been with them the last time they used the cave as a base. Highly doubtful his daemonic buddy put them in danger on purpose. The presence of a supernatural being must have somehow activated the magic in the cave. Blix thought the goblins used it to cross over. Whether or not the creatures came from the woods in this country or some other dimension, he didn't know. After being 'arrested' or kidnapped, he didn't really care to spend time running around the woods hunting goblins anymore—not that the boys *could*. Soldiers hunted them. They had zero choice but to hope to get home the same way they got here.

"I think it just kinda happened because Blix is here." Sam hooked his thumbs in his pockets. "The cave reacted to supernatural energy."

"Darryl's farted in here before, and we didn't end up in Russia." Jordan chuckled. "That's some supernatural energy."

"Blix?" asked Sam.

"Not know." The imp rubbed his pointy chin. "Not purpose. Try figure out."

Soldiers rushed into the cave, pointing rifles at the boys.

Sam, Darryl, Jordan, and Ronan backed up, raising their hands. The men appeared angry and confused. Perhaps they'd expected to find a hidden CIA base, not an ordinary cave. Perhaps they resented having to stop goofing off and spend an hour running into the forest. No reasonable person could blame the boys for the explosions since they'd been nowhere near them, even though Sam technically caused them. Problem being, these guys didn't seem reasonable. Anyone stupid-slash-crazy enough to seriously believe the CIA employed children would probably assume the boys had somehow planted explosive charges.

Ronan burst into tears.

"Little help please, Mel," whispered Sam.

A double-helix swirl of flames leapt up from the cave floor. M'Len D'lar, Matron of Nightmares, appeared in a puff of smoke. Her black evening gown sparkled like a swath of starry sky, second only to the glimmer shining off her diamond necklace. She looked more like a Middle Eastern socialite than an ancient succubus. Sam bit his lip, slightly guilty at the idea he might've interrupted her from a fun party.

"Gladly," said Mel in a sultry voice.

Whew. Sam smiled. She didn't sound annoyed at all.

The soldiers stared at her, seemingly having forgotten entirely about the boys' existence.

"You don't have to kill them." Sam smiled weakly. "They didn't hurt us. Can you just make them leave us alone please?"

"Of course, hon." Mel winked at him. "This way, boys." She sashayed toward the soldiers, gliding through their line and out of the cave.

Like zombies, the men pivoted in place to continue staring at her, then followed her outside.

Darryl, Jordan, and Ronan moved to leave as well.

Sam grabbed his friends. "She's not talking to you. Mel called the soldiers 'boys.'"

"Oh." Jordan exhaled.

Ronan stopped crying suspiciously fast.

"You okay?" asked Sam.

"Yeah. I wasn't really crying. Trying to fake them out."

"Uh huh. Sure." Darryl chuckled.

Ronan shrugged. "Fine. Don't believe me. Everyone thinks I'm a little kid. Tried to make them feel bad so they didn't shoot us."

"So… Sam's got a hot girlfriend." Darryl patted him on the back.

"Well… she is my friend." Sam smiled. "She's also really hot, but not the way you meant."

"Wait…" Darryl pointed at him. "Is she a demon, too?"

Jordan raised both eyebrows. "How many people do you know who just appear out of nowhere in a blast of fire and smoke? Duh!"

"Guys." Sam sighed. "It's really super important you don't tell anyone about them. Okay?"

His friends all swore themselves to secrecy.

"Blix, how do we work this… portal or whatever it is?" Sam again tried to 'feel magic' in the air, but drew a blank.

"It happened by itself when I here." Blix tapped his foot.

"Can you work it on purpose?"

"I think so. Give moment." Blix extended his spindly little arms up to either side. His face cycled through a series of expressions like Dad trying to make sense of Ikea assembly instructions. "Okay. Something happen. Try now."

"Try what now?" Sam blinked.

"Go outside." Blix leapt onto his back.

Sam shrugged and headed up the short passage to the cave exit—and gazed out at a gloomy white glacial wasteland suffering an intense blizzard. Within seconds, the tip of his nose tingled from the cold. A deep, resonant howl echoed out of the murk as if a twenty-foot-tall yeti stubbed its toe.

"Nope. That's not right." Sam backed into the cave. "That's definitely not right."

23

LIES, HALF TRUTHS, AND PLAUSIBLE DENIABILITY

"Sophia?" called Mrs. Brewer. "Girl, where you at?"

She tried as best she could to mentally prepare herself for getting in trouble. It didn't happen often, and she viewed a 'talking to' for being five minutes late to class as dreadfully as if the police picked her up for shoplifting.

"I'm here," called Sophia. "Can't see anything. Careful! There's a hill."

Flashlights angled in her general direction. A moment later, three beams appeared over the top of the ridge, pointing down at her. Sophia raised an arm to shield her face from the glare.

"Good grief, child," said Mrs. Brewer. "What's gotten into you? Running off like that in the middle of the night."

Coleman leaned sideways toward her and whispered, "Want me to give them a scare?"

"Nah," whispered Sophia. "They'll fall down the hill and get hurt. But if they really start yelling at me, maybe let them see you so they don't think I'm crazy."

"You got it, kid."

Mrs. Whitaker and Kayleigh—her troop's dedicated camp counselor—began discussing going back for a rope or something so they could climb down to her. Mrs. Brewer muttered into a handheld radio, telling someone named Byron they could turn around and come back. No need to bother the sheriff.

"Ugh." Sophia cringed in guilt. She almost set off a legit search party. "I'm okay. I can climb."

"That's awful steep, hon." Mrs. Whitaker pointed her flashlight at the hill.

"Yeah, I know," muttered Sophia. "Fell down it already."

She grabbed handfuls of roots wherever possible. Quite unlike Sierra, she rather lacked in physical strength. However, if the Wright family genetics did anything good, being scrawny and light made activities like climbing easier.

Kayleigh and Mrs. Brewer crouched by the top, grabbing her by the arms and hauling her up when she got close enough.

"Let me have a look at you." Mrs. Brewer probably made a face at her. Between the serious darkness and having a flashlight in her face, Sophia couldn't see anything. "Cuts, scratches, dirt. Don't look like nothin' serious."

"What happened?" asked Kayleigh. "The girls said you screamed like Freddy Kreuger kicked in the door."

"I'm sorry. The wind blew the door open and I thought I saw Crazy Coleman coming to kill me."

The ghost story on top of the spirit's warning of a wendigo on its way to wipe out the whole camp genuinely made her shake. Trembling added legitimacy to her story, which really hadn't been too much of a lie. Only claiming she 'thought' she saw the ghost versus *really* saw the ghost had been false. At the time, she'd believed the spirit would hurt her.

"I'm okay now, and I'm sorry for making everyone get out of bed and come looking for me."

"Poor thing, you're scared to death." Mrs. Brewer pulled her into a hug.

"Wow. I... sorry." Kayleigh sighed. "It's just a silly story. Didn't think anyone would take it so seriously."

Mrs. Brewer patted the younger woman on the shoulder. "Don't you worry about it. Sophia's a bit on the delicate side."

The two scout-leader-moms and counselor Kayleigh walked Sophia back to the camp, pausing outside the bunk cabin to look her over more thoroughly under a flashlight. They insisted she go with them to the nurse's station. Once there, Sophia quietly tolerated being wiped down and having her cuts and scrapes treated with alcohol, peroxide, and a couple Band-Aids. While the nurse fixed her up, Mrs. Brewer and Mrs. Whitaker talked outside the door, likely unaware she could hear them. They agreed a kid wouldn't flee into the pitch-black woods at night to the point they banged themselves up so much without being genuinely terrified of something. Mrs. Whitaker even suggested perhaps Sophia might be 'too delicate' to sleep away from home for a whole week.

Hearing that set off an explosion of hope and guilt. While she'd *adore* being able to go home early, leaving would doom everyone here, including her two friends. Staying didn't guarantee anything different. In fact, the wendigo might easily kill her, too.

Sophia trembled at the thought.

"Shh. It's okay, hon. You're safe. There's no such thing as Crazy Coleman." The nurse tended to a small cut in front of Sophia's left ear. "Only a story."

Darn. There's no way I can tell any of them the truth. They'll stop thinking I'm a wimp and start thinking I'm nuts. Maybe if

Coleman shows himself... Ugh. No. It still won't make them close the camp. I gotta do something.

The nurse finished cleaning her up in a few minutes. "You're okay, hon. Try not to think scary thoughts and get some sleep, okay?"

"Okay," mumbled Sophia at the floor.

Mrs. Brewer sent Mrs. Whitaker off to sleep, volunteering to walk Sophia to the bunk house.

Having an adult with a flashlight around made the midnight woods far less scary. Still, a long walk down a dirt path to the sleeping area sucked. At least *this* dirt happened to be relatively soft and free of rocks or roots. Before long, they arrived at the bunk house she'd been assigned to.

"You gonna be okay in there, dear?" Mrs. Brewer patted her back reassuringly. "If you're too wound up ta sleep here, there's a spare cot in my room."

"Thanks. I think I'm okay. Just a scary story." Sophia exhaled.

"All right, hon. Get some sleep."

Sophia pulled the door open and crept inside. Mrs. Brewer pointed the flashlight at the grey-painted ceiling so she could see her way back to her bunk. The other girls all appeared to be asleep. Someone had even put the screen back in. Her head swimming in fear, doubt, guilt, and frustration, Sophia trudged to her bunk and crawled under the covers. Klepto wriggled out from beside the pillow and curled up against her neck. Soon after she pulled the blanket up to her chin, Mrs. Brewer shut the door.

Barely two seconds after the room became dark, the bunk above her shifted. The bunk past her feet also squeaked. Nicole and Priya hadn't been sleeping after all.

"What the heck happened?" whispered Nicole, likely hanging her face over the side of the upper bunk.

"Yeah," whispered Priya.

"The ghost is real. He opened the door."

Neither girl replied. They both knew, or at least mostly believed, she could see ghosts. If any other girl in the room faked sleep to eavesdrop, they'd probably think her a scared little kid making up stories. It didn't matter if anyone overheard her. In two days, Sophia would either find a way to stop a wendigo or everyone here would be dead and unable to talk about secrets.

"The story's wrong," whispered Sophia. "Coleman isn't a bad guy."

"So why did you run?" asked Nicole.

"I didn't know that until he caught me." Sophia snugged the blankets tighter to her chin. "He died trying to stop a monster. It's back, too. He came here to warn me."

"What are you saying?" Priya's whispery voice shook. "Monsters now? Ghosts aren't bad enough?"

"It's a wendigo. It killed Coleman and those college students. Now it's waking up and it's gonna come after us."

"You best be makin' crap up," whispered Shante, Mrs. Brewers' daughter.

"I'm not. Sorry."

"Why didn't you tell the moms?" asked Nicole.

Sophia sighed. "Because they would think I'm crazy. Oh, Mrs. Brewer, Mrs. Whitaker, you have to close the camp down and send us all home or everyone's gonna die because there's a monster in the forest."

"You are right," said Priya. "That does sound crazy."

"Worse, they might send me home thinking I'm 'too delicate' for camp. Then everyone else is in big trouble."

Nicole let out a long sigh. "Maybe you *are* too delicate for camp. Sorry for making you go. I should've known better than to ask a kid who's too scared to watch *Troll* to go camping in the woods."

"That one's scary!" whisper-whined Sophia.

A few girls chuckled.

"You had a nightmare," said Shante. "Ain't no wendigo out there gonna eat us."

Sophia bit her lip. "I didn't say eat. Dunno what it's gonna do. Just kill us."

"Wow. Never saw you lie before." Nicole whistled.

"I'm not lying."

Nicole snickered. "I mean, to the moms. You didn't tell them about the wendigo."

"The truth sounds nuts."

"What are you going to do?" Priya clicked on a blanket-covered flashlight. It gave off enough light to see her face without disturbing anyone trying to sleep. She looked terrified.

Sophia snuggled her kitten close. "Not sure. Still thinking. Cell phones don't work out here. It's at least an hour drive to civilization. Can't call for help in time to matter, and it's not like anyone would believe me, anyway."

The mystics would. Maybe they can help... but I can't call them.

"Yeah," said Nicole, her voice a resigned exhale. "So, are you saying we're gonna die and there's nothing we can do?"

"Can we run away?" asked Priya.

"I dunno. Not in the dark." Sophia squirmed as all of her little scratches and scrapes decided to sting at the same time. "Too dangerous. There's, umm... no one who can really help us fast enough to make a difference. I gotta do this myself."

"Go to sleep," muttered Hadley. "Some of us are trying to sleep and don't believe in ghost stories."

She pondered sending Klepto off in search of Sarah, but the kitten couldn't magically find her the same way she located needed objects. She'd have to teleport to places Sarah might be in hopes of finding her there. Last Sophia heard, Wolent gave her sister some sort of job. No doubt she'd drop everything and come running if Sophia's life was in danger.

It might make the other vampires angry with her. She didn't want her big sis to get in trouble, especially with vampires. Writing a note asking for help that Klepto took to the mystics sounded like a reasonable option. Cell phone reception didn't matter to teleporting kitten familiars.

"I gotta do this," whispered Sophia, more to convince herself of it.

"Tomorrow." Nicole flopped back up onto her bunk.

"Time is short." Coleman appeared, standing beside the bed, making Sophia jump. "But it is safe to wait until morning. The wendigo will not fully wake tonight and the fiend *will* be weaker during the day... a fact I learned too late."

"Too late?" whispered Sophia.

"After I died."

"Oh, yeah. That is a bit late."

"Mmmn," moaned McKenzie. "Please go to sleep."

"Sorry." Sophia curled up on her side, clutching Klepto.

Tomorrow, she'd probably confront a wendigo and still had no idea what it was or how to fight it. She did, however, know one thing for sure: there wouldn't be much sleep for her tonight.

ALWAYS TAKES A FEW TRIES

T he boys retreated from the subzero wind blasting across the cave mouth.

Sam covered his face in both hands, waiting for his nose to thaw. His friends stood around him, shivering. T-shirts, jeans, and sneakers did *not* work for the deep Arctic.

"So cold." Darryl's teeth chattered.

"I bet if we peed, ice cubes would hit the ground." Jordan breathed into his hands to warm them.

"No way." Ronan shook his head. "It would break off in our hand."

"Dude." Sam rolled his eyes. "It's not liquid nitrogen cold out there. Body parts don't start snapping off until you're like negative two hundred degrees."

"I don't care." Jordan shuffled around. "Fix it before we freeze to death."

"Oops," muttered Blix. "Trying again."

The imp stretched his arms out. An expression of sublime contentment spread over his face, part meditating Buddhist monk, part baby loading a diaper.

Howling wind outside stopped.

"Something happened," said Sam. "It's quiet out there now. No more blizzard."

Ronan reached toward the cave opening. "Feels warmer."

Sam waited for Blix to leap up onto his back, then made his way up the cave to the opening. Woods outside looked promising. The trees didn't contain a rotting old missile carrier, angry soldiers, nor epic amounts of snow.

"I think he did it," said Darryl.

"Hang on." Sam pulled his phone out. It got signal. Hopeful, he opened maps. Current location showed him right where he wanted to be, a little under a quarter mile from home. Surprisingly, the time showed at three minutes to seven. It really felt as if they'd been gone longer. "Blix?"

"Hmm?"

"Did we experience time wonkiness?"

"No. Just human time wonkiness."

"Huh?" Sam looked at the imp on his shoulder, almost touching noses. "Human time wonkiness?"

"Yep." Blix grinned. "Do fun, time go fast. Do scary, time crawl."

"Oh. Yeah. I hate that." Sam stuffed his phone back in his pocket. "Guys, it's almost seven. We're late for dinner."

"Crap!" chorused Darryl and Jordan at the same time.

The boys' phones exploded with text message pings.

"Guys," said Sam. "Official story is we lost cell signal in the cave and didn't realize what time it was. Parents are gonna see message delivery failures, so they'll know we aren't lying about not getting the messages when they were sent."

His friends nodded.

"Gotta go!" Darryl ran off.

"Me too." Jordan sprinted in a different direction.

Sam started walking home. "Blix? Has this cave always been a gateway?"

"Mmm." Blix shrugged. "Mystics probably did enchantment long, long time ago. So long, called shamans. Native people."

"Is it gonna open on its own and let stuff in?" Sam peered back over his shoulder at the no-longer-innocent cave. Too many Eighties movies made him worry the Russians had psychic spies who might come to check out the cave based on the soldiers telling the commander the boys had simply vanished. Then, the Russians could invade the USA. "Like bad guys?"

"Nah. Magic old, weak. Only demon can make it work. Humans need to have shaman come back and do ritual magic to recharge it before they can use it."

"Cool."

"Nice," said Ronan, after Sam translated.

The boys headed out of the forest straight to Sam's backyard. Max the hellhound reclined in the grass by the fence in his usual spot, peaceful and content. To anyone else, the creature would've given off a dire aura of dread. Sam found his presence comforting. If Sarah accidentally pissed off some vampires, they'd have a super hard time getting past Max.

Sam headed up the deck stairs. Mom sat at the table staring into space. Her expression meant one of three things. One: Dalton came over and put her on pause. Two: Dad attempted some manner of home repair again. Three: supernatural events occurred in excess of her ability to tolerate or process.

"Mom?" asked Sam, pulling the door open.

A waft of chicken pasta hit him in the face, causing an instant growl from his stomach.

"Where have you been?" asked Mom.

"I'm not exactly sure." Sam walked through the kitchen to the hall. "Be right back. Need bathroom bad."

"Hi, Mrs. W. Bye, Mrs. W." Ronan waved, and hurried upstairs with Blix to use the mirror to get home. He lived too far away to walk or even ride a bike.

Sam washed his hands, used the toilet, then washed his hands again before returning to the kitchen. "Sorry I'm late for dinner. Is there any food left?"

"Of course." Mom got up to fix him a plate. "Where were you and why do you have a filthy rag tied around your head?"

"Somewhere in Eastern Europe." Sam pulled the rag off, grinning. "It was epic. Headband is a requirement."

She shook her head. "You are definitely your father's son. Are you pulling my leg?"

"Nope. Blix accidentally opened a gate in the cave we always go to. We would have been back earlier, but some soldiers thought we worked for the CIA and tried to kidnap us, but we got away."

Mom set the plate down beside the stove, then leaned on the counter as if she'd fall over without the support. "Accidentally?"

"Yeah. He didn't know it would happen. His just being there made it happen."

Sam stared ravenously at the plate of chicken pasta Mom carried over and set in front of him. Only, he didn't dig in right away. As soon as his gaze followed the plate down to the table, he noticed a pair of action figures looking at him. One resembled Sierra—except for being in a pink dress—the other looked like Dad in an Army uniform from a long time ago. The sight would have been weird enough if the action figures *weren't* moving.

Micro-Sierra leaned against Dad, both hands on her stomach like she'd recently eaten too much. Dad appeared similarly overstuffed.

"Umm, Mom?" Sam pointed. "Is... that...?"

"Yes. Something about goblins." Mom flopped in her chair, braced her elbows on the table, and grabbed her face in both hands.

Sierra squeaked at him.

"Huh?" Sam leaned closer.

"I said," shouted a tiny chipmunk voice, "if you put me in one of your toys and fly it around, I'm gonna be mad at you."

"Oh." Sam stuck his fork into dinner, gathering chicken and noodles. "Okay. I won't."

Watching his sister, not much bigger than a GI Joe guy, pace back and forth on the table looking thoroughly furious, caused Sam to laugh.

"Stop laughing at me!" yelled Sierra. "The goblins can shrink you, too."

"There's goblins in the house?" asked Sam.

"I haven't seen anything unusual." Mom sat up straight, then sighed. "Except for all the cats."

"Cats?" Sam blinked.

"Yes." Mom pointed at an orange tabby relaxing on the floor by the garbage can. "There are a ton of stray cats outside."

Sam spotted two lounging on the back of the sofa down the hall in the living room. "They're inside."

"I think Klepto brought reinforcements," chirped Sierra. "Mom, can we tolerate the cats being around for a while? The goblins are scared of them."

Sam giggled.

"Grr!" She shook her fist at him.

"Sorry…" Sam covered his mouth until the urge to laugh weakened enough to resist. "Your voice sounds so squeaky."

Dad smiled in a 'notice I haven't opened my mouth yet' way.

"Fine." Mom sighed. "But how in the heck do we get you two back to rights?"

"We wait for the mystics to respond to the voicemail I left," said Dad.

His chirpy voice sent Sam into another laughing fit.

"Yeah, yeah..." Dad waved. "Yuk it up."

"Dad." Sam snickered. "They probably didn't understand you and think a mouse left them a prank voicemail."

Mom chuckled. "I left the voicemail for that exact reason."

"If they don't call back before Blix returns from taking Ronan home, I'll ask him to go annoy them until someone calls." Sam stuffed a forkful of dinner into his mouth.

"Good idea," said Mom. "Wish I could do that to opposing counsel sometimes. Drives me nuts when they deliberately refuse to return calls or emails until the last minute."

Sam blinked. *Wow. Mom's really stressed out.* "I'll get the dishes tonight."

She stared at him as if she'd forgotten entirely about the mess lurking behind her, then smiled. "I'd really appreciate that."

"So..." Dad walked up to his plate. "Did you say Eastern Europe? See anything cool? I, uhh, notice you didn't forget the headband."

"It's important."

"Good boy." Dad folded his arms, beaming. "I'm proud of you."

"Don't encourage him," muttered Mom, though Sam couldn't tell if she said it as a joke or really meant it.

He decided not to mention the helicopter shooting at them. Mom couldn't handle something like that right now. Except for the Hind opening fire, he more or less told them the truth. Mom stared at him, horrified. Dad appeared torn between thrilled and freaked out. Sierra didn't show much emotion, nor did she say anything. However, the look she gave him had a distinct quality of frustration, like she wanted real bad to protect him but couldn't do anything.

Dad's cell phone erupted with *Don't You Forget About Me*, his ringtone song.

Mom scrambled to grab it. "It's him…" She swiped at the screen. "Hello? Yes. Right, well, it's… a bit difficult to explain. Do you have a few minutes?" She paused. "No, she's away at Girl Scout Camp. They're saying goblins did it, I think. Not really sure. Oh, that's wonderful of you. Thank you."

Everyone stared at her as she hung up.

"Mr. Anderson is on his way here now." Mom slumped over the table, relieved.

"Cool." Sam scarfed down the last of his dinner, then got started on the dishes.

25

COMPANY

My night sucks.

The Odd Sisters hang out with me on the rooftop for a little while before deciding they have better things to do than watch me watch the old theater. Soon after I'm alone, I send the obligatory text messages. One to the parents to let them know everything is more or less fine. I'm not in danger, hurt, or running away—merely busy with a job that's running long. Next one goes to the Wolent contact number to provide an update.

I advise whoever handles the mobile account of the sword's status. At present, recovery would require a direct frontal assault against somewhere between twelve and twenty vampires, all of whom are most certainly older than me. If Wolent wants heads kicked in, he'll need to send the guys here. However, I also mention my plan: wait until tomorrow afternoon and sneak in there during the day. I'm like the annoying little kid who doesn't pick fights unless their older sibling is holding the other kid down while they hit them. In this case, my older sib is the sun and I have no intention to hit anyone.

My guess is sending the brute squad to Olympia would ruffle some political feathers, so Wolent isn't going to go to such a length when a better option remains on the table. I briefly apologize for this taking so long, hint that 'unusual circumstances' are to blame and everything will be explained in detail once I'm back.

Next few texts go to Hunter, Ashley, and Michelle. Gotta do something while sitting here. My friends' and boyfriend's lives appear to be going on normally without me. Wait, that sounds melodramatic. We're college-aged and they have jobs, yes, but it's not like they're burdened down with spouses and kids and whole lives where they can't take two hours out of one weekend a month to hang out with people they knew in high school.

Mom, I'm looking at you.

She hasn't really spent time with her friends in… well… since I was like seven. It's nice being free of that trap in a way. I'll always be able to pop in randomly to visit Ashley or Michelle no matter how busy their lives get. My time will be wide open, free of the demands of a day job, career, spousal obligations, or children. Right now, it feels awesome and liberating. Could always adopt if ever the urge for kids happens, but it might not. Professor Heath telling me a vampire's personality freezes during the Transference implies my outlook on existence is permanently that of a just-out-of-high-school eighteen-year-old.

No sane kid my age—except Ashley—wants kids or a family. And even Ashley knows she needs to wait until she gets herself established before spawning.

The only real downer about becoming a vampire is knowing everyone I love will die, and I'm gonna be here watching them creep along into old age and oblivion. Doesn't have to happen, though. Could spread the vampire love. Ugh. Bad Sarah. Seriously, though. I'm just having idle nonsense thoughts. Hunter's the only one in my close orbit who's open to the idea of becoming a vampire, too. And hey, ghosts are a thing, right? People I care about could stick around if they wanted to.

Yeah, I totally get why vampires normally distance themselves from society and pretend to die. It's stupid though. And selfish. All it does is make the loss happen right away—and make the family go through hell. Like, if I hadn't gone home, my family would all be messed up *and* I wouldn't see them anymore, which is the exact same thing as them growing old and dying. At least this way, *they* aren't forced to deal with the sadness of my death and I get a bunch of decades before I have to suffer the loss I'd have felt anyway.

So, yeah. Good choice.

Sarah happy again.

I sit like a gargoyle watching the theater for hours. Yes, it's damned boring. Fortunately, Dieter doesn't leave with the sword nor does anyone arrive for a visit. About thirty minutes before sunrise, I figure it's safe to leave. He won't be doing anything this close to dawn. If he's made any arrangements to bring the sword somewhere, it's not going down until tomorrow night.

My more immediate problem is finding somewhere to be before the ball of nope is in the air. First things first, though. I fly back to my car and move it out of downtown to a residential area where it won't get ticketed, towed, or stolen. Hey, someone out there might be desperate enough to take a ten-year-old Nissan.

I park under some trees in a quiet little neighborhood with about fifteen minutes left before sunrise. The lights are on in a house three away from my car. Hmm. Works for me. Any port in a storm, right? Cutting it close already.

A sweet-looking elderly woman answers when I ring the

bell. She's gotta be over eighty and looks like she's just itching to give me cookies and tea.

"Hello, dear. You're up awfully early."

"Yeah…"

"Do I know you? You're not my granddaughter, are you?"

Aww. Damn. I feel horrible now. Wait, no… she doesn't have dementia. She knows I'm not familiar and is afraid she *might* be developing Alzheimer's or something because the only young girl she can think of who would show up at her house—especially at such a crazy early hour—is her granddaughter and I'm not her. She's worried she's failing to recognize me.

"No, ma'am. You don't know me." I point to one side. "My car just stopped running. Saw your lights on and was hoping I could use your phone." Wow, Sarah. Lame. Like everyone in the world doesn't have a cell phone. Someone's been watching too many old movies.

Despite being sweet, the woman hesitates. She suspects something's a little off, even if I look too innocent to be part of some nefarious deed. Can't blame her. The 'need to use your phone' line is gallingly stupid.

Heck with it. No time. I charm her into inviting me in. No, she doesn't *have* to. I'm not going to spontaneously melt if I barge in uninvited. Vampires don't work that way. Still, just being nice here. The house smells like toast and coffee. Guessing she hasn't been up for too long. Wow. Early riser. Once the door's shut behind me, I encourage the woman to believe I'm volunteering with a project to visit old people and give them a little company… and she doesn't need to worry about where I am, then cram myself into the closet of her guest bedroom—the nearest windowless space most likely to remain undisturbed for a day.

Good thing it doesn't matter how soft or hard my 'bed' is. Closet floors aren't the most comfortable places to crash.

They're one step down from the sketchy motel next to a gas station by a major interstate in the middle of nowhere a person goes to at two in the morning after the seventh time nearly falling asleep behind the wheel has caused an accident. Much like that motel, this closet is a hasty choice made with no better alternatives.

At least it's free.

26

BENDING BAD

S ophia stared at the empty paper plate on the table in front of her.

She'd somehow managed to fall asleep since the night didn't feel as if it took forever. Klepto purring against her chest probably helped. Being dragged out of bed in the morning stank. By the time she'd finished changing into the Girl Scout uniform, she'd become awake enough to remember everything and fall into a deep pit of worry.

Surprisingly, smelling food chased away the sick feeling in her gut. The scrambled eggs, veggie sausages, and shredded potatoes hadn't stood a chance. Nicole and Priya sat on either side of her in the cafeteria, both of them still finishing up their food.

"Kinda stupid of them taking us canoeing right after breakfast." Nicole wagged a fork-impaled sausage in the air. "What if someone gets sick?"

"We're not going straight into the boats. It's gonna be like an hour or two of teaching stuff before we even touch a canoe," said Priya. "There are over 200 girls here and only twenty-four canoes. Our group is going first or second in the water."

Nicole ate the bit of sausage, then glanced at Sophia. "If you're scared, just say something. They won't force you to go in the boat."

All things being normal, going canoeing didn't rank on the top 1,000 activities Sophia would choose to do. She didn't fear it since she loved to swim—in nice pools, not freezing cold rivers. It simply didn't sound fun. People long ago used canoes because they didn't have cars or needed to travel long distances down rivers.

"I'm not scared. It's just, bleh." She swished her fork back and forth across the crumb remains of her breakfast. Here it was, the moment Sophia Wright deliberately defied all the rules and did something wrong. Innocent girl breaking bad. Granted, she wouldn't be making and selling industrial quantities of meth, so perhaps she didn't 'break bad' as much as 'bent bad.' "Not going canoeing. Gonna sneak off and try to stop the wendigo."

"No way." Nicole grabbed her arm. "You're not going alone."

Priya stared at Nicole. Her face said 'she can totally go alone,' but after a few seconds, she swallowed and whispered, "Yeah. We're going with you."

"You guys should stay here." Sophia put her arms around both friends, pulling them closer. "There's nothing you can do about it but get hurt. I don't want you to get hurt."

"Nope." Nicole shook her head. "We are not going to let you run off alone. The monster isn't the only thing. What if you fall in a hole or wolves show up or you get lost? Buddy system, remember? No one goes anywhere alone."

Priya furrowed her brows. "The wolves around here aren't known to be a threat to people. Besides, I'm good with animals."

"Just saying." Nicole shrugged. "Might be wolves out there."

"Not afraid of animals." Sophia smiled. "They won't hurt me. Seriously guys, this isn't a normal situation. Wait here."

"Nope." Nicole pointed her plastic fork at Sophia's face. "If you try to go alone, we're gonna tell on you."

Sophia sighed at the ceiling. "You wouldn't."

"Totally would... for your own good." Nicole dropped the fork and grabbed her arm. "Seriously. Don't go alone."

"Forget it." Priya nodded toward Mrs. Whitaker. "We're not going to be able to go anywhere without getting in trouble."

Sophia sighed. Taking her friends with her into the woods to hunt a wendigo and stop it from waking up sounded like an exceptionally bad, reckless, dumb idea. Neither Nicole nor Priya truly understood the seriousness. They hadn't seen the jar spirit, brownies, leprechauns, or those creepy-as-hell dark dryads. The world had a whole host of horrible things most people couldn't handle seeing at all, much less trying to fight.

However, even if her friends couldn't do squat to the wendigo, not being alone would make her feel a thousand times better. She had trouble calling on her magic if she became too frightened to concentrate, so in an indirect way, Nicole and Priya might help defeat the monster. Also, if they did tell on her and the counselors found her before she got to the wendigo, it effectively killed everyone here.

No choice.

"Okay. And don't worry about sneaking away." Sophia cracked her knuckles. "I got it covered."

Her friends exchanged an 'I'll believe that when I see it' glance, then resumed finishing off their breakfast. Sophia wrote a brief note on a napkin:

Ghost said a wendigo is going to attack us. It was sleeping for a long time and isn't all the way awake yet. What is a wendigo and how do I stop it? Answer fast, please. I'm going after it in about twenty minutes.

She rolled the napkin up. Klepto took it in her mouth, emitted a muffled, "Mew," then teleported away to the mystics... or at least the lodge. Hopefully, someone would be there.

Sophia bided her time until the scout leaders and counselors gathered the kids from the tables, arranging everyone outside based on troops in preparation of the hike to the lakeshore.

"Here goes. Stay quiet and close to me," whispered Sophia.

Nicole and Priya raised eyebrows at her but said nothing.

Concentrating on her desire to use magic, Sophia extended her arms out in front. She pictured herself and her friends becoming inconspicuous, unnoticeable. She envisioned Mrs. Brewer and Mrs. Whitaker assuming Sophia, Nicole, and Priya were among the group even though they wouldn't be. She held the idea at the tip of her mind that none of the other girl scouts in their troop would notice them missing. No one would wonder where they went. Sophia, Priya, and Nicole would always seem to be somewhere in peripheral vision.

A tingle ran down her body from forehead to the tips of her toes.

She let her arms fall at her sides.

"Nothing happened," said Nicole.

"Are you trying to do like the Jedi?" Priya covered her mouth to mute a giggle.

"Nope. Magic, not the Force." Sophia glanced around. No one appeared to be looking at her. "I think it worked."

"Yeah, sure it did." Nicole folded her arms.

"I'm going. If no one yells at me, it worked. Stay close."

Sophia walked away from her troop toward the middle of camp and the dirt path leading to the bunk houses.

Nicole and Priya followed, initially shaking their heads in disbelief. Priya kept looking back as if expecting someone to call after them at any second... but no one did. When they'd walked fifty feet or so away and *still* had no one yell at them to come back, Nicole's attitude shifted to mildly freaked out awe.

"I don't believe this," whispered Priya. "They are just letting us go away? Do they think we're needing the bathroom?"

"No. They think we're still there." Sophia swallowed a ball of nervousness.

"Cool. How did you do that?" Nicole gawked.

"Magic. And, umm, it's kinda cool, but kinda bad. If something happens to us, no one's going to start looking for at least four hours. Last chance to change your mind and go back."

"No way." Nicole took her hand. "You are not equipped to be alone in the woods."

"I don't feel equipped to be alone in the woods either," said Priya. "But the three of us should be all right."

Hope so.

Sophia led them along past the empty bunkhouses. A crumbling wooden barrier attempted to block the end of the trail. It appeared to be a single segment of ranch fence that would've been easy enough to walk around if not for the wild undergrowth surrounding it. Something felt wrong in the air up ahead. After a momentary pause to search for the courage necessary to continue, Sophia gingerly climbed over the rotting fence.

"I wanna slap whoever decided the uniform should have skirts." Sophia threw a leg over the top railing.

"Right?" Priya chuckled. "Kind of stupid if you ask me."

"What else are *girls* supposed to wear?" asked Nicole in a sarcastic voice.

Priya and Sophia chorused, "Ugh."

She jumped down behind the barrier, then checked her hands for splinters.

Priya's skirt snagged on the fence. She appeared to make a split-second choice between landing on her face or staying upright and allowing the old wood to tear the garment off her, opting for the face plant. Sophia and Nicole reacted at the same time, crashing into each other in their effort to catch their friend. Though they bonked heads, they successfully stopped her fall.

"Thanks." Priya lay draped sideways across their arms. "Stupid fence."

They set her back on her feet, helped dust her off, then resumed walking.

"Where is it?" asked Nicole.

"Umm." Sophia looked around at the woods, realizing she hadn't even thought about direction, merely started going. "Not exactly sure. I think I'm sensing it or something."

About a minute after passing the fence, they reached an area with six huge cabins standing three on either side of a faintly visible suggestion of an old footpath. These cabins looked more like single-story houses in terms of size and because they had porches. None of them appeared to be even remotely usable thanks to massive holes in their roofs, broken out windows, even trees apparently growing inside them.

"What is this place?" whispered Priya.

"It's the old Girl Scout labor camp where we'd spend twelve hours a day chained to a workstation making cookies," Nicole deadpanned. "These are the original bakery prisons."

Sophia might have laughed if not for being terrified about

facing a wendigo... but the frightened look on Priya's face pushed her over the edge into giggling. "She's kidding. The scouts don't do that. It's Sierra's joke."

"Oh. Right." Priya coughed, trying to pretend she hadn't taken Nicole seriously. "What are they really, though? It's kind of scary here."

"Looks like vacation cabins. People probably rented them for a week." Nicole spun around in a 360 as she walked. "Wonder if this is where those college students were staying when they died?"

"Eep!" yelled Priya. "Why did you say that?"

Sophia cringed, not wanting to think about it.

"Are you sure we're going the right way?" Nicole sighed. "We are *so* going to get lost."

Sophia scanned their surroundings. "Mr. Coleman? Are you here?"

"Stop it," hissed Priya.

"I'm not trying to scare you." Sophia kneaded her hands. "I'm really looking for the ghost."

Coralie had been kind enough to reveal herself to Nicole, Priya, and Megan not too long ago. It seemed both a good idea and reasonably safe. Rumors going around about Sophia Wright claiming to be able to contact ghosts didn't in any way involve the existence of vampires and wouldn't threaten Sarah's secrecy. Lots of people claimed to be able to see and talk to ghosts. They even had TV shows about it. *Most* people didn't believe them. The same 'most people' would roll their eyes at Sophia or her friends, too.

"He's real..." Priya gulped.

"Yes, but he's not like the story said. The monster killed him, then killed the college students." Sophia sighed. "He's just an old guy who lived alone in the woods and tried to help."

"I don't regret it," said Coleman.

"Gah!" Sophia jumped, clutching her heart.

Her shriek made the other two girls yell.

Priya rasped 'stop it!' repeatedly while swatting at Sophia's arm. Nicole merely stood still, mouth open, hand pressed to her chest.

"Sorry." Sophia glanced to her left at the spirit. During the day, he didn't look too much different from an ordinary person except for being transparent. Evidently, the sickly green glow only happened at night. "Mr. Coleman is here."

The old guy smiled at her. "Coleman's my first name, hon. S'okay fer ya ta call me that. Or Mr. Emerson if ya wanna be over polite."

"Can you please let my friends see you? They've seen spirits before."

Nothing visible happened, though Priya gasped and jump-clung to Nicole.

"Okay." Nicole appeared to calm down. "For a sec there, I thought you might be playing a trick on us. And... crap!"

Sophia blinked. "What's wrong?"

"Coleman is real." Nicole fidgeted. "That means the wendigo is real."

"Been tellin' ya." Coleman shook his head.

"Umm." Sophia looked down. "Can I ask you a bad question?"

He chuckled. "Can ask anything ya like. Might not answer it though."

"*How* does a wendigo kill people? What does it do?"

Coleman cringed. "Threw me around inta trees a couple times, broke a bone or six. Jumped on me. Last I remember is me heart gettin' all cold like. Then felt all sorts o' strange. Like it squeezed me up into a little wad and pulled me outta my own nose."

"Eww," said Nicole.

"One o' them college kids saw the damn thing. Shot it in

the ass. Err, butt. Sorry. Y'all too young fer language like that."

Sophia waved dismissively. "I've heard bad words before. I don't use them, but they don't make me cry."

"Everything else does." Nicole winked.

Sophia stuck out her tongue.

Priya continued staring at Coleman, her eyes the size of small moons.

"What happened next?" asked Nicole.

"Wendigo seemed ta get mad. Jumped offa me. Landed on him. Poor fella screamed somethin' fierce. It beat on him 'til he stopped movin, then all this weird light and stuff came outta the kid. Started turnin' inta I guess a ghost of him, but that damn wendigo ate it."

Sophia grimaced. It sounded as if the creature killed people in a relatively ordinary manner—beating them to death—then fed off their spirits. Made sense now why only Coleman remained haunting the woods. The college student interrupted it before it could finish devouring his ghost. It must've consumed the others.

"This way." Coleman headed off to the left a bit compared to the direction she'd been going.

"Wait... he's taking us *to* the monster?" asked Priya. "Shouldn't an adult be trying to stop us from going near something dangerous?"

Sophia stared down at where she stepped. Hiking shoes definitely made walking out in the woods much nicer. "It doesn't really matter. Camp isn't safe. The wendigo's gonna get us anyway unless we can talk Mrs. Cartwright into closing the camp and sending everyone home today."

"Yeah, that won't happen." Nicole laughed. "That woman would keep the camp open if four kids drowned in a tragic canoeing mishap."

"Ugh." Sophia shuddered. "Thanks. You just made sure I'm never going in a canoe."

"As if you'd have done it anyway." Nicole nudged her.

"I dunno. It didn't scare me before, just didn't sound fun." Sophia pointed into the trees. "My only chance to stop the monster is to find it *before* it's finished waking up."

Nicole stared at her for a few seconds, then put a hand to her forehead as if checking for a fever. "Are you still Sophia?"

"Yes."

"Okay, so the girl so scared of camp she almost didn't get off the bus is—*on purpose*—going *to* the lair of a deadly monster?"

Priya sighed. "Why do you have to say it like that?"

Sophia clamped her eyes shut, trying to resist the terror gnawing at her spine. This thing couldn't be worse than the jar spirit. Even if it turned out to be a little worse, she'd sent the jar spirit away fairly easily. The mystics already taught her how to banish evil spirits. It had to work on the wendigo, too.

"Can she actually stop this thing?" asked Nicole.

"Got a better chance than I did." Coleman chuckled. "Kid's got enough… something ta wake it up."

Nicole gave her side eye. "What did you do?"

"Nothing on purpose." Sophia swiped her hair off her face, tucking it behind her right ear. "I knew it was a bad idea to go camping."

Priya laughed. "You think this wendigo thing is going to kill everyone because you went to camp? That's kinda stupid."

"No. It woke up because it sensed me here." Sophia sent out a mental ping, asking Klepto to hurry up and come back. She needed something soft, warm, and fuzzy to squeeze. "It smells my magic or something and probably wants it."

"Magic now?" Nicole whistled.

"Not to say something too stupid here, but…" Priya held up a finger. "We did just walk away from camp and no one noticed or yelled at us."

Nicole pondered for a moment. "Yeah, but that doesn't necessarily prove *magic* happened. The adults could have been distracted and just not noticed us."

"McKenzie didn't yell at us and tell her mother we tried to sneak away." Priya folded her arms.

"Ooh." Nicole winced. "Okay, yeah. You're right. Definitely magic."

Sophia almost chuckled. Any opportunity McKenzie Whitaker could take to kiss up to her mom or the other scout leaders, she jumped on and reveled in the 'glory.' Sarah called herself Follows Rules Girl, but McKenzie elevated the concept to a new level. They also came from two totally different directions. Sarah felt horrible doing bad stuff and didn't want to hurt or bother anyone. She also didn't often get in anyone else's face if *they* broke rules. McKenzie demanded rule following because she adored 'bringing rule breakers to justice'.

"I wish I had my dad's gun," said Nicole after a few minutes of wordless hiking.

Priya gasped. "Guns are bad! And it wouldn't help. That one boy shot the wendigo and it didn't do anything."

"Sure it did." Coleman chuckled. "Made the beast leave me be and go after him."

"That's even worse than nothing!" Priya flailed her arms.

"So? If it's about to eat Sophia's face off, I can maybe distract it," said Nicole.

"And have it eat *your* face off?" Priya cringed.

"No. I'm not a stupid college boy." Nicole shrugged. "I wouldn't stand there staring at it."

Sophia mulled, thinking of Klepto. "I can maybe arrange that. Do you know how to use a gun?"

Nicole nodded.

"No. No. No." Priya shook her head so hard her hair flew around like a troll pencil. "We are way too young to handle firearms."

Coleman glanced over at them. "I gotta side with your friend on this one, kiddo. Gun won't help ya much."

"Okay." Sophia exhaled, somewhat relieved. Admittedly, she didn't share Priya's complete fear of guns, but also thought it dangerous for kids their age to have one in the absence of an adult. Mom would completely flip if she ever found out.

"Yanno," said Coleman. "The other two really ought to stay back at camp. They ain't gonna be much use against the wendigo. Just get themselves kilt."

"They are helping." Sophia squeezed Nicole's hand. "I'm too scared to go alone."

"Y'ain't alone, kiddo." The ghost smiled, frizzing up his beard. "I'm wit' ya. Yer friends are only gonna get hurt. You don' wan' that, do ya?"

Sophia sighed, shaking her head. "No. Not at all. I told them to stay but they wouldn't… and sometimes, my magic doesn't work too well if I'm scared. Hey… how do I know you're not trying to lure me into a trap? Is there really a wendigo?"

Coleman regarded her with an impressed look. "A fair question. I am not leading you to a trap. We *are* going to a dangerous place wit' a good chance you get hurt. Maybe kilt. But I think ya kin maybe send the fiend back where it belongs. Don' much matter. You stay at camp, yer gon' die anyway. I get what it sounds like, me tryin' ta get ya alone and all. Just thinkin' these two girls don' need ta be out here. You wan' them to come, go right ahead. Don' say I didn't warn ya if they get hurt."

"If we're going to die anyway, what difference does it make?" Nicole flapped her arms.

Coleman stared at her. "Yah. Good point. C'mon then."

They walked, following the ghost for a little over twenty minutes before Klepto appeared in a purple flash a few feet away from Sophia. Nicole and Priya stopped short, gazing at the spot as if they'd noticed the unusual light but not the kitten.

Sophia stooped to pick Klepto up and hugged her.

"Mrrrp," said Klepto.

"Huh?" Sophia held the furball up to look at her. She had a tiny scroll in her mouth.

"Oh!" Sophia set the kitten on her shoulder and took the scroll, opening it as fast as she could get her shaking fingers under control.

Sophia, we have little information on wendigos as the creatures are native to the Americas. Most of our lore is from the Old World. We do know they are incorporeal entities that possess and mutate a human being. They often prey on those who spend long periods of time alone in the wilderness. At first, the victim experiences violent insanity, which can last for years. Eventually, they die and the wendigo consumes their body, changing it and becoming something neither man nor spirit. Our records offer conflicting explanations of the creatures' feeding habits. Some mention cannibalism, others describe soul consumption, not the eating of flesh. Apologies if this is somewhat graphic for you. We are unfamiliar with any concept of them going into hibernation or slow awakening. Best guess is it ran out of victims and, rather than starve, became dormant. Our opinion is that such a process could leave the creature weakened and vulnerable, stuck between planes. Optimally, you should avoid the beast entirely. If this is not possible, direct your focus on evicting it from this plane rather than destroying it. Ordinarily, confronting such an entity would require at least a week's preparation. However, you are not a ritualist as are we.

Spontaneous magic is not our area of mastery. As you are still a child, our recommendation is to flee if it is at all possible. If you are forced to confront the entity, do so with extreme caution.

— *Regards, Darren, Callum, and Landon.*

She read it twice before sighing and looking up at Coleman. "Please apologize."

The ghost blinked. "For?"

"I think you lied to me."

He tilted his head.

Nicole and Priya stared at each other, then her.

"I believe you tried to stop the wendigo, but not like you said." Sophia stuffed the mini-scroll into the pocket of her uniform shirt. "It was taking *you* over. You're the wendigo... or at least, your body is."

Coleman bowed his head.

"Umm." Nicole backed up. "Is this bad? Is he dangerous?"

"No. He's a ghost. The wendigo stole his body." Sophia tried unsuccessfully to hold the spirit's hand. "He's a victim, too. It made him go crazy... and maybe hurt some people. Then, it took his body and turned it into a monster."

Coleman fidgeted like a boy caught lying. "It's true. Didn't wanna say nothin' case you maybe got scared and ran off. I *did* try warnin' them college kids, but they didn't pay no attention to a ghost."

"So, the college guy didn't shoot in it the ass?" asked Nicole.

Priya blurted a giggle at hearing her friend swear.

"Nah. He shot it a bunch of times. Not in the butt." Coleman chuckled. "Didn't bother it. Gun ain't gonna do no good. I's long dead before them college kids showed up here. All them ghost stories ya hear 'bout me's from tryin' ta scare people away 'fore the wendigo gets 'em. Mebbe few from afore I died when I'd been mad, outta me right mind."

"Did you kill people?" asked Priya in a timid tone.

"Aye. Most after the damn wendigo took my sanity."

"Most?" Nicole raised an eyebrow.

"Yep." Coleman gave a dry, wheezy chuckle. "Others were bandits and such tryin' ta rob me."

"Oh." Nicole exhaled. "It's kinda weird talking to someone who's killed people, even if they had a good reason for it."

Sophia bit her lip. "Weirder than talking to a ghost?"

"Uhh." Nicole fidgeted. "Maybe?"

"Okay. This changes nothing." Sophia patted her shirt pocket. "Mr. Emerson's spirit isn't dangerous. He needs help. Sure, he *is* the wendigo, but it's not really him. It stole his body. Let's go."

Priya grabbed Sophia's shoulder. "Are you sure this isn't a trap?"

"Yeah." She resumed walking, following the ghost.

"What if he needs someone with magic to go to wherever it is so it can finish waking up?" Priya narrowed her eyes at the spirit. "You going there might be exactly what sets it loose to kill everyone."

Sophia stopped walking. *That* she hadn't considered. She looked up at the spirit's eyes. Desperation and longing saturated his features. He didn't *feel* evil... but her first, instinctual reaction to the sickly green-glowing spirit had been dread. Perhaps he pretended to be nice. The longer she stared at him now, the less she thought of him as a threat. Also, the mystics said a wendigo was a noncorporeal entity. They didn't have solid bodies, so needed to steal other people. She could totally sympathize, having suffered something similar. What her body did while the London mystics borrowed it had nothing to do with what *she* wanted to do. Some monster kicked Coleman out of his body. No... she trusted him. The little spark of violent glee in his eye came from hoping she could destroy the monster and give him the revenge he wanted so badly.

"I don't think so." Sophia exhaled. "I trust him."

"You're sure?" asked Nicole.

"Yeah. And if something weird happens, you guys are here to drag me out."

Coleman bowed to Sophia. "I give you my word that I mean you no harm. Can't say the same for my body, though. It's going to try to kill you."

"Yeah. Figured." Sophia let out a shuddering exhale. *How the heck are people in movies so brave? They do stuff like this all the time as if it's nothing.* She frowned to herself. *Because they're actors who know it isn't real.*

The ghost led them deeper into the woods for around another half hour before he came to a stop a short distance from a vine-shrouded cave opening in the side of a giant dirt cliff. A small stream burbled over some rocks near the entrance. Scraps of wood here and there plus a ring of stones suggested the area once served as a small campsite an extremely long time ago.

As soon as Sophia looked at the cave, every fiber of her being screamed at her to run away.

She sucked in a breath. "Eep. I think it's in there."

"Aye." Coleman gestured at the opening. "It is here the wendigo gathers its strength. By tomorrow night, it will cross back into this world and attack your camp. Right now, it's weak enough I think you can stop it."

Sophia clenched her hands into fists. Whenever Dad put on a scary movie, she usually ran upstairs. Whatever awaited them in the cave sounded worse than the 'tame' horror movies her father tried to get her to take a chance on. She couldn't run away from this. Her legs shook at the thought of going in, but having bad nightmares paled in comparison to how awful the guilt would be if everyone at the Girl Scout camp ended up dead.

"Are we really doing this?" whispered Priya.

"I have to." Sophia closed her eyes.

"Mew," said Klepto before purring and nuzzling against her neck.

"I can do it." She opened her eyes. "No choice. Failure is not an option. If I fail…"

"Our troop becomes a ghost story other kids tell to scare each other," deadpanned Nicole.

"I don't wanna be a ghost story," whispered Priya.

Nicole grabbed a branch from the ground to use as a staff. "I don't either."

"A stick? Really?" Priya stared at her.

"Beats not having a stick." Nicole hefted it. "Besides. This is a *big* stick."

Sophia approached the cave mouth. Palpable evil wafted from it like a chilly, humid breeze. Her mind teased her by imagining the air as wispy black vapors. Children often sensed the presence of malevolent spirits adults couldn't feel. Gifted people could sense ghosts. That she happened to be both a child *and* gifted ramped up the dread exponentially. Going into that cave terrified her. She felt like a girl about to be thrown into a volcano for a sacrifice, only one stupid enough to jump in by herself before the islanders could toss her.

No. It's trying to scare me. It's magic fear. Dark energy and I'm really sensitive. I might be a wimp, but I'm not a coward. She swallowed hard.

"I'm going in. Wait out here if you want." Sophia stepped past the opening into a wash of ice-cold air.

27

IT'S A NICE DAY FOR A... BIT OF LARCENY

I wake at 2:33 p.m. to the cacophony of a daytime television show's canned audience cheering.

Theologians have it wrong. Hell is not a physical location in another dimension. Hell is being stuck at home alone with no one to talk to while you're too old to drive and every channel is full of nothing but vapid talk shows and game shows broken up by infomercials pushing supplemental old person health insurance or dietary supplements.

There's a text waiting on my phone from Sam saying something 'super messed up' happened at home, followed by a bunch of laugh emojis and a line of like goblin faces. Oh, boy. I'm not sure I even want to know. Might explain the odd feeling from yesterday. At least he's laughing about it. Can't be too serious.

‹Acknowledged. Proceed› is the response from the Wolent number.

Hmm. The terseness makes me worry he's upset. It might only mean he saw no point to sending a long-winded reply. Not looking forward to the end-of-job meeting this time.

Hey, everyone new at their first real job screws up at least once, right? I'd say something like 'that's why entry level positions pay crap' but I'm not being paid at all. At least, not paid in money. And really, I haven't made an error yet. Dealing with Jake Warner and his wife doesn't count as an error unless you're a heartless douche. Even a vampire like Stefano would appreciate the need to not simply run off after Dieter. If for no other reason than keeping secrets, the situation couldn't be abandoned. Most likely, the ordinary authorities would've chalked it up to Jake snapping and going insane. Does not wanting him to be thought of as a crazed killer make me overly sensitive?

Anyway, even though my presence here had next to zero impact on the old woman, I feel a bit bad for barging into her home. Don't have the time right now, but I'm definitely going to come back here and visit her. Giving her a few hours of conversation and maybe some help cleaning around the place is the least I can do for borrowing her closet.

Her hearing doesn't seem to be the greatest. At least, it's my assumption since she's got the TV up so loud people driving by out front are bidding on prize packages. Contestants on the game show are all losing their minds. I don't get it. An entirely useless prize comes up for grabs like a pair of hideous chairs and a stereo cabinet—people flip out, screaming and jumping around like they won ten million dollars. Relax, people. It's only furniture.

She doesn't notice me creep past the archway to the living room and go out the front door.

I save a navigation point in my phone in order to find the house later, and hurry to the Sentra. Maybe I'm not completely an eighteen-year-old mentally. Having no choice but to drive annoys me. I *should* be thrilled to have a car to myself. Okay, to be fair, *any* teenager who can fly would think of driving as slow and annoying.

Right. Time to go steal a sword.

Or... get viciously shredded in the basement of an abandoned theater.

I love my dad, but sometimes, he gets on my nerves. He's the reason I spend the entire ride humming *White Wedding*. Yeah, it's a Billy Idol song. Not like Dad's a mega-fan, but his mix tapes have a few songs from the guy. No idea why he calls playlists 'mix tapes.' What the hell does tape have to do with music? Maybe when he was my age, he'd like write down the names of songs, cut them out, and tape them in order.

It's bad. *How* bad? I'm *still* mentally humming the song when I'm sneaking down the alley behind the old theater. Signs announcing the property is dangerous, condemned, and off limits are all over a 'temporary' chain link fence surrounding the place. It's temporary because the steel fence posts have feet and aren't drilled into the ground... but it also looks like it's been here for longer than I've been alive. This has to be a situation where vampire influence is preventing demolition or new construction. Dieter and his friends like crashing here, so they're probably making sure nothing happens to it for now.

This is me crapping a proverbial brick.

Follows Rules Girl has issues with breaking and entering. Vampire me is totally okay with what I'm about to do. The problem is... I'm offline. Can't fly over the fence, can't mind-control any cops or security guards who catch me sneaking into the property, and if I fall and impale myself on something, who knows what effect it will have.

Paradoxically, becoming a vampire has turned me into a chickenshit during the day. Nothing quite like immortality to make being vulnerable terrifying. Technically, I'm still a vampire... just all my immortal power is going to not catching fire right now. If I sustained a bad injury, my body would probably attempt to shift power to regeneration, thus taking it away from sun defense. Maybe I'd go up in flames and ash over instead of being stuck permanently maimed.

Joy.

Note to self: do not fall face-first onto exposed rebar.

Urban exploration can be dangerous, but it's usually not quite as dangerous as invading a lair of vampires. At least these guys aren't waging war on the elders of Seattle like Anselme Ernoul. If they catch me, I'm probably in for nothing worse than a light ass-kicking. Then again, non-Innocent vampires who wake up while the sun's out aren't in their right minds. It's about the same as sneaking up on a sleeping honey badger and poking it in the butt with a cattle prod.

I'm in the alley behind the theater because the street out front has traffic and pedestrians. Me climbing the fence or slipping through the gate and going up to the main entrance of a defunct theater would be the exact opposite of subtle. Someone would probably call the police, assuming me a vandal or maybe just an idiot YouTuber or Instagrammer.

Better not to be seen going in here at all.

Unfortunately, in the day, I'm no more equipped to do this kind of thing than an ordinary girl my age. No breaking annoying locks open or cheesing my way past a difficult climb using flight. Speaking of flying... at least now I know how spray-painted graffiti ends up on highway overpasses. It *has* to be vampires messing around.

Right. Enough procrastinating.

After a quick look left and right to make sure no one else is in the alley, I grab the green chain link and climb. It rattles and clatters as fences are wont to do. It's not the most stable thing in the world either, being 'temporary,' and it's like ten feet high. The only good part is there's no barbed wire. Reaching the top isn't too bad, but I kinda get stuck there, clinging to the fence and not being entirely sure how to go about getting to the other side without landing on my face.

Yeah, little bit of my old fear of falling is back.

I feel like a turkey some wiseass put on top of a pole that doesn't know how to get itself down. Is this why cats get stuck up trees? Climbing is easy, but as soon as they look down it's like 'oh em gee, what have I done?'

With a grunt, I try to get my left foot over the top of the wobbling fence, certain I'm seconds away from knocking the entire thing over and making a crapton of noise as the *entire* perimeter fence comes down like massive chain of dominoes. A fall from this height won't kill me. Might break my arm or cost me some teeth depending on how I land, but it won't be fatal. Nothing a little darkness won't fix in a few minutes. There's no logical reason for me to have vertigo paralysis up here.

Oof. Fence bit jabbed me in the thigh. Oh, that's uncomfortable. I'm about to become an internet fail meme like that poor little boy who tried to jump over a fence and wound up snagged and hanging by an atomic wedgie. Oh, power of flight, how I miss thee. Grr. I set my foot on top of the fence, throw caution to the wind, and heave myself over. Pretty sure people passing by out front notice the fence rattling as I crash against the inside face. I consider it a win since I am neither bleeding, dangling from my underwear, nor lying on the ground with a broken ankle.

Can't remember the last time I climbed a fence. Had to be like fifth grade.

Okay. I'm in. It's easy to drop to the ground in the lot behind the theater. It's not large, basically only a loading dock to receive shipments with a handful of parking spaces probably intended for the owner or big stars if they got any to show up. I scurry across the crumbling pavement and jump up to the loading dock, trying one door after the next. All are locked and too secure for mortal strength to dislodge.

Grr.

So close, yet so far.

I head around the left side of the building.

Hey little sister, something something something... it's a nice day for a... Dammit!

Billy Idol get out of my head.

The clunking of a steel door in the breeze distracts my brain from playing old music on loop. I almost end up jumping and carrying on like one of those contestants looking at ugly furniture on whatever game show the old woman had been watching. The sound leads me about a quarter of the way down the side of the theater to a blue door labeled 'staff only.'

Oops. Guess I'm breaking a rule.

I grab the edge, pull it open the rest of the way, and cringe at the run-down hallway in front of me. This is so totally a fire trap. What kind of idiot vampires *want* to be in this place? Well, thanks to the giant holes in the roof, everything here is damp and smells like wet dog. We aren't all that far away from Seattle. Perhaps a fire isn't really that much of a concern.

Invading this place is less nerve-wracking than the last time I snuck into a vampire lair. No huge firebomb is involved. My intentions here are harmless. Vampires have a weird ability to sense danger while asleep. It's not perfect, and depending on one's bloodline, sometimes they don't wake up until *after* the idiot rams a stake into the heart. Sucks to be them when they realize the stake thing doesn't work.

My having zero intention to harm any of the vampires here or cause property damage *should* prevent them from stirring due to supernatural senses.

The hallway leads me past several dressing rooms and costume storage areas. Fading signs on the walls point the way backstage, but the roof's collapsed in, blocking it off. It would take a construction crew—and heavy equipment—to clear it out, two things I don't have. Grumbling, I double back and go the other way past a bunch of unlabeled rooms and around a left corner to a fancy pair of narrow double doors. They open out to the middle of the audience area.

The theater is vast, jaw-droppingly huge from inside. It didn't look anywhere near this big from the roof next door. Balcony seat boxes shed plaster flakes to the ground. Fake gold trim peels away from an elaborately decorated ceiling two stories above me. The soft, scraping grind of a distant jet goes overhead. One of the bigger holes in the roof allows me to look straight up at the passing 737.

My sneakers squish on the dark burgundy carpeting. It's soaked up a *lot* of rain. The amount of mold on everything is staggering. Someone would have to be stupid to be here without a mask on. Oh, hi. I don't count. Breathing is an option for me. Speaking of which, I hold my breath. It would be just my luck to suck up some spores and develop a case of black mold growing inside my lungs. Probably wouldn't bother me too much beyond bringing it home and/or exhaling toxic crap for a while. However, becoming the fourth horsewoman of the apocalypse—pestilence—isn't on my top ten list of things to do.

Unsurprisingly, there are no vampires hanging out on stage messing around with instruments at this hour.

The roof holes let quite a bit of sunlight fall directly on where they'd been last night. Talk about a smoldering guitar riff. Dieter went across the stage into the back, so... it's where I go. Walking down the aisle sounds like repeatedly punching a damp sponge. Yeah, this theater is gothic as hell, but eww. It's one thing to look cool, but this is just nasty.

I jump onto the stage, hurry past the two sofas, three recliners, and a nice, dry area rug to the curtain in the back. The room behind the stage is full of old scenery props, mechanical devices, ropes, pullies, and what I assume to be a cabling system to let actors 'fly' on stage. None of it's moved in fifty years. To call it 'dusty' is a laughable understatement. It's almost like walking on the Moon. No exaggeration, there's like a half-inch-thick layer of it on most things.

Following a trail of obvious footprints, I navigate a maze past giant slabs of wood painted like forest backdrops, crates, mannequins, tiny castle parapets, and other junk. There's something surrealistically nightmarish about being backstage in an abandoned theater. I'm sure the presence of vampires here charging the air is no small part of how creepy it feels.

At the back of the room, I find a crumbling brick wall with a whole bunch of framed photographs of people I don't recognize. About a third are black and white. Guessing they're probably the big-name actors who worked here, or maybe local important people who came to see the shows. The photos don't interest me anywhere near as much as the door they surround, since the footprint trail goes right to it. This backstage area is *almost* dark enough for me to go online. Probably would be if not for all the holes in the roof and walls. Trying to be as quiet as possible, I creep up to the door, grasp the knob, and ease it open.

Stairs down.

Perfect.

I step inside and tug the door shut behind me.

A tingle sweeps down my body. Red light from my eyes appears briefly on the wall before fading. Yes! Online. Old wooden staircases tend to make more noise than a thirty-six-year-old mother of two at a Walmart customer service counter being denied a return because she showed up one day after the cutoff date.

Easy fix. I levitate and glide down to the landing. Before opening the next door, I do some weird zen type thing, 'centering myself' as some people call it. I am not here to cause harm. Peace and harmony with all—or at least the vampires I don't want to rip my face off.

Like some kind of sheltered suburban teenage wraith with limited fashion sense, I float into the basement, my sneakers eight inches above the floor. The room right inside this door appears to be a hangout spot containing more sofas, tables, and an assortment of distractions like ping pong tables and one of those games with the football players on twisty sticks arranged among a ridiculous amount of old theater props, background scenery, and giant wooden crates. Except for the newer games and places to sit, massively thick layers of dust cover everything. Three passages lead out, one at each corner on the opposite wall and another to the left.

I ignore the one with the sign for 'boiler room' and try the left first. Based on the pushcarts in the corridor, this likely used to be more storage space for stage props. I peek in the first door. Two rather dead looking guys in punk clothing lay sprawled on a king-sized bed, surrounded by Victorian-era junk. Rather, pretend Victorian-era junk. It's not really as old as it looks. Neither guy reacts to me. Good. Sleep peacefully, dudes.

Next room has more vampires draped on mattresses. Moving on...

Room by room, I search my way down the corridor, still floating, touching nothing except the occasional doorknob. The lair is as quiet as Bree Swanson's brain during an exam. Wait, no. It's quieter. There's no continuous hissing sound like a radio tuned to a dead airwave.

The fourteenth door I check—holy crap, this place is huge

—shocks me into squeaking.

There he is. Dieter Herbert. Spiky white hair punk himself.

He's splayed out on his back atop a lavish bed modeled after the French Renaissance period. Looks like something Aurélie probably had back in the day. The guy's as naked as a Greek statue, as are the two women sharing the bed with him. One's more or less on top of him with her face buried against the front of his neck. The other's curled against his right side, facing the door. She'd be staring right at me if her eyes opened.

And oof. This is *way* more of Deiter than I ever wanted to see. There's a reason people refer to dead bodies as stiffs. I mean, the dude isn't bad looking, but East German athlete is totally not my type. Not the biggest guy, but he's pretty shredded. I mean muscle definition, not claw wounds. Okay, Sarah, why are you still standing there staring at him? Not like you've never seen a boy naked before. It shouldn't be shocking.

Speaking of swords...

The one I'm looking for is *not* sticking straight up in the air. It's somewhat casually tossed on an ornate writing desk in the back corner of the room behind the foot of the bed, half buried under an assortment of denim, leather, and lacy undergarments. Peeking into a room containing sleeping vampires is one thing. Entering it is different. Vampires can be super territorial.

Not here to hurt anyone. I am no threat. I am silent like a ninja.

Still levitating, I glide into the room, hovering as close to the wall as is possible without bumping it to stay away from the bed. Don't mind me. I'm no one important. Harmless little Innocent. Professor Heath thinks my bloodline actually elevates the idea of 'harmlessness' to a legit power. Yeah, it's the exact opposite of epicness. Some vampires have magical powers to project intimidation. We're the reverse. Yay, I can cower against a wall during a huge battle and no one will pay me any attention. Go me. Sigh. I'm thinking about it wrong. I can scurry around a huge battle carrying intelligence or dragging wounded people out, and no one will care about my presence.

Or, I can sneak into a sleeping vampire's room and steal back a cursed sword without waking them since I seem to be such an extreme non-threat even a snoring vampire's sixth sense can't see me.

Claws are super handy. Great in a fight, helpful getting those stupid blister packages open, and amazing for handling things I don't really want to touch... like the clothing tossed everywhere. I don't know—or want to know—where those women have been. Piece by piece, I pinch garments between my thumb and index claw and peel them away from the sword.

Up close, this thing looks ordinary as heck. It could have belonged to any common soldier centuries ago. Two things make it stand out as unusual. First, it's not the least bit rusted or suffering corrosion. It looks as if someone made it last month. Add to the great condition, subtle stylistic traits in the design that match the way swords were made years ago— and not a modern replica—someone who knows swords would be baffled. The second oddity is the *feeling* it gives off.

Pure malice.

Staring at this blade is like I've been shoved into a prison cell on my first night in jail only to find a six-foot-nine bald cellmate waiting for me who says 'your ass belongs to me now' as soon as the door closes—and he plans to kill and eat me after he's done.

There is some seriously *bad* mojo in this damn sword.

Yanno, it's not supposed to be able to possess vampires...

but I'm not taking the chance. I grab a black T-shirt off the floor, probably Dieter's, and use it to shield my hand from making direct contact with the scabbard. Considering Detective Warner didn't have a sheath on him when I last saw the blade, my guess is this scabbard is on loan from the theater's prop department. Don't care. It's another layer of separation between my hand and the blade.

Okay, this is the moment where something bad happens. As soon as I touch this sword, either Dieter's going to automagically wake up, a random demon is going to attack me, or some other part of my unlife is going to go straight off the rails. I half expect the damn Kool Aid Man to break through the wall and grab the sword before I can get to it.

Silence.

Screw it. After wrapping the T-shirt around my hand, I grab the sword by the scabbard. The instant my fingers close around it, a mild headache squeezes the back of my neck. A sense of ominous doom falls over me like I've got a term paper due tomorrow and haven't even started on it. Ugh. Chill out, sword. I don't want you. I'm only a courier. I'm not gonna keep you.

Strange. I think it's furious it can't take me over.

The mood shifts to a sensation like someone's glaring at me. I freeze like a kid caught raiding the cookie jar before dinner time. Nothing moves or makes noise. No giant pitcher of cherry Kool Aid comes smashing through the wall. After a few seconds, I risk a glance toward the bed. Dieter and his two girlfriends haven't moved... and he's still naked, not to mention a rather... 'upstanding' citizen.

Wow. It takes skill for a vampire dude to fall asleep like that. They had to be in the middle of things when the sun came up and knocked everyone out. Gah. Bad Sarah. Stop staring.

It's not Dieter or the women. Something else is looking at

me. Probably the entity inside the sword. Bet it's furious because it can't take over my brain. Right. Done here. Time to go. I glide across the room to the door as careful not to bump anything as if I carried five gallons of nitroglycerin. Once I'm in the hallway, I'm confident enough to fly much faster since it's a straight line and *now* it doesn't really matter if the vampires around me start to wake. I'll be long gone before they're coherent enough to stand up.

In seconds, I'm back in the hangout room. Zooming across it at high speed sets off a tornado of dust in my wake. My hurry to get the hell out of here as fast as possible overcomes my ability to reason. I'm flying out the door at the top of the stairs before I remember there's sunlight in the backstage area.

Know what happens to a vampire like me who's flying when they suddenly go offline?

Yeah. Flying becomes falling.

Like a dumbass, I instinctively try to shout 'oh shit' when it becomes apparent I'm no longer in control of my flight, but end up inhaling about ten pounds of dust as I crash down on my chest and go sliding face-first across a floor that hasn't been swept since 1956 before smashing into a huge wooden crate. A whole bunch of crap falls on me, but I don't feel much. I'm choking on dust way too hard to notice anything else. Gah. This tastes freakin' awful. It's as horrible as opening up the bag of a vacuum cleaner and pouring it into my mouth.

Billows of dust fly from my mouth on each cough. Tears stream from my eyes. My lungs are about to come flying out of my face. My tongue feels like a dried up wad of cotton. The last message my taste buds managed to transmit to the brain before their position was overrun is a vomit-inducing mixture of wood, paint, dead skin, and oil.

I'm not sure how long it takes, but eventually, the

coughing stops.

Wow, Sarah. That was about as graceful as an ostrich on ice skates being fired out of a cannon.

Thankfully, no one saw me. My clothes are so covered in dust, I could blend into the surroundings full chameleon mode or pass for a terracotta statue. Blergh. I'm going to be tasting this horror for weeks. At least my nose didn't break on impact with the crate. A bunch of mannequins and scenery boards formerly stacked on top of the huge box fell over when I hit it, burying me under a pile of junk. Even if one of the vampires downstairs woke up at the ruckus and came to look, they'd probably not be able to see me. Well... if one of those vampires stepped into this room, they'd have much bigger problems than finding me.

Flame on, bitch.

Whew. I am totally safe now... at least from Dieter's crew.

I gag again, cough a bit more, then start the process of digging myself out. Wow, stupid of me. This sword must be affecting me enough not to think. Only reason for me to run out of here like the lone survivor girl in a horror movie. How can I *forget* there's sunlight upstairs?

Groaning and grunting, I fight my way out of the debris fall, stand, and swat at myself until I no longer look like a sand person. Meaning, a person made entirely out of sand, not the guys from *Star Wars*. I am no doubt filthy, but beyond caring. Trying to summon up spit to moisten my mouth doesn't work. Too much dust.

Oh, hey... the creepy 'I hate you and every ancestor to ever come before you' feeling coming off the sword is gone. Guess it doesn't like the sun either... or my 'receiver' is off now. Could be either one... or both. Not gonna ask questions. I like this much better.

Screw that fence. Don't care if someone sees me going *out* the front door. I'll be long gone before the cops get here.

28

THE GHOST OF VLAD TEPES—NO, SERIOUSLY

Multiple people going by on the street stare at me as I emerge from the theater, go down the long stone staircase, and head for the gate in the fencing.

For the hell of it, I have my iPhone to my ear the whole time, complaining to no one about how much of a hellhole it is in the theater. It's probably confusing them why I sound like a ninety-seven-year-old grandmother who's smoked since age twelve.

"Yeah, I know I'm just an intern, but that doesn't mean he gets to keep sending me to deathtraps. I mean seriously, alone? The whole point of being an intern is someone teaches me how the hell to do property inspections. I fell through the goddamned floor! I'm covered in dust that's probably made of cancer."

Two guys in dress shirts, the closest to the gate and the most likely people to call the police about a break in, stare at me.

I hold the phone away from my mouth while looking at them. "World's worst summer job." As if someone on the other end of the line said something stupid, I gasp, move the phone back in front of my face, and yell, "What? Are you serious? Wrong address? Ooh! Nicky did that on purpose. You know he hates me for some stupid reason."

The men just stand there as I storm off down the street pretending to fume. Maybe they won't call the police. Depends on if they think I'm old enough to be an intern at some city office. Someone up to no good generally doesn't make a loud scene of themselves and *attract* attention. If they think I'm too young and lying, maybe they'll brush it off as a stupid kid doing stupid things. It does look a bit suspicious to walk out of an old theater carrying a sword wrapped in a T-shirt. Most people would assume I stole it from the prop room.

They'd be wrong.

I stole it from the basement.

Really, though, I'm recovering it. Not going to get into a semantic argument with random passersby or cops if I can help it. I don't look back to see if they have their phones out, primarily because they might take a picture of my face. From behind, I'm pretty generic. There are tons of girls my size with long brown hair around here. One of the perks of being painfully average. Okay, so I'm on the reedy end of average, but still. In my own humble opinion, I'm quite forgettable.

Soon, I'm around the corner, hoofing it the two blocks to the Sentra. Maybe it's paranoid of me, but parking an irritating distance away from anywhere 'vampire crap' goes down makes me feel better. Wouldn't be good if my old silver Sentra kept showing up in surveillance photos or random pictures of places where questionable events occurred.

I toss the sword in the back seat, jump in, and drive.

It's *so* tempting to stop at the first store I see and eat/drink something to get the rancid taste of theater dust out of my mouth. Like… munching an entire tin of Altoids at once might do the trick. Or gargling straight Bacardi 151, which is slightly less unpleasant than drinking gasoline. Even offline, alcohol won't do anything to me... but I'd stink like booze. Not a good idea when driving.

Trying to come up with something to eat or drink that's astonishingly strong-flavored yet not going to get me in trouble for driving while consuming it distracts me from looking for an actual place to stop. I end up on mental autopilot and before realizing it, I'm on the highway going back to the Seattle area from Olympia.

Ugh. Too late to stop now.

I summon up a mouthful of saliva, swish it around, and spit out the window. The wad of slime is dark brown. Blech. My mouth still tastes like I cleaned the entire floor of the backstage room with my tongue. My throat kills and my lungs are itchy. Had I not already died once, this would be terrifying. Who the hell knows what manner of awfulness I sucked up? Bacteria, spores, dirt, dead bugs. Ugh. Thinking about it is enough to make a vampire throw up.

This is a new experience for me. I've never inhaled foreign material before. Food goes straight through. Considering how we heal ourselves, there's little chance this gunk is going to take up permanent residence inside me or do damage. Only question I have is, will it migrate out via the usual plumbing or am I going to hack up a filthy 'hairball' like a cat? Or considering it's in my lungs, will it stay there until removed?

Yanno... I had my lungs full of water once already. Compared to this flavor/sensation going on now, intentionally 'drowning' myself again doesn't sound like a bad idea. Just call it a new age vampire 'deep internal cleansing' process.

About six minutes after leaving the Olympia city limits, I

reach to turn on the radio and notice there is a man with long, black hair sitting in the passenger seat, staring at me.

I jump so bad my head hits the roof while trying to shout an F-bomb, shriek, and yell WTF all at the same time. Attempting to yell dislodges some of the crud in my trachea, setting off a wicked coughing fit. The resultant sound of everything all at once is probably the same noise a chicken would make as it's being fired out of a cannon, assuming anyone could hear it over the explosion.

By some miracle, I don't crash into another car or go off the side of the road. A guy in a white pickup truck most likely has a lap full of hot coffee now. He jammed on the brakes when I swerved into his lane.

I'm a little too preoccupied at having a strange dude come out of nowhere in my car to pay much attention to the guy in the pickup truck making faces at me. Of course, I'm still choking on dust so maybe he thinks I'm swerving around due to a health issue.

Past cough tears, I struggle to look at the man invading my personal space. He's like late thirties or maybe early forties. Kinda looks somewhere between Turkish and Roma... we're talking *epic* unibrow. Guy's also giving me this drop-dead serious look as if to say 'you done messed up, kid.'

The blare of a horn jump-scares me for the second time in under a minute.

"Gah!" I yelp, then start choking on dust all over again.

How bad is it? Dust is legit spraying out of my mouth and snowing onto the steering wheel.

Pickup Guy yells something.

Can't make out the words. His tone is loud but doesn't sound belligerent, so I look over as soon as the coughing fit permits me. He shouts again. Lip-reading (sorta) makes me think he's asking if I'm okay. Ugh. Screw it. I pull over and stop. He does the same, parking in front of me. A fairly big guy hops out and jogs to the side of my car.

I open the window.

"You okay, kid?"

"Sorta." I rasp. "Just started coughing real hard. Couldn't breathe. Sorry for swerving."

My passenger momentarily shifts his gaze to the man outside. Even though his expression hasn't changed at all, its meaning in my mind changes from scolding me to 'go away, peasant.'

"Need me to call someone?" asks Pickup Dude.

I take a few slow breaths, patting myself on the chest. "I think I'm okay now. Must have breathed wrong or something."

He looks me over almost like he might be an EMT or maybe a fireman with some first aid training. Seeming satisfied, he nods once. "All right. If you're sure."

"I am. Thanks... and sorry about that."

"No problem, kid." The man stands away from my window, lingers for a moment as if wondering if I might change my mind and ask for help, then walks back to his truck.

Oh, duh. He has firefighter license plates. Wow. How sad is it I'm surprised to run into a genuinely nice guy?

Unfortunately, the man in my passenger seat is still there. Since I'm not presently driving and worried about watching the road, I look at him. It's obvious now his body lacks full solidity, and his clothing is, well, ornate leather armor.

"Oh, shit. You're the entity in the sword, aren't you?" I throw the car in drive, check the side mirror, and pull back into a traffic lane. "Sorry you can't possess me. Nice try getting me killed though."

"You will not succeed, fiend."

I glance at him. "Little harsh, dude. You don't even know me."

"The magic upon you is unlike any I have seen. Yet, the stench of undeath is thick."

"Whoops. Skipped deodorant today." I smirk.

He continues glaring at me.

"Anyone ever tell you it's not really polite to tell a girl they stink?" I sniff myself. "Ugh. I smell like a moldy couch."

"You will be destroyed, fiend."

Sigh. "Really, dude? What's your deal?"

"I do not make deals with vampires."

"Wow. Just… wow."

"Your machinations will fail."

I glance at him again. "Points for melodrama, but you really ought to just chill."

The temperature in the car drops like thirty degrees.

"Literal much? Guess you don't keep up with how 'the kids talk these days,' huh?"

"You would be wise to impale yourself on my blade."

"Hah. Nope. Not happening." I rub my chest. "Already had a bunch of swords stuck through me. Not looking to enjoy that again."

He flashes a dark smile. "I assure you, it would not be enjoyable. Your kind deserve only destruction."

"Hey, easy with the genocidal ramblings, grandpa." I huff —blowing a small cloud of dust into the air. "Not all vampires are evil."

"You are a vampire and must be destroyed."

I stare at him. "Look, dude. Having an attitude like that is how you ended up as a tortured spirit trapped in a sword. Stop being closed minded. Vampires *can* be evil, sure, but we're as varied as normal people."

He continues glowering at me.

So… I start rambling about Scott, my murder, Dalton

happening to be right there, me waking up not even knowing vampires were a real thing that existed… and how I'm a big, homesick sap who couldn't bear the thought of her family believing she died. After like ten minutes of me talking about my family, he finally stops giving me the Look of Death™ and stares straight ahead.

"Your mind tricks are failing."

"Hey, guy. Hate to break the illusion here, but you're dead. You're a ghost. You don't have a mind to trick." I tap a finger to my temple. "Vampire powers do not work on spirits. That thing you're feeling is called 'holy shit, I've been a total dick and this girl isn't evil.'"

He narrows his eyes at me.

"Aww, come on. Enough with the death stare." I make a lane change in preparation for taking the exit I need. "Dude, just relax. I'm not gonna keep the sword. We're trying to put it somewhere it can't hurt anyone. Oh, wait. That's probably why you're pissed off. You can't drive people insane as long as Wolent keeps the blade hidden from the world."

"That's not even close to truth," snaps the ghost. "You know nothing."

"Well then enlighten me, oh scowling one." I give him side eye. "For a dude who looks like you belong in Czarist Russia, your English is really good."

He avoids eye contact while muttering, "Side effect of being a ghost."

"Really?"

"Yes. If I want someone to understand me, they hear whatever I say in their language. I do not know how the mechanism of it. It just works."

"Neat."

He looks back at me. "What does tidiness have to do with anything?"

I whistle. "I mean… that sounds helpful."

"Quite."

Hey, at least he's saying something more than 'you deserve to be destroyed.' Progress.

"Your family knows what you are, yet they tolerate you under their roof?"

"Yep. Dude. I don't know what sort of weird, bogus information you have on vampires, but we are not mindless killers. If I thought for a second I'd be a threat to my parents or siblings, I'd fling myself into the sun."

He points out the windshield. "You have done so and it has not affected you for some reason I am unable to understand. How is it you are not on fire?"

"I'm Innocent."

"I have not accused you of anything more than being a despicable fiend."

"Gee, thanks." I smirk. "I mean... do you know about different bloodlines or are all vampires the same in your eyes?"

"All fiends."

"Riiight. This is going to take way too long to explain. Won't finish before I give the sword to Wolent and we never see each other again, so I'll just say this: vampires have different tribes, basically. Each one has some unique thing. Mine is being able to tolerate mild amounts of sunlight and look like I'm still alive. They call my type of vampire 'Innocent.'"

"A convenient lie, no doubt."

"Hah. No. I'm really kind of a squishy wimp."

"Squishy..." He raises an eyebrow.

"It's my Dad's word. Means I cry at movies, wanna squeeze every kitten I see, that sorta thing. Real sensitive. Not as squishy as my sister, Sophia, though."

He sits in silence, likely pondering. Hey, it's not every day one's worldview gets turned on its head. Got the feeling this guy hasn't had a conversation in a while.

"So, who are you?"

"You do not recognize me?" His dour expression finally changes… to mild surprise.

"No. Can't say I do."

"Damn the fiends."

"Yeah, we established you don't like vampires already. What's that have to do with who you are?"

The man waves a hand around angrily, raising his voice. "The whole world believes me a vampire, a murderer, a monster who tortured children. It is a lie. Upon finally defeating me, the fiends spread falsehoods. It was not enough for them to simply end my life, they destroyed it in perpetuity."

"You wouldn't be the first person in history to be vilified wrongly." I pause to glare up at a red light. Hate it when they change at the last second. It's as annoying as someone slamming a door in my face. "So, who are you, really?"

"My name was Vlad Tepes."

I blink. "Oh, shit. Seriously?"

He scowls.

"No, I mean… not judging. Just surprised you really exist. Thought Dracula was a made-up story."

"Dracula is a lie!" He pounds his fist on the door, shaking the entire car.

Whoa… old spirit. "Calm down. Please. I promise not to judge by anything but what you tell me. I told you about my family and about being an Innocent. Usually, I keep that secret so people can't use it against me. Usually, when talking to ghosts, I find the best policy is full transparency."

He stares at me in Vlad the Impaler.

"Sorry. The puns just happen sometimes. It's in my genes."

"Fiend," he mutters.

"Oh, come on. The pun wasn't *that* bad." I flick my thumb over the steering wheel repetitively. "They say history is written by the victor. Someone wins, they can make up any lies they want. A good first step to not being thought of as an asshole is to stop acting like one. Sure, I'm a vampire, but I'm not a bad person. I could have killed everyone in that theater, but I just snuck in and took the sword."

"You failed to destroy a nest of fiends. You should have done so," says Vlad in a cold tone.

"No, they're just people who happen to be living impaired. Ditch the medieval mindset, dude. The world is way more complicated than"—I do my best impression of Saturday Night Live Frankenstein—"mortal... *good!* Undead... *bad!*"

Vlad stares at me.

"I mean it. Back when you were alive, they'd execute people for being left-handed and stupid stuff like that. The world's changed. There are living people around who are *way* more evil than vampires."

"Why did you take my sword if you do not want it?"

"It's only my night job."

He blinks.

"What, not even a chuckle?"

"Why should I find that humorous?"

Sigh. "Most people have 'day jobs'. I said 'night job' because I'm a vampire."

He keeps staring at me. Wow. Tough audience.

"I'm bringing the sword back to my boss because it's what I was asked to do. He likes keeping it safe so innocent people can't pick it up, go crazy, and kill."

Vlad fixes a piercing stare on me for a long moment, then raises one eyebrow. "Perhaps if you are as you say, you can solve this problem permanently."

"This sounds like it could be painful... but go on. What do you mean?"

"Go into the sword and defeat Iorghu the Destroyer."

Eep. Something tells me despite a name like that he's not a B-league WWE wrestler. "I'm fairly sure I'm a little too small to ride that ride just yet. Maybe in a century, I'll think about it."

"To ride this ride?"

"You're from what, the 1400s?"

"My death occurred in 1477."

"Okay. This Iorghu the Destroyer... what is he?"

Vlad narrows his eyes. "He is the first vampire fiend I slew with this blade. Through my command of the arcane arts, I trapped his tainted soul within the weapon to empower it as a fearsome tool against the undead."

"Sounds complicated."

He strokes his mustache. "It was. But effective. The sword has but to break the skin of a vampire and it will mean their end."

For the second time in one afternoon, I almost crash while suffering a panic flashback of Detective Warner swinging the thing at me over and over again. "Wait, what? Like a tiny cut will kill a vampire?"

"A small cut to a limb will not immediately destroy the fiend. They will turn grey and blow away as ash. It takes a few minutes and I believe it is quite agonizing. Taking off a fiend's head or impaling them in the heart destroys them immediately." Vlad smiles to himself. "If the edge of my blade tastes the blood of a vampire, no matter how small the wound, that fiend is doomed."

"And this thing is in my car!" I yell.

Vlad peers over his shoulder. "Yes. It is on the seat in the rear of this most perplexing wagon that moves with no horses."

Holy crap. I'm gonna throw up. I don't want to be anywhere near this stupid sword. Shit. No damn wonder some vampire out there wants it so bad. Also, no wonder Wolent keeps it hidden. Does *he* know what it can do to us? Is *that* why Dieter put it in a scabbard? Why am I the last person to find out I've got a sphere of annihilation in my car?

"You would not need to fear it if you defeated Iorghu," says Vlad. "I know now that I made a grave mistake binding him to the blade. I never should have done so. Not in my wildest nightmares did I imagine the kind of power he would have over mortals who touched the sword."

I give him epic side eye. "Dude... I've been a vampire for about one year. Whatever this Iorghu the Destroyer guy is, he's at least 700 years old, plus however old he was before you went all *Ghostbusters* on him. When you say 'go into the sword,' I'm assuming you mean some kind of dimensional door type deal where I enter a shifted reality or some kind of demi-plane and meet this guy face to face for a fight. If I beat him, the demi-plane crumbles, the curse ends, you're freed and people stop going crazy when they touch the sword."

"That is surprisingly accurate. How is someone in this modern world so familiar with these concepts?"

"I play a lot of video games and D&D."

He blinks.

"Forget it. Look, I have about as much chance of beating a 700-year-old vampire as a cockroach winning a fistfight against a speeding car."

"I do not understand what you say."

"Iorghu was a powerful vampire when you killed him?"

"One of the most feared vampires in all of Wallachia. It is by sheer luck and tenacity I bested him." Vlad holds his chin up in pride. "I was the greatest vampire hunter in all of Europe."

I'm laughing before I even think about it.

"Do not mock me, fiend."

"Sorry. No. I'm not laughing at you." I cough up more dust, snicker, then wail in agony at having my sinuses packed with moldy dust-mucus. "Ugh. This really, really sucks."

"I do not understand."

"Dust in places dust doesn't belong." I hack a few times. "Just find it hilarious you were a vampire *hunter*. They call you Dracula, say you were one of the most powerful vampires ever."

He scowls. "I am aware. I was never turned to an undead. I killed thousands of fiends. They swarmed over the land like rats. Wild, feral monsters preying on the innocent."

Oh, he must mean the Oblivare... or missionaries. "Umm. Yeah. If the vampires were attacking people like that, they deserved to be stabbed."

Vlad regards me with a look of surprised respect.

"Don't look so shocked. I'm not loyal to every vampire just because they're a vampire. A killer is a killer. So, wow. Vlad Tepes, vampire hunter." Eek. If he carried a sword that killed us from wounds as small as a paper cut to the toe, no wonder he had been so feared and hated by vampires they completely twisted history to make him out to be a psychotic monster.

"You surprise me, Sarah. I am not used to vampires speaking much at all. They often merely snarl, growl, or moan before trying to tear a person's throat out."

"Did you hunt vampires or Philadelphia Eagles fans?"

"What is a Philadelphia Eagles Fan?"

"A violent creature prone to random fits of rage." I smile. "Seriously though, sounds like you ran into a ton of scraps or maybe even *sefil*."

"Scraps?"

"Half-vampires. Accidents. They basically aren't much smarter than dogs."

"I slew many like that. But many others as smooth with verse as you are."

"Right… hey, question?"

"Hmm?" Half of his unibrow lifts.

I come to a stop at another red light, then look at him. "If you are trapped in there, too, why don't you try stopping Iorghu from possessing people?"

"I do try. But the curse has left me weak. The fiends thought it amusing to kill me using my own blade. Iorghu delighted in dragging my soul into his prison as revenge. I have endured centuries of agony. We stalk each other across a stygian maze, both hunted and hunter. He and I have died ten thousand agonizing deaths. Due to the nature of the curse, neither of us can permanently destroy each other. We are bound together in eternal torment."

"You could've just said you work in a customer service call center."

Vlad blinks. "You use words I am unable to grasp."

"I'm making dumb jokes as a coping mechanism in order to avoid thinking about there being a slab of metal four feet behind me capable of *permanently destroying* me if it so much as nicks my skin."

"Ahh, yes. I can see how that would be worrisome."

Argh. I bonk my head in to the steering wheel. What the hell am I going to do with this thing? That part of me driven to help everyone who asks for it is toying with the idea of trying to confront Iorghu. No, I'm not that damned stupid. He'd squish me. Grr. Now, I'm torn. Could there possibly be some way for me to neuter or destroy this sword? Wolent's intention as far as I know is to keep it safe and hidden. Perhaps there's no real urgency here. Of course, if some other vampire successfully stole it once, it could happen again.

"Vlad? How did the sword get stolen? I thought Wolent's place was like an impenetrable fortress."

He makes a blasé face. "Iorghu wanted to be free."

I stare at him so long the car behind me honks. Oops. Light turned green. Once we're moving again, I exhale hard, spraying dust all over the dashboard. "So, you're saying it pulled some *Lord of the Rings* crap where it just decided to let someone take it?"

"I do not know of this lord." Vlad adjusts his mustache again. "Lord of the Rings is an interesting title. Who is this man?"

"Fiction. Made up story. Basically, you're saying the sword called out to some random vampire who then became aware of its existence and sought to steal it... and succeeded in doing so because the sword desired it?"

"No. Iorghu desired it. The sword is merely a container."

"Semantics." I bonk my head on the steering wheel again.

Ugh. No way am I going to be able to kill something like this. Way too powerful. Giving it back to Wolent isn't going to do any good either. As soon as the sword—I mean Iorghu—wants, someone else will take it. I really ought to go drop the damn thing into an active volcano. Knowing my luck, doing that would only set Iorghu's fiendish spirit loose on the world. Also, the sword probably wouldn't allow me to bring it anywhere it thought posed a serious threat to its existence. As soon as it realizes my actions are remotely threatening, bad crap will happen.

Hmm... I wonder...

29

SPIDERS OF UNUSUAL SIZE

T he cave passage ahead of Sophia looked like a tunnel dug by a giant mole.

Dirt walls covered in roots and moss led into the dark, going downhill to a rightward corner. A spectral chill raked at her skin, the unnatural breeze passing through her uniform as if it didn't exist. She didn't really need yet another reason to get out of here as fast as possible. The cold had to be a manifestation of evil, not temperature. Hopefully, she wouldn't get frostbite from dark energy.

"No way." Nicole moved in behind her, brandishing her 'staff.' "Not gonna stay out there alone."

Priya stepped up on her other side. "Yeah. We're gonna die no matter what, right? Go in, go back to camp, same result."

"No." Sophia forced herself to continue deeper into the cave. "Going in, we have a chance of not dying."

Her friends and Coleman followed her along the tunnel. So many roots hung from the ceiling it looked as though she walked under the belly of an enormous, furry bear. Darting shadows among the hairy strands somewhat resembled spiders, but she dismissed it as a trick of her mind and the dark energy in the air. They couldn't possibly be spiders. If they were, they'd be the size of grapefruit, and spiders didn't get that big.

She continued refusing to believe she really saw giant spiders until they reached a chamber littered with more, even larger, spiders.

Sophia screamed.

"Don't worry about the spiders of unusual size," deadpanned Nicole. "They don't exist."

Somehow, Sophia giggled.

Priya edged back a step. "They are quite obviously here… and I think they are looking at us."

"Umm." Sophia clung protectively to Klepto. "I don't think they're normal spiders."

"No kidding." Nicole raised her 'staff.' "Normal spiders aren't as big as basketballs."

The giant spiders charged.

Sophia screamed again.

Nicole smashed the first one to get close, whacking her giant stick down on it like a double-long baseball bat. Yellowish raw-egg slime exploded out of the creature's abdomen. Priya kicked at one attempting to bite her, launching it away into the air. She growled and kicked another, but it clung to her shin. She hopped on one foot, screaming and flailing her right leg while the massive arachnid bobbed up and down like a rodeo cowboy struggling not to be thrown off.

Still screaming, Sophia whirled around and ran… but only took three steps before both of her friends shrieking in terror slapped her back to her senses. She spun again. One spider had gone between the girls, coming straight for Sophia. Nicole backpedaled to the left, swinging the stick back and forth in a gradually losing effort to keep four spiders away from biting range. Priya had one hanging on her back, one still on her right leg, and two approaching from the ground.

Sophia froze, staring at Priya. *Why didn't they bite her yet? She should be stung already. It's like they're only trying to scare us.*

She glared at the one rushing toward her, refusing to be afraid of it. Spiders did not grow so big. It couldn't be real. It *had* to be an illusion. The skittering furry horror reared its gleaming black fangs. The one on Priya's back still hadn't bitten her.

Sophia stared at the one about to bite her on the knee. "You aren't real."

The spider disappeared.

"They're not real!" shouted Sophia, thrusting her hands out while focusing on her desire to dispel magic.

The spiders, including the one Nicole smashed, disappeared.

Priya continued spinning in a one-legged dance, shrieking, mostly because she'd closed her eyes.

"Pree!" yelled Nicole. "They're gone."

The girl didn't stop until Nicole grabbed and shook her. Finally, Priya opened her eyes, realized the spiders disappeared, and nearly fainted.

"Nicole was right." Sophia smiled at her. "The spiders of unusual size *do not* exist. Fear magic. An illusion."

Coleman, once again tinted sickly green in the dark cave, pointed forward. "The wendigo is in there. I ain't gon' hold it against ya if ya run."

Sophia shivered. It finally hit her why she hated the idea of going camping so much, why it had terrified her into three sleepless nights before Friday's bus ride up here. If anything happened to her, screaming for Mom or Dad to come help wouldn't do any good. She'd gone too far away for them to hear her, like a bird fallen out of the nest too young.

Surviving the fall depended entirely on her ability to flap. She didn't want to be independent yet, even for a week-long test flight away from her parents. Being so far from home, her family couldn't be there if she needed them is what truly scared her.

Camping did not leave her at the mercy of the wilderness to survive purely on her own. Scout leaders, counselors, a nurse, a couple maintenance people... plenty of adults were here to take care of her. Alas, they couldn't do anything about a wendigo. Mom and Dad couldn't either. Sure, they'd try. Dad would put a red necktie around his head and try to kill it with a weed eater or something. Mom would grab her and run. Heck, Sarah might not even be able to beat a wendigo. It probably didn't have blood due to being someone's dead body. Her sister's ability to fight it would depend on the effectiveness of claws or a sword.

The mystics didn't have the time to get ready. Before they could take on a wendigo, they'd need to spend days preparing ritual magic tailored to fighting this particular creature. By the time they finished weaving the magic they'd need for the fight, everyone here would be gone already, not even ghosts remaining.

Sophia had two choices. One: she, Nicole, and Priya run away, elude the authorities, and go home. Doing so might spare their three lives, but everyone at the camp would be lost. *Walking* all the way back to Cottage Lake would both totally suck as well as be kinda dangerous. They could get hit by a car, kidnapped robbed, or lost and eaten by bears. Even if they survived to get home, she'd have to live with the guilt of abandoning everyone else to die.

Second choice: go into the next room and metaphorically punch a wendigo in the face. Sure, it might kill her, but for some strange reason, confronting it scared her less than the thought of the long trek home. Her magic had a much better chance of protecting her from a creature like a wendigo than an evil normal person who'd want to hurt three young girls on their own. She'd also caused the creature to wake up. Even if she didn't know her presence here would do something like that, every time she thought 'if I didn't go to camp, they'd all still be alive,' it would crush her.

"Nah," muttered Sophia. "I'm gonna try and stop it. We already sneaked away from camp. If we're gonna get in trouble, we might as well make it worth it."

"Wait, we're gonna get caught?" Priya gasped.

"Maybe not." Sophia approached the opening at the far end of the chamber. "Trying to be funny so I don't start crying."

Nicole walked up behind her. "We got you."

Priya didn't move for a few seconds. As soon as Nicole shot her a 'are you coming' look, she darted forward. "Y-yes. We're here."

"Sec." Sophia tried to calm herself. *Square peg. Round hole. I'm the wimp. I need Sierra to protect me. I shouldn't be the one protecting my friends. They don't belong here. They're gonna get hurt if I mess up.* Exhale. *Sierra likes to protect me. I can protect myself sometimes. If I beat the wendigo, I can go home. I wanna go home so bad. Just gotta stop this monster.* "Okay."

"Did you do something magic?" whispered Priya.

"No. Just trying to psych myself out. Good idea, though."

Sophia grabbed her friends' hands and wanted to use magic to protect them. She envisioned casting a defensive spell to shield their minds from fear and their bodies from harm. The warm tingle she usually experienced whenever her magic did something crept down her arms. Considering the level of fear nibbling on her at the moment, she cringed, half expecting to have turned the girls into turtles by accident or made them weightless.

Nothing *looked* different. She sighed in relief.

Together, they advanced through the opening into a wide, round-walled chamber with a low ceiling. At the center of the floor, a gaunt human figure with gnarled, greyish-black tree bark for skin knelt waist-deep in a gloopy morass of black gunk, as thick and viscous as tar. The creature appeared to be struggling to lift himself out of the substance. Long, untamed hair, stained black by the strange fluid from which he emerged, hung longer than his waist, stuck to his body. Deer-like antlers protruded from his temples, extending straight up the ends three feet above the top of his head. Where eyes should be, empty sockets held a haze of pale white mist.

The wendigo radiated evil as well as frustration. His desire to break free from the mire and feast upon the souls of all who crossed his path fell on Sophia from merely looking at him. Delirious with need, he didn't react to the girls and continued trying to grab at the solid ground at the edge of the bubbling pool of viscous liquid. Even though his arms appeared elongated past human proportion, he couldn't yet reach.

In one day, he'd more than halfway emerged. He would definitely escape tonight.

The mystics advised her to kick him back through the gateway into the other realm. Sophia figured the pool was the opening between this world and wherever wendigos came from.

Nicole and Priya whimpered.

Klepto hissed at the wendigo.

"This is so weird," whispered Nicole. "It's like I'm so scared I want to scream and pass out, but I can't do either one."

"Fear magic." Sophia stared at the monstrosity struggling in the muck. "People looking at it get terrified by magic. My spell is protecting you."

"You really believe you cast magic, don't you?" asked Priya.

"Pree…" Nicole pointed. "Do you or do you not see a wooden deer man stuck in a tar pit?"

"I do."

"What part of normal reality includes tree men with deer antlers and glowing smoke for eyes?" asked Nicole.

"Okay. Fine. Maybe Sophia has magic." Priya gazed around the otherwise empty chamber. "Hurry up and use it. This place is scary."

Sophia raised her arms, fingers splayed. "You don't belong here. Go back where you came from!" She poured all the terror she'd felt at going to camp, all her need to go home as fast as possible into a spell, trying to push the monster back down into the muck, across planes, back to where it came from.

Greenish light flashed over the wendigo's body. An invisible force knocked him into a backward lean. He waved his long, slender arms frantically, black goop flying from them, while roaring in a deep, completely inhuman voice.

She growled, pushing harder. The tingling of magic down her back increased to near burning.

Another green flash hit the wendigo, knocking him over. Sophia started to smile—until he shoved himself back up into the same kneeling posture as before. The pale mist hovering in his wooden eye sockets coalesced into brighter points. Eerie, soulless 'eyes' locked on her, giving off pure malice.

Sophia gulped.

Shadows thickened on the far side of the chamber, gathering into the forms of two large, black wolves. The furry horrors stalked around the tar puddle toward the girls. Their yellow eyes held more intelligence than a wolf ought to have.

Priya stepped forward to the right, holding a hand out to the wolf on that side. "You are a magnificent creature. Can I give you skritches?"

"Uhh, that's not a normal animal, Pree." Nicole raised her stick. "Get away from it."

Both wolves lunged at the same time, one at Sophia, the other at Priya.

Nicole leapt in front of Sophia, thrusting her stick sideways into the wolf's mouth. The huge canine tackled her over onto her back, snarling viciously.

Priya shrieked and ran to the side, going in circles around the wendigo's pool, trying to stay as near the wall as possible, out of his reach.

Splintering crunches came from the stick.

Sophia stood there frozen, rapidly glancing back and forth between her friends. One wolf would bite through the stick any second. The other knocked Priya to the ground. She screamed in pain and pleaded with the animal not to hurt her because she was its friend. If the girl had any real ability to soothe beasts, it did *not* appear to have any influence on these wolves.

"No!" yelled Sophia, making a shoving gesture at the wolf attacking Priya.

The dog went flying away from her as if struck by a heavy thrown object. It flipped over, hit the wall upside down, then fell to the floor. Priya struggled to her feet and limp-ran. The wolf shrugged off the double hit and bolted after her, gaining fast.

Creating the enchantment for Sierra taught Sophia a few new tricks. She concentrated on Priya, casting a spell to make her faster. If it worked right, it would last only a minute or two—but she didn't need a permanent boost. Priya zoomed forward, the wolf's lunging bite missing her skirt by three inches. Like sped-up video, Priya and the wolf ran around and around the chamber.

Crack!

Sophia spun toward Nicole. The huge stick gave out in the middle, breaking inside the wolf's mouth. Saliva covered splinters flew from its mouth as it chomped down on Nicole's arm. Before Sophia could do anything, hard wooden cords closed around her neck. Gurgling, she twisted her head to look up the length of the wendigo's unnaturally long arm. Narrow fingers, pointy and rigid like the branches of a tree coated in slime, tightened around her throat. Thinner branches extended from his fingertips, threading in the neck opening and sleeves of her shirt, constricting around her chest. Squeezing.

The creature lifted her off her feet, drawing her in closer.

Sophia's head pounded. She couldn't breathe. Near panic, she grabbed at the wooden vines tightening around her throat. Kicking wildly didn't help. Her chest ached. Any second now, her ribs would start to crack. Perhaps she'd get lucky and pass out before she felt any pain.

Klepto darted up the wendigo's arm, yowling, screeching, and hissing. The kitten flung herself in a clawing frenzy at an eerily familiar face… the wendigo looked like someone carved a statue of Coleman Emerson from a tree.

Sophia couldn't scream or breathe. Her fingertips wouldn't fit between her throat and the impossibly hard hand squeezing it. Ever-growing branches continued slithering around her body, scratching her skin like wooden snakes. She stomped him in the chest over and over again to no avail. Somewhere behind her, Nicole screamed in pain. Priya continued blurring around in circles. Her friends kept the wolves off her… and she messed up. She stopped paying attention to the wendigo to protect them. She missed the chance her friends gave her.

The instant she started to see flashes of home and her parents play across her mind, an all-consuming sorrow crashed over her, killing panic. Her parents would be destroyed if she died, as bad as they'd been when they thought Sarah was gone.

Get off me! screamed Sophia in her mind.

A blast of invisible force radiated out from her chest. The wendigo's hand exploded in a shower of tree bark, rotten meat, and human bones. Thick, goopy black ooze spurted from the stump of a forearm.

Sophia dropped straight down, landing on all fours, her hands almost up to the elbows at the edge of the slimy pool. She sucked in a huge breath. Glowing spots danced in her eyes. Fragments of broken branch scraped at her skin under her shirt. The wendigo leaned back, moaning in pain. His arm squished and crunched, regenerating fast. He didn't appear to be made of solid wood. Only his skin hardened. Inside, a rotten human corpse.

Sophia recoiled from the puddle, scooting backward in a rapid crawl. The muck she assumed to be viscous and sticky released her as easily as water, not even staining her arms. Priya jumped over her. The chasing wolf leapt over her as well.

Nicole yowled in pain.

Ack! Sophia shoved her left hand toward Nicole, hurling a 'telekinesis' type spell at the wolf biting her. The large canine gave a yelping wail as her magic punted it into the air. Nicole rolled onto her side, clutching her bleeding arm.

Sophia rose up on her knees, again focusing all her willpower, magic, and emotion into trying to shove the wendigo back across the gateway. Green light flashed around the creature's body. He recoiled back under the impact of a great force, yet still didn't go anywhere.

This isn't working... He's too far into our world. Too strong a hold. She sighed as the last bits of his hand regenerated. *Branches... he looks like a dried out old tree.*

Priya zoomed by again.

Dried out... wood.

"Fire..." Sophia held her hands up as if cradling a basketball.

Desperate to do *something* so she could go home again, she pictured a rolling sphere of flames forming in her hands. Naked elemental magic like this shouldn't be possible anywhere outside of movies. The mystics didn't think it ever worked. The Tome of F Knowledge disagreed. The book advised her against doing it, due to the uncontrollable nature of such forces... and because it would kinda kick her butt. Being tired for a week definitely beat dying. Anything beat how much it would hurt Mom and Dad to be told Sophia died.

Tears ran down her face.

With a roaring *whoosh,* a bright orange orb of flames burst into existence above her hands. The instant she desired it to, the fireball rocketed into the wendigo's chest. As fast as an electric light turning on, flames engulfed the creature's entire body. It roared in agony, its voice so deep and loud everyone back at camp probably heard it. The wendigo's hair vanished. His antlers and fingers crumbled away to ash. Large patches of its bark-like skin turned pale grey and disintegrated, revealing bubbling flesh and glowing embers inside.

Hope glimmered in Sophia's heart... right up until the ashing spots began to regenerate. The flames showed no sign of weakening any time soon, feeding off the tarry slime as greedily as if the wendigo bathed in lamp oil. Alas, his regeneration appeared to be almost keeping up.

Sickly green light flickered in the corner of her vision.

Sophia glanced over at Coleman. The spirit hovered at the entrance to the chamber as if afraid to come inside. He stared at the conflagration, eyes wide, fists clenched, a 'come on and die already' expression on his face.

Ooh... Coralie said I could take my body back whenever I wanted and kick Pippa out, but I didn't know I could.

She reached out both hands in a grabbing gesture at Coleman, invoking magic as she pictured herself tossing the spirit into the floundering wendigo. The ghost gave a startled yelp as he flew into the air, a life-sized action figure grabbed and thrown by a huge child. Coleman tumbled head over feet across the chamber.

She pictured him taking his body back, kicking the bad spirit out, and smashed him into the monster's chest as hard as she could.

Amid a green flash, Coleman's ghost disappeared into the body at the same time a sickly, pallid white apparition burst out of its back. The wendigo spirit looked far more like a narrow tree with two branchlike arms than anything human. Dark spots near the top of the trunk where it split into a short fray of branches gave the suggestion of eyes.

"Gotcha," whispered Sophia.

She drew in a deep breath and lashed out with the ghost-banishing spell the London mystics taught her. With a keening, high-pitched wail, the wispy white form collapsed into a mass no bigger than a tennis ball... then burst apart, filling the air with a million tiny ethereal scraps.

The tar pool shrank away to nothing, swallowing the unmoving wooden-skinned remains as the fire completely consumed them to ashes. Silence filled the chamber. No sign of the wolves remained. Nicole whispered 'ow' repeatedly, curled up on her side not far away. Priya, having stopped running, leaned against the wall and tried to catch her breath.

A few seconds after the cave floor once again appeared to

be ordinary dirt, Coleman's ghost reappeared—no longer sickly green, more of a bluish-white. "Sophia... thank you."

She slouched, exhausted. "You're welcome. Holy crap, we did it."

"You did." He smiled.

"Are you going to be happy now, haunting the woods?"

"Nah." He turned away. "I've had enough of haunting. Time to move on." Coleman walked off, disappearing in a few steps.

"Ow." Nicole sat up.

Priya stumbled over. "I agree. Ow."

Sophia looked her friends over. Both bled from multiple dog bites, though Nicole got the worst of it. Her shirt had been ripped completely to pieces, only the collar remained around her neck plus a few bloody tatters hanging from where they tucked into her skirt. Scratches and tooth marks crisscrossed her entire chest. The girls looked as if they'd gone mud surfing.

"Klepto, can you please grab a new shirt for Nicole?"

"Mew." The kitten disappeared in a violet flash.

"Sorry you guys got hurt." The reality of the moment finally hit her and Sophia broke down crying. "You really stayed with me."

The girls flopped to sit beside her.

"Yeah." Nicole winced, poking at a bite on her arm. "You didn't warn us about giant wolves, though."

"Sorry." Sophia sniffled.

"I'm teasing." Nicole grabbed her head in both hands, forcing her to make eye contact. "We got your back, Soph. I might go scream and cry in a corner now, but we weren't gonna let you deal with crap like this by yourself."

"I don't believe this is real." Priya brushed at dirt on her arm. Except for a scuffed elbow, her injuries appeared confined to her legs from the wolf trying to drag her to the ground. "Was I really running so fast?"

"Yeah." Sophia wiped tears.

"I should've run too." Nicole shot a nasty look at her broken stick. "Didn't think a dog could bite through a stick as big as my arm."

"Not normal dogs." Sophia sighed.

"Those were not illusions like the spiders." Priya poked at a bite mark on her leg.

Klepto reappeared in a flash, a new Girl Scout uniform shirt still in its plastic wrap hanging from her mouth.

"Thank you." Sophia patted Klepto, took the shirt, and gave it to Nicole.

"Sweet. Thanks." Nicole ripped the old shirt collar off her neck, then opened the packet.

"We will need a story for the nurse." Priya sighed. "Some of these might need stitches."

Sophia hugged her friends together. "You guys… saved my life."

"We didn't really do anything but get chewed on," muttered Nicole.

"You kept the wolves away from me and… if you weren't here, I'd have been too scared to think straight. You guys beat the wendigo as much as I did."

"Can we go back to sanity now?" asked Priya. "These cuts are starting to sting."

"Yeah." Sophia stood. "We don't need a complicated story. Tell the sorta truth. We got attacked by a wolf."

"Are they going to believe that?" Nicole buttoned the last button on her new shirt.

"Why wouldn't they?" Sophia grinned. "It's the truth."

30

THE STRONG SCENT OF CATS

A year and a month ago (roughly) when I woke up in a body cooler, it seemed the most surreal experience likely to ever happen to me. Driving home from Olympia while having a conversation with the 700-year-old ghost of Vlad Tepes beats it. I'm no longer on Earth. Maybe my last meal dosed some serious LSD a few minutes before I bit him. The dude doesn't really trust me much, but he did spend his entire adult life hunting down vampires. During the course of the ride, he tells me Wallachia (what they used to call the area of Romania where he lived) had a serious vampire problem. During his childhood and teen years, it sounded like an Oblivare's paradise. People hiding in their homes at night, afraid to open windows. Few dared to go outside after sunset, and the ones who did often disappeared or came back... changed.

As a young man, he set off on a crusade against the evil plague, as he called it. What can I say? Steal a man's young wife a month after the wedding, it tends to cause some emotional issues. She turned out to be the one vampire he couldn't kill. No, it's not Ladonna. Imagine the crazy odds of that, right? No idea if we're talking about Oblivare, though his description does sound like the sort of reality they'd absolutely love to bring back.

He doesn't know how many vampires he killed, but it's somewhere in the thousands. Considering the supposed power of his sword, it's plausible. Pretty easy to nick a vampire on the arm or something, even as an ordinary mortal. Thing is, Vlad had some advantages... magic. Back then, anyone who did stuff like what Darren Anderson and his friends do didn't have to hide underground. They legit had 'wizard guilds' on street corners. All that stuff got swallowed into myth in the late 1600s. Cities where one could go buy an enchanted potion for whatever reason at a walk-in store stopped believing magic existed in a little over a single generation, as if their great grandmother hadn't used magical brews as routinely as my Mom gets Starbucks.

Anyway, Vlad mastered the art of swordsmanship as well as necromancy. It's not the raising legions of undead Hollywood and D&D turned it into. According to him, *real* necromancy is any magic designed to affect dead things as well as ghosts and soul energy. It allowed him to enchant the blade in my backseat into a pan-dimensional prison and twist the negative energy of the vampire it ate in a way to unravel the forces keeping vampires 'alive.'

Again, this is only his word, so it may or may not be perfectly true. He claims to have been such a prolific vampire hunter, elder vampires from multiple neighboring countries lured him into a trap. He admits to not thinking many of our kind possessed reason beyond bloodthirsty animals. My guess is he killed off a bunch of scraps or maybe an older bloodline prone to losing their humanity and becoming monstrous. Either way, smarter vampires tricked him into an abandoned castle and filled him full of arrows in nonlethal places. When he could no longer move, an elder kicked him over onto his back and plunged the sword they all feared into his heart.

He's been stuck inside it ever since.

And no, he's not happy. We're not talking a paranormal version of *The Odd Couple* in there.

No surprise Vlad doesn't think I should give the sword back to Wolent. He confirms the blade has been in the same place for ninety-three years. We're both fairly sure Wolent has no intention to use it. The man might not even know the sword has the capability to destroy any vampire it so much as makes a cat scratch on. Doubtful. He's not the sort of man who half-asses anything. If an object of any importance is in his possession, the man knows everything possible to know about it short of knowledge only divination or precognition could divine. I can also see him omitting the 'trivial' detail because he didn't want to scare me into saying 'screw that' and not doing his job. It's unlikely he expected this to be anything more complicated than me simply walking into a vampire nest while they all slept, taking the sword, and leaving.

Honestly, it *did* end up being that simple—eventually.

I shudder again, thinking about Jake swinging the damn Sword of Doom at me. Worse, I toyed with him, letting his attacks come close. Good grief, Sarah. Don't be a dumbass. Never do anything like that again.

Multiple serious problems are on my plate. Not returning the sword to Wolent may be a good idea, but it will bite me in the ass... with large teeth. Keeping the sword in my presence is also a massively bad idea. As soon as the sun sets tonight, Dieter is going to wake up, discover the sword gone, and probably lose his mind. He may or may not know where to find me, but he's certain to come looking. Whatever vampire is pulling Dieter's strings is also going to be on the hunt for this sword. I don't want to take it near any vampire I care about, like Aurélie or even Wolent himself. Accidents happen. Weird as it sounds, I'd feel better letting Sophia hang onto the sword, and that's an *incredibly* bad idea.

So, yeah. I have to come up with something to do about this stupid blade before the sun goes down tonight... or at least soon after.

Speaking of Sophia... she's going to help. If Iorghu has Sauron-level powers to influence people miles away to come get the sword, he's definitely going to make things complicated the instant he believes any serious threat to his existence is approaching. Fingers crossed he doesn't feel at all threatened by my adorable littlest sister. Poor kid's probably hiding under her cot at camp, counting the seconds until she gets to go home.

Plan: go home, shower, rinse out my lungs, wait for it to become dark enough to fly... and rush to the Girl Scout camp hoping no angry vampires intercept me on the way. It's the last place anyone would expect me to be taking the sword. I should be safe at home thanks to the hellhound. Hmm. Two hours by car. That might be doable via mirrorverse instead. Maybe there's no need for me to wait until dark. There has to be at least one decent-sized mirror at the camp. Question is, do I want to deal with the crazy weirdness on the other side for however long it takes to walk there?

There's a question for Blix.

Getting home is as wonderful as if I'd been gone for half a year at college in California. I only spent one night away and I'm excited to see the house. Ashley's right. I would totally have been homesick going to school out of state.

Vlad disappears when I stop the car. Okay, whatever. It's a little early in our relationship to introduce him to the parents anyway. I get out, open the back door, and gingerly grab the sword. It's still in a scabbard and a stolen T-shirt. No idea if scratching myself on the cross-guard is enough to destroy me or if it *has* to be the sharpened edge. Don't really want to test it. I'd go off on a rant about what kind of dumbass idiot of a vampire would *want* to possess this thing, but then I remember humans invented stuff like VX gas. Inventing a weapon that will instantly kill you from even the slightest mishandling is not unique to vampiredom. There's always someone out there looking to make something stupidly lethal and never stops to consider how easily said overly lethal thing could be turned against them.

People are stupid.

I hurry to the front door, duck inside, and kick my shoes off. Being home is a relief for multiple reasons, including getting out of direct sunlight. Yeah, I've gotten better at resisting the sun, but it's still a noticeable exertion to do so.

Strange. The house smells like cats. And not cat. I mean, *cats*. It's like walking into an animal shelter. This isn't the fragrance of litterbox in need of change or random rug peeing. Merely the ordinary cat smell mortals don't usually notice unless they stuff their face into fur. There's no way Mom got thirty cats. Something weird happened.

Another weird thing: the living room is empty. TV's off. No Sierra playing games. Crazy for a Saturday afternoon these days, especially considering Nicole went to Girl Scout camp. Sierra doesn't really have any other friends she'd be inclined to hang out with. She *should* be here playing games unless Mom or Dad took her shopping somewhere.

Dad's office is quiet, too. No clicking from the keyboard. He does throw a few hours at work on Saturdays more often than not. But he also isn't in the living room watching TV. I check the kitchen. Nothing. No one in the back yard. My concern grows, so I start checking room by room. There's no one in the house but me downstairs. Basement is empty. I put the sword down on my computer desk, grab a nearby towel from the dirty laundry pile, and cocoon the stupid thing. There. No part of the sword is visible to the outside world and capable of scratching me.

So tempting to jump right in the shower, but I'm too worried. This house is not supposed to be as quiet as it is on a Saturday afternoon.

Upstairs I go, trying not to cough too much on dust.

As soon as I reach the hallway, the soft tapping of Mom working on her laptop tells me at least one thing is normal. Her keyboard isn't as loud as Dad's. He's got a mechanical one. I bee-line to the 'rents' bedroom. Mom's at her desk. Nothing weird.

"Mom?" I walk closer. "What's going on? Where is everyone?" Before she can answer, I notice a Ken doll sitting on the desk next to her laptop... with Dad's face. "Aww! That's so adorable. You had a custom doll made to look like Dad?"

"Sarah..." Mom puts a hand to her forehead.

"No, hon," says the tiny Dad. "It's me."

"Yikes!" I stare. "Ack! WTF?" (I actually say W-T-F so Mom doesn't yell at me.)

"I don't know." Mom goes to hug me but stops. "You are filthy."

"Little bit of dust, yeah."

She hugs me anyway. "You went somewhere with a serious mildew problem."

"Yep." I gesture at Dad. "Whoa. Why is Dad ten inches tall?"

Mom flashes an impish smile. "Not the first time he's been ten inches tall."

Dad fist pumps, muttering, "Yes," to himself.

I gasp, turn a thousand different shades of red, and nearly pass out from embarrassment. "Mom! You did not just say that."

"Gotta let this crazy out somehow." She leans back in her chair. "I don't know what happened, hon. I really should just stop asking why anything happens."

"Sarah," chirps Dad, "your friend, Darren Anderson, said it's a dark faerie curse and should wear off in around seventy-two hours. Faster with direct exposure to iron. Unfortunately, the only pure iron we have in the house is your grandmother's skillet. Sierra is currently using it."

I blink. "She went to cooking school?"

Mom laughs.

"No," squeaks Dad. "She's *in* the skillet basking in the iron-ness of it, trying to make the curse wear off faster."

Blink. "Sierra's shrunk, too?"

Dad nods. "We had a goblin problem. They got into Sophia's crystals and blasted us tiny."

Facepalm. I give him this 'you have to be kidding me' look with one raised eyebrow. My expression remains the same as curiosity drags me out of their room to Sierra's. A big iron skillet sits on the floor in the middle of the room with a washcloth in it. Looks as though a small GI Joe action figure is under the washcloth.

"Sierra?" I ask.

The tiny figure jumps. "Don't look!"

Either we have a talking mouse or Sierra really is tiny.

"What the heck are you doing?"

"Please don't move the washcloth. I don't have anything on."

"Umm." Well, this certainly explains why Dad is not sharing the skillet. It's got plenty of room given their size. "Why?"

The tiny figure under the cloth crawls to the side. Micro-Sierra sticks her head out into view. "Maximizing contact area to iron. The more of me touching iron, the faster it eats the curse. It's like charcoal drawing up the bad energy. I want this stupid curse *gone*. Effing goblins."

Ugh. I hang my head. "Sorry."

"Stop blaming yourself for the weird stuff. This just happened." Sierra squirms. "Actually, it's kinda my fault. Maybe I shouldn't have killed the first one, even if it's true what Mr. Anderson said about them."

I sit on the rug next to the skillet. My poor sister looks like a wingless faerie. She has to be terrified Sophia is going to find her like this and squee so loud every window in the house shatters. "What did he say about them?"

"They're a type of goblin called a 'breathweaver.' Really evil and they steal kids' souls while we sleep." She folds her arms, holding the washcloth up to her neck. "Cats can kill them. Some stories claim those goblins are the reason people got into the habit of keeping cats as pets."

"Cats, huh? Is that why the house smells like a pet store?"

"Yeah. Klepto somehow made a bunch of stray cats come over to help. They're all gone now, but so are the goblins."

"Good, I suppose. The breathweavers can probably smell the cats and aren't risking coming anywhere near the house. Anything I can do to help?"

"Umm." Sierra opens her mouth to say something, but stops, looking as if she's about to vomit all over the place.

"You okay?"

She goes cross eyed, hiccups twice, then abruptly inflates to normal size, sitting in the skillet with the washcloth in her lap.

"Sweet!" Sierra pats herself down as if making sure she's real, then dashes over to the bed and throws on her bathrobe. "It's gone! It's gone! Moooom! It worked! I'm okay!"

Mom sprints down the hall. She rushes in, sees Sierra back to normal, and grabs her in a fierce hug.

Sierra looks over at me, pointing one foot at the skillet. "Would you mind giving that to Dad?"

I pick it up. "Sure. But... I really don't need to see Dad on pot."

Mom groans.

Sierra frowns. "That's not a pot. It's a pan."

"Hah." I glance down at it. "Well, let me go help Dad iron out his problems."

Mom throws a pillow at me.

Heh.

I head down the hall, set the skillet on Mom's desk, then hurry off before Dad gets any crazy ideas about wardrobe adjustments in front of me. No idea where he found a tiny set of Army fatigues. It's bath time. Convenient since I'm basically already at the upstairs bathroom. After flinging my dusty clothes off—and locking the door—I jump in the tub. As soon as there's enough water in it, I submerge and force myself to breathe in water.

It's *way* uncomfortable, but nowhere near as bad as inhaling the dust. My first exhale launches a plume of brown fog into the water. Not gonna say what it looks like. Horrible enough I'm tasting it again. I refill my lungs with water and breathe out over and over. Yes, it feels incredibly odd to breathe water. However, this is far preferable to filling my lungs with water via direct access courtesy of having a sword poked entirely through me. Eventually, the water coming out of my mouth no longer looks dirty and the scratchiness is gone from my throat. It's too bright in here to be online, so I'm forced to do a handstand instead of flying to drain my lungs. It is so awesome to be able to suck in a breath of air and *not* cough. It's super tempting to flood my lungs with

Mom's Scope mouthwash but… no. Something tells me that would be unpleasant. Might burn just a touch.

I do, however, use some in the ordinary manner. Maybe by next week, I'll stop tasting moldy floorboards.

Awesome. Now for a hot shower, soap, and scented shampoo.

31

THE DIFFERENCE BETWEEN ACTING AND LYING

S ophia emerged from the cave, looked around, and almost started crying because she had no idea where to go. Her mind tormented her with the idea they just stopped a wendigo from re-entering the mortal world and now she'd get lost and die of starvation.

She fixated on the idea of defeating a wendigo, even if it had been stuck in tar and weakened by daylight. *I am a magical badass bitch... who would get grounded for saying that out loud.*

"Which way is it?" asked Sophia, keeping her voice from sounding scared—mostly.

"This way." Priya marched off, no hesitation at all, though she did limp somewhat.

Nicole looked around, shrugged once, and followed her.

"You're sure?" Sophia hurried after them.

"Yes. I never get lost." Priya pointed forward. "That tree there, with the egg-shaped hole and broken branch. We passed it before."

"Pree is good at navigating." Nicole climbed over a mossy log. "She's got the badge for it and everything."

"It is not difficult," said Priya. "It is simply a matter of observing your surroundings and remembering those observations."

Sophia gazed at the tree with the hole, feeling a sense of awe. She hadn't noticed it at all before, not that it happened to be a particularly important tree. It did, however, stand out as different from other trees. A good landmark. "The hard part is being able to do that when you're scared. You really are good at it. Maybe you should like become a forest ranger or something."

"I'd like to." Priya smiled. "I love nature." Her smile dropped off as she pointed back over her shoulder. "Whatever that thing was, it did not come from nature. Neither did those pretend wolves."

"No. Those were manifestations of pure hatred and evil the wendigo gathered into solid form hoping to kill us," said Sophia.

"Math tests?" Nicole raised both eyebrows.

Priya and Sophia laughed.

"Stop. Math is fun." Sophia jumped over a rock. "Not as fun as reading, but still fun."

"I don't like math." Nicole gave a faint whimper as a branch swiped across the wolf bite on her arm. "It's pointless."

Sophia sighed. "It is the exact opposite of pointless."

"No... I mean the problems in class. It's just busy work. I wish they'd let us do math that mattered. Like how to figure out things we'd actually need to know." Nicole rolled her eyes. "Not doing variations of thirty-two-times-ten fifty times in a row."

"We have a problem now." Priya stopped, turning to face them.

Sophia and Nicole also stopped, staring at her.

"We have to go to the nurse." Priya gestured at her bitten

legs, then at Nicole who got worked over even more. "How are we going to do this without getting in trouble? They're going to know we ran off."

Sophia pondered. "Should be easy to sneak in there using the same magic we used to get away from camp."

"And…" Priya rubbed her chin. "You expect the nurse to help us without asking what happened? What do we say when none of the scout leaders know where we've been?"

"They think we're canoeing," muttered Sophia.

"Your cat could yoink some Band-Aids, right?" Nicole smiled.

"Mew," said Klepto.

"She could, but you guys need more than Band-Aids." Sophia scowled to herself. "We can't just sneak into the nurse's office. It might break the effect of the other spell and people will remember watching us walk away."

Nicole and Priya exchange a glance.

Sophia paced. "Gotta work it all together somehow."

"They think we went on a canoe." Priya pointed again. "The river is that way. We could hike back into camp beside the river and say our canoe flipped over and we lost it."

"Ooh, yeah. Good idea." Nicole's face lit up.

"I dunno." Sophia shook her head. "The nurse is going to recognize dog bites. She won't believe we hit rocks or something in the water."

"So, tell her we got attacked by a wolf." Nicole flapped her arms. "It's technically not a lie. Even you should be able to say that with a straight face."

Sophia's expression said 'you have a point.' "True, but one more problem. The camp knows how many canoes they have. Someone will start asking questions when none of them are missing."

"Wouldn't they just assume someone else found it and put it back?" Nicole scratched her head.

"Maybe." Sophia narrowed her eyes. "We can try to sneak back into camp, take a canoe and pretend to come back."

"Mew!" said Klepto, insistently.

"Huh?" asked Nicole.

"Seriously?" Sophia gawked. "You can get a canoe? It's like a thousand times your size."

"Mew…. Mew." Klepto tilted her head.

"Wow." Sophia whistled.

Priya absentmindedly fussed at her hair. "Don't tell me you can understand her."

"No, she's just mewing. I can read her mind." Sophia hugged the kitten. "She said she can yoink a canoe. Can't move it once she gets here, but she can teleport a canoe to us."

"That's insane," whispered Nicole.

"So insane it might work." Priya grinned. "If Soph can lie convincingly."

"We are screwed." Nicole slapped herself in the forehead.

"Soph." Priya grasped her by both shoulders and stared into her eyes. "Think of it like acting, not lying."

She smirked. "What's the difference?"

"Acting doesn't hurt anyone." Priya smiled. "Sure, we're trying to avoid getting in trouble, but it's not like you can tell everyone what *really* happened, right? You're protecting secrets."

"Yeah." Sophia exhaled. "I think I can do it."

"Good." Priya veered to the left and resumed walking.

A few minutes later, they fought their way out of the undergrowth to the relatively steep banks of the river. Sophia asked Klepto to take their phones and stash them in the bunkhouse. Mixing expensive electronics with a canoe trip did *not* sound smart. Within seconds of the kitten disappearing, Sophia stepped on a chunk of dirt that gave way, dumping her into the water. Despite it being summer, the river proved exceedingly cold, like falling into a basket of needles.

She resurfaced, flailing and gasping.

"Good idea," said Priya. "This is going to stink."

"Wha?" Nicole stared at her. "She didn't jump in on purpose. She fell."

Priya jumped in, then squealed. "Oh, god. It is cold."

"Why did you do that?" whispered Nicole.

"I tripped!" yelled Sophia. "Didn't mean to."

"No." Priya rapidly gasped for air. "If we say the canoe flipped but our clothes are dry, they will not believe us. The cold water is kind of nice on the bites."

"I hate you all." Nicole closed her eyes, clenched her hands into fists, and jumped in.

A moment later, an aluminum canoe appeared in a flash of purple light.

"Mew," said Klepto, her tiny voice echoing inside the boat.

Sophia grabbed the side and tried to climb into the canoe, but ended up pulling it over. Thanks to the water here being quite shallow, sinking it didn't cause too much of a problem. Working together, the girls lifted the canoe out of the water, righted it, and pushed it against the bank. The kitten fetched three oars.

It didn't really occur to Sophia she'd climbed into a canoe and begun paddling out onto a river for the first time in her life without any instruction until they'd gotten a scary distance away from the bank. She vaguely knew canoeing a river could be dangerous. Something about rapids or rip currents or crazy water physics stuff capable of dragging the boat under and drowning them. She definitely didn't know enough to feel comfortable with only sheet metal between her and water. Also, her nightmare about zombie hands *definitely* did not help.

I am a badass magical bitch. She swallowed a trickle of salvia. *Come on, Soph. It's just a boat. Paddle a bit more and I get to go home.*

The current, alas, traveled away from camp. However, the water didn't flow at too great a speed. They paddled feverishly, Nicole and Priya doing most of the work until Sophia realized she essentially flailed at the water and started copying how her friends did it.

Soon, the river widened into the lake. From the mouth, they had a clear view of about twenty-two other canoes all migrating in the direction of the dock.

"Holy cow," said Nicole.

"Not funny." Priya smirked.

"Sorry. It's just a saying." Nicole pointed. "Felt like we were gone much longer. They're still on the water."

"Confronting a source of primordial evil and having a near death experience kinda makes time feel funny." Sophia scrunched up her nose.

"Yes." Priya laughed. "Okay. Time to act upset."

"Not gonna be hard," deadpanned Sophia. Being in a canoe scared her enough to pull off a highly convincing 'freaked out.'

"Do you wanna eat this one, Soph?" asked Nicole.

"Huh?" She blinked.

"We need a reason we got separated from everyone else. How about we say you didn't know how to paddle and got us stuck in a current and pulled down the river?"

Sophia looked at the oar in her hands. "I really don't know how to paddle. Okay. We can use that story. If I get in trouble, no big deal. You guys got hurt. I should get in trouble."

"Naw. That's not your fault." Nicole resumed paddling for the dock. "I jumped in front of that thing on purpose. D&D rule number two. Protect the mage."

Sophia gave a nervous laugh. "I'm not a mage."

"You're more of a mage than I'm a fighter." Nicole nodded at the front of the canoe. "Pree is definitely a ranger."

"What is this D&D you keep talking about?" asked Priya.

"Explain later. Start crying and screaming now," whispered Sophia.

As they neared the dock, it became obvious other girls and scout leaders noticed a straggling canoe far behind the others. Nicole, Priya, and Sophia put on a convincing show of being terrified and freaked out. While the true source of their emotions happened to be coming face to face with a wendigo, ordinary wolves would get the blame. As soon as the scout leaders noticed the girls were soaked, two of them bloodied, every adult in sight came rushing over to help pull the canoe in and lift the girls out to dry land.

"Girls!?" gasped Mrs. Brewer. "What happened? Where have you been?"

McKenzie Whitaker rushed over to Nicole. "I got my first aid badge. I can help."

"The boat just kept going down the river," said Nicole, acting freaked. "We couldn't stop it."

"I'm sorry." Sophia sniffled. "It's my fault. I don't know how to paddle and I was doing it wrong. We got in a current and pulled out of the lake."

"The canoe hit something and flipped over." Priya shivered. "We swam to the bank and got attacked by a wolf."

Nicole held up her arm, showing off the nastiest bite.

The adults, and McKenzie, all gasped or made concerned noises. At the sight of all the blood on Nicole, Hadley went cross-eyed and fainted. Shante caught her before she hit the ground. Mrs. Brewer and Mrs. Whitaker started talking to some of the counselors about wolves in the area, and what to do about it.

"There were cubs," said Priya. "I think the wolves were

just protecting their babies. They're not a danger. We jumped back in the water and they didn't chase us."

Scout leaders and counselors looked back and forth at each other as if having a little trouble accepting the totality of the story. Sophia figured their confusion came from their inability to remember watching the girls get into a canoe in the first place or anything about them all morning. Spotty memory—courtesy of magic—didn't disprove or even cast enough doubt on the story of a rogue current and bizarre wolf attack for anyone to challenge the story.

Mrs. Whitaker escorted Sophia, Nicole, and Priya to the nurse's station while the rest of the girls and adults headed to the cafeteria for lunch. When the three of them entered the medical room, the nurse took in the sight of three soaking wet, two bloody, tweens and stared in bewildered shock.

"What happened?" The nurse hastily opened a cabinet, rummaging for supplies.

"Pillow fight got a little crazy," deadpanned Sophia.

Nicole and Priya giggled.

"At least your sense of humor is intact." The nurse shot her a mildly scolding look. "Be serious, Sophia. What happened?"

"We got attacked by a wolf. Nicole and Priya basically saved me."

"I'm all scratched up." Nicole opened the front of her shirt to show off more tooth marks and scratches. "This is gonna sting a lot, isn't it?"

"Maybe a little." The nurse patted the cushioned table. "Hop on up. Looks like you got the worst of it."

Since Sophia needed only dry clothing and not medical help, she went with Mrs. Whitaker out of the room to wait in the hall. Klepto, somehow still dry and fuzzy, curled up on the seat next to her.

"Don't look so guilty, hon." Mrs. Whitaker patted her shoulder. "It's not your fault a wolf attacked your friends."

Sophia bit her lip. She could have told them to stay at camp. They only got bit because she let them go with her to face the wendigo. Good chance she wouldn't have survived without them, though. And she didn't exactly trick them into doing something dangerous without warning. Maybe she could accept what happened simply happened and not carry a burden of guilt for it. Telling the scout leaders Nicole saved her might even get her friend an achievement badge for heroism or something.

Sophia managed a smile. "Okay. I'll try not to feel guilty."

OBLITERATION CAN BE FLUFFY

Mirrorverse travel can be incredibly bizarre.

The world on the other side takes many forms, most of them dangerous. It's like being in a Hellraiser movie where they hired MC Escher to do the set design, Hieronymus Bosch to paint the backgrounds, and everyone involved in script development took large doses of the good drugs.

Case in point: a room full of eight-foot-tall anthropomorphic mice sipping martinis and wearing fancy plumed hats.

It's really not worth it, neither for the risk it involves or my sanity, so I don't bother asking Blix about helping me get to the Girl Scout camp via mirror. It's saner (and less dangerous) to gamble on getting out of here (my house) as soon as it's possible for me to go outside and be online before any problems come knocking.

It is, as they say, a safe bet. I'm already fully awake and functional. Other vampires only *start* to wake up at sunset. It takes them a few minutes to shake off the grogginess of sleep. Then, they'd have to travel from wherever they lair to my house—assuming they even know who I am, where I am, and that I'm involved.

This should take more than thirty seconds.

It's not like a hundred bad vampires will magically appear in my backyard the instant the sun vanishes. Besides, we have a Max. Our yard is quite safe from vampires, burglars, and overly pushy missionaries. You know that thing about answering the door-to-door cultists naked and they'll leave you alone? Imagine how they'd react to seeing a legit hell hound?

Yeah, no. Can't do that to people.

Dad and Sierra are both back to normal. They told me the whole story about the goblins and their adventure in Mr. Niedermeyer's house. Amazingly, Sierra's taken the whole thing in stride and is already back on the PlayStation like yesterday and Saturday-so-far have been completely ordinary. I think she's just so damn happy to be back to full size it overpowered any other emotion.

Mom walked in on Dad a few seconds after the iron skillet absorbed the curse out of him and he returned to his usual size. I will say only this: doll (or action figure) clothing did not expand with him. Mom, seeing him in his birthday suit, decided to instigate certain activities which my brain refuses to associate with parents.

Yes, I know I—and three siblings—exist. Incontrovertible proof said 'events that do not occur' have, in fact, occurred. Leave me alone. I am in a fantasy world where parents just don't do that. Eww. Reality is like the Sims. After two people live together in a house long enough, kids just kind of appear. Parents do not have sex. Ever.

Shudder.

So... we have a totally normal family Saturday late afternoon, hanging out together over a board game while Sam and Ronan tell us about their little adventure somewhere in Eastern Europe. Sam sounds like his usual 'unimpressed' self, but he isn't making eye contact with anyone while talking about what happened. He's scared... or *was* scared. Kid doesn't like to show it. He and Sierra have that in common, only my brother doesn't compensate by acting angry.

This, I can help with.

I change seats and pull him into my lap, wrapping my arms around him. He leans back into me, approving of the new seating arrangement. This confirms my guess his trip to wherever-i-stan rattled him somewhat.

All is back to normal by the time it starts to get dark. I feel a little guilty not telling anyone about what's sitting on my desk downstairs. Enough crazy happened to them already where it seems cruel to add more wood to the fire. No one went anywhere near the basement stairs, so I didn't have to warn them under no circumstances touch the sword.

"Need to finish running an errand for Wolent." I scoot out from under Sam and set him on the chair. "Shouldn't take me too long. Just need to drop something off."

"All right." Mom looks at me like she's either going to ask me to pick up bread and milk on my way home or caution me not to instigate a political confrontation between elders. "Sarah?"

"Hmm?" I stop two paces from the table and spin around to look at her.

"Would you mind maybe flying out to the campground and checking on Sophia? I had the oddest feeling she's in trouble." Mom fidgets. "All day long."

"She's probably throwing off psychic screams for help because she's throw-up levels of homesick," says Sam.

Sierra sighs. "I should have gone to camp with her."

I smile. Funny she should say that... little does she know, I'm already intending to go up there. Or down there. South is generally considered 'down' in casual conversation where exactitudes of navigation aren't important. "No problem. Consider it done."

"Thanks." Mom examines her cards. "You have permission to use your mental powers to exact appropriate revenge on anyone who has teased her."

"Hah."

Dad and Sam laugh.

"I'll keep that in mind." I wave and hurry out of the dining room.

This sword needs to be as far away from my house as possible as fast as possible compared to sunset. I don't even waste the time it would take to put my sneakers back on. Gonna be flying anyway. After jogging downstairs to grab the sword, I zoom up the stairs and exit the house via the sliding glass door in the kitchen. No sooner does my foot touch the deck than three punk vampires jump over the fence at the rear of the yard.

Ugh. How the hell? There's no possible way Dieter's people could have found me so fast. I eye the blade. Oh, right. Ring of Sauron type bullshit. This thing probably drew them here since it doesn't want me bringing it back to Wolent. Honestly, no idea why. It managed to effectively escape once. Unless, of course, it wants to mess with me out of revenge or something. As evil as the vampire soul trapped inside it is, according to Vlad, the idea seems legit. Violence for violence's sake and all.

"Oh boys..." I point. "You might want to look behind you."

None of them take me seriously... until Max snarls.

I leap straight up into the air at the same time the hellhound drops his invisibility, showing himself to the three idiots. Never heard grown men scream like that before. It's kinda funny. Two sprint away from the dog while one launches himself airborne and chases me. Tactically, I should turn around and fly back toward Max so he can reach the flying guy, but I don't. Too much could potentially go wrong. I'm still at the low end of vampire power, being young, so my immediate assumption is every other vampire is older than me and will kick my ass. Running is always the best option. They even say so in karate class.

I'm vaguely aware of the hellhound flame-roasting the two flightless vampires. Most of my attention is on the guy coming up to say hi in much the same way a surface-to-air missile wants to hug a plane. Pretty sure he's not going to explode on contact, though.

Every so often, being an Innocent is inconvenient. Like now. Sure, I can fly but compared to other bloodlines, my flight isn't the fastest. Dude catches up to me in under a minute. Expecting claws or a knife, I spin away, clutching the sword to my chest like a mother protecting her homicidal demon baby.

The guy grabs the sword bundle.

We're not vampires having a mid-air sky battle. We're a pair of five-year-olds engaging in a playground fight over a toy, pulling it back and forth. The only thing missing is us shouting 'mine!' over and over again. I plant a foot on his chest and shove him off. We break apart. His grip on the bath towel is too strong. The fabric fails, ripping the towel away from the scabbard. Crap. Crosspiece is exposed. I stare at it like a scientist realizing they're carrying unshielded weapons-grade plutonium.

The guy snarls, throws the towel aside, and launches himself at me. I spin to my left and dive. He grabs me from behind in a bear hug, trying to wrestle the sword out of my grasp. This is not a fair contest. Except for us being a couple hundred feet in the air cruising around in a drunken corkscrew, it feels more or less like I'm twelve and my fifteen-year-old brother is slowly but surely prying the television remote out of my grip because he wants to watch 'something cool.' He's noticeably stronger than me but not ridiculously so.

We spin around and around, grabbing at the sword, yanking it back and forth while trading the occasional punch or kick. He grabs the scabbard around my hand, twisting. My grip starts to fail, primarily due to my fear of the weapon making me afraid to want it anywhere near me.

With a metal scrape, the sword slides eight inches out of the scabbard, the pristine—and razor sharp—blade glinting blue in the moonlight right in front of my face. Eeeeek! Dude pulls the sword mostly out of my grasp while I'm paralyzed in terror over what the thing is capable of.

Hang on.

Could Vlad have been lying? I mean, the guy hates vampires and knew I am one. He might have been trying to scare me into wanting to get rid of the sword carelessly. Foolish or not, I set aside the giant weight of existential dread, growl, and try to yank the sword back from the guy with as much strength as my muscles can generate.

The sword lurches toward me. He growls and pulls back, slowly overpowering me. I struggle to fight him off, but my hold on the scabbard and handle fails. The sword jumps entirely out of my hands, his own strength snapping it up into his face like that YouTube prank... only I didn't let go on purpose, and this isn't a plate of shaving cream. The exposed blade smacks him on the chin, leaving a fairly deep slice. Trivial to a vampire, likely a hospital visit to a mortal.

"Bitch," he mutters.

Ack! I grab the sword before the shock of being bonked wears off and he flies away. He starts to pull it back from me again, but hesitates, the anger in his face melting to confusion. Color fades out of his lower jaw, the skin around the cut fading from pale white to ashen grey. The cut itself turns black. In seconds, the ashy patch spreads up past his nose and his jawbone disintegrates into powder.

He lets go of the sword to clutch his face, letting out an agonized scream.

I hang there, too stunned to do anything but watch as he careens over backward, disintegrating from the head down. In like eight seconds, all that's left of him is a cloud of ashes and clothing fluttering to the ground.

"Holy shit," I whisper, shaking.

It's a damn miracle I haven't thrown the sword. F this thing. My mouth goes dry. C'mon, Sarah. Can't hover here forever. Still trembling, I carefully slide the weapon back into the scabbard. If I had Krazy Glue, I'd make sure it never came back out. No such luck.

Holy crap. Holy crap. Holy crap.

Vlad didn't lie. This freakin' sword destroyed that dude from a shaving cut. Okay, a *nasty* shaving cut but still... a little slice like that is nothing to a vampire. So many F-bombs explode in my thoughts my mother's Spider Sense must be shrieking. Somehow, she knows when we curse even if she can't hear it.

Not gonna lie. My pants would be wet right now if there had been anything in my bladder. Thinking about Jake swinging this freakin' thing at me makes me want to zoom home, clamp-hug my parents, and spend the next four days whimpering under a blanket. This thing is serious.

Oh, please let my idea work. Pleeease.

ABOUT FORTY-FIVE MINUTES AFTER LEAVING HOME, I'M cruising around over the Girl Scout camp.

At least, I assume it's the Girl Scout camp. Seeing a couple hundred preteen girls in uniform sitting in clusters around campfires is reasonably strong evidence I'm in the right place. If this damn sword can attract problems to our house, it can attract problems wherever it is. Don't have a lot of time.

Sophia is sitting in one of the groups beside Nicole and Priya. The kids are making S'mores and probably listening to scary stories. Or maybe not. My kid sister doesn't look terrified. Shockingly, she also doesn't appear to be miserable. Couldn't describe her as having a blast, but she's tolerating it.

I glide down to hover over her troop, just out of reach of the firelight, fixing my stare on Sophia. *Hey, kiddo.*

She looks around, thinking, *Sarah?*

Don't scream. I'm here. Look up.

Sophia spots me in a few seconds. An emotional bomb goes off in her mind like a kitten who's been floating on a piece of debris in the midst of a flood finally sees a human reaching to save it. She calms surprisingly fast, though. Wow. Guess she really is tolerating camp. *You're too low. The fire's making you look orange, like a demon.*

I float up. *Need your help. Can you get away for a few minutes?*

She nods, then stands. "Gotta go to the bathroom."

Nicole and Priya get up to go with her, all three of them whipping out flashlights. Hey, it's a girl thing. Going to the bathroom in groups I mean, not the flashlights. Though, she doesn't tell them not to follow her. Probably because it would seem weird and they'd get suspicious. Hmm. No worries. I can make them forget. I follow them in the air across the center area of the camp to a relatively large cabin, probably the cafeteria or meeting hall. After they go in the door, I spin around to make sure no one can see me, then land and follow them.

Feels like being in a country school after hours. For a

'camp,' it's fairly built up. Only real thing about it close to 'roughing it' is the lack of lights. No electricity at all here. Works for me. The girls shine their flashlights around while making their way down the hall to a bathroom. They're kinda hesitant, like a paranormal investigation group checking out a haunted hotel. Admittedly, there *is* something about the place setting off my creep detector, but I'm sure it's purely the spartan, rustic design and lack of electricity. Can't say I've ever peed by flashlight before. Total rustic moment, right?

"Sarah's here," whispers Sophia. "I don't really have to go."

"I do," says Priya.

"Might as well since we're here." Nicole opens the door.

"Don't scream." I walk up behind them.

Priya jumps but manages not to shriek. Nicole responds to my sudden appearance by punching me in the arm. Sophia, despite expecting me to show up, 'eeps.' She's *really* susceptible to jump scares.

"Inside," whispers Sophia. "Why did you scare us?"

"If I wanted to scare you, I wouldn't have said anything... just appeared and grabbed you."

She gives me a narrow-eyed 'you still scared me' stare, then goes into the bathroom.

Her friends duck into stalls. Ooh, perfect. The mirrors on the wall above the sinks are on the small side. Ugh. They could be larger but still big enough to squeeze through.

"What's up?" asks Sophia.

"Mom had a weird feeling all day like you were in trouble."

Sophia's face gives away massive amounts of guilt. "Yeah, but I'm fine now."

"Uh oh."

"A monster was going to kill us all and eat our souls." Sophia clamp-hugs me. "We stopped it."

"Are you okay?"

"Little freaked out but I think so."

"Wanna talk about it?"

"Yeah, but I need a couple days to think." Sophia exhales.

"Want me to bring you home?"

"Yes." She fidgets. "But I should probably stay the rest of the week. It's not really *that* bad."

"Wow. Seriously?"

She grinds her sneaker into the floor. "Yeah."

"Okay. Umm, need your help with something if you're up for it. It's extremely important and we don't have a lot of time."

Her fearfulness evaporates. "Must be important if you're actually involving *me* in something. You hate putting us in danger."

"You can say that." I point at the mirror. "Can you open it?"

"Umm. Yeah. Are you sure?"

"Working theory. I'm sure it might work."

She blinks. "That doesn't make sense. A 'definite maybe' is stupid."

I make a silly face at her.

"Fine. Whatever." Sophia approaches the counter, holds her arms out toward the mirror and stares at it.

In a few seconds, it stops reflecting the room and becomes more like a window into a creepy horror movie version of the bathroom, decayed, black vines growing on the walls, broken toilets, mold.

"Eww." Sophia gulps.

I climb up on the counter and duck into the mirror. It's like squeezing through a tiny window. But hey, I'm skinny and I can fly. Sophia has a much easier time of fitting. She jumps from the sink counter to the floor on the other side, then leans her head back out into the real world.

"Guys, wait here. I'll be back in a minute."

"Back?" calls Nicole. "Where are you going?"

"No time to explain. Just stay in the bathroom." Sophia leans away from the opening and faces me. "Okay. We're here. What do you want to do?"

I take her hand, lead her out of the bathroom and down the hallway in the shadow version of the giant cabin until we're outside. The building behind us appears to be the only trace of the Girl Scout camp to exist here. Wilderness surrounds us. "Soph... I need you to summon Fuzzydoom."

She gawks at me. "You are playing with powers beyond your comprehension. I... dunno. What you're asking me to do is..."

"Maybe. Just do it, okay? Don't let him out of the mirror. I just need to see him over here on this side."

Sophia bites her lip. "This is going to go wrong in an untold number of ways, but... okay. If it's that important."

Asking my kid sister to conjure up the substance of her absolute worst nightmare is a certain measure of cruel. "I know this is difficult and dangerous, but I came within a literal half inch of being permanently destroyed. I don't want it to happen again, or to anyone else. So, Fuzzydoom."

"Gah!" She stares at me, stuck between wanting to cry and go full Mom and yell at me for being reckless. She assumes I was reckless since something almost 'permanently destroyed' me.

Perhaps the only thing that frightens her more than Fuzzydoom is me dying. Or really, anyone in the family dying. We're all neurotic now. Who'd have thought something like death would make us hyper close.

Sophia closes her eyes and concentrates.

A few seconds later, a ten-foot-puffball of infinite blackness with teensy little wings on top comes gliding out of the forest about a hundred yards away from us. Maybe I'm being ridiculous here. What are the odds a three-year-old's nightmare monster is truly dangerous? Stuff that scares little kids is often laughable to adults. I mean, it's barely possible for me to look at the creature without cracking up. When Sam called it the 'pom-pom of annihilation,' I nearly lost it.

Here goes nothing. I walk toward it.

Eager to kill us, Fuzzydoom creeps at me at the speed of a sprinting snail. The DMV moves faster than this thing. Uncle Hank could outrun it without his wheelchair. Yeah, it's kinda mean to say that, but he's a butthead, so I don't feel too bad.

"Get away from it!" yells Sophia, who hasn't moved from where she'd been standing. "Don't let even one hair touch you or you're gonna be destroyed!"

I continue walking closer. "Not planning on touching it. Just don't want to miss."

"Miss?" yells Sophia.

"Yeah." Once I'm near enough to feel confident in my aim, I raise the Tepes sword over my head in both hands. "Vlad, you might want to eject if you can." I hurl the blade at Fuzzydoom, scabbard and all.

The sword spins end over end at ridiculous speed thanks to vampire strength. An instant before contact, a smear of yellowish spectral light zooms up from the blade, which whiffs straight through the middle of the apparently intangible giant mass of black fuzz, comes out the other side, and lands about fifty feet behind it with a *thump*. Nothing noticeable happened except for the monster's tiny wings fluttering rapidly for about a second as the blade vanished into the furry ball.

"You can't kill him!" yells Sophia.

"Not trying to hurt Fuzzydoom." I fly up into the air, going over the ridiculous monster in an arc, and land beside the sword.

The pom-pom of ultimate ruin stops in place, then

reverses its creeping drift, heading toward me. Oh noes. I only have about twenty minutes before it gets to me. Moment of truth time. I force myself to crouch and grab the sword's handle. Whoa. The *lack* of animosity coming from the blade is stronger than the rum and cokes at Mom's office Christmas parties. Yes, I got one by accident the last Christmas I'd been alive. And yes, my parents were not exactly pleased. Not my fault I grabbed the wrong glass from the bar. It looked the same as normal coke. Don't look at me like that. I only took one sip. Didn't keep drinking it once I knew what it was.

"Holy shit. I think it worked." I glance over my shoulder at the big black furball. "Yikes! Fuzzydoom is seriously dangerous."

"I told you!" yells Sophia. "Why do you think I'm so scared of him?"

A flight-assisted jump avoids the creature *I* am now frightened of. Sophia hugs me when I land next to her.

"Okay. Send him away and let's get out of here."

Sophia fidgets. "I can't. That's the problem. He's my nightmare. All I can do is run. If I could send him away whenever I wanted, he wouldn't be my nightmare."

"So..."

"We just have to get to the mirror before he catches us." Sophia backs up.

"Not hard."

"If you stop looking at him, he'll be right behind you the next time you look."

I shake my head. "Stupid movie monster nonsense."

She flails her arms. "Hello? Nightmare. It does what it wants."

"Right..."

We walk backward into the big cabin, keeping our stares locked on Fuzzydoom, then back down the corridor into the bathroom and climb through the same mirror we entered from. Sophia cancels the magic and the reflection of this room once again appears. The demon pom-pom can't get us.

Nicole and Priya, no longer in the stalls, stare at us in shock.

"Oops. They saw us come out of the mirror," I say.

"Umm." Sophia fidgets. "It's okay. They saw some... stuff."

"Stuff?"

"Wendigo," mutters Sophia.

"That sounds bad."

"It kinda was."

It occurs to me Nicole smells like vanilla-cherry ice cream. "Is she hurt?"

"Got chewed on by a wolf." Nicole holds up her arm, showing off bandages.

"Are you *sure* you don't wanna go home?" I ask.

"I'm super homesick." Sophia pauses, waiting for her voice to stop breaking. "But... I'm going to stay because I said I would. Not going to do this ever again, but I can survive four more days."

"Okay."

"Everything okay at home?" asks Sophia.

"Yeah. Dad and Sierra had a tiny problem, but nothing our family can't handle." I wink, then glance at the seemingly mundane and no longer cursed sword. "Gotta go give this to Mr. W."

"Okay." Sophia hugs me again. "Tell Mom I'm fine. If you want, you can tell her I had a monster problem, and I'll explain everything when I'm back."

"Probably better to do that so she's expecting something, rather than dump it on her all at once." I wave. "See you girls in a couple days."

"Bye," chime Nicole and Priya together.

I lurk in the bathroom until they leave, and when no one is looking, sneak outside and throw myself into the air.

Wow. The idea worked. Iorghu didn't do anything to stop me from hurling him into Fuzzydoom's furry embrace. Guess he thought the monster is as ridiculous as I used to. Wow. It destroyed a 700-year-old horror who probably would've had little trouble killing Aurélie. Amazing. Then again, Fuzzydoom came from the mind of three-year-old Sophia. Small kids think in total absolutes. *Ultimate* destruction—will destroy *anything*—really means ultimate.

Wonder where Vlad went. He's finally free of the arcane prison he made. Ugh. I really hope warning him and setting him free isn't going to come back to bite me in the ass. He was a bit of a dick, but his motivations made sense. I would have felt bad destroying him.

I toss the ordinary sword up and catch it, smiling. "And you... you're going back to Wolent."

GIRLS' NIGHT OUT

I hadn't known what to expect from Mr. Wolent, but uncontrollable laughter wasn't on the list.

At first, he thought I brought back the wrong sword since it didn't give off any strange energy. After I told him everything, he couldn't stop laughing. He appreciated me not being upset at him for neglecting to inform me about the sword's lethality to our kind. My guess summed it up. Wolent figured I'd go in, pick it up, and leave without being at risk.

He really didn't want the sword at all, considering it far too dangerous to exist. His only goal had been to keep it shut away. It took me longer to explain what I meant by Ring of Sauron effect than to tell him how I got rid of the curse. He called it an 'assassin in a clown suit,' referring to a hitman pretending to be something ridiculous like a birthday party clown or mime in order to get close to a target who'd never suspect anyone dressed like that as a threat. Pretty sure his looking into my thoughts and seeing Fuzzydoom is what made him laugh.

So, yeah. Even though I went off script and did

something he hadn't asked me to do, Wolent didn't get angry at me. In fact, he seems quite happy this sword is no longer a threat. It's like a president who thinks some weapons are simply too dangerous to exist and won't consider using them.

We still don't know who Dieter may have been working for, though once Wolent understood Iorghu set things in motion from inside the sword, it no longer seemed to be an issue worth worrying about. The vampire who developed the sudden craving to possess the blade might not even remember why he or she wanted it.

My unlife is back to normal, for however long it will last.

It's Monday night after a relaxing Sunday spent with my friends and Hunter.

My plan is to hang out with Ashley and Michelle again tonight once they are done at work. Their summer jobs have predictable hours and don't require overnight sleeps in random elderly people's closets. Using my time wisely, I fly to Seattle to feed before they're home.

Right as I finish enjoying some mocha mud pie flavored blood from a guy in a Starbucks polo shirt, the sense of being stared at intently hits me from behind. Uh oh. Expecting Dieter or one of his minions, I whirl into a fighting stance.

Two gold eyes glare at me from the alley between where I am and the street.

Tilloa.

Oh, okay. Not an attack. She doesn't look combative, more distraught. Crap. Now what?

I give Starbucks guy a compulsion to go eat some cookies. Wait, no. A scone... then walk over to her.

She stares at me, radiating jealousy.

"Something's wrong. Can I help?"

Tilloa swipes at her hair, as if attempting to salvage some dignity. It's obvious she's been crying pretty hard for a while.

If my girl-dar is working properly, she's recently been dumped.

"He left you?"

"Yeah." She folds her arms. "I… after you said… I tried to tell Lincoln the truth. He flipped out when he saw me at the door."

"Thought you died?"

"Yeah." She sniffles. "Then he started accusing me of messing with him by faking my death. He didn't believe me at first until I showed my fangs, then he completely lost his mind."

"Oh, no."

Tilloa breaks down in sobs.

"What happened? Is he okay?"

It takes her a moment to compose herself enough to speak. "No. He's not hurt, but he's either gonna end up a drunk or in a mental hospital."

I blink. "You didn't make him forget?"

"What?" She stares at me. "Make him forget?"

"Uhh… are you like really new or do you not have mental powers?" I raise an eyebrow. "You read Hunter's mind, didn't you?"

She lets out a long sigh. "It's been three weeks. And yeah. I know about *reading* minds. Didn't realize we can change shit."

"Oh, wow. Okay." I throw an arm around her shoulders. "So, you're a vampire now… it comes with some really awesome perks. I can help make him forget before he does anything stupid, then show you how it works."

Tilloa gazes at me, hope in her eyes. "Really? You'd do that?"

"Sure. We girls gotta stick together, right?" I smile.

"Can you make Lincoln okay with this vampire stuff?"

I cringe. "That's a bit more difficult. If he reacted that

strongly to you telling him, it's probably too deep in his nature. Giving him a mental compulsion to ignore it will almost certainly fail eventually… and be much worse after it does than the reaction you got."

"No…" She sobs. "I love him."

"There's time to sort it out. Take me to him."

"Umm, it's a bit far."

"Can you fly?"

"Fly?" She stares. "You're kidding, right?"

I float off the ground. "Nope."

"How do I do it?"

"Not every vampire can… I did it by accident the first time by simply not wanting to fall. Think about wanting to fly."

Tilloa makes a series of faces ranging from 'what is that smell' to 'constipation.' Two-ish minutes later, she floats a few inches off the ground. Her mood shifts in an instant from weepy to giggling. "Oh, wow. This is amazing!"

"Isn't it?" I grab her hand and tow her up into the air. "Let's go find Lincoln."

TILLOA AND I WALK OUT OF LINCOLN'S APARTMENT AN HOUR later.

She's got a grim 'well, that sucked' expression of a kid who just had their favorite toy confiscated for a week of grounding. As far as the ex-fiancée goes, he's back to believing Tilloa died during a mugging three weeks ago. Any scraps of memory he has of seeing her after her 'death', he'll blame on a nightmare.

Sadly, he wasn't as into her as she's into him. The guy never cheated or anything, but he's already moved on.

Honestly, if a dude gets over her *that* fast, he never really loved her. Just my opinion.

"Hey, wanna hang out tonight?" I raise an eyebrow at her. "Was probably going to spend the night on my friend's couch watching movies and stuff. I'm sure they wouldn't mind a girls' night out instead if that's your speed."

"I dunno."

"Something to take your mind off boys and mortals." I wag my eyebrows.

"Are your friends mortals?"

"Yeah."

She sighs. "That's not fair."

"I don't know why they're cool with the supernatural stuff, but they are. Trust me. They won't freak out. Don't feel guilty about Lincoln. Having a mortal boyfriend is really complicated and probably stupid."

"But you have one, right? The boy I saw you with is alive. That's why I tried to get back with Lincoln. Seein' you two made me think it might be possible."

Exhale. "Yeah. I do. But... problems."

"You guys fighting?"

"No, not that type of problem. We are awesome together. He loves me so much it's almost painful. I mean... he's going to get older. I'm not. At some point, he'll look like my dad. Then grandpa."

Tilloa cringes into a laugh.

"Yeah, it'll get super creepy." I fuss at my hair. "Basically, I've got a few years to decide whether or not to break his heart or end his life."

She gasps.

"Make him a vampire, too. Not just kill him." I bite my lip.

"How does he feel about it?"

I kick at the ground. "He wants to join me. I think he

loves me so damn much a mind-erasure won't hold forever and when it breaks, he'd do something stupid."

"Why haven't you turned him yet?"

"It's stupid." I fold my arms.

"Spill, girl." Tilloa grins.

"Two reasons. He's still got a mom and little brother. I'm hesitant to mess up their family. And secondly, have you seen *any* vampire movies lately? The mortal girlfriend/boyfriend *always* ends up turning into a vampire before the movie's over. It feels cliché."

"So, you're gonna lose the love of your life because you think it's cliché?" She blinks. "Screw what people think. What do you guys want?"

Exhale, harder. "Yeah, I guess."

"What do vampires do with all that free time?" asks Tilloa.

"Umm. Speaking for myself, reading or video games. Normal ones? I dunno. Clubs? I never really got into the whole nightclub or bar scene." I shrug. "Guess it's better than running around doing random mischief and vandalism."

"Say what? We're a little old for nonsense like that. Least I am. You're still a kid."

"Right... some vamps I met in Portland have an odd opinion of a fun night."

Tilloa shrugs. "After dealing with Lincoln tonight, I really wouldn't mind a couch and movies. You sure your friends would be okay with a total stranger invading your space?"

"Yeah. You seem pretty cool for an old woman."

She gives me the finger. "Girl, I'm only twenty-four. Just because your ass is fourteen don't make me old."

"I'm eighteen."

"No way."

"Yes way."

She whistles.

"Seriously." I show her my license.

"This your older sister? Doesn't really look like you."

"Pre-V picture."

"Oh. Damn, girl. You're right we changed a bit. I got the hotness, you got the adorbs."

Grumble. "Don't rub it in."

"No wonder you don't wanna go clubbing, hon." Tilloa grins. "They'd never let you in the door."

I flash a sly smile. "Sure, they will. I have the best fake ID in the world."

She laughs.

Hmm. Maybe we will escape from Ashley's couch for a girl's night out. Been a while. We could all use the break. Or maybe we'll end up hanging out together. Either way, should be fun.

Tilloa squeals in delight as we take to the air again.

So, yeah. I have a new pet project. This girl got Dalton-ed. Whoever gave her the Transference abandoned her. Guess I'll step in and show her how to vampire.

Should be fun.

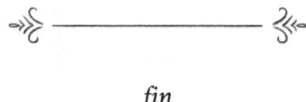

fin

NOTES

10. DAD WOULD LOVE THIS

1. It's good. Unload it.
2. What are you doing here?
3. Is that your mother there?
4. Is that English?
5. I think so.
6. American spies?
7. Americans would do anything, but these are kids. They can't be Americans, they're not overweight.
8. Who are you and where are you from?
9. This is not the time to play, boy.
10. Speak.
11. Commander, I think they are Americans.
12. What on Earth are American children doing inside our security zone?
13. Find out who they are and why they are here.

ACKNOWLEDGMENTS

Thank you for reading Vampire Innocent book 13! Sarah and the Littles will return in book 14.

Much appreciation to Lee Sheridan for editing. It's wonderful to work with someone who is tangibly excited to get their hands on the latest installment.

Additional thanks to Alexandria Thompson for the cover and interior art.

ABOUT THE AUTHOR

Originally from South Amboy NJ, Matthew has been creating science fiction and fantasy worlds for most of his reasoning life. Since 1996, he has developed the "Divergent Fates" world, in which *Division Zero, Virtual Immortality, The Awakened Series, The Harmony Paradox, and the Daughter of Mars series* take place. Along with being an editor at Curiosity Quills press, he has worked in IT and technical support.

Matthew is an avid gamer, a recovered WoW addict, Gamemaster for two custom RPG systems, and a fan of anime, British humour, and intellectual science fiction that questions the nature of reality, life, and what happens after it.

He is also fond of cats.

Visit me online at:
Facebook: https://www.facebook.com/MatthewSCoxAuthor
Pinterest: https://www.pinterest.com/matthewcox10420/
Goodreads: https://www.goodreads.com/author/show/7712730.Matthew_S_Cox
Email: mcox2112@gmail.com

OTHER BOOKS BY MATTHEW S. COX

Divergent Fates Universe Novels

Division Zero series

- Division Zero
- Lex De Mortuis
- Thrall
- Guardian
- Harbinger
- The Shadow Fixer
- Neuroshock

The Awakened series

- Prophet of the Badlands
- Archon's Queen
- Grey Ronin
- Daughter of Ash
- Zero Rogue
- Angel Descended

Daughter of Mars series

- The Hand of Raziel
- Araphel
- Ghost Black

Virtual Immortality series

- Virtual Immortality

- The Harmony Paradox

Prophet of the Badlands Series

- Prophet's Journey
- Prophet's Mercy

Divergent Fates Anthology

(Fiction Novels - Adult)

The Roadhouse Chronicles Series

- One More Run
- The Redeemed
- Dead Man's Number

Faded Skies series

- Heir Ascendant
- Ascendant Unrest
- Ascendant Revolution

Temporal Armistice Series

- Nascent Shadow
- The Shadow Collector
- The Gate to Oblivion
- The Queen of Discord
- The Burning Alchemist

Vampire Innocent series

- A Nighttime of Forever
- A Beginner's Guide to Fangs
- The Artist of Ruin
- The Last Family Road Trip
- The Phantom Oracle
- How Not to Summon Demons
- Ordinary Problems of a College Vampire
- A Vampire's Guide to Surviving Holidays
- An Introduction to Paranormal Diplomacy
- A Vampire's Guide to Adulting
- How to Stop a Vampire War in Six Easy Steps
- Ancient Vampire Death Cults and Other Annoyances
- Hunting Vampires for Fun and Profit
- A String of Seriously Unlucky Events
- The Summer of Completely Usual Strangeness
- Demonic Crisis Management for the Modern Vampire

Standalones

- Wayfarer: AV494
- Axillon99
- Chiaroscuro: The Mouse and the Candle
- The Spirits of Six Minstrel Run
- Sophie's Light
- The Far Side of Promise anthology
- Operation: Chimera (with Tony Healey)
- The Dysfunctional Conspiracy (with Christopher Veltmann)
- Of Myth and Shadow
- The Girl Who Found the Sun

Winter Solstice series (with J.R. Rain)

- Convergence
- Containment
- Catalyst
- Catacombs

Alexis Silver series (with J.R. Rain)

- Silver Light
- Deep Silver
- Silver Quarrel
- Silver Crucible
- Silver Heart

Samantha Moon Origins series (with J.R. Rain)

- New Moon Rising
- Moon Mourning
- Haunted Moon

Vampire For Hire series (with J.R. Rain)

- Moon Master
- Dead Moon
- Lost Moon
- Vampire Destiny
- Infinite Moon
- Vampire Empress
- Moon Elder
- Wicked Moon
- Moon Blade

Maddy Wimsey series (with J.R. Rain)

- The Devil's Eye

- The Drifting Gloom
- Dark Mercy
- Primal Wrath

<u>Samantha Moon Case Files series</u> (with J.R. Rain)

- Blood Moon

Immortal Operative (with J.R. Rain)

- Broken Ice
- Broken Wing

Four Elements series (with J.R. Rain)

- The Elementalist
- The Black Rose
- The Wakefield Curse

Witches series (with J.R. Rain)

- The Witch and the Hangman

Zeb Clemens series (with J.R. Rain)

- The Beast of Devil's Creek
- Wanted: Undead or Alive

Young Adult Novels

The Eldritch Heart Series

- The Eldritch Heart

- The Cursed Crown
- The Sapphire Soul

Evergreen Series

- Evergreen
- The World That Remains
- The Lucky Ones
- Nuclear Summer
- The Nuclear Frontier
- The World We Make
- The Threat Unseen

Progenitor Series

- Out of Sight
- Out of Mind

Diary of a Teenage Fey

(Short story series)

- Elder Horror
- The Hag of Barrow Falls
- Babysitter's Nightmare
- Lharakki
- Bauble for a Soul
- Simulacrum
- Amorphous
- Manticore

Standalones

- Caller 107
- The Summer the World Ended

- Nine Candles of Deepest Black
- The Forest Beyond the Earth

Middle Grade Novels

The Adventures of Ubergirl series

- My Dad is a Mad Scientist
- Aliens Ate My Homework
- The End of all Halloweens
- Dr. Infinity and the Soul Smasher

Tales of Widowswood series

- Emma and the Banderwigh
- Emma and the Silk Thieves
- Emma and the Silverbell Faeries
- Emma and the Elixir of Madness
- Emma and the Weeping Spirit

Standalones

- Citadel: The Concordant Sequence
- The Cursed Codex
- The Menagerie of Jenkins Bailey